YORBA LINDA PUBLIC LIBRARY

MW01127604

"... if trickster can disguise his tracks, surely he can disguise himself. He can encrypt his own image, distort it, cover it up. In particular, tricksters are known for changing their own skin."

Lewis Hyde,
Trickster Makes This World: Mischief, Myth, and Art

YORBA LINDA PUBLIC LIBRARY
CITY OF YORBA LINDA
4852 LAKEVIEW AVE.
YORBA LINDA CA, 92886-3433

FATES: I BRING THE FIRE PART IV

Copyright ©2016 C. Gockel

All rights reserved. No part of this publication may be reproduced, distributed, or transmitted in any form or by any means, including photocopying, recording, or other electronic or mechanical methods, without the prior written permission of the publisher, except in the case of brief quotations embodied in critical reviews and certain other noncommercial uses permitted by copyright law. For permission requests, write to the author, subject "Attention: Permissions," at the email address: cgockel.publishing@gmail.com

ISBN-13:978-1530424078
ISBN-10:1530424070

SF
GOCKEL

FATES
I BRING THE FIRE PART IV
C. GOCKEL

YORBA LINDA PUBLIC LIBRARY
CITY OF YORBA LINDA
4852 LAKEVIEW AVE.
YORBA LINDA CA, 92886-3433

Acknowledgements

First and foremost, I want to thank my editor, Kay McSpadden. Kay read and reread this story more times than I can count. I also would like to thank Gretchen Almoughraby. Her suggestions helped me clarify situations and make the action more believable. Also indispensable was Patricia Kirby. She consulted on aspects human and horse. My brother, Thomas, was great as a myth reference. Shelley Holloway was the final editor of grammar and content and a delight to work with. A shout out must also be given to Mr. Lewis Hyde, author of Trickster Makes This World: Mischief, Myth and Art. Mr. Hyde's work was the chief non-fiction inspiration behind I Bring the Fire and he generously let me, or rather Loki, poke fun at the unerring accuracy of his vision of tricksterdom.

I also want to thank all of my readers. Your continued encouragement helped give me the confidence to write this story. I love you guys!

Finally, thanks must go to my husband Eric. If he hadn't nagged me to give original fiction a try, this story never would have happened.

Special Note:

This is a fourth in series (plus one-half!) I've tried to include brief descriptions at the introduction of each character to get readers up to speed. However, I've also included an appendix of names and places at the end of this story, for those who want more background.

PROLOGUE

Bohdi Patel shifts in his seat, eyes glued to the white door in front of him. The door leads to the familiar halls of the FBI's Department of Anomalous Devices of Unknown Origins Chicago headquarters. It is locked. They locked him in. Like a criminal. Was it Hernandez who turned the bolt, or Steve? He bites his lip. Running his hand through his hair, he looks around the room. He sees thin, dirty, brown carpeting, and a single foldout table. The chair he's sitting on creaks.

The radiator in the room is ticking, and it's probably too hot—must be too hot because there is the tiniest prickle of sweat on the back of his neck—still, he shivers.

He turns. There is also a window. Standing up and walking over, he presses his hands to the cold glass and peers through the grime. He's three stories up, facing an alley, but there is a fire escape a few feet to the left. He shakes the hand crank on the sill and feels it give a little.

Bohdi swallows. With trembling hands, he pulls out his wallet and flips it open. He has $23.00. No credit cards. The only ID he has is his badge for HQ. "Bohdi Patel" it says below his picture. It's a lie of course, just like the ID he had been found with—credit cards, driver's license, social security card—were lies. He is not Bohdi Patel. Bohdi Patel was an American citizen who died twenty-six years ago at the age of six months. The only reason ADUO calls him Bohdi is because no one knows what else to call him.

Six weeks ago, Loki, so-called God of Mischief, Chaos, and Lies, attacked Chicago, let loose trolls and wyrms and other nasties, killed thousands of people, displaced hundreds of thousands more, and in a comparatively trivial bit of mischief, wiped Bohdi's memory. All Bohdi knows about the time before Loki comes from Steve, and even that's not much. Apparently, during the chaos, Bohdi had shown up at HQ, given his name as "Bohdi Patel," and volunteered to help ferry people out of the city, in what later turned out to be a stolen cab. Kind of heroic. According to some people in the office, kind of criminal.

Bohdi is probably Indian, but he doesn't have a passport. He shivers. The only reason he wasn't deported was because no one knew where to deport him to. He frowns. He also suspects that Steve had wanted to keep an eye on him—after the accident his brain had briefly hummed with magical energy.

Bohdi flips past the ADUO badge. There is only one piece of authentic identification in his wallet. It is a photo of a dark-skinned man in white shirtsleeves and a woman with slightly fairer skin in traditional Indian attire punctuated by a bright orange sari. Both are smiling widely, all their attention on a chubby baby balanced on the man's knee. The baby has a lop-sided baby smile and is looking toward the camera, oblivious to the rapt attention but obviously thriving under it.

The photo isn't labeled. Bohdi's not sure if he is the child, or even if the couple is his parents, but usually he likes to think that they are. Not so much today. They look so clean, happy, and so good—what would they think of him if they knew what he'd done?

He had done it with the best of intentions. The security loophole was glaring and dangerous, even if it was only on the intranet, and behind firewalls and logins. After weeks of alerting ADUO and nothing being done, he'd proven it.

A true criminal would have put the personal details of all of ADUO's personnel on the Internet. Bohdi just changed all the names to Pig Latin—a silly language he had learned from Claire, Steve's eight-year-old daughter.

A true criminal's hands wouldn't tremble at the memory of the confrontation with Steve afterward.

"Do you think this is funny?" Steve had demanded, hovering above Bohdi's desk.

Unable to suppress a smile, Bohdi had replied, "Esyay?" He'd meant to launch into a defense, an explanation of how easy it would be to change the names back, and how now Steve could get funding for more tech support. He'd never gotten the chance.

"Don't you understand we're busy protecting people out there," Steve had shouted, pointing to the ruins of LaSalle Street where magical beasties still had a habit of popping up.

"Of course," Bohdi responded. "But this is about protection, too...protecting your employees' identities from espionage and blackmail!"

Face going a shade darker, Steve snapped, "You acted unilaterally—without respect for authority. You made this department look bad, and me look bad, at the worst possible time."

Bohdi's skin heated. That was what Steve thought this was

about? Trying to make him look bad? His vision had gone red around the edges.

"There's no 'I' in the word team, Bohdi!" Steve shouted.

Bohdi's lips curled into a snarl. "But there's a 'U' in fuck." As soon as he had said the words, he regretted them.

Steve's face melted into a look of such unmitigated rage that Bohdi shrank in his chair, all his own anger vanishing. "I'm sorry," was on his lips, but Agent Hernandez had interrupted him. "You do realize, you are now a felon?"

Bohdi hadn't even realized Hernandez was there. Chin tilted low, eyes glinting in Bohdi's direction, Hernandez said, "You're not an American citizen. Do you know what we could do with you?" Hernandez shook his head, his fists tight at his sides. When Steve had fought to keep Bohdi at ADUO, Hernandez had argued he should be deported—or even sent to Guantanamo.

Fear twisted so violently in his stomach, Bohdi felt like throwing up.

"Get up," Steve said, jaw tight. Bohdi just barely managed to stand. His legs felt like rubber.

Hernandez and Steve had led him to this room. Steve ordered him to sit; then they left and shut the door. He heard the lock click.

Bohdi looks down at the picture in his hands. The man, woman, and baby are seated outside, behind them rises dark green vegetation. The sunlight makes flecks of dust glimmer in the camera's eye and burnishes his parents' shoulders. He imagines that is how the sun is in India, a warm hand on your shoulder all the time. Not like the sun in Chicago in winter. He looks out the window. The sun's position is impossible to know behind the gray of the clouds and smog.

He imagines what the smiling woman would say to him. "You had a good thing, with good people, and now you've ruined it!" He wipes his face with his hand. He did have a good thing. Steve looked out for him. He'd gotten him a job—and okay, even if it is just as a glorified receptionist, it's probably better than driving a cab—and set him up with his parents in their enormous greystone out west near Garfield Park. Ruth and Henry Rogers fuss over him like a second son.

Now they might deport him... If he's lucky.

He looks toward the fire escape. He thinks if he just opens the window, he can make it. And then where? He'd have to leave Chicago.

His breath steams the glass. The only frame of reference he has for the country beyond Chicago is the child's map in Steve's boyhood bedroom. In Bohdi's mind, each state is a different bright color, with some landmarks—the Grand Canyon, Mount Rushmore, the Statue of Liberty—drawn in friendly caricature. Beyond Chicago, nothing is real. He'd be no one in nowhere.

Bohdi backs away from the window, nearly knocking over the chair.

The door clicks and he drops quickly into the seat.

Steve walks into the room, shutting the door behind him with a bang.

Not meeting his eyes, Bohdi stammers, "I'm sorry."

Steve doesn't respond until he's sitting down on the table. "You've got to be more than sorry."

Bohdi looks up in alarm.

Silhouetted against the cheap fluorescent lights, Steve's skin looks so dark it is almost flat black. His expression is difficult to read. In low, clipped tones, Steve says, "It is not without precedent for the US government to hire talented pranksters with the idea it's better you're with us than against us."

Leaning forward in his chair, Bohdi feels a weight lifting off his chest.

"But I can't do that because you're not even a goddamned citizen," Steve says.

Bohdi shrinks back in the seat. Shoving his hands in his pockets, his fingers go to his lighter. He begins to nervously play with the thumbwheel.

"What do you want me to do?" Bohdi says.

Without a word, Steve holds out a hand with a Post-It note. Taking it, Bohdi sees an address and phone number on it. "That is the nearest Marine Corps recruitment center," Steve says. "I'll hold off the filing of the charges...somehow. If you prove that you are willing to fight and die for this country, I'll have something to tell the higher ups."

Bohdi stares at the handwritten scrawl. Die?

Steve exhales sharply. "I'll have to think of a way to get you out of the Corps later."

Bohdi looks up.

Steve shakes his head. "Your brain is too valuable to lose if you get shot."

Bohdi almost smiles.

"But boot camp may teach you some discipline," Steve says.

Bohdi fiddles with the corner of the Post-it as Steve says, "Stodgill's already working on the recruiter to deal with the paperwork that will result from your special situation..."

Bohdi nods at the mention of the legal counsel's name. He's needed her help a lot. It seems like you need a social security number for just about everything in this country.

"...all you'll have to do is show up and sign the papers."

Blinking up at Steve, Bohdi nods again, hoping he looks sufficiently grateful.

Raising an eyebrow, Steve says, "Just don't wander off into the desert and die during boot camp. Someone always does that."

Bohdi's eyes go wide. Beyond the door, shouts can be heard. Bohdi hears the words "troll" and "new gate."

Grumbling, Steve slides from the table and heads to the door.

Standing shakily, Bohdi says, "Thank you."

Steve meets his eyes just before he leaves the room. "My mother would kill me if I let them send you to Gitmo."

Before Bohdi can respond, Steve's gone. But he leaves the door open.

Bohdi looks down at the address in his hand. He can picture it. Not the building, but the blue dot on the public transit map he's memorized that marks the Blue "L" line stop nearby. He takes a shallow breath. What choice does he have?

Crinkling the paper in his hand, he heads toward the door, the nearest "L" station, and the recruitment center.

He almost makes it.

Why the University of Illinois Chicago Medical School hasn't been used for a horror movie's set Steve will never know. The centuries-old, gothic-style building is a hulking dark form on the downtown's southwest horizon. It's the sort of place you'd expect a troll to pop by. Thankfully, the creature was quickly dispatched with goat meat loaded with explosives.

Now Steve is standing in a crumbling archway with other ADUO agents and police, fielding questions from the press, as cameras flash in his eyes.

"Director Rogers, when will the troll sightings stop?" someone asks.

Most likely never. "As yet, that is uncertain," Steve says.

"Is it certain whether or not you'll be running for mayor?" someone else asks.

There are shouts and cheers through the press corps.

"What about president?" someone else shouts. "We need you to take on the trolls and wyrms in D.C!"

There are some more cheers and the adoration feels like electricity under his skin. His mind feels sharp and clear; he feels strong and alive. "Uncertain at this time," he says and the crowd gives a collective "aw" of disappointment, and it just buoys the rush.

Fighting to keep from smiling, he wonders if this is what drugs feel like. Someone else raises a hand, but an obnoxious ringtone that Steve certainly didn't download begins to blare over his phone.

The moment is over; his jaw ticks. He doesn't have to look at the ID to know who it is. Giving a quick excuse to the press, he turns and walks back through the arch, clicking to accept.

"Bohdi," he grinds out. "Tell me you are at the recruitment center."

"I was almost there," Bohdi says, sounding a little frantic, "but then I ran into Amy Lewis."

Steve starts to pace when he hears the name of the girl who had been Loki's...well, something. "What happened?"

"I was just walking, and I saw her as she fell. I ran over

to help. She didn't have her phone, so I couldn't call her grandmother..."

"Bohdi, what happened?" Steve snaps.

"We're at the hospital. She's having a miscarriage."

Steve stops mid-stride. He hadn't realized Amy was pregnant. Had she hidden that tidbit of information from him deliberately?

"Can you call her grandmother?" says Bohdi.

Steve draws his tongue across his teeth. Amy's grandmother, Beatrice Lewis, is Amy's only real family.

"Sure," says Steve, motioning with a hand for Hernandez's attention. "What hospital are you at?"

Bohdi gives him the hospital name and Steve says, "I'll be right there."

"What about her grandmother?" says Bohdi.

"Hanging up right now to call her," says Steve as he hangs up on Bohdi. He immediately turns to Hernandez. "Get the car started."

With a nod, Hernandez takes off. Steve stares at his phone. The FBI has been waiting for an opportunity like this. He doesn't look for Beatrice's number. Instead he makes another call. After a few short words with the agent at the end of the line, he heads over to the waiting car, smiling and waving for the press as he goes.

A few minutes later, Steve is at the front desk in the ER, holding up his badge. "I'm here to see Amy Lewis. She was brought in about half an hour ago. She was having a miscarriage—"

The nurse behind the counter looks at his badge and her brow furrows. "You'll have to wait; the doctors are in with her now."

"This is very important," says Steve. It's been only eight weeks since Loki disappeared, and he has no doubt whose baby it is.

"Then maybe you should talk to the father," snaps the nurse, pointing down a nondescript hallway. "He's in the waiting room around the corner."

"The father is here?" Steve says.

"Yes, he—"

Before she can finish, Steve is bolting down the corridor, nearly colliding with an attendant pushing a wheelchair. As he slides around the corner, his hand falls to the Glock at his hip. He almost pulls it out before he remembers it would be useless.

Breathing heavily, he enters the waiting room. Magic detector silent, his eyes scan over the dozen or so people seated there—the only person he recognizes is Bohdi.

Striding over to him, Steve says, "Where is he? Where is Loki?"

Murmurs go up around them. Bohdi glances around. "I don't know."

"The nurse said the father is here!" Steve says, grabbing Bohdi by the collar.

The lights above them flicker. Meeting his eyes, Bohdi swallows. "I lied to get into the ambulance."

For the second time in one day, Steve resists the urge to strangle him.

Behind him he hears the sound of rapid footsteps. Bohdi's eyes slide to the side. "Why are all the agents here?"

Men in black file by them and head down the hallway beyond Bohdi and Steve. The recovery team. Steve watches them go and reminds himself it's not a baby, it's a fetus, and it is already dead.

Turning back to Bohdi, he lies. "Someone told the hospital that the father was here, I had to be prepared."

Bohdi's nose wrinkles up like he might sneeze, and Steve lets go of his collar.

"Where's Beatrice?" says Bohdi, falling back into his chair and rubbing his nose.

"She's coming," Steve lies.

Bohdi lets loose a furious, sneeze, and looks up at Steve with weepy red, narrowed eyes.

Steve feels a twinge of guilt. Putting a hand on Bohdi's shoulder, Steve says, "Come on, I'll make sure you get to the recruitment center."

Drawing back, Bohdi wraps his hands so tightly around the chair's armrests, his knuckles go several shades paler. "No. I have to make sure my wife's okay." He says it loud enough for a passing orderly to hear. The man gives Steve a dirty look.

Rolling his eyes, Steve waits for the man to pass, and then says, "Why is this an issue for you?" He's hoping the question will help Bohdi cut through the clutter of his own internal bullshit. The kid doesn't talk about Lewis, they're not friends, and they've said maybe a dozen words to one another since Bohdi "arrived."

Bohdi drops his head. His long bangs falls in front of his eyes. Steve expects him to confess something along the lines of, "I'm afraid to join the service..."

Bohdi shrugs and swallows audibly. "She and I..." he shakes his head, looks up, and gives Steve a bitter smile. "We were both screwed by Loki," says Bohdi.

The kid's eyes are a little unfocused. He sounds so lonely and so lost. With an exasperated sigh, Steve sinks into a seat beside him.

CHAPTER 1
2 YEARS LATER

Stepping out of the coffee shop, Amy glances down LaSalle Street. Lifting her head, she gazes up at the former Chicago Board of Trade building, still listing to one side. The windows are dark. Weathered scaffolding protects the sidewalk below from falling rubble. The building has been leaning since the largest earthquake in Chicago's history wrecked its foundations. Coincidentally, at the exact same time, Loki had been dancing in an ADUO interrogation room.

"Such a lovely day!" says Amy's grandmother, Beatrice, cheerfully.

Amy blinks at the sky. There is no snow, just a blanket of early morning fog. It's warm for December, but gloomy. Turning to her grandmother, her lips quirk. "Do you mean the weather... Or are you referring to the troll this morning?"

Amy's staying with Beatrice until she finds an apartment. This morning, a troll popped up in their neighborhood, and their commute involved an hour-long detour. Periodic trolls, wyrms, and others visiting Chicago through magical World Gates is why the city hasn't been repaired.

"It is just so nice to have you back!" Beatrice says, sipping at her coffee. Her pink flower umbrella swings on her free arm.

Amy raises an eyebrow. "Grandma, you drove down to check on me every weekend while I was at school in Oklahoma."

Beatrice nods and smiles happily. "And now I can check on you every day while you're in the office, too."

Amy stifles a sigh. Not that she doesn't love her grandmother, but Beatrice has been a little over-protective of late. Amy only managed to keep Beatrice from moving to Oklahoma with her by finding her a job at ADUO. Beatrice is fluent in English, Ukrainian, and Russian. Just before Loki attacked Chicago, the city had been visited by Dark Elves bearing AK-47s. After the attack, Russia, the Ukraine, and Belarus had pushed for the elves to have the rights of the Geneva Convention. The US government even released the captured elves to the Russians. No one knows precisely what the elves are offering the Russians in return for weaponry, but Steve has Beatrice monitoring communications from those countries, looking for clues.

Amy appraises Beatrice. She walks with a spring in her step that belies her gray hair and wrinkles. Beatrice has the energy and sharpness of mind of a twenty-something. Before Cera and Loki destroyed Chicago, her grandmother had been in a nursing home, unable to remember her own name. And then…something happened.

Suffering from wounds inflicted by an ill-advised SWAT team raid, Amy watched the battle of LaSalle Street from Loki's apartment. When the battle was over, Amy's injuries were healed and Beatrice was there, her mind and body restored, the outrageous flower umbrella in her hands.

Steve and Beatrice posit that Loki healed Amy and Beatrice as a parting gift to Amy.

Amy rubs her temple. What Loki did give her as a final parting "gift" was his memories…and in all his memories, Loki was incapable of healing. Someone else had healed Beatrice and Amy, someone who was a master of biology, someone immensely powerful, and it could only be…

Pain flares behind her eyes, and she stops sharply. She winces. Sometimes this happens when she tries to think about that time…

"Are you alright, dear?" says Beatrice.

Amy drops her hand from her temple, and finds her grandmother's eyes peering at her from beneath neat, gray bangs. Beatrice has a rather fashionable bobbed haircut. And she's wearing a sharp white skirt beneath her fitted, black down jacket. She looks more put together than Amy does in jeans, tennis shoes, and casual ponytail; but Steve promised Amy a troll to dissect today. No way is she getting formaldehyde on good clothes.

"I'm fine, Grandma," Amy says, trying to give a reassuring smile. Why should she care how she and Beatrice got better? The important thing is that they are better…

"Hmmm…" says Beatrice.

As they resume walking, a shiver runs down Amy's spine. But she shakes her head, and it's as though her apprehension is swept away by invisible hands. Her mood lifts, and she takes a sip of her coffee. It's delicious, and she finds herself smiling.

They pass under some scaffolding. Construction has stalled, and there are no workers about. Across the street, a park appears. Off in a corner of the park, Amy notices a woman in garb that looks vaguely priestessy, talking to a group of camera-toting tourists. A bus bearing the slogan "City of Gods Tours" is idling on LaSalle a few feet away. For a minute, Amy gawks, but then she shakes her head. Scientists, the military, and tourism are the only things keeping Chicago afloat.

"This is the place I was telling you about," says Beatrice. "Lovely spot for a coffee break."

The park is pretty. There is a gentle bluff in a wide-open clearing. At the top are semi-circular half walls made of smooth stone sheltering a seating area. At the center is a statue commemorating the fallen firemen, police officers, and city council members who died defending the city. Following her eyes, Beatrice whispers, "Some people said it should be a statue of Steve. That man is golden in this town. If he doesn't run for mayor…" she shakes her head.

But Amy's eyes have alighted on the four men sitting at the bottom of the statue. There is Steve, Brett, and Bryant, but it's the last person that makes her smile. "Look, Grandma! It's Bohdi Patel. I thought he was in the Marines?"

Beatrice taps her chin. "Oh, he was. But he was discharged…something about a bum spleen."

"Let's go sit with them," Amy says as they approach the gentle sloping walkway that leads up to the seating area. "I'd like to talk to him."

"Hmmmm…." says Beatrice. "That boy…" she tsks.

Amy bites her lip, a little nervous as they cross toward the bottom of the stairs. To most people, Loki isn't the person who saved the world from a mind-warping source of infinite magical power bent on world domination. Instead, he is a psychopath who took out a large portion of the city, its defenders, and thousands of civilians. Most of those who know of Amy's "association" with Loki do not care for her. Or even feign respect. She smiles ruefully.

Bohdi has as much reason—or more than most people— to hate Amy. But when she'd woken up in an unfamiliar bed after her miscarriage, in a haze of blood loss, the first thing she'd seen was Bohdi's eyes on her. Framed by startlingly long lashes, they were warm, wide, innocent, and earnest. "Hi," he whispered.

And then he'd taken her hand in his. She'd followed the motion with her eyes. Leaning closer, Bohdi whispered, "I lied and told them we were married." He licked his lips nervously. "I'm sorry, I just had to make sure…" He stammered. "I'm glad you're okay." And then his face had gone a little pale, and his eyes had opened wider. "I mean…you're not okay, but…I'm sorry."

Amy had squeezed his hand. She didn't know Bohdi really, but she was grateful he was there. She felt lost, empty, and alone. His hand was like an anchor to humanity, and the look of concern on his face was like a balm. If he could care if she lived or died, she could care. And if he could forgive her, then she could forgive herself.

She'd dozed off a few minutes later, but she remembers waking a few more times after that, just briefly, to see him sitting there, hand still in hers, gazing at her intently, Beatrice standing just behind him.

Now, as she and Beatrice approach the first of the stairs, she begins to hear the murmur of the men's conversation, and she has a little flutter of panic. What must Bohdi think of her? He's a nice Indian boy, probably from a nice Indian family— even if he can't remember them. All of his compassion in the moment aside, what must he think of her getting "knocked up" by the guy who wiped his memory?

Beatrice and Amy are almost at the top of the stairs when the first of the conversation becomes intelligible.

"You did not," says Bryant.

"I did too," says Bohdi.

Amy's and Beatrice's heads clear the stairs. Bohdi's back is to them; all of the men's eyes are on him.

"I'm telling you, I slept with her!" Bohdi shouts, whipping something hot pink from his pocket and hurling it at Bryant.

Amy gasps. Brett's eyes meet Amy's and go wide.

Bryant shouts as whatever it is lands on his shoulder. Amy blinks. It's a thong.

Hopping and shouting, Bryant flicks it back at Bohdi who snatches it from the air and stuffs it back in his pocket.

Brett clears his throat loudly. Beatrice huffs. Rolling his eyes, Steve says, "Hello, Dr. Lewis. Welcome back."

"Hi, Amy," say Brett and Bryant in unison, Bryant still wiping at his shoulder.

Bohdi spins around, his eyes wide, mouth open in a startled "O."

Amy's coffee crashes to the ground at her feet.

Bohdi has filled out over the past two years, in a good way. He's still a little on the skinny side, but his shoulders are broader. His hair is also neater. His face, with his wide almost orange brown eyes, adorable slightly squished nose, and full lips, is just as open and innocent-looking as she remembered.

She feels a blush rising to her cheeks. Innocence—that's a lie, obviously. Maybe it's Amy's imagination, but the sky above her seems to darken.

With a shaky exhale, she looks down at the spilled coffee

at her feet. "Grandma," she says, "I think I need to go back to the café."

Beside her, Beatrice says, "Of course, dear."

As they turn and walk down the steps, Amy tries not to take off in a jog. Beside her, Beatrice tsks. "That boy is an alley cat…"

A strong wind buffets Amy's back. She and Beatrice look up. The sky had been clear when they left the office, but now dark clouds are moving in.

Beatrice scowls. "I don't remember rain in the forecast."

The crimson that had crept into the edges of Bohdi's vision when Bryant had taunted him starts to recede. Bohdi's eyes are trained on the retreating forms of Amy Lewis and her grandmother, but in his mind, he's seeing only the look on Amy's face—her blue eyes very wide, her full lips parted in shock. His throat feels tight. When had she come back to Chicago? Why hadn't anyone told him she was back?

Why had she just looked at him like he was a puppy kicker?

He straightens his shoulders. And why should he care? He thought they'd shared a moment there back in the hospital—but who was he kidding? She had been practically unconscious the whole time. And Amy's not just cute, she's a doctor of veterinary medicine, which makes her smart. Caring what smart, cute, girls think is just asking for trouble. You go gaga for them and then they dump you for a neurosurgeon because you don't have a college degree.

From behind him, Steve says in a dry voice, "And that is why I have told you time and again, gentlemen tell no tales."

Bohdi turns. Steve is cradling his coffee in one hand, arms crossed over his chest. The expression on Steve's face is so severe and unforgiving—like every drill instructor Bohdi ever had in the Corps—that Bohdi's body automatically snaps to attention. He almost blurts out "Yes, sir," before he catches himself. Face heating, he slouches deliberately and gives Steve a devil-may-care smile. "I thought you kept me around because you like living vicariously through my tales?"

And besides, Steve had also told him never to "get involved" with anyone in the office, but Bohdi had with Marion, and that had turned out all right.

Steve raises an eyebrow, his jaw set into a hard line. "I keep you around for comic relief," he says, his tone hard, and not comical at all.

Bohdi winces and averts his eyes. Besides being his boss, Steve is probably Bohdi's best friend. But the bastard's taller than Bohdi's six foot and change—which gives Steve the unfortunate ability to *literally* look down on Bohdi when he's *figuratively* looking down on Bohdi. Like now.

"We'll just head back to the office now," says Brett, making his way to the stairs. "Right," says Bryant, following his brother.

Steve doesn't budge.

Bohdi's eyes slide to the side. "You're not mad at me, are you? You left the bar, and after you did, Frieda seemed upset so I…"

"Offered to comfort her?" Steve supplies.

Bohdi rotates his shoulder and pats his arm. He's still sore from last night's comforting session. "Errr…"

Steve rolls his eyes and looks away. "I'm not mad at you," he says. It sounds a little forced. "Better it was you." He shakes his head and lets out a huff. "If it had been me, it would be all over the news that the black mayoral candidate couldn't keep it in his pants."

Rotating his shoulder again, Bohdi says, "But you're not even officially running yet."

Still not meeting his eyes, Steve says tersely, "Doesn't matter."

Bohdi takes in the hard set of Steve's jaw. Steve doesn't talk about racism much. Bohdi has experienced racism from the opposite end of the spectrum. He's taken for the nice Asian boy—not the stereotype you want attached to you in the Marines—but in the real world, kind of convenient. He doesn't know what to say to Steve, so he says nothing.

A wind buffets Bohdi's back.

"Come on," Steve says, voice still tight, walking toward the stairs.

Bohdi remembers how Steve had been so animated talking to Frieda, the woman who'd approached them—well, Steve—last night. It suddenly occurs to Bohdi that the tight set of Steve's jaw isn't about sex, or even racism. Steve's lonely.

"So, that date your mom set you up on last weekend…" Bohdi starts to say.

Steve's eyes slide toward him. They're dangerously narrow. Bohdi belatedly remembers that little tidbit is something he learned from Steve's mom, Ruth. Bohdi doesn't live with Steve's parents anymore, but he regularly shows up at their house for dinner. He likes Steve's parents. Also, there is free food.

Steve's glare shifts to an indefinable point in the distance. Feet flying down the steps in an unbroken rhythm, Steve grunts noncommittally. "I don't have time for dating right now."

"But when Claire moves with her mom—"

"We're not talking about that," Steve snaps.

Shoving his hands in his pockets, Bohdi finds the familiar comforting cool surface of his lighter. He looks down at the sidewalk. Steve's ex-wife, Dana, just married the US Ambassador to the Ukraine. Dana and Claire are relocating there to be with him.

Claire's smart, daring, and funny. Although Bohdi doesn't really know what it's like to have a sister, he thinks Claire is like a little sister to him. He'll miss not seeing her around.

Steve won't just miss her. Steve sees his divorce and inability to provide Claire with a stable two-parent home as the two greatest failures of his life. Having someone else step into the role of father, and not being able to see his daughter more than a few times a year...

Steve lightly swats the back of Bohdi's head.

Bohdi lifts his eyes.

"Throwing underwear? What were you thinking?" Steve says.

Recognizing the change in subject as an escape from unpleasant realities, Bohdi gives his most charming smile. "I wasn't really thinking." He feigns a yawn. "Probably because of all the sleep I didn't get last night."

Steve scowls at him. "You need to take a sexual harassment seminar."

"What?" squeaks Bohdi. "No, I was..."

Above their heads comes the sound of loud rawking. Bohdi and Steve both look to the sky. Two ravens are circling between the skeletal remains of unfinished construction.

"Huginn and Muninn," Steve says, jaw tightening again.

"It's been two years…Why are they back?"

In the sky, Odin's winged messengers laugh. "Hey, Steve, miss us?" Bohdi squints up at the birds, he's only seen them a few times. They used to trail Steve quite a bit, but had stopped shortly after Loki blew up large sections of downtown.

The wind picks up behind them and Bohdi stares at the clouds. When had they gotten so dark? "I didn't think the forecast was calling for rain," he says.

Steve's face hardens. "We're about to get company," he says, increasing his stride. Bohdi has to jog to keep up.

Snapping his phone open and putting it to his ear, Steve says, "Lewis? I think I'm going to need you at HQ." An instant later, he's shouting in the phone at Bryant, but Bohdi is too distracted by a flash of lightning and almost immediate roll of thunder to pay attention to the conversation.

On the sidewalk, people stop and stare at the sky. Steve walks around them so quickly Bohdi loses him for a second. When he catches up, he sees Amy down the street, just outside HQ's revolving doors. Her grandmother is with her, pink umbrella unfurled, despite the fact there is no rain.

Falling behind Steve again, Bohdi scampers to catch up but then stops in his tracks. A cold feeling of dread rises in his chest, and a sense of déjà vu. They are only a block away from Bohdi's first memory—being found by Steve. The thought still brings the taste of dust to his mouth.

A shape comes hurtling through the sky around the corner where LaSalle Street meets Jackson Boulevard, a lightning bolt streaking out in front of it, crackling down the center of LaSalle. Cars and messenger bikes dart to the sides; a flurry of horns and curses rise from the vehicles and are almost immediately drowned out by the boom of thunder.

The dark shape plunges down to the center of the street, and cars swerve to the side. Bohdi blinks and realizes it's a chariot, drawn by no visible means, with two men in it. One man is red haired, tall, and muscular. He wears Viking-meets-futuristic-video-game armor and a helmet that seem to melt into the scene behind him. Bohdi's seen plenty of footage from the battle with Loki to recognize him—it's Thor. During Loki's attack, Thor had stood beside the police, government agents, and firemen who tried to defend the city.

The chariot bounces to a stop on the ground in the very center of the street, and for a few heartbeats, Bohdi and the rest of the crowd stand immobilized in collective shock. It strikes Bohdi that in real life, Thor is a lot bigger and more imposing than in YouTube videos. Without pausing, Steve walks right out into the street to meet him.

"Well met, Steve Rogers!" booms Thor, as camera flashes wink from the sidewalk and windows of cars.

Shaking himself out of his personal bout of shock and awe, Bohdi slips out onto the street to stand behind Steve. He's just close enough to hear his boss say, "What brings you here, Thor?"

The space Viking nods his head. Bohdi had nearly forgotten the chariot's other passenger, but now that man exits the chariot and walks around to stand before Steve, his head held high. The man's hair is bright blond, nearly white, and his skin is very pale. He is wearing metal armor. A sword is sheathed at his side. In one hand, he bears a thin wooden stick like Bohdi had seen the conductor use when Steve's mom dragged him to the symphony. The man doesn't give the street, or the throngs of humans pressing closer, a single glance. He just looks at Steve and says nothing.

Exiting the chariot, Thor nods in the man's direction. "This is the mage Skírnir. We are here, Steve Rogers, to ask you for a boon."

As agents spill out of headquarters to contain the crowd that is forming around the two alien visitors, Skírnir raises his chin. Eyes on Steve, he says, "We wish to speak with the Frost Giantess Gerðr you hold in your custody."

Bohdi blinks at mention of Gerðr. "Giants" is a bit of a misnomer when used to describe the people of the planet Jotunheim. The Jotunns visited Earth in the age of the Vikings. Gerðr is only about as tall as Bohdi, but the average Viking male was only five foot six. To them, the Jotunns must have appeared to be giants, and the name "giants" stuck. Bohdi doesn't know whether the adjective "frost" before the word "giant" is due to the average temperature of Jotunheim, or if they all share Gerðr's frosty personality.

Beyond Thor and Skírnir, Bohdi sees Amy making her way forward. Beatrice is at her side, umbrella closed and raised like a sword. Frowning in Steve's direction, she nods her head in the negative.

Steve's eyes flick from Amy back to Thor. "Let's discuss it in our boardroom," he says.

Thor nods, but Skírnir pulls his head back as though Steve has just slapped him.

Steve gestures toward the HQ's door and says, "After you."

As Skírnir and Thor walk toward the door, the crowd surges. The black-suited agents can barely keep it in control. Flashbulbs go off around Skírnir, Thor, and Steve. Bohdi hears someone that must be in the press shout, "Rogers—did you know about this visit? Is this something you planned to boost your rankings in the mayoral race?"

"No comment," says Steve, his face grim as Bohdi sidles up beside him.

They've just cleared the doors, and Bohdi's about to ask Steve if he did know, but Steve steps away from Bohdi, holding up a hand in Amy's direction. "Lewis!"

Amy and her grandmother are at Steve's side a minute later. She meets Bohdi's eyes very briefly, and then turns away. Bohdi finds himself staring at the back of her slightly messy, light brown ponytail.

"What do you know?" Steve asks her.

Amy whispers, "Skírnir's presence may be triggering to Gerðr. Don't make her be in this meeting."

The hushed tone of her voice, the set of her shoulders— Bohdi doesn't have to ask triggering for what.

Jaw tight, Amy says, "Skírnir forced her to marry his master Freyr by threatening to destroy her homeland and her people…and then later, as Freyr grew tired of her…" There is anger bubbling in her voice.

Lifting his head, Bohdi looks at Skírnir walking a few meters ahead of them, armor glittering. The Frost Giantess Gerðr has remained in ADUO's custody as a "prisoner-consultant" since her team tried to steal Cera, the World Seed, years ago.

Bohdi doesn't like Gerðr. No one does. She has, upon occasion, loudly declared humans to be on par with snow weevil shit. But still…he narrows his eyes at Skírnir's back and his hands clench at his side. Glancing down, he sees Steve is having a similar reaction.

Steve tilts his head. "I'll look out for Gerðr. I need you in the meeting though, Lewis."

She nods. "Of course. By the way…the little stick he's

carrying is Gambanteinn, a magic wand."

"Like Harry Potter?" says Bohdi without thinking.

Glancing back to Bohdi, Amy says to Steve, "It's not really like a Harry Potter wand." Her voice goes soft. "It's not as versatile. I think it may have some powers of compulsion... but in some stories, it was also used as a sword."

They step into a hallway, and Beatrice falls back until she's walking side by side with Bohdi. They're just past a service hallway when Thor and Skírnir, escorted by Bryant, Brett, and Hernandez, slip between two armed guards into the magically sealed conference room. Steve and Amy follow them in, and Beatrice and Bohdi step forward as one to do the same—and both of them run into a hand of the guards

"Excuse me, young man," says Beatrice, glaring up at her guard, the tip of her umbrella just beneath his chin.

Giving his guard a smile, Bohdi says, "I'll just go in in case they need audio-visual help."

Both guards step sideways so they're blocking the now-closed door. The one in front of Beatrice says, "Sorry, Ma'am." The one in front of Bohdi—Smith, or Jones, or something—just glares at him and says, "No."

Beatrice backs up a step. "I'll just wait for my grand-daughter here, then."

"Could be a while, Ma'am," says one of the guards, his voice apologetic.

Bohdi's eyes dart to the side. The hallway is pretty clear. "Hmmm...well, I'll just get back to work," says Bohdi.

"You do that," says the guard whose hand he'd run into earlier. The guy doesn't even look at him. Which is good. Bohdi walks casually down the hall. The guards continue to talk to Beatrice. Which is also good—it keeps them distracted.

"Do you want to pull up a chair?" he hears the nice guard say to Beatrice.

"Are you offering to get me one?" asks Beatrice.

"Well—"

"We can't leave," says the other guard.

Bohdi checks over his shoulder. No one is looking. He sidesteps into the short service hallway and hears Beatrice's voice echo behind him. "Well, I'm not leaving either."

The service hallway is only a few feet long. Besides some dust bunnies, there is a dirty window, an emergency exit that leads to a fire escape, and a non-descript door. Pulling out his wallet, Bohdi extracts a credit card and checks over his shoulder one more time. He's still alone. With a quick movement, he slides the credit card between the door and the wall and feels the lock give. Checking one more time over his shoulder, he opens the door, steps into the room, and then shuts the door quietly behind him.

He looks around. It's the same room Steve and Hernandez had locked him in two years ago and it brings a bitter taste to his mouth. Of course, Steve would have him enlist into the most fucking gung-ho branch of the armed services. If Bohdi had known what a shit deal joining the Marine Corps would be and how easy this particular lock was to unlatch, he'd have taken his chances being no one in nowhere. He shakes his head. But of course, if he'd run away, he wouldn't have Steve's parents to retreat to on Sunday nights for dinner. And enlisting did get him his current job—it's a job he usually loves—spending all day trying to hack into the classified files of the FBI and ADUO. When he's successful, he's not supposed to read the files, but of course, he does. It's awesome.

He looks around the room. His job may be awesome, but

listening in on Thor and Skírnir's conversation with Steve right now? He's betting that's even better.

They've changed the space into a storage area since he was last here. Unused desks, folded up and coated with dust, lean against one wall. Fortunately, they've left the wall with the air-conditioning intake free. Bohdi smiles.

Instead of being cooled and heated by a central air conditioning and heating system, ADUO's headquarters have heavy-duty industrial heating and AC units set into the walls at regular intervals. Most of the units cool more than one room. The unit with the intake vent in this little room cools the conference room next door. The units are so loud that in the winter, the office just relies on the building's ancient radiators.

Quietly unfolding a foldout chair leaning beneath the window, Bohdi steps up. Through the vent, Thor's voice booms, "We have come to your realm seeking passage to Nornheim."

Amy's voice isn't as loud; Bohdi has to press his ear to the vent to hear her reply.

"Asgard has its own World Gate to Nornheim," she says, her voice firm and clear even if it's soft. "What are you hiding from us?"

Drawing back, Bohdi scowls and takes out his knife. If he's going to hear all of this conversation, he's going to have to get a little closer. Flipping open the Phillips-head screwdriver hidden in the knife handle, he begins to work on the grate.

CHAPTER 2

The conference room is windowless and lined with magic-blocking Promethean Wire. The wire makes the conversation invisible to Heimdall if he's looking this way. It also makes it impossible for magic to work in the room, making Skírnir's wand just a stick, and Mjolnir, Thor's hammer, just a hammer. Steve is at the head on one end of a long, oblong table. Thor is at the other. Amy is sitting stiffly on one side, half way between them. Brett and Bryant are seated next to her. So is Agent Stodgill, ADUO's legal counsel. Hernandez and some other men are standing along the walls, eyes on Thor and his companion. Skírnir is sitting directly across from Amy, his very pale eyes trained on her.

Amy glares right back at him. Loki's memories of Skírnir make Amy wish that he'd do something threatening. It would be nice if one of the agents had an excuse to shoot him.

"What are you hiding from us?" Amy says, directing the question at Thor. Skírnir hasn't spoken since they entered the room. And she doesn't want to speak to him.

Feeling something wiggle in her pocket, she blinks. Eight tiny feet scamper up onto her lap. Keeping her eyes on

Thor, she reaches down and gently wraps a hand around Mr. Squeakers, the eight-legged venomous spidermouse that Loki had given to her over two years ago. Squeakers doesn't like it when people upset her. Slipping the stowaway back into her pocket, Amy glances around the room. No one seems to have noticed her tiny protector.

Thor leans forward and meets Amy's gaze. "The Norns have closed all known gates to their realm."

Tapping a finger on the table, Amy says, "Why doesn't Odin just create a new World Gate?" Creating a World Gate isn't as simple as opening one to walk thru, and yet she has this feeling...

Across the table from her, Skírnir's head does a quick jerk. "What makes you think that Odin can do that?"

Amy's heart beats fast. Loki's memories don't normally come to the surface unless she stumbles upon something relevant. Now they come forth in a deluge.

Loki awakens to darkness, lying on his side. He tries to open his eyes and finds he can't. He tries to move his arms to wipe away whatever is obstructing his vision and feels the bite of bonds at his wrists. Dull pain throbs through his shoulders, and his shins and ankles. He tries to move his legs, and succeeds in yanking his own wrists backward. A shocked yell comes unbidden to his throat, but all that comes out of his mouth is a muffled whine and the taste of linen invades his senses.

From a few feet away, a rough male voice says, "Oh, look, he's awake."

"Broken bellows," mutters another voice. "The draught of potion should have kept him knocked out longer." Loki hears

more grunts, and the sound of steel against stone.

Draught of potion? Above his blindfold, Loki's brows constrict. The last thing he remembers was being in Svartálfaheimr, realm of the dwarves, on a diplomatic mission with Odin. He'd been escorted to the servants' kitchens, and offered a draught of mead…

His eyes scrunch tighter. "Broken bellows." Loki's mind whirls at the curse words. Dwarves. His eyelids flutter beneath his bonds. He should have realized that immediately from the Dwarven tongue they're speaking, but he'd magically translated the language without a thought.

He squirms. Something enters his nostrils. Dust maybe? And are those pebbles beneath him? Is he lying on the ground? If he is, it hasn't rained in a long time; it's as dry as the stones of the World Gate in midsummer. Very little light is filtering through his eyelids. Is it nighttime? He strains to hear the sounds of night animals. There is a humming, but nothing like he is used to.

"He might be more fun awake," says the first voice. "What is he? Sixteen or seventeen years old? He's pretty enough to be a girl."

There are chuckles around Loki. His body goes still. It's not the first time he's heard such words, but never while in such a vulnerable position. The sound of his heart pounding in his ears grows so loud it is almost deafening.

"Don't get close to him, Longbeard. He's scrawny, but closer to twenty-three and made his first kill when he was naught but a boy. Killed a foe too wicked for even Odin."

Loki tries to inhale deeply but barely fills his lungs. He tries to swallow, and feels drool trickling down his chin. He hadn't been trussed up like a helpless blind worm when he'd slain the giant Cronus.

Longbeard snorts. Loki can't help but notice that he's drawn closer. "*This boy? Impossible. I've never seen a lad this pretty. The Norns said they wanted him intact, but they didn't say we couldn't play with him. What could be the harm?*"

"*Rites of War,*" someone chuckles.

Loki's breath comes in short shallow bursts, and he wiggles away from the sound of Longbeard's voice. Unfortunately, it takes him closer to the sound of the other voices.

"*Look!*" someone shouts. "*I think he understands you.*"

"*He squirms like a worm!*" says someone else.

There are a few dark chuckles. "*Longbeard will give him a worm!*"

Curling his body into as tight a ball as he can manage, Loki concentrates. He imagines a hulking troll stomping through the camp—

Yelps rise up around him. Longbeard gives a satisfying gasp of fear. There is the sound of metal on metal, and then someone snorts. "*Don't let him stoke your battle fires, men. That is just an illusion. Real trolls don't step into flames...or through trees...*"

"*You won't get away from me that easily,*" says Longbeard.

There are dark murmurs around camp. Loki lets the illusion fade and scowls beneath his blindfold. Hoenir and Odin had always told him he should learn to use his illusions as eyes and ears; they'd even shown him how, but he hadn't bothered to practice. If he could see the dwarves and their fires, his illusion would have been more convincing.

There is the sound of approaching feet.

"*Don't go near him!*" the owner of the first voice shouts. "*If we fail, the Norns will never reveal the location of Andvaranaut, and our land will continue to be blighted with its curse!*"

"*I don't plan on not delivering,*" says Longbeard, drawing closer.

The sound of Loki's heartbeat is so loud and strong now, it sounds like hoof beats.

Something tickles his cheek. Loki writhes in his bonds, his vision going red. Heat flashes against his face and Longbeard screams.

"Longbeard's beard is on fire!" someone screams. "Drop and roll on it."

Loki would laugh, but he's too terrified.

Screams erupt around the camp. "Einherjar! We're being attacked! Grab the boy! Grab the boy."

Loki feels himself hoisted up onto a burly shoulder. He hears a hiss and a thunk beneath him. The wind is knocked out of him as his captor falls and Loki lands on top of his fallen body. Around him, steel rings on steel, and hooves beat in every direction.

Odin's voice cuts through the din like thunder. "Find Loki!"

Wiggling his way onto his knees, hands still tied behind him, Loki tries to let out a cry, but his voice is barely audible even to him.

"Loki!" Odin roars from behind. Loki tries to turn toward the sound.

Crossing swords clang in Loki's ears. Horses whinny and bellow. A hand touches his blindfold. Loki screams beneath his gag, the blindfold disappears, and he blinks and sees a blur of flame dancing before him. Loki screams again and the fire snuffs out.

"Loki!" shouts Odin.

The blur in front of Loki comes into focus, and he's staring into Odin's single eye. The Allfather's eyebrows are smoldering slightly. Surprisingly, Odin, Loki's king and guardian, looks more relieved than angry.

Loki swallows and feels tears prickle behind his eyes. He wants to throw his arms around Odin, as he did when he was a child. Perhaps it's best he's still trussed up like a pig. Odin is a king, and Loki is not a child, nor his kin.

Loki closes his eyes. Patting him once on the cheek, Odin says. "Easy, I'm going to cut you loose." Opening his eyes, Loki sees Odin pulling out a long knife. The Allfather walks around him, and Loki feels the knife slice through the bonds. His limbs snap free with such force, he almost topples over, but Odin catches him.

Loki's wrists tingle and burn with the sudden rush of blood. "Give yourself a minute," Odin commands. Loki looks down alarmed. He can't feel his feet, and his legs feel as limp as newly tanned leather. Rubbing his wrists together, he looks around.

Surrounding Odin and Loki, backs to them, stand the Einherjar, the human warriors recruited from every corner of Midgard, and made immortal by Idunn's apples. Their swords are drawn, but no one seems to be confronting them.

Near Loki's head, Odin whistles.

Sleipnir, Odin's enormous, eight-legged steed, emerges between the other horses, pale as a moonbeam, his halter glowing faintly. Sleipnir's halter is magical. Woven from the strands of Gleipnir, the rope that can hold anything. Mimir always said that an ordinary stallion was difficult enough to control; give a stallion eight legs and you need magical control...

Sleipnir snuffles against Loki's cheek, gently nudging Loki from his reverie, and then the horse pricks his ears toward the darkness.

Around them, the Einherjar begin to fan out. The night is very dark. Loki cannot even see the stars, but he thinks he makes out the shapes of dwarves lying on the nearly barren ground, arrows protruding from their bodies. He hears a few low groans.

Odin hauls Loki to his feet and surveys the scene.

Loki eyes the Einherjar with apprehension. Odin always says their gratitude makes them braver and more loyal than any Aesir or Vanir warrior. That Odin would think he needs them to fetch Loki suggests Odin suspects a dangerous foe, and yet they seem to have dealt with the dwarves quickly enough.

A tall Einherjar, his skin nearly as black as the night around them, approaches Odin. "We've dispatched the dwarves, Your Majesty."

Guiding Loki by the shoulder, Odin says, "Good, let's get back to the World Gate."

Shaking, Loki says, "The dwarves were going to take me to the Norns."

Hoisting himself up onto Sleipnir, Odin grunts. "Yes, Heimdall heard that just before they slipped you through Svartálfaheimr's World Gate." Almost to himself, he says, "The Norns requested you in exchange for information the dwarves were seeking."

Loki feels as though his stomach has suddenly shrunk to the size of a robin's egg. Odin and Frigga have told him that the Norns know everything that has ever happened and is happening—some say they even know what will happen—though Frigga long ago disabused him of that notion. The Norns will provide information to requestors at a price: either an object of power, or a nearly impossible favor. Loki isn't an object of power, and capturing him doesn't seem so impossible.

"Why would the Norns want me?" he asks, wincing at the whine in his voice.

From the saddle, Odin offers a hand to help Loki up behind him. Loki takes it—he needs it. Sleipnir's back is nearly as high as the top of his head, and Odin's got the stirrups. Hoisting Loki up, Odin says, "I do not know. It's a question for later—we need to escape quickly."

"Escape…what?" says Loki, swinging up behind Odin.

"Everything wicked in the realms eventually makes its way to Nornheim," Odin says, holding up a hand for silence.

The tall Einherjar who'd just spoken to Odin follows the direction of Odin's gaze. "Hoof beats," he says.

A horse comes galloping out of the darkness, the whites of its eyes visible as they roll in terror. The beast's saddle is askew; its rider has slumped forward and is dangling dangerously over the animal's side, groaning loudly. Wispy gray ropes cling to both steed and warrior.

Running to grab the horse's reins, one of the Einherjar shouts. "It's Hsu! He was with the others guarding the World Gate."

In the saddle, the warrior Hsu groans. "They took the gate… they…"

A bolt of gray-white rope the width of a man's arm shoots from the darkness above and affixes to Hsu's mouth. The warrior's head is yanked up by the rope with such force his neck cracks. An instant later, his corpse is ripped from his saddle and pulled up into the darkness above. More bolts of rope shoot from above and affix to the Einherjar and their mounts. The horses scream as they and their riders are pulled into the air.

"Follow me!" Odin shouts, drawing a sword and severing a rope that has affixed to Sleipnir's neck.

Some of the Einherjar are able to slip from their mounts and jump to the ground, only to have the ghostly ropes shoot from the sky and affix to their bodies and the flat edges of their swords. Sleipnir rears, and Loki clings to Odin. The Allfather curses, and Loki glances above to see Odin's sword has been ripped from his hands. More ropes affix to Odin. One lands on Loki. Frantically trying to shake the wet sticky thing from his arms, Loki looks around in horror. His arm tightens instinctively around Odin's waist. They are now surrounded in a forest of glistening gray-white strands.

Before Loki, two ropes affixed to either shoulder start to drag Odin out of the saddle. Loki locks his arms around the Allfather's waist and his legs around Sleipnir's sides trying to pull Odin down.

"Loki!" Odin screams. "Fire!"

"But I might set you aflame!" Loki cries.

Another bolt of rope shoots from the darkness to Odin's back just in front of Loki's nose, and Odin starts to slide from his arms.

Loki gives a cry of rage and fear, sees red, orange, yellow, and blue light before his eyes, and every inch of his skin burns. Beneath Loki, Sleipnir screams, and Odin falls back into the saddle. The heat fades from Loki's skin, but around him, fires still crackle in clumps of dry grass and dried up husks of bushes on the ground.

In the flickering light, Loki can see the terrain around them for the first time. The earth is almost completely barren, the sky above…He gasps. They appear to be in a huge tent of some kind. Red lights glint amid the eaves. Around him swing warriors and horses encased in hammocks of sticky rope.

He jumps in the saddle as a loud crack sounds to his right. Turning with a gasp, he sees the skeletal remains of a tree burst into flame, fire dancing up its trunk to branches hidden beneath the tent's white eaves. Close to where the tree burns, a horse falls from the sky and lands on its feet with the sound of splintering bones. The horse screams in pain and tumbles to the ground. A few of the Einherjar fall from above and stumble to their feet. "Grab hold of Sleipnir's mane and tail!" Odin commands.

Hastening to obey Odin's words, the warriors run through curled blackened ends of rope to Sleipnir's sides.

A bolt of the sticky rope lands on the ground before them, and Sleipnir rears. "Steady!" Odin commands, and Sleipnir stills, shaking his head and snorting. More ropes fall around them. To the warriors around him, Odin says, "Sleipnir will slip through time. Whatever you see, feel or hear, do not let go!"

Loki barely has a chance to digest those words before Odin gives a tap to Sleipnir's haunches. Loki instantly feels lighter. Another bolt of rope shoots from the sky—and then appears to stop in midair. Tossing his head nervously, Sleipnir begins to thread his way through the small clumps of fire and sticky rope pillars.

Staring at the flames, Loki almost falls from his saddle. The flames aren't flickering, they are just columns of colored light, as though intricately carved and painted statues of fire.

One of the Einherjar mutters a swear and releases Sleipnir's mane...Loki blinks...and the warrior is no longer at Sleipnir's side. Craning his head around, he sees the soldier, body seemingly frozen in place, hand outstretched toward them far off in the distance. Odin doesn't turn Sleipnir around.

The sky above them goes from black, speckled with a few distant clusters of red lights, to navy blue, lit by three moons, and unfamiliar stars. Tightening his arms around Odin, Loki looks back again and sees the tent-like structure they emerged from already far back in the distance. Suddenly around them trees rise. Some look familiar. Others look completely alien, leaves like feathers or dinner plates visible even in the low light. In only a few falls of Sleipnir's hooves, the forest falls away, and they are standing on a bluff. Odin draws Sleipnir to a halt. Loki's body suddenly has weight again, and his ears are assailed by the sound of chirping insects. The soldiers still holding onto Sleipnir's mane and tail gasp and murmur. The hum of insects rises around them.

Gentle mountains covered by forest stretch all around them. Between some of the mountains, Loki sees more tents. From the outside, they glisten white in the moonlight. He squints. Because of the distance, it's difficult to gauge their size, but he'd guess each tent to be the size of a small city.

Those observations are secondary to the true defining feature of the Nornheim landscape. Scattered about, seemingly at random, are enormous columns. Each must be as wide as Odin's great hall. Their bases are not smooth and circular; rather, they seem to be composed of many great tree trunks merged together. Near the ground, they are covered with plants, but as they rise into the sky, their surfaces shimmer with color and appear to be lit by inner light. They stretch so high, their tops are invisible, but Loki thinks he makes out the faint shadow of branches slightly obscuring the faces of the moons.

In the saddle, Odin lifts his head and roars. "Hoenir, create a new gate!"

Tense minutes tick by, with Odin saying nothing. Sleipnir stamps the ground and shifts beneath Loki. The buzzing of night insects grows louder.

Odin grunts, and says, "The branches of the columns obstruct Hoenir and Heimdall's vision. I'll have to create a new gate myself."

Loki sits back in surprise. "You can open World Gates?" he whispers. Through clenched teeth the Allfather says, "Not well."

He turns his head to the side. In profile, Odin's face is haggard, weary…and it strikes Loki, maybe even fearful.

If Odin is worried, Loki is worried. He shivers.

Patting Loki's hand, Odin chuckles. "The odds are I will fail…but then again, I have you."

Loki's brow furrows. He can't imagine what could be worse

than what they've already come through.

Nervously stepping sideways, Sleipnir lets out a nervous whinny.

"Sire, behind us," says one of the warriors.

Loki turns. In the night sky behind them, he sees a swarm of shadows rising into the air. They look like giant dragonflies, but where he'd expect the bodies of insects, he sees slender, hominid-like forms.

"Adze," a dark-skinned Einherjar says. "Cursed bloodsuckers."

Loki's mouth goes dry. There are hundreds of them.

"Loki, hold tight!" Odin commands. "That goes for the rest of you, too."

Without further warning, Odin gives Sleipnir a kick in the haunches. Loki feels his body go light, the humming of insects stops, and Sleipnir launches himself down the bluff, leaping in such great bounds that the bones of a normal horse's legs would crack. But Sleipnir and the Einherjar land lightly. On Sleipnir's back, Loki would not know the beast had leaped if he hadn't seen it for himself.

Bohdi pushes his head a little further into the air duct between the two rooms. The back of Steve's head comes into view and then the rest of the room's occupants. He sees Amy, looking a little lost in space, staring above Thor's head. Skírnir is glaring at her.

Eyes on Steve, Thor says, "If it were so easy. My father can create gates, but only at great expense."

"What does this have to do with us?" says Steve.

Turning to Steve, Skírnir says, "The World Seed's residual magic is still creating gates in your city. Depending on their proximity to the Norn's stronghold, it is possible that the Norns have not been able to close them. All we require of you is that you take us to a gate that leads to Nornheim. Then I will open the gate, and Thor and I will be gone and trouble you no more."

Tilting his head, Steve says, "We have gates, but we don't know where they lead."

In the duct, Bohdi's nose starts to itch. Rubbing his upper lip, he restrains a sneeze. He can't help but notice that, at the conference table, Amy's eyes have gone wide as though she's surprised.

Voice tight, Skírnir says, "Surely *your whore* Gerðr has told you?"

Steve's shoulders tighten like he's restraining the urge to lunge across the table and strangle someone. Which he probably is.

Bohdi feels his skin heat. Steve has worked hard to ensure Gerðr is treated with more decency than the cranky giantess gives any human. She only has female guards. She's never alone with any one person, male or female, and all her interactions are on camera—precisely because Steve doesn't want any allegations like the ones Skírnir just tossed into the room.

Steepling his fingers, Steve says coolly, "The *lady* is not a whore. And frankly, that you suggest she is treated as one under my roof insults me."

Thor casts a dark look in Skírnir's direction. "Excuse him. Skírnir does not know your ways. He did not mean to cause offense."

For his part, Skírnir, the magician guy, looks both annoyed and perplexed. "Indeed, I did not. But she is your prisoner so I assumed you would—"

Straightening in his chair, Steve says nothing. Bohdi's lip curls. His boss has way too much self-control. If Bohdi were in the room, he'd strangle Skírnir on Steve's behalf.

Clearing his throat, Thor says, "Gerðr is capable of knowing what realm any World Gate leads to without traversing it."

Leaning forward, Skírnir says, "Has she not told you?"

Bohdi knows she hasn't, but Steve does not respond.

Looking pleased, Skírnir says, "If she has not, leave her to me, and I will extract the information for you."

Voice flat, Steve says, "I'll have to run it by my superiors."

Clearing his throat, Thor says, "He means magic compulsion, Agent Rogers. Not torture."

Skírnir raises an eyebrow in Thor's direction that clearly says, "Say what?" Bohdi feels a little sick.

"I'll still have to clear it," Steve says.

Skírnir's eyes narrow. "How long will it take?"

"Oh, it could take quite some time, months…" says Steve. He gives a shrug and a casual wave that clearly say "maybe never."

Bohdi almost snorts. If Steve had a magic power, it would be clearing hurdles of bureaucratic bullshit in the blink of an eye.

Skírnir glares, but Thor grunts and says, "Do what you must." He gives Steve a tight smile. "We are not authorized to interfere with the internal workings of your affairs."

"Yet," says Skírnir.

Bohdi's fingers tighten at the edge of the grate.

Looking genuinely weary, Thor slumps in his seat. "Enough of this politicking. Agent Rogers, it is truly good to see you again."

Summoning up more self-control than Bohdi's ever had,

Steve says, "And it is good to see you."

Thor visibly brightens. "Does your cafeteria still boast the magical chocolate elixir?"

"Yes, it does," says Steve, and Bohdi can hear the smile in Steve's voice. Steve can bullshit in ways Bohdi never can.

Bohdi smirks. If Steve can cut through bullshit as well as he can deliver bullshit, does that make Steve the King of Bullshit? He restrains a chuckle. He's going to declare that Steve's title...but maybe after a few beers.

"Let us adjourn there," says Thor, banging his fist on the table. There is a loud crack, the table shudders, sags, and the middle drops to the floor with a bang. Everyone that wasn't already standing jumps from their seats. Every agent along the room's perimeter has his Glock out and pointed at Thor or Skírnir.

Thor stares at the table and says sheepishly, "No offense meant."

Steve steps over, puts a hand on Thor's shoulder and turns him toward the door. "None taken. I'll let my people escort you to the cafeteria. I need a few words with Dr. Lewis."

Thor stares blankly at Steve for a few long seconds, and then his eyes widen. Looking back at Amy, he dips his chin in a gesture that looks respectful. Bohdi almost sighs. No one gives him that sort of respect.

With a final parting nod to Steve, Thor and Skírnir step out of the room with a gauntlet of agents surrounding them, magic detectors beeping as they leave the confines of the Promethean Wire.

And then it's just Steve and Amy...and Bohdi, if peering through the air duct counts.

Leaning two hands on the back of a chair, Steve says,

"Well, Dr. Lewis, do you have any insights into the meeting?"

Amy puts her hands in her pockets and looks down. She prods the table with the toe of her sneaker. Bohdi leans closer. Amy isn't gorgeous, but she is really, really cute. And she's a *doctor.*

There are people at ADUO who say less than nice things about her—how she isn't very bright to have hooked up with Loki, and how His Mischievousness just wanted someone who was easy to control. Amy's file is so well protected that even Bohdi hasn't been able to read it. But gossip isn't as easily contained. She helped Loki escape from Alfheim, realm of the elves, and ran over Thor with her car *on purpose.* Bohdi was also there when she opened a portal to another dimension and when she came back from said dimension…*by herself.*

Bohdi thinks that, super-villainy aside, maybe Loki just had good taste.

The piece of wood Amy was prodding settles with a creak and a bang. Bohdi snaps out of his reverie.

Slipping her hands into her pockets, Amy says, "Well, the Norns know everything that has happened and is happening…and people go to them with questions in exchange for an item of power or a heroic deed…"

Bohdi jerks so quickly, he nearly bangs his head on the top of the vent. His hand starts to slip toward his wallet.

"Any idea what sort of question Odin would find so important that he'd send his son?" says Steve.

"No, I…" Amy's eyes grow wide. "I think Odin's still looking for Loki."

Bohdi's body stills. Loki is dead. That's ADUO's official pronouncement, and Steve's said it and…

Steve's eyes widen a fraction. "I think you're right."

Bohdi's body goes cold.

Putting his hand to his chin, Steve says, "But if the Norns and Asgard are not on speaking terms, how does Thor expect to pry any information from them?"

Shrugging, Amy rolls on her feet. And then she says in a small voice, "What about the gate to Nornheim in Loki's old apartment?"

What? Bohdi leans forward in the duct. How in all his online snooping and offline eavesdropping does he not know there is a World Gate in Loki's apartment?

Steve waves a hand. "Loki's apartment is cordoned off and constantly monitored. To get in, you'd need to get past armed guards, fingerprint and retina scans, and a door that would put most bank vaults to shame."

Bohdi shakes his head but doesn't sigh. There is a way into Loki's apartment. But when Bohdi pointed it out, ADUO had deemed it "too preposterous to occur" and "too expensive" to fix.

In a light tone, Steve says to Amy, "How did you know Odin can open World Gates?"

"Oh." Amy shifts from one foot to another. She gives Steve a small smile, meets his eyes, and says, "Loki told me."

A sneeze wracks Bohdi's body before he can contain it.

Steve looks toward the vent. "Damn mice!"

Amy eyes the air vent. "Sounds more like a rat."

Well that... Bohdi draws back and bangs his head on the corner of the duct and the wall.

Steve snorts. "I think you just insulted it."

And then Steve looks back to Amy. "Exciting first day back?"

As Bohdi massages his head, he hears Amy say, "Thor...

Skírnir…the thong."

Steve sighs. "Oh, Bohdi is all right."

Still massaging his head, Bohdi frowns. Can't Steve say he's a little better than "all right"?

"Any idea why Loki stole his memories?" Amy asks.

Bohdi opens both eyes to see Steve stop in his tracks by the door. "The only thing that comes to mind is Bohdi flipping Loki off right before it happened."

Bohdi's breath catches in his throat. Steve never told *him* that. That sounds almost…heroic.

Amy rolls her eyes. "So he's always been kind of an ass, then?"

With an indignant huff, Bohdi pulls back so quickly his head bangs against the metal ductwork.

Amy stands at the coffee dispenser in the cafeteria, finally getting the cup she'd said she'd get after the thong incident.

Beatrice is beside her, umbrella swinging on her arm, eyeing the table where Thor, Skírnir, Steve, and a few other agents sit surrounded by armed guards. Magic detectors are beeping faintly, picking up on Thor's hammer and Skírnir's wand.

Skírnir's not eating, just picking at some food with a plastic fork.

Shaking her head, Amy turns toward the door and whispers to Beatrice. "Steve asked me to talk to Gerðr before I dissect my troll's anterior cruciate ligament."

"I'll come with you," says Beatrice as they step into the hallway. Amy feels a bright light of pride. "You've never been interested in my dissections before! It's so exciting, I'm working with a veterinarian in Indonesia and we're comparing the knees of trolls to orangutans and—"

"I meant I'd go with you to visit Gerðr," says Beatrice. Her grandmother pats her arm. "Not that dissecting a troll doesn't sound…" Beatrice swallows audibly. "…lovely."

Amy *does not* pout at Beatrice's lack of enthusiasm. At least not very much.

It will be nice to have some company when visiting Gerðr. It's not that Amy doesn't have sympathy for the giantess— Gerðr's been branded a terrorist, even though, when she attacked humans, she was being controlled by Cera. And now Gerðr is trapped here on Earth as a prisoner of ADUO without a way to go home—at least that they know of.

Nonetheless, Amy doesn't *like* Gerðr. The giantess is fond of calling humans "the magically retarded worms of the World Tree." Unfortunately, Amy speaks Frost Giant—courtesy of Loki. Gerðr's rooms are lined with Promethean Wire, and within them, Gerðr can't use magic to translate English. Amy is the best worm to visit and talk to the cranky giantess. She sighs.

Beside her, Beatrice says, "So much excitement today. Aren't you glad you came back to Chicago?"

Amy raises her head at the question. A movement in a dead-end hallway to her left catches her eye. She glances in that direction and sees Bohdi there. His eyebrows go up in surprise. Is it her imagination, or does he look vaguely guilty?

"Amy?" says Beatrice.

Amy blinks. How had Beatrice forgotten the excitement in Oklahoma? "Grandma, Oklahoma was exciting—I discovered a new species of toad in my backyard."

"Yes, dear, you've told me," Beatrice says, patting her on

the arm.

"*Bufo laugauz* is such a cutie, too," says Amy wistfully. "...with his black skin and cute little yellow spots." She named the toad after a version of Laugauz, Loki's Fire Giant incarnation.

Beside her, Beatrice protests. "They're warts, not spots."

They turn a corner and Gerðr's rooms come into view. "They are not warts," says Amy, frowning at her grandmother's prejudice. Poor toads.

But Beatrice doesn't answer her. Instead, she puts a hand on Amy's arm. "Amy, there should be guards here."

Staring down the empty hallway, Amy feels her heart sink. Poop. Another delay. "Huh. Yeah, I'll have to call someone to open the doors for us."

"Call security. Now," Beatrice says, stepping in front of Amy.

Holding her coffee in one hand, Amy fumbles for her phone with the other and finds Mr. Squeakers instead. "I think maybe I..."

There is the creaking of hinges down the hall. Amy lifts her head to see the door to Gerðr's room swinging open. Skírnir steps out, Gerðr slung over his shoulder. A magic detector in Amy's pocket begins to chirp and Skírnir and Gerðr begin to flicker into invisibility.

Amy's gasps. No. If they become invisible, Gerðr—

She stops thinking. Dropping her coffee, she pulls Mr. Squeakers from her pocket. In front of her, Beatrice shouts, "Stop!" With too much grace and speed for a woman her age, Beatrice opens the umbrella and holds it in front of them like a shield.

Against all possible logic—or magic—the flickering around Skírnir and Gerðr does stop. Amy's jaw drops. Mr.

Squeakers gives a tentative squeak and Skírnir's eyes fly wide.

"What enchantment is this?" the mage demands.

Before Amy can fully process the question, Beatrice whips out a handgun from her pocket.

"Put her down!" Beatrice snarls. Amy's eyes nearly pop from her head. Beatrice has a handgun?

Letting Gerðr slide from his back into a careless heap, Skírnir's lips curl in a sneer. "Out of the way, old woman."

"No, Grandma…" Amy says.

But the words aren't even fully out of her mouth before Skírnir lifts his wand. Beatrice drops the umbrella and wraps both hands around the handgun. There is the blast of a gunshot and then the sound of a bullet ricocheting off of metal.

Skírnir laughs, and an orb of something orange and molten-looking begins to form at the end of the wand. There is a ring of gunshot, and Amy barely sees the orb shoot off the tip of the wand a second later—she's already being tackled to the floor by Beatrice.

Heat flashes over Amy's back and legs, and she turns to see molten goo smoldering on the carpet just past her feet.

Beatrice is on top of her, pressing her into the ground. In front of her, all Amy can see is the open umbrella. Mr. Squeakers is hissing in her hand.

Beyond the flimsy shield of garish pink and flowers, Skírnir says, "You will pay for this."

CHAPTER 3

Bohdi hears the sound of a gunshot and Skírnir's laughter. He races in the direction of the sound without thinking, his hand going to his knife, the only weapon he has. He turns one corner, and then another and arrives just in time to see Amy and Beatrice huddled behind Beatrice's umbrella. Something molten and glowing is smoldering in the carpet just beyond their feet.

"You will pay for this," Skírnir says.

Bohdi lifts his eyes to see Skírnir raising his wand beyond the two women on the floor. The magician is standing over the crumpled body of Gerðr.

Without thinking, Bohdi flips open his blade and prepares to throw it. Before it leaves his fingers, Skírnir sways on his feet, his gaze going somewhere off into the distance.

It's only then that Bohdi sees the dark circle of a bullet wound square in the center of Skírnir's forehead and the thin trail of blood trickling down one side of his nose. For an instant, his eyes meet Bohdi's. He looks—confused. And then he falls to his knees, wavers, then falls face-first onto the floor.

Beatrice lifts her head in the magician's direction. "First

shot was a warning," she grumbles.

Behind Bohdi comes the sound of footsteps. He snaps his knife shut, slips it into his pocket, and backs around the corner, just as agents rush past him. He sees his buddy Marion with them, she gives him a barely perceptible nod, but then rushes down the hall.

Bohdi turns to see Steve and Thor walking shoulder to shoulder.

Scowling, Steve says, "What happened!"

Bohdi shrugs and shakes his head, still a bit in shock. "Beatrice shot Skírnir?"

"Skírnir is still in the cafeteria…" says Steve, his voice trailing off. Pulling out his phone, Steve calls someone while barreling past Bohdi with Thor a step behind. Bohdi hears shouts beyond them, and then Thor's voice. "What treachery is this?"

Without really thinking about it, Bohdi backs into the dead-end hallway. As he watches the agents race past, he has a revelation. Thor needed Skírnir to open World Gates.

His heart starts to beat fast. Despite Steve's words to the contrary, humans do have a working theory about how to open World Gates…He takes a ragged breath, remembering what Amy said. The Norns will tell you anything, in exchange for an object of power or an impossible task.

Turning, he takes a few more steps down the hallway. Fingers shaking, Bohdi touches his back pocket where his wallet with the picture of his maybe-parents is.

The FBI has an ongoing investigation into Bohdi's past. But so far, they don't even know his real name—and the people in the picture, his maybe, probably, parents—their identities are even farther off. Ruth has told him how much she and

Henry worried about Steve when he was in Afghanistan… how they still worry about him every single day.

Do the man and woman in the picture worry about Bohdi?

He hears Thor shout, "The old woman killed a loyal subject of Asgard!"

Bohdi's attention snaps to the present as Steve roars back, "That loyal subject was trying to kidnap one of our own!"

Thor shouts again. There is the sound of something hitting a wall hard. Above Bohdi, some plaster falls to the floor, and then he hears Thor's footsteps thundering closer. The giant man passes the hallway that Bohdi is in without even glancing up, hammer gripped tightly in his hand.

Bohdi blinks at the hammer. He remembers Amy holding Laevithin, Loki's magical sword, two years before in a broken cage of Promethean wire. An instant later, she had vanished into another dimension.

Bohdi hesitates only a second more before racing after Thor.

Thor is past security and out the revolving doors before Bohdi catches up to him. Police are redirecting cars and foot traffic away from the sidewalks and street surrounding Thor's chariot. Even though it's Chicago, and nearly noon, Thor and Bohdi are oddly alone. If Bohdi is quiet, and Thor doesn't get too close to the agents guarding his chariot, they won't be overheard.

Sprinting forward, Bohdi grabs hold of one of Thor's forearms. "Wait!" he shouts.

Thor's response is instantaneous. Whipping his body

around he wraps a huge hand around Bohdi's neck and raises his hammer over Bohdi's head.

The ADUO agents by the chariot start to move in their direction, but Bohdi waves a hand. They slow but do not stop completely.

"What do you want?" Thor snarls, the hand around Bohdi's neck tightening a fraction.

Bohdi grins, even though the pressure on his windpipe is making his eyes water. "To help you!"

Thor snarls.

"I know where the Norn...gate...is," Bohdi grinds out.

Thor releases his neck, and gasping for air, Bohdi turns to the guards, smiles, and waves. They stop, though their leader's scowl is visible over his sunglasses.

Leaning forward, Bohdi whispers, "And I can take you to Nornheim myself."

"You're lying!" says Thor.

Actually, Bohdi is just maybe over promising. ADUO's research is mostly theoretical.

"No," Bohdi says. He lowers his voice to a barely audible whisper. "Here's how...."

When he's done, Thor nods his head, though his eyes are narrowed. The agents are still far enough away that they can't have heard, but their eyes are fixed on Bohdi and the Viking.

Giving them a smile, Bohdi takes a pen out of his pocket and a battered business card from his wallet. Thrusting them into Thor's hand, Bohdi shouts at the ADUO agents. "Just asking the big guy for his autograph!"

They're a little too far away to hear—but Bohdi thinks he sees a guy's nostrils flare in a snort.

CHAPTER 4

Even though she's wearing a thick fleece sweater under her lab coat, Amy shivers. She's in the magical creature morgue in ADUO's basement.

The room is white walled and has steel operating tables. It would almost look like a human morgue except that the operating tables are elephant sized. A single troll cadaver covered by an enormous swath of fabric lies on a table at the center of the room. She shivers again, not because the morgue creeps her out; it's just *really* cold.

Putting a hand in the pocket of her lab coat, Amy idly rubs her thumb between Mr. Squeakers' ears. The little mouse makes a tiny sigh and curls into a tighter ball in her pocket, apparently untroubled by the nearly overpowering smell of formaldehyde in the room.

Brow furrowing, Amy remembers Beatrice's words as her grandmother followed Steve and Laura Stodgill into Steve's office.

"Don't worry, dear, Steve is very competent at these things. He'll get me off the hook," Beatrice had said.

"It's a good thing we were already in the process of

getting you authorized to carry a weapon on premises," Steve grumbled.

"You were?" Amy said. Her grandmother hadn't told her that. Her grandmother hadn't even told her that she could fire a gun—let alone fire a gun so *well*.

Steve, Laura, and Beatrice had all stared at Amy. She'd felt her face flush as she realized she was missing something. Patting her arm, Beatrice leaned forward and whispered, "I think that's the story we're going with."

"Beatrice, shut the door!" Steve shouted.

With an apologetic look, Beatrice had shut the door, but not before Amy heard Steve grumble. "You're going to help me deal with the blizzard of paperwork this is going to cause."

Amy had found herself staring at Steve's door, still shaken by the sight of Skírnir planted face-first in a puddle of his own blood, Gerðr's guards in a bleeding heap just inside the giantess's cell door, and Gerðr herself, concussed and barely conscious, being carried away on a stretcher by ADUO's paramedics.

But it was what she signed up for when she chose to come back to Chicago. So she'd taken a deep breath and come to her lab.

Now in front of the covered cadaver, her nose wrinkles at the smell of chemical preservatives. The only good thing about the morning was that Odin's plans to contact the Norns had been delayed.

Bowing her head she tightens her ponytail. Maybe Steve can convince Gerðr to open the gate to Nornheim for them? If ADUO could get to Nornheim first…if they could find the Norns….

Hoping for some clue that could help, she closes her eyes

and picks up the strand of memory she'd seen before.

In an impossibly short time, Odin, Sleipnir, and the Ein-
herjar are standing in the shadow of the cavern formed by the
enormous column's roots. The ceiling of the cavern is at least as
high as seven men, the mouth at the base more than thirty paces
wide. They have too few men to defend the place adequately, and
yet it's the most defensible position they've seen.

Odin pulls Sleipnir to a halt and Loki has weight again.
Dismounting, Odin barks at the two Einherjar closest to him.
"You two with me." Gesturing toward the rest of the men, he
says, "Prepare for the adze attack!" Loki looks behind and sees
the shadows in the sky. They look to be in the same position they
were before, but now they're closing fast.

Loki prepares to dismount from Sleipnir. "Can I help you
make the gate, Allfather?" he asks. To see a World Gate created,
not just opened, might make all this terror worthwhile.

But Odin holds up a hand. "Your talents are not in this,
Loki."

Loki stills on Sleipnir's back. Odin comes and lays a hand on
top of Loki's own. "Help the Einherjar, but stay on Sleipnir—
I've gone through too much to lose you again."

Blinking, Loki nods, tightening his hands in the animal's
mane. Odin murmurs a word to Sleipnir, and the great animal
turns back toward the warriors.

As they stride away, lights flickering in the great column catch
Loki's eye. Whispering for Sleipnir to halt, he turns to look. The
column's surface shimmers, and Loki begins to see shapes forming,
as though reflected in a milky mirror. Before his eyes, the shapes
coalesce into a scene: an infant with pale, nearly translucent

*Jotunn skin and a shock of bright orange hair, lying in a smol-
dering pile of rubble. Loki's mouth gapes. The picture is so life
like…An Aesir man who looks vaguely familiar, with wide green
eyes, approaches the infant and—*

"Loki!" barks Odin, so forcefully Loki jumps in the saddle.
Turning, he meets the king's gaze. In his deepest, most command-
ing tone, Odin says, "Do not look at the pictures in the column.
You'll drive yourself mad."

Loki nods, and faces forward again. Behind him, he hears
Odin start to chant. He swallows. The images in the column
are so bright in his mind. He tries not to look, but finds himself
turning his head to see the babe and the familiar yet unfamiliar
man again…

Before his eyes have a chance to focus, Sleipnir sidesteps so
quickly, Loki almost loses his seat. "Whoa, boy," says Loki. Wondering what has the great animal spooked, he looks beyond the
cavern in the direction they came from. His breath catches in his
throat and his body goes cold. The swarm of adze is so close, he
can see moonlight glinting on their bald heads, the talons at the
ends of their long spindly fingers, and the whole of their hairless,
weirdly sexless bodies.

The Einherjar fan out at the mouth of the cavern. For the first
time, Loki notices many don't have swords, shields, or bows and
arrows. They must have lost them in the battle in the tent. Some
have found long sticks in the underbrush around the column and
in the cavern, others are merely brandishing their knives. None of
them wavers or shows any sign of fear. They simply stand watchful and waiting, gazing up into the night. It makes Loki's urge
to slip beneath Sleipnir and hide just that much more cowardly.

The Einherjar that had identified the adze turns to Loki and
pushes a tree branch half as long as Loki and nearly as thick as

his forearm into his hands. "Do you think you can set them on fire?" the warrior asks, eyes flicking to the swarm.

Loki nervously eyes the distance between the adze and the pitiful band of Einherjar. The swarm can't be more than five hundred paces away. He's so frightened, his legs are vice-like on Sleipnir's sides, making the great horse paw the earth nervously. He's never set anything on fire from so far away. He doesn't have the courage—or even the voice—to admit that to the Einherjar. He just stares wide eyed at the approaching shadows.

From the swarm, one of the adze gives a blood-curdling cry that makes the hair on the back of Loki's neck stand on end. The cry is echoed by the others in the swarm, and as one, they begin to glide to the ground. Loki's vision blurs with fear, and a little bleep comes from his mouth; simultaneously, a few dozen of the adze's wings burst into flame. Those adze drop like stones, but the sky remains thick with their twisting, pale, hairless bodies.

Still, the Einherjar give a cheer. And the one closest to Loki says, "Well done!" Raising his voice, he shouts to the others. "They cannot hover! They are weak flyers, and they will land and then attack. Their strength is in numbers only!"

Looking up at the hundreds of swirling, shrieking, shapes, Loki isn't comforted by that information.

While most of the swarm coast overhead just outside the cavern, a dozen adze hurtle to the ground. Raising their weapons, the Einherjar easily evade the clumsy bombardment. The warriors lash out with their knives and makeshift staves, but the creatures keep coming.

Loki raises the branch in his hands as an adze lands to Sleipnir's right. With a cry, Loki aims the butt end of the branch at the creature's face. There is the sharp crunch of bone and the sickening squish of pulverizing flesh. The adze drops quickly, but

another falls from the sky to take its place, one of its brothers land-
ing to Loki's right, and then another and another all around.

Some instinct in Loki's mind kicks in. He doesn't think; he
just acts. Snarling, guiding Sleipnir with his legs, he urges the
mighty animal to pivot on his hind legs. The turning, rearing
animal bowls over the adze that wind up in the path of its with-
ers, and strikes at them with its four forward hooves. The ones the
horse doesn't hit, Loki dispatches the same way he did the first,
his staff sliding left and right, a shout of rage rising from his lips.

Loki's blows land every time, and a dim part of his mind
wonders at how easy it is. Whatever sliver of triumph he feels
evaporates as he looks up. The adze keep coming, and even though
they fight without finesse—and aren't agile enough for true aerial
assaults—there are too many of them.

Before Loki's eyes, one of the swarm manages to drop from the
sky directly upon the back of the dark-skinned Einherjar who had
praised Loki moments ago. Loki brings his staff over the creature's
head even as it sinks its teeth into the Einherjar's neck. The staff
hits home, the adze falls—but although the warrior's wound
is minor, the man wobbles on his feet, and then crumples—his
body disappearing as adze pile upon him and each other with
frenzied shrieks.

Loki doesn't have time to be horrified. More of the swarm is
landing, slipping between the warriors, behind and in front of
them. Loki pummels with his staff in every direction at the same
time he tries to guide Sleipnir like a battering ram into the fray.

"To me!" shouts Odin above the sound of the shrieking swarm.

Loki turns to see Odin, silhouetted by a circle of light just
large enough for Sleipnir to slip through. The Allfather is swing-
ing his sword, but his movements are wild and there is no energy
behind his strikes. He looks like he has been fighting for hours, not

just minutes. Two Einherjar are beside him, guarding his flanks, but they fall even as Loki watches.

Loki sends Sleipnir barreling in the direction of his guardian. A few of the swarm land between Loki and the Allfather, and Loki roars in fear, hatred, and desperation, his skin heating so much, he thinks his blood is boiling, his vision turning to a tunnel of red, the sound of the swarm's shrieking being joined by a sound like a thousand twigs cracking.

The adze in front of him drop out of view, and Sleipnir hops over their bodies. Dismounting, even before the horse has stilled, Loki is at Odin's side a minute later. For the first time, he realizes that what he took for a tunnel of red is a tunnel of flame, the sound of twigs cracking the sound of adze's wings on fire.

Odin falls into Loki. It is all that Loki can do to keep the heavier man upright. Beyond Odin, the circle of light is dimming. "Quick, we must get through the gate," the Allfather mutters. Pulling Odin to Sleipnir's side and helping him into the saddle, Loki looks back the way he had come. Only one Einherjar is still standing. The warrior breaks through the dwindling flames toward Loki and Odin but is set upon by dozens of screaming adze. An instant later, he vanishes into a pile of writhing bodies. More adze fall on the smoldering remains of their own kindred and the fallen warriors. Loki's jaw drops.

"Loki!" Odin says. "We must leave."

Odin's voice shakes Loki from his stupor. Fear and adrenaline give him enough strength to leap onto Sleipnir's back. Bracing the Allfather's dangerously listing body, he gives Sleipnir a quick kick. The horse darts forward. Even though the circle of light has gone out, Sleipnir has the ability to open World Gates and walk between realms, just as the beast's mother had, just as Odin and Hoenir can do…and as Odin says Loki will one day be able to do, too.

There's a flash of rainbow colored lights. For an instant, Loki can't see Sleipnir's ears, then his neck, and then the shrieking of the adze is gone, replaced by the clatter of Sleipnir's hooves on stone. Instead of darkness, there is sunshine pouring through a window. Instead of a sky filled with the darting bodies of adze, there is a ceiling. Loki looks up to see an ornate mosaic, a depiction of the Greek myth of Leda and the swan.

"Father," calls a small voice, as the last of Sleipnir's hooves clacks into the room. Loki brings his gaze down. Odin has opened the gate directly to his own chambers. To one side, there is an enormous bed with heavy draperies. To the other side is a fireplace, above which is a painting in the realistic perspective that is the new-elfish style; it features Odin, Frigga, and a golden-haired, straight-limbed, clear-eyed, pink-cheeked Prince Baldur.

Leaping from a plush chair by the fireplace is Baldur himself. To nearly everyone, the painting is the spitting image of the prince—but Loki sees something very different. Loki sees a four-teen-year-old who is chubby, his hair a dingy brown, his eyes a muddy hazel. And his face is peppered with acne. Loki supposes if no one can see your imperfections, it's very difficult to fix them.

In front of Loki, Odin lists dangerously. Loki manages to keep him on Sleipnir's back, but it's a close call. "Guards!" shouts Baldur.

Loki hears several sets of footsteps behind Sleipnir and another voice, this one feminine. "Odin!"

Loki turns to see Queen Frigga striding into the room with Odin's two most trusted servants. They run to Odin's side and Loki eases the Allfather into their arms.

"You see, Mother," says Baldur. "I knew if he was forced to make a gate, he'd open it here. He'd never let the court see him

so weak." At those words, Baldur narrows his eyes at Loki.

"The prince is always wise," says one of the servants, carrying Odin to his bed with his comrade. Normally Loki would roll his eyes at the sycophantic words, but he can't bring himself to care. As he dismounts Sleipnir, he notices his hands are shaking.

Baldur trails after the servants. Frigga and then Loki follow, Sleipnir tagging behind Loki like a dog.

Odin's eyes flutter a bit as they prop his head on a pillow.

"Get him some water and food!" Baldur commands the servants. The men bow and leave the room. Baldur sits on the edge of the bed beside his father and takes one of Odin's limp hands. Climbing onto the bed, Frigga sits next to her husband on the other side. Laying a palm upon his forehead, she murmurs, "He is warm, he was not scratched or bitten."

Loki swallows. Feeling relieved, but anxious to see Odin recover completely, Loki stands a few feet away, head bowed. He wants to sit on the bed, too, but that would be overstepping his station.

Baldur's eyes go to Sleipnir, then to Loki. "Wonderful, the whole family is here."

Behind Loki, Sleipnir lets out an angry sounding snort—perhaps picking up on Baldur's tone? Loki blinks. It's the only time that Baldur has ever called Loki one of the family.

Baldur drops his head to his father's hands. "Wake up, Father," the prince says. Voice cracking a little, he whispers, "I hate seeing you like this."

Loki bows his head again…and the images of the falling adze flash before his eyes. Maybe Odin was bitten or scratched, maybe he is more than just magically exhausted…

Taking a step forward, Loki says, "Are you sure he will be all right…"

Voice not unkind, Frigga says, "He is just magically exhausted from creating a New World gate. He cannot do it with the ease of Hoenir."

Raising his head like a viper, Baldur hisses. "You weren't worth the risk."

Taking a step back, Loki bumps into Sleipnir and the horse gives a whicker, then drops his head over Loki's shoulder and stamps all eight of his feet.

On the bed, Odin's one eye opens. "No, Baldur."

Baldur and Frigga turn their eyes to Odin. "It was terribly risky," Frigga says.

Patting her hand, Odin says, "Yes, but as soon as I found Loki, we both knew the odds would rearrange."

Frigga sighs. Loki sees only the back of Baldur's head and can't see his expression.

Odin's gaze finds Loki's. "You fought well."

Loki remembers all the Einherjar they'd lost. The praise feels hollow, but he nods.

Odin smiles gently. "Now would you mind taking Sleipnir out of my bedroom?"

Loki flushes and stammers, "Yes, of course."

As Loki turns to grab Sleipnir's magic bridle, he sees Baldur frowning at him. He's just entered the hallway when he hears the prince say, "The court will say that he's your toy, that you're buggering him—"

Loki draws to a halt.

"Baldur!" says Frigga.

"Any man that says that will have his tongue cut out," says Odin. "I am Loki's guardian, and I treat him as a guardian should—such rumors would dishonor me as much as him." Standing a bit taller, Loki smiles. Whistling loud enough for the

royal family to hear, he leads Sleipnir down the hall.

Eyes still closed, Amy brings a hand to her forehead. To see Loki so young…so distraught by violence and bloodshed, and so different than the Loki she knew… It makes her hurt, and miss him…even though that was a Loki she never knew. But she had seen that Loki, in bits and pieces, hadn't she?

She lifts her chin and exhales. It doesn't matter. That Loki is gone. All that matters is finding the new Loki and letting him—or her, or it—know what he is. She presses a hand to her temple. As interesting as the family dynamics in the memory were—Odin's protectiveness, Baldur's jealousy, and Loki's obliviousness—there isn't anything that will help her find the Norns.

Still, when Steve is done with Beatrice's paperwork blizzard, she'll talk to him. They have to try and find Loki.

She shakes her head. But will Steve agree?

She opens her eyes and turns her attention to the task in front of her. Work is always a good distraction from unpleasant thoughts. Straightening her shoulders, she pulls the sheet off the troll's body, and her heart quickens.

Normally, she'd rather put critters back together, but being able to dissect a troll—a real-life alien—is pretty darn amazing. Laid out on the operating table, the chest of the beast is a foot above her head. If the troll were standing, it would be as tall as an elephant, and perhaps broader side to side. It has some greenish hair on its head and greenish skin marked by regions of swelling that look a lot like boils.

She blinks, and another Loki memory comes to her. Loki, was a little boy, sitting on a workbench beside a rough-hewn table. He was playing a hand-slap game with a hand that was protruding from a box...much like the hand from The Addams Family. Only this hand was giant, green, and covered with boils.

Next to the box was Mimir's head, propped up against a crate. Long ago, Mimir had been decapitated by the Vanir for talking too much. His body had been lost, but his head had been magically preserved and animated so that all of his wisdom would not be lost.

"Trolls' native habitat is the surface of Svartálfaheimr, land of the dwarves," Mimir said, in his most officious, school master voice. "Svartálfaheimr's molten core is hardening, its magnetic field weakening, and its surface is buffeted by cosmic rays. The dwarves moved underground long ago. The trolls stayed above ground, their hides becoming tougher and tougher to resist radiation. But water is scarce on Svartálfaheimr's surface, and most other species have gone extinct. Trolls derive some of their nutritional needs from the symbiotic bacteria that make their skin green, but it isn't enough. Whenever a troll discovers a World Gate, it will open it and cross through in order to find food. That is why they now inhabit all the known worlds."

"Except for Earth, right?" said Loki. He couldn't have been more than eight; the troll's hand was easily as large as his head.

"Well, Hoenir is working with Odin to get all the trolls off Earth..." Mimir said.

Beside Loki, there was a cough, and he turned to see Hoenir approaching. An apron was pulled over Hoenir's paunch, and what was left of his hair was pulled back in a ponytail. The older man held a nearly barrel-sized jar of a purplish liquid with hand-sized bobbing eyeballs.

On the table, Mimir said, "Loki, would you please stop playing with the troll hand? Hoenir needs it to open the velociraptor treats."

Hoenir cleared his throat, and Mimir added too quickly, "Did I say velociraptors? Having velociraptors about would be against Odin's orders…"

"Then who are the treats for?" said Loki.

Mimir's eyes slid toward a doorway at the far end of the room. "Loki, did you know the spidermice that moved into Hoenir's dresser just had kits? Wouldn't you like to see them?"

"Yes!" Loki shouted, standing up and dashing from the workroom.

The memory ends and Amy is staring at her troll again. Scrunching her eyes shut, she tries to recover any memories involving troll anterior cruciate ligaments.

Nothing comes.

Opening her eyes, she sighs. But not unhappily. Really, even if she could find those memories, she'd still want to see the ligament for herself. Putting on a pair of goggles and reaching for a scalpel, she approaches the cadaver's left kneecap.

Forgetting the day's trauma turns out to be easier than Amy expected… partially because dissecting the troll is much more difficult than she expected. The troll's skin is so tough that after her fourth scalpel blade is dulled to the sharpness of a butter knife, she gives in and takes out an electric bone saw.

She's finally through the outer layer of dermis, turning off the saw, and picking up a new scalpel when there is a knock at the door.

Shifting the plastic bags from 7-11 to one hand, Bohdi checks the time on his phone. Scowling, he knocks on the door to the morgue again. The duffel bag on his shoulder nearly slides off with the movement.

Bohdi checks his pocket one more time for his lighter and his knife. He's not authorized to carry a gun, and hadn't had time to surreptitiously borrow one from an agent. Patting his stomach, he looks down. But at least he is wearing his lucky pink shirt that ticks Steve off; he's set.

Adjusting the bag and his shoulders, he waits for the door to open.

And waits.

And waits.

He's reaching forward, about to knock again, when the heavy metal security door groans inward.

Bohdi's jaw drops, and so do the 7-11 bags he's holding. Propping the door open with a hip, Amy's holding a wicked tool that looks like the baby of an electric drill and a saw, and she's got a scalpel awkwardly clutched in the same hand. Covering her eyes are goggles flecked with what looks likes the remains of bugs that met a windshield...but that's not what makes him gape.

Behind the plastic lenses of the goggles, Amy's eyes widen a fraction, as if to say, "What?"

Swallowing, Bohdi points very slowly to the top of her head. "I, umm...I think a tarantula is eating a mouse..." He winces. "In your hair."

Amy stares at him for a few heartbeats. And then she backs up so fast the door nearly slams in his face. Catching it with a sneakered foot and grabbing his bags, he enters the morgue.

Backing up, Amy drops the drill-saw and scalpel on a small rolly table in front of a very large, dead troll that smells like chemicals and cold. Bending slightly, she reaches up to the top of her head.

Holding up a hand, Bohdi blurts out. "Do you think you should…"

…touch it.

Before the words are out of his mouth, the spider-eating-a-mouse comes hurtling toward him and lands on the top of his outstretched hand. Bohdi is too shocked to move.

"Don't hurt Mr. Squeakers!" Amy says.

Bohdi looks to Amy. She has one hand pressed to her mouth, and she's pointing at the thing that has just sprung on him. The gears in his brain start to turn again, and he looks down at the critter that must be Mr. Squeakers. It isn't a spider eating a mouse; it's a little gray mouse with eight long black spider legs.

"He's a friend…pet…spidermouse," says Amy quickly.

Oh. Well, then. Peering closer, he drops his duffel and the 7-11 bags. He holds out a finger to the little guy. Mr. Squeakers grabs it with his two front legs. Bohdi grins. "He's kind of cute."

And then he feels a familiar sense of disorientation. "Are spidermice something else I've forgotten, or are they new things?"

"Ummm…" says Amy. "He's a magical creature, if that's what you mean…and new. I don't think you'd have ever heard of one…"

Bohdi lets out a relieved sigh and brings the spidermouse up to his face to get a closer look. Mr. Squeakers pokes his little nose at Bohdi and wiggles his whiskers.

"Please don't tell Steve," says Amy quickly. "He's just a harmless mouse."

The only warning Bohdi gets is the tickle at the back of his nose. He pinches his nose and closes his eyes, but it's too late. He barely turns his head in time to miss sneezing on Squeakers and Amy. Sniffling and looking for a Kleenex, he hands the mouse back to Amy. "Sorry, little guy, I think I might be allergic to you," he says.

Tucking the mouse into her lab coat pocket, Amy takes off her goggles. "Why are you here?"

Bohdi reaches into his pocket and finds the comforting shape of his lighter. Why is he here? He must be crazy—his life is good, great job, great friends, and what he's about to do will terrify Ruth and Henry. He swallows and thinks of the man and woman in the picture.

He knows more now about the immigrant experience than he did when he first "woke up." A lot of immigrants send money back to their families. Bohdi's parents are wearing simple clothing in the photo. They don't look particularly wealthy. But even though he's lost some of his mind, what he has left works rather well. Bohdi speaks English, Hindi, and the same regional language that is spoken in Bangalore—but with a Kashmiri accent. He also knows the three regional languages of Kashmir—but speaks them with a Bangalore accent. He reads mathematical notation with ease, and several computer languages. And even if his knowledge of recent history is nearly non-existent, he has weirdly accurate knowledge of the WWII era and prior. He may not have a college degree, but someone made sure he had an education.

He takes a breath…There's no way he would have gotten

his sweet job with the FBI without them. And if he'd been smaller, and weaker while he was in the Marine Corps...

He has to find his parents. He owes them everything.

Shifting on his feet, his fingers tighten on his lighter. He can't bring himself to say all that. Instead he just smiles as cockily as he can and says, "Want to go to Nornheim?"

Amy says nothing for a few long seconds. And then her gaze becomes hard and calculating. "How?"

It takes a moment for it to register in Bohdi's brain that she hasn't said no, or called him crazy. But then, Amy hasn't traveled just between realms; she's traveled between *universes* if what he overheard her telling Steve once is right.

Feeling a little small, he spins the wheel on his lighter and says, "With Thor."

"Thought he lost his ride?" Amy says.

Picking up his duffel, Bohdi opens the zipper to reveal two spools of Promethean wire, each about two feet long and a foot in diameter. "We're his ride to Nornheim. He'll show us the way to the Norns once we get there. All we need is the exact location of the gate in Loki's condo..."

Amy's face softens at the mention of the "secret" gate in her ex-boyfriend's old apartment. It makes Bohdi weirdly uncomfortable.

Amy's eyes drop to the Promethean wire. Two years ago, Amy held up Laevithin, Loki's magic sword, in a room sealed with Promethean wire. Bohdi had walked into the room, broken the seal, and allowed some of Laevithin's magic to open a pathway to the In-Between. The physics guys theorized that Promethean wire, when forced to contain too powerful a magic source and not sealed completely, can create tears in space time. Picking up on what he plans, she speaks quietly,

"We need a magical power source."

Laevithin, the power source she'd inadvertently used for her unplanned trip between universes, had been taken by the guys in DC. Bohdi jokes that it is in the same warehouse as the Arc of the Covenant. Steve says he shouldn't watch so many old movies with Brett and Bryant. However...

"I think Mjolnir will do the trick," Bohdi says.

Amy lifts her eyes. Voice a little shaky, she says, "You know...if we accidentally open a pathway into the In-Between, we won't be able to get back...when I did it...I had..." she crosses her arms over her chest. "Loki's..." Biting her lip, she looks down. "The baby was magical and saved me."

Bohdi's mouth goes dry. He can't help but remember that night when he found Amy lying in the snow, calmly and matter-of-factly asking him to call an ambulance as blood bloomed like a crimson flower around her. That memory made missing pieces in a puzzle click in Bohdi's brain. When Amy had opened a pathway to the In-Between, instead of turning into a spacecicle, she'd gone into another universe. Bohdi had wondered how. Now he knows—and he feels like he just punched her in the gut. He wants to say sorry...or... something...but they're running out of time. He says what he's sure she already knows. "That's why we need you to show us the exact location of the World Gate. The physics guys are pretty sure if we set the wire where a branch of the World Tree connects with Earth, we'll slip right past the In-Between and into another realm."

Head still down, Amy nods and crosses her arms. Looking up at him abruptly, she says, "Does Steve know about this?"

Bohdi grimaces.

Rolling her eyes, she turns away and waves a hand. "Then

there's no way for us to even get past security and into Loki's apartment. Talk to Steve, come up with a real plan, and then…"

Stepping forward, Bohdi catches her shoulder. Spinning, she reaches into her pocket, grabs Mr. Squeakers, and holds the little guy up in the space between them as though the mouse is a can of mace. Her nostrils flare slightly. For his part, the mouse just wiggles his whiskers.

Backing up, Bohdi holds up his hands. "I *know* how to get into Loki's condo. If we wait for Steve to do this officially, it will take…weeks…months…Thor isn't going to wait that long, he'll go home, find another wizard guy, and find another way."

Amy purses her lips. Bohdi's eyes catch on them. They look extra kissable when she's pouting.

Mr. Squeakers gives a cheery cheep from her hand, bringing Bohdi's attention back to task. He looks at the mouse, and then back up to Amy. Smiling and giving a shrug, Bohdi says, "See, even the mouse agrees with me."

Amy looks down at the mouse, and her eyebrows rise. Sighing, she closes her eyes.

"All right," she says. "I'll do it. When did you plan to leave? We need supplies, camping gear, food, and my grandmother will want to come. Considering what a good shot she's become, that might be a good idea."

Whipping out his phone, Bohdi checks the time. "We have fifteen minutes."

"What?" says Amy.

Sliding the phone back into his pocket, he says, "In fifteen minutes, Thor is going to kidnap us while we're having a romantic picnic on the roof." He holds up the 7-11 bags triumphantly and smiles. He's really got this well thought out.

Amy cocks her head to the side and puts a hand on her hip. "Kidnap us while we're having a romantic picnic?"

Bohdi shrugs. "It has to look like a kidnapping so we have plausible deniability."

Amy doesn't move.

Bohdi tries again. "A platonic picnic celebrating your return to ADUO?" he suggests.

Amy rolls her eyes and turns away, but this time she says, "Let me get my coat and first-aid kit."

Bohdi blinks. That actually...was easier than he expected.

"This is what you call a romantic meal?" Amy says, holding up an unopened protein bar and wrinkling her nose. They're atop ADUO's "green roof." In winter, it isn't so green, and in the lowlight of the evening, it is positively gray. She and Bohdi are sitting on two benches in an open rectangular area among raised beds filled with the husks of dead grasses and spotty snow.

Strands of Amy's ponytail are whipping around her face in the frigid Chicago wind, but she doesn't look at all cold. She's dressed in a cozy-looking down coat. The messenger bag with the first-aid kit is draped over one shoulder.

Shivering in his cheap winter coat, bristling at her insult, Bohdi says, "Well, it's a good thing it's only a welcome back meal."

She raises an eyebrow at him. Mr. Squeakers, peeking from the pocket of her down coat, gives a squeak that sounds strangely disappointed and then pulls his head back and disappears.

"I wanted something that could double as rations," Bohdi adds defensively. "We don't know how long this trip will take."

Both of Amy's eyebrows go up, and she looks down at her protein bar.

The wind increases and whips her ponytail around her face. Brushing it back, she looks up to the sky. Handing Bohdi the protein bar, she says, "I'm saved."

Turning, Bohdi sees Thor in his chariot hurtling down from the sky. Bohdi and Amy both jump from their seats as the chariot whips past them, bouncing to a stop on a patch of grass.

At that moment, the door to the stairs creaks open and Brett and Bryant come through, coffee cups in their hands.

Uh-oh.

"Thor?" says Brett.

"Amy and Bohdi?" says Bryant.

Amy grabs Bohdi's arm and pulls him in the direction of the chariot, even as Thor shouts, "Get in!"

"Where y'all going?" says Bryant.

Following Amy through the snow and dead grass, Bohdi manages to say, "Ummmm…"

A weight falls on his shoulder. Bohdi turns his head and sees Thor's enormous hand; and then he's yanked back so quickly he falls on his butt on the floor of the chariot. His duffel bag lands on his lap, and the 7-11 bags cut into his wrist. The chariot immediately starts to lift, Bohdi's feet hanging over the edge.

"We're being kidnapped," Bohdi shouts as they rise vertically into the sky.

"What?" says Bryant, lifting his head. "Going for a joy

ride?"

Bohdi opens his mouth to respond, but they zip forward so fast his reply is lost to the wind.

"That was convincing!" Amy shouts over the rush of air around them.

Scowling at her, Bohdi whips his phone out of his pocket, presses a few buttons, and holds it up. "Thor," he shouts to the Asgardian warrior standing beside him, "I programmed directions to Loki's condo into my iPhone just in case…" In case Thor forgot. According to the classified reports Bohdi wasn't supposed to read, Thor's been to the apartment before. It suddenly occurs to Bohdi that Thor might be insulted if his sense of direction is questioned. Bohdi really doesn't want to insult him. The big man's calves are right by Bohdi's nose—and look about as wide as Bohdi's head.

From his hand, Siri's voice is barely audible over the wind. "Four blocks west…"

Grunting, Thor takes the phone and holds it up. "Chariot!" he bellows, "Follow the Myeyephone sprite's directions!"

Bohdi's eyes go wide and shift to Amy. Standing on the other side of Thor, she meets Bohdi's gaze, winces, and shakes her head.

In Thor's hand, Siri says, "One block south."

The chariot careens left so fast, Bohdi slams against the right wall and Amy crashes into Thor—who doesn't budge. The giant man gently rights her as the chariot's course evens out.

In the distance, Bohdi thinks he sees a traffic helicopter. He squints. Is it his imagination or is it coming in their direction?

Amy slides down the opposite wall of the chariot and

tucks her knees up to her chin. "So how do we get past security?" she shouts above the wind.

Feeling instantly more confident, Bohdi smirks. "By going past security..."

He doesn't get to finish the details of his brilliant plan. Above them, Thor shouts, "Cover your heads! There may be falling glass!" And then the large warrior drops a visor Bohdi didn't realize his helmet had and raises Mjolnir.

There's a flash of light and Bohdi feels a prickle, as though every hair on his body is standing on end. Above the rushing of the wind comes a crack, and then a sound like discordant chimes. Beside him, he sees Amy tuck her head beneath her hands and draw her legs in even tighter.

Bohdi barely has time to do the same before they are swooping down into a shadow—sharp splinters prickling his shoulders, hands, and scalp as they do. The chariot's wheels connect with something hard, and they bounce—again and again. Bohdi's teeth are still rattling when they lurch to a stop, snapping his head against the chariot wall behind him.

Thor strides from the chariot and surveys the room, "I will hold back any guards that attempt to come through the door. You will need Mjolnir..." Bringing the hammer to his lips, he whispers some words in a strange guttural language. Thor nods once and hands the hammer to Bohdi. "Call for lightning when you need it," he says.

Groaning, Bohdi gets to his feet, clutching the duffel bag, shards of glass falling from his shoulders. He hesitates, eyes glued to the hammer. It's surprisingly crude up close. The handle is too short and...

"Take it," says Thor. "It won't bite you..." He smirks. "Unless you attempt to betray me."

Bohdi lets the 7-11 bags fall into the chariot and gingerly takes the hammer. It's heavy, but lighter than he expected. He's vaguely aware of Amy going around them to stand near the open window.

Lifting Bohdi's iPhone to his eyes, Thor asks, "Can Myeyephone work any defensive magic?"

"No," say Bohdi and Amy at the same time.

Thor sighs. Eyes still on the phone, he says, "Never fear, sprite, I will keep you safe as well."

Bohdi's eyes go wide, but he decides not to correct the big guy. Instead he quickly surveys what was Loki's apartment. He's not sure what he expected—but the place is modern, sleek even, with two walls made of floor-to-ceiling windows. Well, one wall has a window. The wall they just crashed through has a jagged hole of glass.

Thor presses the iPhone back into Bohdi's hand, snapping his attention back to the present.

Tilting his head at Bohdi, he says, "Get to work."

Amy steps forward. "No, wait! Before we help you, do we have your oath that you will return us to Earth safely?"

Thor blinks. From somewhere in the background, Bohdi hears muffled footfalls and shouts.

Thor's eyes slide to the door and then back to Amy. "We don't have time for this."

Amy puts her hands on her hips.

Grumbling, Thor says, "Fine. You have my oath." Shaking his head, the big man jogs away in the direction of the muffled voices.

Amy turns and goes back to the window. Kneeling, she says, "Ratatoskr slipped through right...about...here." She holds up her hands, spreading them about two feet wide.

"There was a little circle of light…"

Opening the duffel, Bohdi drops to the floor beside her. He can hear more muffled shouting in the hall, much louder this time, and a bang.

Thor's shout echoes through the apartment. "I've blockaded the door, but it won't keep your warriors at bay forever."

"They'll call helicopters," Amy whispers.

Bohdi nods as he unwinds one of the wide spools of Promethean wire. It's a little like chain link fencing, but the holes are octagonal, the wire itself is coppery, and it's more flexible—still his fingers are starting to stiffen with the bitter wind coming through the broken window—making working with the metal difficult.

He unspools enough of the Promethean wire to make a loop in the space Amy's still patiently indicating the location with her hands. The finished loop is slightly wider in diameter than Mjolnir's length. Then a horrible thought occurs to him. Turning his head to Amy, he whispers, "If this is the width of the gate, Thor is too large to get through."

Amy meets his gaze. Jaw hard, she says, "Put the hammer in and fire it up. We'll worry about that if this works."

Bohdi blinks. She's right. Dropping the head of the hammer onto the part of the loop that's on the floor, he clears his throat and pulls back his hands. "Umm…lightning?"

The hammer trembles and sparks fly. Bohdi drops his head and gazes through the circle. Peering through the loop, all he sees is the city of Chicago. His hands suddenly get clammy and his heart rate quickens. It's not working.

Ignoring the sparking hammer, Amy sticks her hand into the loop. About halfway through, her hand disappears. She gasps. "It's working!"

Bohdi's jaw falls, the Promethean wire trembles, Mjolnir sparks more brightly, and then the loop starts to grow, drawing more wire from the spool as it does.

"Wha—" says Bohdi.

Amy pulls her hand back out. The wire loop stops growing...but now the loop is wider. Without a word, Amy sticks her head into the loop...and suddenly Bohdi is staring at a headless Amy, the Promethean wire shuddering around her, Mjolnir sparking madly, and the loop continues to grow—but it's still not large enough for Thor.

From behind him, he hears Thor shout. "How goes it, son of Patel?"

"Uhhhh..." says Bohdi staring at the widening loop, "just a minute."

Sitting back on his haunches, he gazes at the unspooling wire and Amy's shoulders. The gate is still too narrow. This is never going to work. He winces at the sight of her headless body. Is she even still alive? This is creepier than he anticipated.

Amy's hand lifts and makes a beckoning motion.

And suddenly Bohdi doesn't care about creepiness or if this is going to work; he has to see whatever Amy sees.

Ducking his head, he fills his lungs like he's about to dive into a pool, grabs the handle of Mjolnir to steady himself, and plunges his head through.

There is the brief flash of light in every color of the rainbow, and he finds himself...or at least his head, in pink-tinged sunlight, a gentle breeze ruffling his hair. He laughs aloud.

"Welcome to Nornheim!" Amy says.

Bohdi is too excited to question how she can verify where they are. He starts to push further through the gate, but something grabs him by the shoulder and holds him back. He looks down. Where his one shoulder has pressed through, Amy's hand has grabbed him.

Lifting his eyes, he sees Amy's head...weirdly cut off at the neck. "Look down," she says.

Bohdi's eyes drop. About ten feet below him is what looks like a fine latticework of glass through which he can see the ground. It's very far away...like up in an airplane faraway-faraway... He makes an undignified-sounding noise.

Amy inclines her head in the direction of the latticework. "My guess is that it can hold a squirrel's weight, but I'm not sure about ours."

Bohdi nods.

Amy's head, eerily suspended in midair, turns to him. "So, if our heads are here and our hearts are there—" she looks in the direction that would be Bohdi's body. "How come we're still alive?"

Bohdi raises an eyebrow and gulps. "Probably best not to think about that right now?"

Of course, now that she's raised the question, Bohdi can't not think about it.

In his hand, Mjolnir trembles, and Bohdi feels the bite of sparks against his skin. "Something's happening," he says.

With a jerk, he pulls his head back through the loop and feels the bitter cold of Chicago's wind whipping down the neck of his coat.

The loop doesn't look like it's increased in size, but as soon as he takes his hand off Mjolnir, it suddenly expands to a width that even Thor's chariot can fit through. If they all huddle together, they'll make it.

Amy emerges an instant later. The expansion stops, and

she looks up and gasps. "The loop has gotten larger. How?" Amy says.

Bohdi's mind races. "I don't know why it got bigger, but you know how we stayed whole when half of us was here and half of us was there? Maybe it isn't so much a 'gate' as an envelope in space time…but at a certain point light can't escape and so…"

Beside him, Amy inhales sharply.

He stops. His eyes slide to her. He licks his lips nervously, prepared for, "What are you talking about?" or "Wha—?" or as Marion would affectionately say, "You weirdo."

Instead, Amy says, "Like a magical event horizon!" Her eyes are sparkling, and she's smiling at him.

Bohdi's heart rate increases. He licks his lips again, this time for a completely different reason. He opens his mouth… and lets out a startled, "Erp!" as Thor lifts him and Amy both by the collars of their coats.

"Eep!" says Amy.

"They've almost broken down the door!" shouts Thor, getting into the chariot. He pushes them in the direction of the vehicle. Picking up the duffel bag with the remaining spool of wire, Bohdi darts with Amy toward the chariot.

Behind him, Thor yells, "Chariot, back up!"

The chariot rolls toward Amy and Bohdi and they leap in. A loud boom echoes through the apartment and Bohdi hears shouts of, "This is the FBI." He's aware of the sound of a chopper behind them getting louder very quickly.

Turning his head, he sees Thor lifting Mjolnir so that the head of the hammer is at the top of the loop, now about four and a half feet off the ground.

"Stop!" someone shouts. Bodhi turns in the direction of

the door and sees three agents striding forward, guns raised. He's not sure if he's sad or relieved his friend Marion isn't with them. He and Amy both drop their heads behind the front wall of the chariot. The chariot keeps rolling backward. There is the sound of gunfire and bullets ricocheting off the chariot. Thor's body is suddenly pressing between Amy and Bohdi, squeezing Bohdi's shoulders against the chariot wall with such force, Bohdi grits his teeth. Bohdi's eyes slide to the big man ducking beside him, holding up the hammer, keeping it in contact with the Promethean wire even as gunfire slams into the armor of his wrist…and then the back of Thor's shoulders disappear. A heartbeat later, Amy, Thor, and Bohdi are suspended midair in the pink light of Nornheim.

The chariot drops and so does Bohdi's stomach. Thor pulls Mjolnir to his side and shouts, "Chariot, level!"

Their descent halts so fast Bohdi's teeth rattle, and he laughs in relief.

Gasping for air and smiling, Amy meets his eyes.

Thor stands and looks to the sky. The sun is almost directly overhead. Muttering a few words, Thor tracks it with his thumb. "It is mid-morning here."

Breathing heavily, Bohdi scans the sky. "The light is so pink…" He'd thought when he first poked his head through that it was sunrise or sundown.

Beside him, Amy speaks, her voice far away. "The sun is a red dwarf…"

"Aye," says Thor. It strikes Bohdi that he is breathing hard, too. Also, the air is warmer than in Chicago, but it's still cold.

Thor nods to himself. "We aren't at the highest level of filaments, but the air is thin here…"

Grabbing the lip of the chariot wall, Bohdi stands as Amy

rises shakily beside him. Gazing upward for the first time, he sees a glint in the sky—another latticework like the one below them?

Amy gasps. "The lacey glass filaments—they're the branches of the giant columns."

"Yes," says Thor. He spreads his feet and the chariot wobbles at the movement.

Holding on more tightly, Bohdi turns and looks down. The latticework he'd seen earlier rolls out beneath them, getting thicker and sturdier looking as it approaches what looks like a tree of sparkling glass about thirty meters away. The tree's trunk keeps rising beyond where his eyes can see, similar lattices stretching out from it along the trunk above them.

"The branches of the columns catch cosmic rays and solar radiation," Thor says. "The Norns convert those forces into magic and use it for their own purposes. The Norns are three of the most powerful beings in the Nine Realms—but only here on Nornheim."

Bohdi turns his head sharply to Thor. Somehow, solar radiation and cosmic rays were the last words he'd expected to hear from the space Viking. He sees Amy looking at the big guy with a similar look of surprise on her face.

Raising an eyebrow at them both, Thor says, "I am over one thousand years old. I have picked up a bit of mag—" Speech halting, he tilts his great head. "*Scientific* knowledge."

Bohdi swallows. "Ummm…right, sorry."

"Errr…yes," says Amy. "Of course."

Shaking his head with a bit of a smirk, Thor gazes downward. "Now to discover where we are so that we may make our way to the dwellings of the Norns." He looks at Bohdi. "I don't suppose Myeyephone would know where we are?"

"No," say Amy and Bohdi in unison.

Thor nods, sagaciously. "Of course, of course, the sprite has never been here before…ah, well."

Before Bohdi or Amy can respond, Thor shouts, "Chariot, down!" and the floor beneath Bohdi drops so fast he almost flies out. They crash through the latticework below, it tinkles like breaking glass, and Amy gives a startled yip.

The world below comes into more vivid focus—forested hills interspersed with more columns—and are those swaths of white tents? Smiling, Bohdi shakes his head and grins. They did it! They made it to a new world without major injuries and only minor property damage. He almost laughs. It went so perfectly… Usually, his plans have a way of going horribly wrong.

"The news says that Thor took Bohdi and Amy!" Steve's daughter's disembodied voice rings so loudly that Steve pushes the phone away from his ear.

"They're fine," Steve says, pacing the length of the hallway in Loki's building. "They're with Thor. They're not in any danger."

Even as he says it, Gerðr's words ring in his mind. "They are in Nornheim, the realm of everything dangerous, dreadful, and deadly."

"He kidnapped them!" says Claire.

Rubbing his temple, Steve scowls and remembers Bryant's and Brett's descriptions of events and doubts it. All he says to Claire is, "That has not been confirmed."

And then another thought hits him. "You're ten years old—what are you doing watching the news?"

On the other end of the line Claire huffs. "It's called Social Studies, Dad. We're doing a unit on current affairs. You have to get them back!"

"I know," says Steve. He respects Lewis, and needs her skills and knowledge. And Bohdi...

When Steve first took Bohdi in, it was partly out of charity, and partly out of curiosity. When they had found him, the kid's brain was temporarily humming with magic. Why, out of millions of people, had Loki wiped Bohdi's memory? Did Bohdi know something? It was a situation Steve wanted to keep an eye on. Over the past two years, Bohdi's become something of a friend. Or maybe a sidekick. Or an obnoxious little brother. And even if Steve wants to strangle him half the time, he doesn't like the idea of him dying in pain and agony on some far off planet.

Trying to switch subjects, he says, "How is your arm?"

"Daddy!" Beatrice's voice rings behind him. "Director Rogers!"

Steve rolls his eyes. "I have to go, honey. Love you."

"Get Bohdi, back," says Claire just before Steve clicks his phone shut.

"Director Rogers!" says Beatrice, holding up her umbrella. "Why don't we send in paratroopers?"

Steve turns around and finds himself face to face not just with Beatrice, but with Gerðr and two female agents.

Gerðr had opened the gate for ADUO...well, for Beatrice. The giantess hadn't been completely unconscious when Skírnir tried to kidnap her. In thanks she offered to cooperate with the agency. She was able to verify the realm that Thor had taken them to was Nornheim, and had even allowed Steve and Beatrice to peek over her shoulder for a few moments when she'd opened the gate.

The magic shielding bracelets and helmet had to be removed for her to open the World Gate. They still haven't been put back on.

Gerðr's wearing nearly formless winter clothes, and Steve's eyes go to the face of the giantess, the other women around her fading to just amorphous clouds at the edge of his consciousness. Gerðr's skin is so pale it's nearly transparent, her eyes are a cold gray, and her hair is so blonde it's nearly white. The giantess narrows her eyes at him and her nostrils flare slightly. Her looks and personality are as bitter and cold as the Chicago winter. But Steve still feels his body heat when he looks at her, feels his pulse rate increase, and can't help but think of what his dark skin would look like pressed against hers.

Beatrice clears her throat, and Steve spins on his heels, averting his eyes and licking his lips. Damn magical glamour.

"Paratroopers, Steven! Why don't we send them?" Beatrice says.

Keeping his body carefully turned away from the giantess, Steve meets Beatrice's gaze. "We have no idea where they went, Beatrice, and they are in a flying vehicle—"

"We could send in gliders!" says Beatrice.

"We're sending in drones, Beatrice! Intelligence-gathering drones. For now, nothing, and no one else!" Steve snaps.

From over Steve's shoulder, Gerðr speaks. Without magic blocking cuffs, her English is flawless. "The Director's plan is wise, Beatrice. It will do the most to find your granddaughter, and will be the least offensive to the Norns."

Steve's not sure if he turns to look at Gerðr because it's one of the very few civil things she's ever said about any human...

or if he just wants to look at her... His eyes fall on her lips. They're not particularly full, but they are well shaped...as is her whole face. It's like she has been carved out of marble. Steve thinks he could spend hours tracing the perfect angles and valleys of her silhouette with his eyes, his fingers, his tongue...

Beatrice clears her throat again, and Steve throws a hand up in front of his eyes. "Can you just turn off the glamour?" Steve snaps.

Leaning forward with snakelike speed and grace, Gerðr hisses. "You're a dog!" The two agents behind her grab her elbows and pull her back, scowling at the giantess as they do.

Keeping his hand aloft, Steve sighs and rolls his eyes, "Believe me, I feel like one."

Down the hall, Hernandez pokes his head out of Loki's apartment. "Sir! We have a press conference at the front of the building in three minutes."

Steve sighs. "Thank God," he mumbles as he strides past Gerðr and the agents, now wrestling with the giantess's arms.

As he steps into the elevator beside Hernandez, he's still thinking about Gerðr, his mind wandering off in uncomfortable trajectories. Rubbing the back of his neck, Steve grumbles, "Is it just her magic or—"

He lets out a huff, and shakes his head. Or *loneliness*. He can't bring himself to say it out loud. He'd thought, when he'd been talking to Frieda, the lawyer he'd met the other night, that there was something there. She'd been sexy in the best kind of way—the kind of way that came with confidence, success, and a passion for life. He thought she was someone Claire could look up to.

But then she'd gone back to her hotel with *Bohdi*... Is

desperation causing Steve to lose his ability to read people?

"It's magic," Hernandez says. "We've got to keep the Promethean cuffs and the helmet on Gerðr or one of our guys is going to get in trouble."

Steve snaps out of his reverie, his brain catching on the words, "one of our guys will get in trouble." What about Gerðr, herself? After the ill-fated meeting with Skírnir, when Beatrice was busy filling out forms, Steve had taken some time to reacquaint himself with the myths surrounding Gerðr. Her husband Freyr had fallen in love with her from afar, but she'd wanted nothing to do with him. So Freyr sent his servant Skírnir to convince Gerðr to allow him to court her. Skírnir had tried to convince Gerðr with threats of pain and death. Gerðr had refused. And then Skírnir had threatened her father, and in some stories, her father's lands and people. Skírnir had also promised to "wed" her to a three-headed giant. In the end, Gerðr had married Freyr.

Steve had always taken the myths with a hefty grain of salt—there were some stories where the union between Gerðr and Freyr was a happy one. But then Amy had confirmed that a darker interpretation of the couple's origins was the truth.

"We need her magic, and she's been very cooperative since Beatrice shot Skírnir," Steve muses almost to himself.

"We only need her magic when she's opening the gate," says Hernandez.

"But without magic, she can't communicate as well," Steve counters.

"It's for her own protection," says Hernandez.

Raising an eyebrow, Steve says, "That's what the Taliban says about burkas."

Staring at the numbers above the elevator door, Hernandez

says, "That's a fallacy, sir—this is magic we're talking about, not just ordinary urges."

The elevator dings and the doors slide open.

Steve rubs his temple. "I think I'm getting a headache."

"Magic will do that," says Hernandez as they walk through the lobby.

When they step out into the frigid air of the Chicago night and are instantly set upon by a gauntlet of the press, it's actually a relief. As flashbulbs go off in his face, he feels his adrenaline surge, and a smile comes to his lips.

Above the din, a man's voice rises. "Is it true that Thor kidnapped two American citizens?"

Steve raises his voice. "There is no solid evidence a kidnapping has occurred, Frank." Steve makes a point to address the investigative reporters that trail him by name. They eat it up.

There are a few more questions that Steve answers deftly enough, carefully restraining a mischievous smirk. Steve's used to leadership, but the tango he does with the press is new. He can't help but think of it as a game.

An unfamiliar woman's voice, precise, clipped, and British, comes from Steve's left. "Thor apparently entered this building in his chariot, but hasn't exited the building. Is there perhaps a portal to another realm in one of the flats above?"

Steve's head snaps in the direction of the voice. His eyes settle upon a woman with skin nearly as dark as his own. She's either very tall or wearing impressive heels; her eyes are just a few inches below Steve's. Her unstraightened hair is tied up into a soft bun at the back of her head. Her eyes are warm and brown. And she's beautiful. Not in the perfect way Gerðr is beautiful. This woman is beautiful in a way that's real—there's a dimple in one side of her face and not the other. Her bottom lip is a little too large for her top, she has smile lines, and two lines between her eyes. A woman who thinks, worries, and laughs about things—a human being.

Steve tilts his head. "I'm sorry, I don't know you," he says, and it's not just an evasion.

Thrusting a hand between the other reporters, she says, "Tara Inanna, BBC science correspondent."

She's wearing a fitted coat, and Steve gets just the barest hint of curves beneath it. He smiles, takes her hand, and feels the sharp edges of a business card in his grip. "What do you know about inter-realm portals?" he asks.

"Is there a portal?" another woman shouts.

Without turning his head, Steve says, "Unconfirmed, Miss Andrews."

In front of him, Tara smiles and pulls her hand away. "I may know more than you. I have a degree in physics from Oxford."

Steve's eyebrows lift, and his stomach does a weird little flip flop.

Another reporter shouts, "How will this affect your candidacy for mayor?"

Turning his head, Steve smiles. "Did someone write me on the ballot, George?"

There are chuckles all around. Hernandez suddenly grabs Steve's elbow and drags him out of the way just as the door to the condo building swings open. Steve had forgotten the agent was still next to him.

Beatrice shoots out of the door and walks directly over to Steve, Gerðr and her two agent minders trailing behind. The giantess is still not wearing magic blocking cuffs or a helmet.

"There has to be more we can do!" Beatrice says.

Shouts and flashbulbs erupt from all sides. Steve grabs Beatrice's elbow, consciously avoiding looking at Gerðr. At the same time, he motions for Hernandez to start clearing a line through the crowd to the waiting car.

As he guides Beatrice forward, he cranes his neck around to look for Tara, but she's disappeared.

When they reach the car, Beatrice slides in first, which means Steve gets the awkward honor of sitting next to Gerðr. He inclines his body in Beatrice's direction, but swears he can feel Gerðr's body heat radiating off her, even through his clothing. He's dimly aware of Beatrice saying, "The drones should be armed," and of one of Gerðr's female guards slipping into the front seat.

He looks down at the business card in his palm. On it, in neat blue ink, Tara has written, "Let's discuss physics over dinner sometime."

Steve grips the card in both hands and imagines the dimple on Tara's cheek, large full imperfect lips, and warm brown eyes.

"Strange, I thought I sensed magic," Gerðr says, shifting slightly, her knee brushing Steve's briefly and sending a lightning bolt of heat jolting up Steve's spine.

Steve's phone rings, but he's afraid to reach for it, afraid to even lift his eyes from the business card. The message goes to voicemail, and then Beatrice's phone rings. A moment later, she's pushing it in Steve's face saying, "Steve, it's your mother."

Steve's eyes slide to Beatrice.

The old woman lifts an eyebrow. "Your mother and I are on the Inter-church Chicago Reconstruction Committee, have you forgotten?"

Steve's vaguely aware of Gerðr turning her head in their

direction.

Steve takes the phone. Rubbing his temples and closing his eyes he says, "Yes, Ma'am?"

Steve's mother is usually a very calm woman. From the South, she usually speaks with a cadence slightly slower than the Chicago norm. But now she is speaking rapidly, and the tone of her voice is unusually high pitched. "Steve, I just got off the phone with Claire. Thor, that giant space alien has got Bohdi—and Bea's girl, Amy, too!"

Bea's girl? It takes a minute for Steve to realize that his mother has a nickname for Beatrice, not just her phone number.

"You know, Bohdi's like a another son to me!" Ruth says.

"Painfully aware," says Steve, the headache he'd felt earlier suddenly blooming full force.

"Where has Thor taken them?" says Ruth.

"I'm not really sure exactly, Mother," Steve grits out.

Gerðr shifts beside him again, and she's not really touching him, but she's almost touching him...and good Lord, what is Steve, thirteen?

Beside him Beatrice pipes up, "The drones should be armed!"

On the phone Steve's mom says, "You have to find him!"

The car turns sharply and Gerðr slides into him.

Steve stifles a whimper even as his mother says again, "Find him. Claire is so upset," Beatrice says, "What is the range of a drone?" and Gerðr, oddly deciding to be solicitous, says, "Excuse me."

Find Bohdi? Steve wishes he could join him. No matter how deadly Nornheim is, Steve is being crushed between magic-induced lust, a protective grandmother, and his mother—who is invoking his daughter's name.

There is no way Bohdi could be any more miserable than Steve is right now.

CHAPTER 5

A man rides a battered, three-speed bicycle on a narrow
street. On the front of the bicycle is a basket. A little boy is
sitting in it, legs dangling over the side. The street is packed
with other cyclists, a few mopeds, women in brightly colored
saris, and even one cow with enormous curved horns.

Someone is calling, "Bohdi!"

The boy and the man stop at an intersection where some
mopeds pass in front of them. As the mopeds pass, the man
reaches down and runs his hand through the boy's hair,
tweaking the boy's ear as he pulls away. The boy smiles and
bats at the hand.

"Bohdi!" someone shouts again, a woman with a strange
accent. The little boy doesn't pay any attention. Bohdi is not
his name.

What is his name?

Smiling, the man puts both hands on the handlebars and
begins to peddle again. A woman gets in the way of the scene,
her pale face suddenly entering the frame of the camera…

"Bohdi!"

…In front of him is Amy. Her blue eyes are wide and

worried. Her hands are on either side of his face.

Grabbing her wrists, he pushes her aside, a cry of abject misery leaving his throat.

He lifts his eyes and sees the milky white surface of the column sparkling with flickers of light from within. And then the flickering solidifies, and he sees the man and the boy again; his heart lifts even as heavy hands land on his shoulders and spin him around.

The man and the boy vanish. Bohdi screams. It feels like he's lost everything and everyone he's ever loved.

Something shakes him, and suddenly Bohdi is staring into Thor's dark blue eyes. Words are spilling from Thor's lips, but Bohdi can't make out their meaning. He tries to spin back to the column, but Thor grabs his shoulders and smaller, softer arms wrap around him from behind.

"You must not look at the Columns of Fate!" Thor shouts.

Gasping, Bohdi screams. "I have to! That's why I came! That's what I have to know!"

From behind him, Amy's voice rises, "No, Bohdi, you'll go crazy if you look into the columns." Her hands tighten on his chest.

In front of him, Thor's lips form a hard line. "She speaks the truth. Stare into the columns and you'll lose yourself."

"But…" Bohdi blinks. The last few hours come rushing back to his mind.

After arriving in Nornheim, Thor had circled until he'd found a stream. According to the space Viking, all water in Nornheim flows to the Norns. They'd flown down low enough to see the direction of the current, and then returned the chariot to higher altitudes. They'd flown for hours. After a while, even being in an alien realm had ceased to be interesting.

A few minutes ago, Thor had touched down near one of the giant "Columns of Fate." He'd said the columns would keep some of the predators at bay but had warned Bohdi and Amy not to look too closely at the column surface…and then Thor had walked off to scout for a bit, and Amy had started taking pictures of alien insects with her iPhone…and Bohdi… Bohdi had peeked at the column.

He's panting. And his eyes are wet. Amy's still standing behind him, arms wrapped tightly around his chest. She's shaking. He gulps. No, he's shaking.

Alien insects trill in a strange mournful harmony. The trees in this part of the forest are white-trunked with fern-like leaves that are such a dark green they're nearly black. The ground is covered in a carpet of shredded white bark and dead leaves. The undergrowth is thin, but here and there plants with burgundy leaves and lavender flowers peek from the ground. Light blue insects with bat-like baby blue wings dart about.

He stands frozen, the strange surroundings making him feel like he's trapped in a surreal dream.

He wants to go back to the place he saw in the column. He wants to feel like he did looking at the man and the boy. His brain is screaming at him to turn his head, just to take one more look…

Closing his eyes, he brings his hands up to where Amy's hands are on his chest. Bohdi can't bring himself to push them away, and when his hands touch hers, she responds by squeezing them. Bohdi bows his head. It's pleasantly warm on the surface of Nornheim. He's only wearing the button-down shirt he'd worn to the office this morning. Amy's shed her heavy coat and is only wearing a fleece sweater. He can feel the softness of her breasts pressed against his back. The sensation is sweet; it mutes the empty feeling in his gut, softens the edge of the niggling feeling at the back of his brain telling him just to turn around…

"We need to eat," Thor says, dropping his hands from Bohdi's shoulders. "Come."

Lifting his head and opening his eyes, Bohdi stares at him briefly and then nods. He gently disengages his hands from Amy's. As Thor walks ahead, Amy steps around Bohdi, and her eyes meet his.

He remembers her look of shock and disappointment early this morning, the look of anger when he'd grabbed her in the lab, and her look of incredulity as she'd wrinkled her nose up at the protein bars he'd gotten them from 7-11. Now she only looks concerned. His stomach twists uncomfortably as he looks down at her. In the Marine Corps, he made it all the way through boot camp, infantry training, and had even attended several weeks of schooling before Steve got him out of the Corps with a bogus medical discharge. He should be looking out for *her*.

Averting his eyes, Bohdi manages to murmur, "Thanks."

She just shrugs and nods.

Trying to regain some of his dignity, Bohdi calls to Thor a few paces away. "I have some food—"

Thor grunts and says. "Keep it." He pats a tiny leather satchel no bigger than a wallet and a small flask attached to his belt. "I have an endless supply of food and water right here."

A few minutes later, Bohdi is sitting with Amy and Thor on boulders by the chariot. They are munching on rectangular biscuits that are savory, delicious, and strangely satisfying.

Bohdi's eyes slide to his companions. They're both looking apprehensively at the sky. Thor says that Nornheim is full of dangers, but so far, the worst encounter they have had was with a particularly nasty low hanging cloud filled with biting shards of ice. Bohdi can't bring himself to share their unease. The column rising up behind him dominates his thoughts. Was the little boy him, was the man on the bicycle his father? Their trip down the crowded street loops in his mind.

Maybe if he just tells Thor and Amy he's going to hit the head, he can sneak back and…

Bohdi sits upright. He's thinking the same way he did when Ruth wheedled him into giving up smoking. He swallows; he's thinking like an addict, and he had only stared at the column for a few minutes.

Hands starting to shake, Bohdi reaches into his pocket and feels the familiar shape of his lighter. He closes his eyes, and the images on the column begin to replay.

"Would you like some water?" says Thor.

The words shake Bohdi out of the addictive feedback loop. Nodding, he takes the flask, tips it back, and drinks water as sweet and pure as any he's tasted.

Handing the flask back, he thanks Thor, and the big man only nods at him then settles back into silence. Amy also eats quietly. The only sound is the drone of the insects. In his mind, he hears the ring of a bicycle bell. Had the bicycle had a bell?

The lack of conversation is suddenly oppressive. Unable to take the silence anymore, Bohdi pulls his lighter out of his pocket and spins the flywheel. Opening his mouth, without really thinking, he says, "So…everyone but me is here to find Loki."

Sitting up very straight, Amy says, "How did you know about that?"

Bohdi's face heats up. Whoops.

Avoiding that question, he turns to Thor. "Mind if I ask why? I mean, we've had two whole years of peace and quiet. Why not let sleeping dogs lie?"

He flicks the lighter in his hand and feels the burn of flame. The nameless boy and man in the image in the column fill his mind, the memory of the brief sense of contentment flits by him like a will-o-wisp. How many other families had Loki torn apart?

"Did I say dog? I meant psychopath."

It's only when Thor makes a loud rumbly noise and Amy makes a startled little hiccup that Bohdi realizes he's said that out loud.

He flicks the lighter again. Steve always says Bohdi just can't help stirring the pot. His nostrils flare. "Someone's got to say it," he mumbles, because obviously Amy and Thor are too nice to see it for themselves. He's doing them a favor.

Standing from his boulder, Thor roars. "How dare you!"

Bohdi leans back. Before he can retort, Amy is up and standing between him and the space Viking. "He doesn't know what Loki did!"

Bohdi's memory isn't that bad. "Yes, I do," he snaps. "He killed thousands of people, turned some of them into popsicles, set cars on fire, destroyed buildings—"

Thor rumbles, and Amy shouts, "Loki wiped Bohdi's memories—he's got reason to be upset—and he doesn't know!"

Bohdi's nostrils flare. Standing, so he can look over Amy's shoulder, he shouts, "Doesn't know what?"

Snarling, Thor meets his gaze. "Loki saved the Nine Realms, including yours!"

Bohdi's brows furrow as he glances back and forth at them. "By destroying Chicago's financial district?" Bohdi says, impressed that he mostly managed to keep the sneer out of his voice. He feels the bite of flame on his thumb as he unconsciously flicks his lighter again.

Looking up at him, Amy says, "No. Cera the World Seed did that. She was controlling him. It took him awhile to trick her."

Bohdi's eyebrows jog up his forehead in disbelief.

Eyes still on Bohdi, Thor says, "Ratatoskr was there! He saw the whole thing with Dr. Lewis and delivered the message to the Nine Realms."

With a snarl the big man turns and walks a few paces away. In a voice more anguished than angry he says, "Yet no one believes."

"Yeah," Bohdi mumbles. "Who wouldn't believe a talking squirrel?" Not that he's met the rodent in question. "Hey, isn't this the Rat's home realm or something? Shouldn't he be here saying hello since he and Amy are buds?" He looks down at Amy, but her eyes are on Thor, her mouth pressed in a thin line.

Thor spins toward him. "But it is true! Loki took the World Seed into the In-Between and tricked it into destroying itself…giving birth to a new universe…and sacrificing his own life in the process!"

Bohdi stares at the large man, lip twitching. He glances at Amy for her reaction to that craziness.

She meets his eyes. When she speaks, her voice is sad. "It's true."

"Would that the honor was mine!" Thor rumbles. Bohdi's gaze shifts to the large warrior. Thor has one fist over his chest, and he looks for all the world like he is about to cry.

Bohdi's eyebrows hike, and the circuits in his brain start to work again. "Wait, Loki *is* dead?"

He finds himself looking at Amy, his chest suddenly feeling oddly light. Even in a shapeless fleece, she's still cute. And she understands magical event horizons.

"Yes," Amy says. "He's dead."

Bohdi's mental circuits short. "But if he's dead, why are we looking for him?"

"Chaos can't die," Amy says, cryptically.

Bowing his head, Thor says, "He will assume another form."

Bohdi tilts his head. "Like reincarnation? Are we looking for a baby?" Wait, why is he saying we?

Shaking her head, Amy says, "Maybe...it's not really like the Hindu concept of reincarnation. It's more like chaos picks a body and hitches a ride. Or the universe picks a body...or..." She shrugs.

Bohdi squints and looks toward the bubble-gum pink sun a few hours from the horizon. A baby wouldn't be so bad, but a full-grown Loki in any form...

"So, why exactly the big pressure to find him? I mean chaos..." Bohdi winces. "It's not something most people want to find, right?" Chaos has a way of finding Bohdi, and he *knows.*

"He must be brought to Asgard. My father will care for him," Thor says.

Amy spins to face Thor. "No, Thor! No! Your father will use him—and take advantage of him."

Thor's face goes blank.

Dipping her chin, Amy whispers, "You know he will."

Something mournful enters Thor's expression, his eyes don't leave Amy's, and for an uncomfortable moment, Bohdi feels like they're having a conversation he can't hear.

Thor drops his head. "Loki was my friend."

Bohdi snorts. He does know something about the Norse mythology—having your brain wiped by a so-called Norse god will do wonders to stoke your curiosity.

Flicking his lighter, Bohdi says, "Didn't Loki once steal a falcon cloak, go on a joy flight to Jotunheim, get his ass caught by some giant, then promise to bring you back to the giant's castle unarmed so said giant could kill you?" His lips curl in an incredulous smile. In the myth, Loki lied to Thor to bring him to the giant's doorstep without his hammer. "Didn't you almost die due to your friend?"

Thor's nostrils flare. "Do you take me for an idiot?"

Bohdi looks to the sky. "Well..."

Thor lifts his hammer, and Amy lunges to grab the big man's arm. Practically dangling from Thor's biceps, she looks over her shoulder and shouts. "It didn't happen that way!"

Odin sits upon his throne. At Odin's left, Baldur sits upon a high-backed chair, nearly as grand as Odin's seat. To Odin's right there is a small table; a plate of Idunn's immortality-bestowing apples sits upon it. Odin doesn't need Idunn's apples to keep from aging, but he always partakes; he has a fondness for their taste.

As he stands obediently behind the Allfather, Loki's eyes fall on the apples. Their wonderful aroma perfumes the air. He hasn't had his share of Idunn's harvest this year, and his mouth waters obscenely.

From the back of Odin's seat, Huginn the raven clacks his beak at Loki. *"Don't even think about it."*

Loki scowls at the bird, but tries to turn his attention to the meeting at hand.

Odin's advisers stand below the raised dais the father's and son's seats rest upon. Among the advisers are Heimdall and Thor.

Bowing his head, Heimdall says, *"There have been attacks on Jotunn by the World Gates that lead to Asgard."*

Muninn rawks from a chandelier. *"We can't see under the attackers' hoods!"*

"Magic! Magic!" Huginn clacks.

Heimdall nods at the birds. *"The attackers aren't ashamed to use magic."* His eyes flick briefly to Loki. Loki sticks out his tongue.

Gaze snapping back to Odin, Heimdall says, *"No Aesir used the World Gates immediately before or after the attacks. I believe the attackers to be Jotunn... Nonetheless, popular sentiment in Jotunheim declares the culprits to be us."*

From his seat, Baldur says, *"Perhaps one of the Jotunn kings is trying to sow dissent against us?"*

There are murmurs of agreement among the advisers, and Heimdall says, *"I suspected as much."* Of course, everyone always agrees with Baldur...although even Loki thinks he has a point in this case. Jotunheim is a mess of warring kingdoms. If they were ever to unite, they would become a serious threat to Odin's power. A perceived injustice of sufficient magnitude would be just the thing to make the Jotunn leaders cease their squabbling, and turn their spears toward Asgard.

Muninn rawks from the chandelier. *"Tricky, tricky Jotunn."* He aims a beady eye at Loki. Loki is a full-blooded Jotunn.

An orphan, he was rescued by Odin as a baby and brought to Asgard. Jotunn are normally regarded as the Aesir's backward kin…though Odin himself is at least half Jotunn, and the mother of Thor is rumored to have been Jotunn as well.

Shaking his head, Heimdall says, "I have not been able to determine the identity of the culprit."

On the throne, Odin runs a hand through his beard and sighs. "The Jotunn bristle at the increased tolls at the World Gate…"

Loki snorts. "Can you blame them? Their northern hemisphere is in the midst of a famine. It's hard to use gold to purchase grain from the Vanir when you've already spent it to cross the World Gate."

Several of the advisers grumble.

But Odin waves a hand at them. "Loki is right. Still, we cannot lower the toll for fear of encouraging similar acts of subterfuge in the future."

Hefting Mjolnir in his hands, Thor says, "Let us declare war on Jotunheim! If the giants' unrest is so easily incited, it is because in their hearts they are ready to wage war against us!"

Loki winces. He respects Thor…sometimes. Odin's bastard son, Thor is one of the few Asgardians who doesn't condemn Loki for allowing his half-blue daughter Helen to live. But sometimes Thor thinks only with his hammer. An Asgardian invasion would be just the thing to unite the Jotunn kings. And a war with a united Jotunheim would only be winnable at great cost—if it could be won at all.

Some of the advisers murmur in assent. Someone says, "Our young men grow restless. It would be a good distraction. And it would be an excellent opportunity for Prince Baldur to lead our armies."

Loki sees Baldur pale. Clearing his throat, the prince says, "To punish all of Jotunheim for the machinations of a few is not noble."

Loki doesn't sigh. Although Baldur's fear at the prospect of leading armies is very much evident to Loki, he's sure that to the rest of the men in the room Baldur sounds merely wise.

Tapping his fingers nervously on the arm of his chair, the prince adds, "Nor is it a great victory to slaughter those who are already weakened by famine."

Loki lifts an eyebrow. He very much doubts that a campaign in Jotunheim would result in slaughter for just the Jotunns. Even starving Jotunns are deadly; they'll turn to eating their own dead rather than submit quietly to Aesir boots in their lands. And the southern kingdoms are still very strong. Loki smirks. A campaign by the Aesir might be just the thing to unite the kingdoms of Frost Giants—and that would spell disaster for the "stability" Odin prides himself in keeping in the Nine Realms.

"We must weed out the troublemakers," Odin says.

Bowing his head, Heimdall says, "I will redouble my efforts."

Huginn and Muninn flutter their wings. "We will fly now."

Odin nods at the birds and they take to wing, flying through an open window in the great hall. To the rest of the room, Odin says, "Dismissed!"

There are bows around the room. Turning as a group the advisers file out. Thor, apparently upset that he won't be smashing any Jotunn heads anytime soon, crosses his arms over his chest and doesn't budge; his lips turn down in an obvious pout. Baldur starts to stand, but Odin motions for him to sit.

Hopping down from the dais, covertly palming one of Odin's apples as he does, Loki pats Thor on the shoulder. "Better luck next time, Thor. Let's go eat."

"Stay, Loki," says Odin. Loki sighs but stops and pulls the apple out of his sleeve. Turning to give it back to the Allfather he says, "It was only a little joke—"

Baldur rolls his eyes and leans back on one elbow. Waving a hand, Odin says, "You can eat the apple. Thor, leave us."

Shrugging, Loki takes a bite of the fruit. His eyes slide back into his head at his first taste of the season's harvest. Idunn's apples are tart-sweet and sour like life. A trickle of juice threatens to escape down Loki's chin. He catches it quickly with the flick of his tongue, unwilling to let even a bit of the fruit's magic escape.

Thor does not budge. Uncrossing his arms, he reaches for his hammer with one hand and gestures toward the heavens with the other. "If Heimdall and your ravens haven't found the instigator yet, what makes you think they'll find him now?"

As Loki chews on the apple's crisp flesh, Odin sighs wearily. "I don't expect them to," Odin says.

Thor tilts his head. "Then how—"

Leaning back on his throne, Odin says, "Loki will find him."

Loki almost spits out the bite of apple in his mouth. "Pardon?"

Turning his gaze to Loki, Odin says, "You will leave immediately."

The tangy taste of apple turns to dust in his mouth. "Surely I'll have time to say goodbye to Aggie—"

Will his wife believe that he's leaving on Odin's orders? Or will she think he's running from her and Helen? Everyone blames Aggie for Helen's twisted frame and half-blue skin—though Loki knows it's his fault. Nothing he does ever goes quite right.

Odin shakes his head. "The sooner you leave, Loki, the less chance Jotunn spies will be able to inform their masters of your visit."

Loki's heart drops. He can send a projection to say goodbye to *his wife and child...but that isn't the same.*

Thor claps a hand down on Loki's shoulder. "And I will go with you!" As usual, Thor's aggressive affection nearly makes Loki fall over, but he's never been so grateful for the weight.

"No, Thor," says Odin. "This is a task Loki needs to do alone."

"Alone?" squeaks Loki. In Jotunheim?

"How will he even survive?" says Thor. "The Jotunn view him as a traitor—" Shaking his great head, Thor says, "You ask him to do the impossible!"

Odin nods at Thor. "Which is why he will succeed."

"How?" says Loki.

Odin meets his gaze and gives him a surprisingly warm smile. "I don't know. But you will figure it out."

Loki stares at the king, his stomach twisting into knots. On the one hand, the display of faith is oddly touching. On the other hand. "Aggie," he whispers.

"Will be taken care of," says Baldur too quickly.

Loki's head snaps in the direction of his former romantic rival. Thor's hand tightens on his shoulder.

"Of course, of course, I will assure you of her welfare indefinitely no matter what the outcome," Odin says, waving a hand absently. His gaze falls hard upon Loki. "But I know you will succeed. You're dismissed, Loki."

Loki's eyes fall on Baldur. The other man is looking at him, his gaze as fierce as a hawk.

"Come on, Loki," Thor whispers, pulling him toward the door.

"You will not go with him, Thor," Odin says. Turning, Thor bows once and says, "You have my word, Father." And then he hastens to Loki's side.

As Loki stumbles, eyes unseeing, out of Odin's great hall, Thor says, "How does the Allfather expect you to manage traveling through Jotunheim alone? It's not just the Jotunn you must fear, it is the yeti and the—"

"Shut up, Thor!" Loki says.

Thor shuts up. For all of three seconds. "I am just worried about you. Jotunheim's lands are perilous!"

"You're not helping, Thor!" Loki spits, rolling his eyes heavenward. His eyes catch on some sparrows fluttering in the eaves of Odin's hall.

"Why would the Allfather give this task to you alone?" Thor grumbles, but Loki's barely listening.

If he avoids the land of Jotunheim, the journey will be far less perilous...

"Do you think Frigga is wearing her feather cloak today?" Loki asks absentmindedly.

"No, too warm," says Thor. "Why do you ask?"

"Oh, no reason," Loki says. He suddenly realizes he still has Idunn's apple in his hands. He takes a bite.

To Amy's surprise, Thor backs away from Bohdi. Suddenly she's aware she's holding an arm that has all the pliability of an oak tree. She drops her hands.

Straightening, Thor looks down at Bohdi. Bohdi is tall— but next to Thor, he looks small and positively scrawny. Still, Bohdi grins mischievously. The glazed look Bohdi had when he was watching whatever he saw in the column is gone. Normally, his eyes have a slightly orange cast, but in Nornheim's pale pink light, they look nearly red, and at the moment, they're glinting.

Thor huffs. "Of course, you think I'm an idiot." He smiles

bitterly. "Even if Loki did borrow Frigga's cloak without asking..."

Bohdi snorts and Amy blinks. A memory of Loki defying Odin's orders, illusioning the guise of a falcon and going to his wife and child to say goodbye, fills her mind.

Thor's voice continues to rumble. "Why would Loki fly of all places to Jotunheim? It is not a place one goes to for a *joy flight.*"

Amy winces, remembering the sharp bite of ice on Loki's skin as he flew over plains of snow covered mountains, and pine forests punctuated by a few primitive forts and castles. He'd found the giant, King Geirod, not by spying on kings— as he knew the ravens and Heimdall undoubtedly did. He'd learned about Geirod's plans by spying on Geirod's daughters. Loki, sitting on the gates of Geirod's castle, still wearing the illusion of a falcon, had overheard the girls describe how they would torture Thor after their father's plans were fulfilled. Unfortunately, Geirod's daughters had a bit of magical training; they'd seen through his illusion and called the guards—just as Frigga's magical feather coat ran out of magic. Loki had been captured and dragged into a dungeon that was cold, wet, and filled with rats. They'd shackled his wrists and ankles and...

Amy's eyes go wide, and her stomach falls. She gasps for air and wills her legs to remain steady, forcing the images from her mind. Amy turns to Thor. His nostrils are slightly flared, his face is flushed with anger. Even as she sees his barely restrained irritation, she sees another Thor in another time...

When Thor had broken into Geirod's dungeon, Loki had been in too much pain to even realize who it was. As his shackles had fallen away and he'd been lifted to a sitting position, he'd thought he was due for another torture session. He'd been too weak to fight. When a flask was pressed to his lips and he heard Thor's voice say, "Drink," he'd opened his eyes. Thor's face was framed above him by flickering torch-light, his eyes very soft.

Loki thought he was hallucinating, but he managed to whisper, "I hope you brought Mjolnir...to smash us...out of here..."

Thor just chuckled as he pushed the flask more firmly to Loki's lips. "No, I left it at home. Geirod wouldn't allow me to come negotiate for your release if I brought my hammer."

Loki almost spit out the water. "You idiot! It's a trap."

Thor snorted. "But I saved the son of an enchantress on the way here, and she gave me the most marvelous staff..."

Amy swallows. The magical staff had been strong enough to crush rock. Thor had destroyed Geirod's castle and Geirod himself. All that was left of the king's forces had scattered.

Suddenly feeling literally and figuratively small, Amy says to Thor, "You marched into Jotunheim knowing it was a trap, didn't you?" Saving the enchantress's son had been a happy accident.

Dropping his eyes, Thor shrugs.

Voice hushed, she says, "Did Odin and Baldur know you were going to do that?"

Wincing, Thor puts one of his meaty hands behind his head and scratches the back of his neck. "They were concerned that if I was captured, it would enrage public sentiment and cause a war. Which was Geirod's aim to begin with so..."

"You went without their permission," she whispers.

Shrugging again, Thor sighs. "I missed Loki. I always miss him when he's gone." Lifting his great head, Thor meets her eyes. "My greatest adventures always came about because of Loki…" He smiles a little ruefully. "I honor and strive for peace, but I have found the most clarity and the truest tests of character come with chaos."

Amy feels her breath catch…and her heart sink. She thought that this trip would be about battling Odin, and his schemes to use Loki. But really, the true battle will be convincing Thor that Asgard might not be the best place for his best friend.

She bites her lip. She has to let Thor knows she cares, too. Win him over to her way of thinking with subtlety, tact, and—

"So is it true you and Loki dressed up as girls?" Bohdi says.

Amy's eyes snap to Bohdi. Idly thumbing the wheel of his lighter, he's giving Thor a mischievous smirk that is so *familiar* that Amy's stomach twists.

"Why, you little…" Thor strides toward Bohdi, lifting his hammer. Amy gasps, but then Thor drops Mjolnir to his side with a growl, and pokes Bohdi's chest with a finger. "If I hadn't given you my oath…"

The poke doesn't quite knock Bohdi over, but he just laughs. "Not that there's anything wrong with that!" Bohdi looks positively delighted…and slightly devilish. Amy's heart rate speeds up.

Thor stammers. "No! It…No, that story is…was…just silly gossip!"

Bohdi's smile drops and his eyes cross. A ferocious sneeze wracks through his body…right onto Thor who barely throws up an arm in time.

"Ugh!" says Thor. "Control yourself, human!"

Bending over and turning his head, Bohdi stammers. "I'm…" he sneezes again. "Sorry…I…"

Staggering away, he sneezes twice more, and then proceeds to sniffle piteously.

Amy sighs and shakes her head. Reaching into her pocket, she pulls out a packet of tissues. As she does, Thor announces, "We will rest here. The adze swarm at night, but if we are at sufficient altitude by dusk, we'll avoid them completely. Try to sleep—I will take first watch." With that, he stalks off toward a bluff a few paces off.

Walking over to Bohdi, she offers him a tissue. Taking it, he sniffles. "Thanks…stupid allergies."

Amy tilts her head. Allergies typically only manifest themselves on second exposure to the allergen, but Mr. Squeakers hasn't come out of her pocket, and this is an alien world so—

"What's an adze?" Bohdi sniffs. His eyes are tearing, and his nose looks a little swollen. Amy swallows. He's just Bohdi. And if he reminded her of anyone else a few moments ago… well, that's to be expected. She's trying to find the next incarnation of her…well, of Loki…and she's carrying his memories, and once carried his child. If she sees "ghosts" of Loki occasionally, it's probably a normal thing.

Shaking herself from her uncomfortable musings, Amy says, "They're sort of hominid things with dragonfly wings and a taste for human flesh."

Amy looks toward the chariot. She suddenly has the desire to wrap herself up in her down coat. "We should sleep."

"How am I supposed to sleep when you tell me about flesh-eating dragonfly people?" Bohdi says. Amy blinks at him. One of Bohdi's eyebrows is up, one eye is wide, one eye is narrowed, and his lip is curled in an expression somewhere between horror and disgust. The overall look is so comical, she actually laughs.

He grins brightly. Leaning in close, Bohdi whispers conspiratorially, "So Thor—he totally dressed up as a chick, didn't he?'

She's ridiculously grateful for the distraction. Checking to make sure that Thor is out of earshot, she whispers, "Yeah, this is what I heard…"

As she tells the tale, Bohdi interjects with amusing little quips that keep her from thinking…too much. She still has reservations about The Thong incident, but maybe Steve is right; Bohdi is all right.

CHAPTER 6

Steve is going to kill Bohdi. Steve rubs one hand over his head as he holds a phone to his ear. He knows why Amy would go to Nornheim, but why would Bohdi do this to him?

The voice of Steve's father, Henry, comes from the other end of the line. "Any news on Bohdi and Bea's girl?"

"No, Dad."

"It's Saturday," Henry says. "Why are you at the office?"

Steve restrains the urge to pound his head into his desk. "Because Bohdi and Bea's girl are missing, Dad." And missing people, opening World Gates, sending off drones, and shooting sorcerers—even in self-defense—generates a lot of paperwork.

"What about Claire—"

Steve's gut clenches. "She's with her mother." Unexpectedly. Steve was supposed to pick her up at noon, but Dana had decided spur of the moment to get Claire's teeth cleaned before she goes to the Ukraine. They're leaving in just three days. Steve takes a breath. He'll get her tonight.

Changing the subject, maybe out of pity, Henry says, "You still haven't announced if you're running for mayor."

"Because I haven't decided if I am yet," says Steve.

"You either want it or you don't," says Henry.

Does he want it? Steve doesn't like setting himself up to fail. Even if he won the election, can he do anything to help the city? Chicago, Cook County, and the State of Illinois are notorious for corruption, inefficiency, and being flat-out broke. The destruction of the financial district and the subsequent visits by trolls and wyrms don't help Chicago, either. Besides losing its downtown firms, large swaths of the population have left. The only people who come to the city now are scientists, government workers, and some religious sects.

Chicago is a sinking ship, and Steve doesn't want to go down with it. If he stays in the FBI and keeps the trolls and wyrms from slipping out into the 'burbs, he stays the hero on the front lines of the new war. When he wants to jump into politics, he'll have a good shot—*someplace else.*

All Steve tells Henry though is, "I'm not giving you any gossip to feed the guys at the barbershop."

Henry grumbles but doesn't say more.

A few minutes later, Steve flips his phone closed. The only sound in the office is the tick of the radiator. He checks his email hoping to see something from the contact that calls himself Prometheus, but there is nothing.

All his paperwork is done. There are no plans to open the gate again for another twenty-four hours when they'll get readings from the drones. He can leave. But his apartment is an empty place.

He glances at the clock. It is lunchtime. He takes Tara Inanna's card from his pocket. Lunch is a good time for a chat about physics—or a first date. Dropping his hands to his keyboard, Steve Googles her name, because, doesn't everyone?

He gets zero results. Steve pulls back from the computer. A BBC science correspondent who doesn't have a web presence? He looks down at the card and rubs his eyes. A fake. Just his luck.

There is a knock at his door. "Come in," says Steve, pushing the card to the side.

Beatrice enters the office.

Steve goes for the preemptive strike. "I don't have anything new for you, Beatrice."

Beatrice frowns. "I know that. I just had some translations to finish, and I'd just rather be at work than at home right now."

Steve sighs. And that's the truth of it for both of them. "Well, what can I do for you?"

Helping herself to a seat, Beatrice says, "We still don't know what the Russians, Ukrainians, and Belarusians were getting from the Dark Elves in exchange for AK-47s?"

Steve leans back in his chair. "No." Or if they do, no one is telling him. Dale, an old Marine buddy who went into the CIA after his service, is somewhere off in Eastern Europe, but he wasn't able to shed any light on the situation, other than to say, "Weird things are happening."

Beatrice nods. "Well, you know I used to come from that region. When my schedule allows, I take a peek at the bloggers from those regions who post their pickle recipes. We have so many more varieties of pickles than you have here in the states."

Steve stares at her. Maybe he should go home. "And this is important to ADUO...*because?*"

Beatrice's eyes get sharp. "Well, they've had access to extremely good produce in the last few years at extremely competitive prices. And recently someone traced where the produce came from. And some of it is coming from just outside Pripyat, in the Ukraine."

Steve's jaw twitches. *"And..."*

Beatrice's eyes narrow at him. "That's inside the Chernobyl control zone, Steven."

Steve blinks. "Is produce contaminated with radiation showing up in produce stands? That's terrible, but I'm not sure—"

"It's not contaminated. One of the bloggers measured it with a Geiger counter."

Steve blinks again.

Leaning closer, Beatrice whispers, "And some people are talking about the lights in the Chernobyl power plant and in Pripyat proper going on at night."

Steve crosses his arms. None of the countries in the former Soviet block are particularly strong on environmentalism, but if lights are going on...

Standing up from his chair, he says, "Come on, Beatrice. We're going to talk to Gerðr."

He instantly feels his body flush at the memory of the last time he spoke with Gerðr...and sits right back down again. Putting his head in his hands, he says, "No wait, Beatrice, I need you to talk to Gerðr..."

He rubs his temples. Steve can handle rabid press, hungry wyrms, angry trolls, and playing the diplomat when it comes to interdepartmental BS.

He glances up at Beatrice. But a magical science mystery through an interpreter?

Why not bang his head against a wall? He already has a headache.

Had Amy thought she'd reach Thor with subtlety and tact?

Trying to be diplomatic is a pain in the ass.

Wind is whipping her hair, three glorious moons are hanging in the sky. Here and there white canopies cover the dense dark trees in the low rolling mountains below them. The river they're following glitters like a silver snake in the moonlight as it twists through the mountains. Now and then, they see the iridescent glint of adze wings below them—from this height, they look like nothing more than a swarm of large dragonflies. To the east, the hints of a pale pink dawn are on the horizon.

All awesome wonders of the Nine Realms. None quite so awesome as the deliberate density of Thor's big head. She can't get it through to him that Asgard might not be the best place for Loki.

Standing beside her, he laughs good-naturedly as he recounts a story. "So because Loki was being blamed for stealing more than his fair share of Idunn's apples, I built a squirrel trap, he made it invisible, and we caught Ratatoskr in it! Odin ransomed the rat for one free answer from the Norns, Ratatoskr being their most faithful servant and—"

"Doesn't it bother you that when apples first started disappearing, everyone's first impulse was to blame Loki?" Amy says. She digs her hands into her down coat to ward off the chill. Down on the ground, Nornheim is comfortably warm, but up here, at high altitudes it's cold. She and Bohdi have both put their winter coats back on.

Thor waves a hand. "My father believed in Loki's

innocence. That is all that matters."

Beyond the great man, Bohdi lifts his hand to his mouth in a yawn.

Amy's tired, too, and her feet hurt. "Your father will treat him as a servant!" She says, the words snippish. She blames her exhaustion.

Thor's good-natured chortling stops. "Aren't we all at our best when we are servants of peace and order?" He brings a hand to his chest. "And my father will never abuse him."

The slight inflection on abuse makes Amy's memory flash to Baldur's comments about buggering, and Odin's response. Her skin heats. But before she can respond, Bohdi says, "You keep saying he, what if the next incarnation is a she? How would Odin treat a *her?*"

Coming from Bohdi, the question leaves Amy a little imbalanced. He doesn't seem particularly sensitive to gender issues. Her eyes slide to him. He's leaning against the wall of the chariot on the other side of Thor, one side of his mouth quirked. He's just asking the question to provoke a reaction. Still...she looks expectantly at Thor.

Thor's jaw is set in a hard line, his nostrils are flared, and his flame-red hair whipping about his head makes him look just that much more angry.

"Loki wouldn't come back as..." Thor's voice trails off.

Amy rolls her eyes. Bohdi grins. "Wasn't he sort of the god of transvestitism? One of his better qualities—"

Thor spins to him, the chariot lurches and Amy barely holds on. Bohdi makes a strangled "gurp" as Thor grabs his collar and snarls. "You *little...*"

Stamping a foot, Amy shouts, "It's a valid question, Thor! How would Odin treat a girl?"

As soon as the question is out of her mouth, she feels like she might throw up. She knows...

Dropping Bohdi, Thor stammers, "I'm sure he'd treat a... woman with respect."

Bohdi promptly sneezes all over the back of Thor's head. Thor turns with a snarl, and the chariot lurches again. "Watch yourself, human!" Thor shouts.

Memories start to spill before Amy's eyes. Her legs give out beneath her. Grasping the side of the chariot, she slides to the floor.

It's Baldur's birthday, but Baldur is dead. Loki saw to it, giving the human warlord Hothur the secret of Baldur's allergy to mistletoe. That doesn't keep the Aesir from celebrating the birth of the golden prince. Loki stares at the gigantic golden statue in Baldur's likeness that stands just outside Odin's hall. Even more flower wreaths than normal adorn its base.

Beside him, Tyr says, "So, Loki, are you going to Aegir's feast?"

Loki doesn't bother to respond. Of course he and his wife Sigyn haven't been invited.

Baldur killed Loki's daughter Helen. So Loki killed Baldur, or rather, helped a human warlord kill Baldur. But even though Loki carefully covered his tracks, he's still blamed for the crown prince's demise.

Irritated, and a little depressed by how events have conspired against him, he veers from the main pathway and into the gardens. He needs to be with someone who is nearly always on his side. Also, he's hungry.

Before long, he has reached Hoenir's hut. The main door

stands ajar. Sleipnir grazes outside. Loki looks around the hut; Odin must be here, but where are his guards?

Giving Sleipnir a friendly pat, Loki goes to the door. Before he enters, Odin's voice makes him pause. "I haven't been able to sleep, not since Baldur died."

Loki hesitates. This is a conversation he is sure Odin does not want overheard. The polite thing to do is walk away. Loki doesn't. But he refrains from interrupting—which he thinks shows amazing self-control.

Odin continues. "Would you give me some more of that sleeping draught, Hoenir?"

Loki blinks. The mighty Odin, in such a state, because of the death of his worthless son? "I fear I won't be able to sleep tonight without it…"

The hairs on the back of Loki's neck stand on end, and he feels like he's covered in ants. Odin is lying.

"He was my boy, the most beautiful of all my sons…" Odin says. Loki's jaw twitches. Odin has had many healthy, hale, and distinguished sons. The Allfather's descendants litter the royal lines of Midgard's Europe. But the words don't make Loki itch; Odin believes them. Loki frowns. Frigga all but put an end to Odin's whoring centuries ago, and Odin's mortal sons are now dead. But there is still Thor. Thor is dense at times, not imbued with Baldur's glamour, and not conniving enough to be a king. But Thor is real in all his faults and strengths. Even Loki will admit Thor has more character and a greater sense of justice than anyone he's ever met. Foolish traits, but Loki has benefited from them and doesn't chide Thor for them—not much, anyway.

From Hoenir's hut there is the sound of creaking floorboards, and then Odin says, "Thank you."

Hearing footsteps coming his way, Loki slips quickly over to

Sleipnir. Odin emerges from the hut. Hoenir comes with him, carrying a staff with the head of Mimir mounted on top.

Sleipnir nuzzling his hand, Loki says brightly, "Hello, Allfather!"

Mimir raises an eyebrow at Loki, and mouths the word, "Hush." Odin doesn't do more than grunt. Giving a nod to Hoenir, Odin mounts Sleipnir, gives the horse a quick kick, and rides off.

The Allfather's lack of acknowledgment niggles at Loki, like a splinter too small to pull out. His skin heats and a spark lights in his fingers. He has done nothing wrong. Odin asked Loki to kill Baldur, and Baldur was vile.

"You know, Loki," Mimir snips. "Things would be better between you and Odin if you showed some remorse."

"I have no remorse for Baldur's death," Loki snaps. "Why should I? Odin himself said his golden son would bring Asgard to ruin."

Hoenir sighs.

Mimir huffs. "Odin sacrificed Baldur for the sake of Asgard! But no matter what sort of monster Baldur was, Baldur was also Odin's son, and Odin loved him, even if he wasn't perfect. Surely you can identify with that?"

Loki's skin heats at the implied reference to Helen and her blue skin and twisted limbs. He takes a step toward the head. Hoenir draws Mimir, and the staff he is mounted on, back quickly beneath the eaves of the house.

Loki restrains the fire itching to spring from him for Hoenir's sake. But he is unable to keep from shouting at Mimir. "My daughter. Was not. A monster!"

Mimir closes his eyes, and inhales—though he has no lungs for air to go to. Opening his eyes, he says, "Odin came here because he can't sleep. He had to borrow a sleeping draught from Hoenir to—"

Loki cuts Mimir off with a sharp laugh and a slow, "Pffffftttttt!"

"I beg your pardon!" says Mimir. Even Hoenir puts one hand on his hip and fixes Loki with a glare.

Rolling his eyes and waving a hand, Loki says, "He's lying about the draught."

"What?" says Mimir. The glare washes off of Hoenir's face and he just looks confused.

Loki shrugs and says, "I overheard."

Hoenir's eyes go wide. Mimir's eyebrows rise. They both know Loki can detect lies.

Motioning for Loki to follow him, Hoenir abruptly turns into the hut, thunking Mimir's staff hard on the ground as he does. As Loki enters, he finds himself in Hoenir's kitchen. From his perch, Mimir says, "Hoenir, you shouldn't get involved. You can't confront Odin."

Ignoring Mimir's words, Hoenir leans Mimir's staff against the wall and grabs a nearly empty teacup from the table.

Mimir sighs exasperatedly. "I know you think you know what he'll do with the draught—"

Hoenir cocks an eyebrow and glares in Mimir's direction.

Mimir looks to the side, "—and I know he's done it before, but it's been a long time…not since that business with Andvaranaut."

Andvaranaut? Loki tilts his head. He feels like he's heard that name before.

Atop the staff, Mimir continues. "Do you think you're letting your…sensitivity…to this subject cloud your judgment?"

Hoenir's nostrils flare, but he doesn't acknowledge Mimir. Lifting his balding head, Hoenir gestures for Loki to approach.

Loki does tentatively. He's never seen Hoenir this agitated before.

From his perch, Mimir rumbles. "Hoenir, he could be any-where in the Nine Realms."

Peering into the cup, at first Loki sees only the dregs of tea, but then a scene appears: the honey-colored plains of Vanaheim, filled with peacefully grazing unicorns.

"Well, he wouldn't be there," snorts Mimir. "You don't know where to look. The odds of you finding Odin are impossible—"

Scowling at Mimir, Hoenir thrusts the cup toward Loki. Holding up his hands, Loki catches one side of the tiny cup auto-matically, lukewarm tea sloshing onto his hand. Hoenir doesn't release the cup, and his fingers brush Loki's. Mimir abruptly goes silent.

Loki blinks. What does Hoenir expect? He's never been able to manage the trick of sight and... He blinks again. In the tea-cup, he sees snow-covered mountains jutting into an overcast sky like wicked teeth. Just before the mountains is a utilitarian for-tress, surrounded by a ramshackle village.

Loki smiles in recognition. "Oh, it's King Billings' fortress on Jotunheim." Pulling the cup back to himself, Hoenir swirls the contents, and suddenly, Odin appears beside Sleipnir in a copse of trees in front of the fort. Loki blinks. Odin shimmers, and in his place stands an ancient Frost Giantess wearing the robes of a medicine woman. Loki's eyes go wide. He never thought the Allfather would stoop to disguising himself as a woman.

The hag that is Odin lifts her eyes and looks directly at Hoe-nir and Loki.

Mimir sighs. "He saw you. Now he'll block your view."

The image in the teacup swirls and disappears.

From where he leans, Mimir says, "Told you he'd do that."

Hoenir frowns and swishes the cup.

Loki grins. The sly old fox knew he was being watched. But it's too late, Loki knows his shame. What fun!

Hands shaking, Hoenir drops the teacup onto the table. It rolls onto its side, spilling its contents, but doesn't shatter.

From his perch, Mimir says, "If he is up to what you suspect, Hoenir, you can't stop it."

Hoenir runs his hands through his hair. He looks like he will cry. Mimir continues. "You don't even know where he's gone! He could have gone into the village, the fortress, or to some remote hut in the mountains."

Hoenir begins to pace the room, hands still in his hair. Maybe he needs a distraction? Clearing his throat and rubbing his stomach, Loki smiles and says, "You know...it's always easier to think on a full stomach."

Hoenir doesn't even lift his head.

In a pitying voice, Mimir says, "There's nothing you can do, Hoenir. You can't kill a bug, let alone fight Odin."

Loki knew that about Hoenir, that he can't kill or maim, but he can't remember ever being told. His eyes flash toward Mimir. There's no need for the head to rub in Hoenir's inadequacy.

Hoenir stops pacing and abruptly grabs Mimir's staff. He pulls back a hand as though he might strike the head. Mimir doesn't even flinch. Hoenir's hand begins to shake and then abruptly drops.

Loki swallows. He doesn't like seeing Hoenir so vulnerable and exposed.

Hoenir's eyes flick to a nearby door.

Mimir's nostrils flare. "What? Do you intend to set the velociraptors loose?"

Loki's eyebrows rise. Hoenir still has those beasts?

"You'll be responsible for more innocent blood than Odin if

you do!" Mimir snaps.

Hoenir's eyes slide to Loki. He leans Mimir's staff against the wall again, points at the teacup, and then at Loki.

"Oh, no, no, no…" says Mimir. "No, don't do that."

Loki looks at Mimir and then at Hoenir. Hoenir's nostrils are flared. Scowling, Hoenir points at the teacup again, and then again at Loki.

Hoenir has occasionally used sign language in the past. Cocking his head, Loki says, "You want me to go to Jotunheim?"

Hoenir nods.

"No, Loki, don't! It's none of your business," Mimir says. "Trust me, it's best to stay out of it."

Loki scowls at Mimir. He doesn't like being told what to do, he doesn't like how Mimir's talking to Hoenir, and frankly, at this point, Loki's just plain curious. Raising an eyebrow he says, "To do what, exactly?"

Hoenir makes a slashing motion across his chest.

"And kill Odin?" says Loki, eyes widening. His anger at the Allfather minutes ago abruptly changes to horror.

"Erm…" says Mimir.

Hoenir stares at him, looking vaguely thoughtful.

Loki steps back. He doesn't think he could kill Odin. Odin is as close as Loki has to a father—not to mention ruler of the Nine Realms, and Thor's father.

But then Hoenir shakes his head. He makes the slashing motion again.

A misunderstanding. Sighing in relief, Loki suggests, "Stop him?"

Hoenir nods vigorously.

"Don't do it," says Mimir.

If Odin is as close as Loki has to a father, Hoenir is as close as he has to a mother. Loki shrugs. "Alright. I'll have to go to the World Gate, and I don't know if Heimdall will…" His voice drops off, a little ashamed. Mimir says Loki is capable of opening World Gates on his own if he'd just practice. And Loki has tried…a few times…but his efforts only end in frustration. Besides, it's so hard to find the time—what with his duties to Odin, chasing his sons, drinking with Thor, and as Mimir snarkily remarked, "watching grass grow." Odin says the only way Loki will ever learn is if someone chains him to a rock for a few centuries.

Hoenir walks quickly over to another door leading off the kitchen. Leaning his forehead against it, he grabs the handle and begins to silently move his lips. As soon as he finishes, he steps away, cheeks flushed as though from exertion, forehead slightly damp. He turns the doorknob and opens the door.

Loki finds himself looking through the doorway and into the courtyard of King Billings' fort. The king is not about, but the yard is milling with peasants, soldiers, and the odd courtier. No one seems to notice Hoenir or Loki standing in the doorway.

Hoenir nods at Loki. Mimir grumbles.

Hesitating, Loki wills an illusion around himself of an ancient Frost Giantess in the same medicine woman robes Odin had worn. Hoenir nods and smiles encouragingly, at the same time making a fast rolling motion with his hand.

Reading the signal, Loki concentrates on the task at hand. "Alright, I'll be quick…"

"He'll still be too late, Hoenir!" Mimir says. "Pick your battles!"

Before he really knows what's happening, Hoenir gives Loki a shove. Loki hears the door close behind him. Looking back, he sees only a crude stone wall. He restrains a shiver. Jotunheim is *much colder than Asgard, and the fort's walls radiate chill. He's not dressed for this. Letting his shoulders stoop as though with age, Loki makes his way into the courtyard proper.*

It takes nearly half an hour to find someone who can help him. No one seems to remember another medicine woman in the vicinity. Finally, Loki gets the attention of an elderly courtier. Loki tells the man that he has come to help his "sister" on "her errand."

The courtier, a tall, painfully pale man with a balding, uncovered head protruding from voluminous robes, accepts the lie easily enough. Fingers fluttering, he says, "Oh, yes, she is already with the Princess Rind. I will take you there immediately."

Loki resists the urge to sigh. Apparently, Odin has gone through ridiculous lengths to gain a paramour. Still, he says, "Lead the way, young man," making a show of gathering skirts.

With a smile and a bow, the courtier leads Loki from the courtyard, and into the fort, at a painfully slow pace.

As the minutes slip by, Loki begins to second-guess his reasons for being here. Why would Hoenir intervene in an affair? Hoenir has turned a blind—albeit, perhaps a slightly disgusted—eye many times as Odin seduced women with baubles, magic, and gold. This is Frigga's business, not Loki's…He fidgets with his illusionary skirts. Also, Mimir's words are beginning to sink in. Odin sacrificed his son for Asgard; Loki doesn't think he could sacrifice his sons for anything. No matter what. But Odin…Odin isn't just Loki's protector, he is the protector of the Nine Realms. Odin won't just give his life like he'd nearly done in Nornheim… he'll give the life of his son.

Loki's stomach feels hollow—with regret, remorse—and maybe awe for his mentor. Suddenly feeling small, he wishes he were on Earth, where he could just disappear. But he is among

Frost Giants. If he draws too much attention to himself, they might call on one of their sorcerers, and he might wind up in another Frost Giant dungeon. He shivers, and it is not from cold. They turn down a dark stone hallway, and climb a narrow staircase. His guide is gasping for breath by the time they reach the top. As they enter a dark drawing room, Loki estimates at least another quarter of an hour has gone by. In the room, King Billings sits upon a rough bench, head bowed, clutching a pewter tumbler of something in his hand.

Necessary courtesies drain away more precious minutes, and then Loki gives the king the same lie he gave the courtier. When Loki is finished, Billings says, "Old woman, your sister is already with my daughter. She warned me not to disturb them."

Loki smiles as kindly as he can manage, and says, "Your Highness, she meant you, not me, her kin."

Billings accepts that easily enough. The king leads Loki to a wide corridor and then stops. "Her chambers are at the end." Eyes still on his daughter's door, the king says, "It's quiet at last…" He swallows. "She is delusional. Paranoid. She imagines the Allfather himself has come to claim her. She sees his face in the faces of her suitors…and even screamed at first at the presence of your sister…I was almost too fearful to leave my daughter alone with her."

Loki feels his jaw go slack. And then shakes himself. Odin does not have to stoop to force to get what he wants. Perhaps the girl carries Odin's child and has concocted some elaborate tale to hide her part in her loss of virtue?

Walking as quickly as he dares in his guise as an old woman, Loki reaches the end of the corridor and tries the princess's door. It's locked. His skin prickles as he draws some dwarven tools from his cuffs. He feels like time is rushing by, even though it only takes him a few seconds to open the lock and slip into the room.

Princess Rind's chambers are deathly silent, and darker than the hallway. Odin's voice cuts through the gloom. "Hag! What are you doing here?"

Shutting the door, Loki allows his illusion to drop and lets a flame dance from his hands to the sconce on the wall.

Beyond a bed where Rind lies bound, her head listing to the side, he sees Odin, sitting naked on a chair, legs crossed.

"Loki, what are you doing?" Odin says. He sounds annoyed but not particularly angry.

Loki's eyes fall to the bed. Rind's clothes are torn open. Blood stains the bed between her thighs. Loki's jaw drops and then he catches himself. It's a lover's game. It must be. Loki has been asked to play such games—and Loki has asked Sigyn to truss him up much the way Rind is now.

He takes a step closer, and then another. Rind does not move or make any sign that she is aware of his presence.

"Why are you here, Loki?"

"Hoenir...was concerned," Loki says, unable to meet Odin's gaze. He draws closer to Rind. Her eyelids don't even flutter.

Odin snorts. "Hoenir and his silly notions. It's not like..."

Loki lifts his gaze sharply.

Standing, Odin says, "They're women. They're made for this." Odin turns and his voice grows louder and angry. "And yet she refused me!"

Loki lowers his head so his face is just inches from Rind's. "She's unconscious."

Odin shrugs. "I did not want to hurt her. I want her to bear me a son. She is the second strongest enchantress in Jotunheim."

A flame leaps to life on a carelessly tossed-aside bed covering, a twisting, bright after effect of the churning in Loki's gut. Mimir was right. Loki is too late.

Odin makes a sound of exasperation, waves a hand, and the flame extinguishes.

Loki stands rooted to the spot. He has seen scenes like this before after battles. He understands it's a show of dominance. But to Loki, when you've razed a village to the ground, and have the inhabitants on their knees with blades to their necks, rape just seems petty, the perpetrators, bullies.

He looks at Odin standing naked and unashamed at the foot of the bed. The guilt he'd felt minutes before, the flutterings of respect for his mentor, they both vanish. Looking at Odin, for the first time, instead of seeing a powerful warrior, sorcerer, and ruler of the Nine Realms, Loki sees a weak old man.

"How could you?" Loki says, and he doesn't know if he means what Odin's done to Rind, or what he's done to Loki. He feels centuries of respect and admiration are slipping away like grains of sand through an hourglass.

"I need another son!" Odin spits. "And Frigga's womb is as conducive to life as your—"

Loki takes a step back, his arms trembling at his sides—the way Hoenir had trembled.

Rolling his eyes, Odin says, "I sometimes forget how sickeningly sentimental you always are. When you fuck, you just want them to like you, don't you?" His lip curls. "Because in most other respects, no one wants anything to do with you."

Still trembling, Loki takes another step back.

Waving a hand, Odin says, "Be off with you. I think I'd like to go for another round."

The old man walks toward the bed and the woman who may as well be dead. Loki can't watch, and can't leave. "No!" Loki shouts.

Flames leap in the curtains, and in the bedclothes, on the chair, and on a rug upon the floor. Rind does not stir. Backing off the bed, Odin's lip curls. "Are you trying to burn her alive?"

"Andvaranaut!" The name tumbles from Loki's lips. He suddenly remembers the story—of Lothur, or was it Lopt? One of them found the cursed ring Andvaranaut, and Odin had touched it briefly. In the stories, to rid himself of the ring's taint, Odin had slept with a virgin, willing or unwilling, every night for a year. Loki had always thought those were just stories. The flames in the room spark higher.

Odin spares him an angry glare. He raises his arms, and the flames still. But then they rise up again.

Cursing, Odin illusions his guise of a medicine woman around him and begins freeing Rind from her bonds. The hag that is Odin snaps at Loki. "Are you going to help me or let her die?"

Loki can only stare. Odin has Rind untied and in his arms before Loki regains himself. Creating the illusion of a medicine woman, Loki goes forward to help, but Odin grunts and pulls Rind away.

With a sharp nod from Odin, the door flies open. "Fire!" Odin calls, his voice shrill and crackling like an older woman.

Guards come running, King Billings at the lead. As Odin drags Rind from the room, he says, "The room was cursed, we cleansed it with flame. Visions of the Allfather will haunt the girl no more."

King Billings takes the still unconscious form of his daughter from Odin's deceptively frail-looking arms without question or comment.

Loki can only gape.

As the guards slip into the room to extinguish the fire, Odin

turns to Loki. In his hag guise, one of Odin's eyes is brown, the
other is blue. The brown eye slips sideways as the blue eye fixes on
Loki. "Remember, you were the one who nearly killed her. I was
the one who saved her and gave her a son."

Loki backs up until his back connects with one of the stone
walls, still cold despite the flames in the princess's quarters.

Odin waves a hand and disappears.

Across from Bohdi, Amy slides to the floor of Thor's chariot. Bohdi wants to follow her lead, to sit on the floor, tuck his
knees up to his chin, stuff his cold fingers into the pocket of
his coat, and sleep. He stifles a yawn. He barely got any sleep
the night he spent with Frieda, and only grabbed an hour or
so at most on the ground before nightfall. Being in Nornheim
is kind of like the last weeks of infantry training, but without
the occasional grenade blast and gunfire to keep you awake.

If he just sits down for a moment…

Amy pulls herself up sharply and yells at Thor. "You know
he'll take advantage of her, Thor! You have to know about
Rind! And after Andvaranaut. How many girls did he attack
then? How many? A few dozen? A few hundred?"

The fog of exhaustion in Bohdi's brain clears. His skin
heats and his fingers fumble with his lighter. It takes him a
moment to realize he's shaking.

Turning to Amy, Thor roars, "Stories! Stories only!" Every
inch of Bohdi's skin feels like it is being poked by pins and
needles. The chariot bounces, as though a barometer of Thor's
anger. Bohdi barely manages to hold on.

The chariot swerves as Thor shouts, "The Allfather respects
women enough to let them fight alongside men as equals!"

"Women shouldn't have to be warriors to be respected!" Amy yells.

Bohdi thumbs the wheel on his lighter. He's only half baiting her when he says, "Why only women?" No one, man or woman, who's not gung-ho should have to go through fucking bloody boot camp.

Over Thor's shoulder, Bohdi sees Amy's eye go wide. She puts a hand to her mouth. "Oh. You're right, I shouldn't have said it like that."

Bohdi blinks. She didn't ignore or contradict him.

Thor gives a loud snort.

Amy's eyes narrow. Her ponytail is whipping furiously in the wind, the sun is rising beyond her, haloing her head with light and...are those butterflies? Bohdi leans forward, mesmerized by the tiny delicate shapes fluttering beyond Amy.

Thor grunts, the chariot shakes, and Amy gives an exasperated sigh. "Be honest, Thor. If Loki were a woman, would you trust your father with her?"

Thor glowers at her, and then turning abruptly, stares silently ahead. Bohdi's jaw twitches at the unspoken answer. He remembers the way Skírnir spoke about Gerðr, and other rumors he's heard about what the Asgardians do to their conquests. The edges of his vision darken. His mouth opens with something sharp at the tip of his tongue, something that will really get Thor worked up, but then the chariot shakes with such force that Amy slips and falls, and Bohdi barely keeps his feet.

Bohdi glares up at Thor. His eyes slide to Amy. She's pulled herself back up, but she seems to have given the debate a rest.

Standing at the helm, Thor is taking deep breaths, like

he's trying to calm himself. Bohdi can't help noticing that the chariot's course becomes smoother.

Bohdi fumes; if he wants to survive, he may have to hold his peace. His fingers thump against his lighter.

He looks back to Amy, the butterflies behind her catching his eyes again. They seem larger now. Their wings are every shade of pink, baby blue, lavender, and soft yellow. But how can butterflies fly so high? Maybe he is hallucinating? He squints. No, they're real, but they aren't butterflies, their wings are shaped more like birds. What kind of birds fly at this altitude? Raptors maybe? They there are no landmarks at this height to help ascertain distance, but whatever these flying creatures are, they're appearing larger with each passing minute.

He blinks at the birds. As they draw closer, the wings become brighter colored. Are those claws on the wings? "Um…" says Bohdi.

Eyes on Thor, Amy says, "I'm just asking you to consider that maybe Asgard might not be the best place for Loki… man or woman."

Bohdi leans sideways to see better around Thor's huge hulking form. The raptors, or whatever they are, have reptilian bodies, covered in brilliant red, yellow, and blue scales…or are those feathers? The creatures look the size of hawks maybe. Probably not dangerous but… "Um…Thor…" says Bohdi.

The big man grunts, eyes straight ahead.

Bohdi clears his throat. The raptor things seem to be picking up speed, and they're bigger than any hawk he's ever seen. Bohdi's heart stops. No, they're not raptors. "Thor!" Bohdi shouts.

Hand going to Mjolnir, Thor turns toward Bohdi. The

chariot lurches at the same time. Lifting a hand, Bohdi points beyond Thor's shoulder. Thor's head whips around again. It is at that moment that Mr. Squeakers, oddly quiet through most of the trip, decides to peek his head out the collar of Amy's coat.

Thor screams. "A spidermouse!" The chariot lurches, and Thor backs into Bohdi so fast, Bohdi almost falls over the side. He only manages to stay in by hanging onto Thor's cloak.

Amy's face flushes, and as soon as the chariot rights itself, she captures Mr. Squeakers in her hand. "He won't hurt you!" she says, putting Mr. Squeakers in her pocket.

"How can you be sure?" says Thor.

Still clutching Thor's cape, Bohdi's eyes go beyond the space Viking and Amy. He gulps. Pushing Thor off of him, Bohdi shouts. "Forget the mouse! Pay attention to the dragons!"

Thor's gaze shifts upward, and he lifts Mjolnir with a mighty yell. Clouds begin to form, as five dragon-like creatures come barreling toward the chariot. Each is about the size of a minivan. They have powerful hind limbs with long, sharp claws and lizard-like tails with a sharp points at the end. Every time their brilliantly colored wings flap, Bohdi feels it on his cheeks.

Thor points Mjolnir in their direction and a bolt of lightning tears off the hammer. The dragons dodge, barely slowing their onslaught.

"They look like giant Archaeopteryx!" Amy says.

"Get down!" shouts Thor, pushing Amy's head down and firing another blast of lightning from his hammer. One of the dragon's wings is sheared at the tip by the blast; it teeters in the air and begins to fall. Halting their forward momentum, the dragons hover in the air and let loose ferocious screams.

The hairs on the back of Bohdi's neck stand on end as he gets a good glimpse at their glistening teeth, that even from this distance seem to be oozing thick, shiny saliva. The creatures' heads draw back, their jaws snap shut, Thor thunks down his visor, and on instinct Bohdi dives to the floor.

Something hits the side of the chariot, throwing it off course, and sending Bohdi rolling into Amy. She has her hands over her head, but when Bohdi collides with her, she lifts her eyes and asks, "Are you okay?" Bohdi can only stare at her open mouthed.

More lightning rips from Thor's hammer, thunder booms with such force the chariot floor reverberates beneath Bohdi's fingers. The dragons scream again. Bohdi catches a glimpse of something green and oozing slinking down the edge of the chariot wall behind Amy's back.

"Look out," he says, pushing her to the side. Her messenger bag had been behind her, and whatever the gooey stuff is lands on the bag and then begins to sizzle.

"Acid? They spit acid!" Amy squeaks, reaching up to clutch the side of the chariot where Bohdi had been standing seconds before.

Eyes still on the ooze, Bohdi reaches for the wall, for a handhold. "I…"

Thor shouts, lightning blazes from Mjolnir, thunder roars, and the dragons scream again. The chariot is hit four times in rapid succession by bolts of acid saliva. The vehicle spins wildly from the blows, and Bohdi slips backward over the edge. For a fleeting instant, he's horizontal in the air, staring down at one of those brilliant white canopies that cover the trees. For a heartbeat, he thinks he's flying, and then his body swings downward. Pain shoots from his fingertips, and more pain races through his wrist. It's only then that he realizes he's still hanging on to the lip of the chariot by his fingertips, and Amy has grabbed his wrist with one hand, her nails biting into his flesh.

Lightning flares in the air, thunder booms, and dragons wail. Gritting his teeth, Bohdi tries to pull himself up. He can do this. Even if he doesn't usually do pull ups with the tips of his fingers, he's still in shape. Steve's always dragging him to the gym, and Amy's pulling him, and...

The chariot abruptly shoots upward. The pressure on Bohdi's fingers increases, and he loses his hold completely. His heart stops. He thinks he's lost, but then he feels the bite of Amy's nails again and realizes he's dangling in her grasp. His eyes go to Amy. She's gritting her teeth and pulling with all her might, but he can see her hand slipping from the chariot's side. He wants to shout to let go of him, and at the same time wants to beg her to hang on.

"I won't let you go!" Amy screams, and Bohdi's not sure if he said anything out loud.

Thor's eyes slide to Bohdi. He looks down and past him, and his eyebrows go up. Bohdi follows his gaze and sees one of the dragons is at his level, coming straight for him, snapping its jaws.

The chariot drops straight down, and Bohdi is staring mercifully at only empty air.

"Thor!" Amy shouts. "I can't pull him..."

"A little longer!" Thor shouts, letting loose a bolt of lightning that shears another dragon's wing. The beast tumbles from the sky, and the three other dragons draw back a little further as the chariot continues to plunge. Body swinging, feet helplessly flailing in the air, Bohdi looks down. The white canopy below is rapidly getting closer. Thor gives a shout, and the chariot stops its downward descent with a jolt.

The shock dislodges Amy's hand from the chariot wall and Bohdi's weight drags her toward the edge. Time seems to stop. He's staring at her wide blue eyes. Her lips part in a gasp. His heart sinks. The moment is backward and wrong, he's supposed to be saving the girl, not getting the girl killed, and he doesn't know why he thinks that. Is it something from his forgotten past, or something he learned in the States, or just an instinctive law of guydom?

"Let me go!" Bohdi tries to shout, but it comes out more of a whine. Her body inches farther forward, his heavier weight drawing her down, but she doesn't heed him. He feels something like anger twisting in his chest. How can she do this? How can she make him responsible for her death? He can't even fight for fear it will pull her over the edge.

Thor turns and leans down, his hand almost on Amy, when a bolt of oozing green comes shooting toward them. "Thor!" Bohdi screams.

Cursing, Thor hits the chariot's equivalent of the accelerator. Amy flies toward Bohdi, and then she and Bohdi are suspended in midair. Their eyes meet briefly, and Bohdi is hit by a horrible all-encompassing sense of failure. Then dragons scream, a shadow passes over them, and they fall.

CHAPTER 7

A light at the bottom of Steve's computer screen blinks, and Steve hits accept. Beatrice's plucky countenance appears in the video feed. "Okay, Steve, I'm going to put her on."

Steve nods, and then Gerðr's face appears on the screen, pretty, but not excessively so. Also, she needs a haircut. Steve sighs, and smiles. "It's working, Beatrice."

Beatrice pokes her gray head over Gerðr's shoulder and gives the thumbs up sign. "Now I don't have to translate your science!" Beatrice says, and vanishes from the screen. Gerðr stares at Steve, looking slightly confused.

Steve jumps right in, "Gerðr, do you know what radiation is?" She's in an unshielded room on the next floor up. Steve's pretty sure she'll be able to use magic to translate. Loki did fine in multiple languages over the phone. But the magic that makes Gerðr irresistible apparently doesn't translate over electrical lines. Thank God.

Gerðr scowls. "Why do you want to know?"

Steve's right hand curls into a fist. Of course he still has her lovely disposition to deal with. Leaning on his elbows, smacking his fist into his hand, he smiles tightly at the screen.

"I just want to know if it's harmful to magical beings."

Gerðr's nostrils flare. "Do you think you can torture me with radiation! Is this a threat?"

And suddenly he's had enough—of her condescension, her paranoia, and suspicion. Leaning toward the screen, he shouts, "When have I ever tortured you, Gerðr? When have I ever treated you without the utmost respect?" His lip curls in a snarl, angry at her—and at himself for losing control.

Gerðr pulls back in her chair, and averts her eyes. Even on screen, Steve can see her chest is rising and falling too quickly.

She licks her lips. Gaze still not meeting his, she says, "It is true you have never..." She doesn't finish. And Steve feels his gut clench at what is unsaid. He slumps back into his chair. She hasn't always been treated well. Are her unfinished words referring to Freyr and Skírnir? Or to her time at Gitmo?

Her eyes flash to the screen. Her head tilts. Her voice is soft and quizzical. "But then why would you want to know this?"

Steve rubs his jaw, debating how much he should tell the giantess. He takes a deep breath and says, "Some nations on Earth are trading Earth technology with certain magical species for something." He's deliberately obtuse, wanting to see how she reacts.

Gerðr's face hardens. "Yes. The elves must have exchanged something for weapons from the Russians, Ukrainians, and Belarusians."

Steve lets his eyebrows go up at her knowledge of the details. He could play it cool, but he decides to allow her to see his surprise, give her a sense of control in the conversation.

Dropping her eyes, Gerðr says, "In the other prison, they asked me about that...often." Lifting her chin she gives a tight smile. "Threaten me with all the torture you like, I won't give you the answer because I don't know!" The last words come out a growl.

Steve's stomach twists into a sick knot. So Skírnir and Freyr are not the only ones who have mistreated her. He's suddenly ashamed of his own species, and he doesn't know what to say. I'm sorry seems hollow.

He bites the inside of his lip and then says, "A few decades ago, a region between those three countries was contaminated with deadly amounts of radiation, and now it is apparently being thoroughly cleaned up, which, quite frankly, is beyond the capability of human technology." Probably not something he should admit to Gerðr, but he'll throw her a bone, see if she takes it. "Do magical creatures have the ability to eliminate radioactive contamination?"

Gerðr's lips purse. "How could so much radiation be concentrated in deadly amounts?"

"We use radioactive material to make electricity," Steve says, undoubtedly, brutally summarizing nuclear fission. "Sometimes there are accidents."

Gerðr leans forward. "You are utilizing the power of atoms?"

"Yes," says Steve, beginning to feel impatient. "Can magical creatures clean up radiation?"

Gerðr sits back in her seat. She licks her lips in a way that is thankfully not seductive, just nervous. "Yes, it would take some knowledge. Trolls, for instance, though magical, cannot manage it. It would take concentration, and there would be waste products from halting the motion of the atom's splinters—but since atomic splinters are so close to magic anyway, even a very inexperienced mage could manage it."

From behind Gerðr comes Beatrice's disembodied voice. "What type of waste product?"

Gerðr looks away, toward Beatrice's voice. "Well, I could choose. When I took away the atomic splinter's motion, I would have to change the force of that momentum into something else. Maybe light, or heat, or—"

"Could you use it to make electricity?" Beatrice asks. Steve raises an eyebrow. Heat is used to make electricity, but maybe Beatrice doesn't know that. Then again, if the "clean up" is generating electricity without first converting it to heat, it might be more efficient.

"Yes, I suppose," says Gerðr. "But why would anyone want electricity when heat and light are so much more practical and controllable?" Beatrice coughs. Steve's eyes widen. Amy has said that in Alfheim, magic is the only source of power. They don't use electricity. Maybe to beings of the other realms, electricity would seem...magical? Still, Gerðr's been here for a while. Steve taps his computer screen. "Ummm...Gerðr," he says.

Gerðr's mouth drops open, and her cheeks go red. "Ah, yes...human...magic." Maybe it's just a shock to not have her deriding the human race, but her embarrassment over something so trivial is almost charming.

Beatrice leans over Gerðr's shoulder. "Steve, if the lights are on around Chernobyl, our satellites have to have seen it."

Steve's jaw twitches. "You're right. But why isn't our government sharing this information with us? Haven't they figured out that Dark Elves could take care of our nuclear waste problems?"

As soon as he says that, he knows it's not true. Steve's not scientifically brilliant. If he knows, they have to. But they're not acting on it.

Gerðr swallows. "King Utgard of Jotunheim, and Sutr, of the Fire Giants, both might be willing in exchange for weapons, though it would greatly anger Asgard."

Beatrice's blue eyes glint. "Something smells mighty fishy here…"

Steve runs a tongue over his teeth. "Agreed. Why aren't my superiors pushing me to open up lines of communication with the Dark Elves or other magical creatures?"

Beatrice crosses her arms, and backs away from the camera.

It's Gerðr who responds to Steve's question. "Because at least some of your superiors are already being controlled by Odin."

The hairs on the back of his neck prickle. "How?" he asks.

Gerðr lifts a hand to her chin. "He has many ways. Usually, by offering immortality, and access to the Bifrost."

The prickling sensation moves down his neck and to his entire back, and Steve is suddenly very conscious that he is in an unshielded room. He glances over his shoulder. Huginn and Muninn aren't outside his window, but Heimdall can see anywhere. Steve hopes he's busy watching Thor.

At that moment, Steve's phone alarm goes off. Glancing down, he sees a text from his ex-wife telling him she'll drop off Claire in twenty minutes.

"I have to go." He nods at Gerðr and is suddenly struck by inspiration. It would be better to talk in a magically shielded room, but then Gerðr couldn't use magic to communicate, and Steve would need an interpreter. Except for Amy, Steve's not sure if he trusts any of them. Glancing quickly over his shoulder, he makes sure he sees no ravens or squirrels. Leaning in toward the screen, he whispers to Gerðr, "Maybe you can help us negotiate with your people?" Even if some of the Fed is controlled by Odin, Steve is pretty sure once the press finds out magical creatures can clean up nuclear waste—and convert it into power—Odin's influence could be negated.

Gerðr lifts her head and looks at Steve, hope in her eyes. "That would mean…"

"We, or more precisely, you, need to figure out a way to go home," says Steve, his brain spinning with possibilities and logistics.

Gerðr's jaw drops. "I…really?"

"Yes," says Steve. If anyone finds out he's made the offer, he'll lie, say it was to encourage the giantess's cooperation. "Think about it." He looks at Beatrice, and then back to Gerðr. "I don't have to say that we need to keep this among ourselves?"

Beatrice nods. Gerðr swallows and says, "Of course."

Standing up, Steve reaches for the disconnect button, but then Beatrice says, "Time to pick up your little girl?"

Steve says nothing, keeping his face blank. He's not sure he wants Gerðr knowing about Claire.

Unfortunately, Gerðr perks in her seat, and says, "You have a daughter?"

Before Steve can say anything, Beatrice jumps in. "Claire is the spitting image of Steve." She gives a cackle, "But attractive!"

Raising an eyebrow, Steve smiles at the jibe despite himself. "I've got to go," he says, swinging his jacket on.

Right before he clicks the mouse, Gerðr says, "Be careful."

Something in her tone makes Steve pause.

Biting her lip, Gerðr says, "Odin has many ways of

exacting control."

Steve thinks of Huginn and Munnin, nods, and clicks the mouse. The video feed goes dark.

As he's leaving the office, he's attacked by the usual throng of press, with the usual questions. Among them is Tara Inanna, just as attractive, wholesome, and appealing as Steve remembers. Steve keeps his face neutral as she asks him if there is any status on Bohdi and Amy. Tilting his head, he says, "Not at this time...Tara? Is that your name?" He gives her what he hopes is a charming smile, gauging her reaction to the question.

From somewhere in the crowd, a familiar reporter's voice asks, "So how does this affect your run for mayor?"

Steve turns to the man who asked the question. "My people are missing right now, can you ask me something a little more pertinent, George?"

He glances back to Tara, but she's gone.

Bohdi falls backward. Amy, slightly above and a little to his left, falls in a belly-flop.

Bohdi's whole life doesn't flash before his eyes—maybe because he's missing large chunks of it—but his thoughts race. Amy's still holding his wrist. She's not screaming or anything, she's just looking straight at him, and he knows she can't look away because he can't look away. And in the milliseconds before he dies, he thinks about that, and how maybe it is a very human thing not to want to die alone. He curls his hand up and around her wrist and squeezes. She squeezes right back.

He   doesn't   even   blink   in   those   last   few

seconds—milliseconds—before impact, because that would be abandoning his fellow human being.

And then his back connects with whatever it is, Amy's wrist is yanked away, and he braces himself for pain, and blackness.

Pain he gets, along every inch of the back of his body—but not like he was expecting, more like being thrown on the dirt during training, jaw rattling and wind stealing, but not anything extreme—and there is no blackness. The impact is strange, too. Instead of coming to a stop, he finds himself slowing. A dragon dives above his prone body, and he thinks he'll be swooped up as a snack, but it shrieks in fury, pulls up sharply, and flies away.

He has no time to think about it. Instead of going down, he is suddenly going up. Beside him Amy gives a loud, "Yeep!" Bohdi feels something yanking him down by the back and shoulders, and pressure on his chest. He watches wide eyed as Amy rises so high she actually is suspended in midair before tumbling down. Another dragon drops from the sky, and its hind claws almost connect with her shoulders, but then it rises fast, and flies away.

Bohdi's descent stops with a snap, and he springs up, Amy rising beside him, a little further away than she was before. Bouncing… They're bouncing! They've landed on the canopy thing, and they're not dying, they're bouncing. He almost laughs, but the force of the bounce whips the air out of him.

Bohdi's still riding up and down in crazy waves when he hears Amy say, "Mr. Squeakers! You're okay! I was so worried! Oh, no…Thor…"

Still attached somehow to the canopy, Bohdi's body ricochets up in the air. Turning his head, he sees Amy hopping on her feet as carefree as if she were on a trampoline. The canopy is more netlike than fabric like, though he can't see the ground, so there must be layers and layers of the stuff. She's holding Mr. Squeakers in one hand, and studying a point far up in the air, behind Bohdi's head, out of his line of vision. How come she's on her feet?

He tries to sit up, mid-bounce, and gets nowhere. "How come I can't move?" he says, the wild trampoline ride easing to a gentler spring.

He's almost steady when he hears a hiss and a squeak, and then all of a sudden, Mr. Squeakers pops out of nowhere and lands on his chest.

He stares at the mouse, the mouse stares at him, nose twitching.

"I'm coming!" says Amy. Mr. Squeakers, turns around quickly, stands up on four back legs, lifts his four front legs, and starts hissing.

About six feet away, Amy draws to a stop, her eyes wide. "Bohdi, are you okay?"

Gritting his teeth, he tries to move. "Upper body...can't move."

"Oh my God! Your spleen, did it rupture?" Amy says.

Lifting his head, Bohdi blinks at her. And then he understands. "No, my spleen is fine," he says, his skin heating.

"But my grandmother said your spleen—"

"Is perfectly fine!" Bohdi snaps. Dropping his head back he grumbles. "That's just a bogus thing Steve made up to get me out on medical discharge." Just when the Marines was getting interesting, too. Bohdi liked the Marine Corps Explosive Ordnance Disposal program. Of course, someone was bound to find out he wasn't really a citizen and kick him back to the infantry anyway, so…

Amy takes a step forward, and Mr. Squeakers gives another hiss. Amy pulls her foot back. She looks up briefly, bites her bottom lip, and then she looks down at Bohdi again.

Her voice weirdly steady and about a half octave lower than normal, she says, "Can you move your legs?" She's speaking like a doctor, he realizes. Cold and professional. It's kind of sexy.

Bohdi wiggles his feet, then his legs, and finally his butt. He smiles. "Yep, It's just my upper body." Walking parallel to his body, she says, "I think I know what's happening." Stopping, she turns, and walks slowly toward his feet. Mr. Squeakers sinks down to all eight legs and gives a cheep.

"I don't have my first-aid kit, so I can't cut you out of your coat," Amy says.

"Cut me out of my…" Bohdi frowns and then he wiggles his shoulder blades inside his winter coat. They move, it's just his coat that is stuck. "Hey, yeah," he says with a grin. "You're right." Lifting his chin, he looks down at the zipper. "Can't you just open it?"

"We don't have time for you to struggle!" Amy snips.

Bohdi blinks at her tone, wiggles his hips, and feels a familiar lump. "My knife is in my pocket if—"

Amy doesn't so much lean down as dive. Mr. Squeakers hops off Bohdi as she does. Hands on either side of him, she crawls up his body. "Which pocket?"

Is that a note of frantic worry in her voice? Bohdi looks up in the sky. It's a beautiful crystalline blue, empty of everything but a few distant clouds. "Left," he says.

Amy sits back on his knees and puts a hand in his pocket. Bohdi feels his skin heating in an actually rather nice way, blood rushing to a place that he'd rather it didn't go.

She pulls his knife out of his pocket, and quickly inspects it. Just to take the edge off his discomfort, he gives her a grin. "Why, yes, that was a knife in my pocket. I'm not just happy to see you." She glares at him as she pries it open.

Bohdi lifts his eye to the sky again. "I don't see any dragons." Which is kind of odd. They're in an open place and kind of helpless. Why aren't there dragons?

"Archaeopteryx," Amy mutters, not looking at him. "Bracing myself on your right shoulder." She crawls forward, until her hips are just above his, and Bohdi tries to shrink back into the canopy as much as he can.

As she puts a hand on Bohdi's shoulder, he can't help but notice she's trembling. So he's not the only person who's discomfited by this. That would be flattering, but she's holding a really sharp knife.

Levity is obviously required. "Braving a belligerent thunder god, going to other realms, and fighting dragons. This is farther than I've ever gone to be tied up by a cute girl." Bohdi's actually only gotten tied up once, and it was without any effort on his part. He can't remember if the sex was good… He was pretty drunk at the time.

Amy doesn't reply. She just mutters something about archaeopteryx and lifts her bracing hand so she's hovering over him. She grabs the wrist of his coat and puts the knife to it. She's still trembling.

"I don't bite," he says. He smiles and bats his eyelashes. "Unless you ask nicely."

Slicing through the coat, Amy snarls. "I am not worried about *you* biting me!"

"Just trying to make you laugh," Bohdi snips.

"Don't!" says Amy.

"A sense of humor makes everything better," Bohdi says, as she cuts the fabric down to his chest, and then down to his hips.

Sitting back on his knees again, she surveys her handi-work. "Is that enough for you to get out without touching the web around your upper body with your hands?"

Bohdi shifts, keeping his upper body on his winter coat, and easily slides his right arm free. "Yep," he says with a grin, raising himself to a sitting position. Even though he's only wearing a sport coat, and it's morning, it's warm enough.

"Good, let's go now," says Amy.

"Shouldn't we—" *talk about this.*

"No," says Amy, as she dips her chin and slowly shakes her head from side to side.

"What about—" *Thor.*

Amy interrupts. "No."

Shrugging, Bohdi twists back to his coat, and says, "I need my wallet."

"You really don't," says Amy, sounding distinctly agitated. Mr. Squeakers gives an uneasy peep.

He really does need his wallet; it has the picture of his parents in it, and even if he has copies, they're only copies. Jaw tightening, he sits back up, and smirks. "But it's where I keep my condoms."

Hopping up, Amy glares down at him. "You plan on hav-ing sex with giant spiders?"

Bohdi's jaw drops at the randomness of her reply. "What?"

Amy looks at her mouse, "Squeakers, let's go!"

With a cheep, Mr. Squeakers hops along until he's in front of her, then turns around and looks at Bohdi.

As Bohdi scrambles to his feet, Amy says, "Walk only on the web where Mr. Squeakers hops, or you'll wind up getting stuck again."

"Uh," says Bohdi, standing up and looking around. For the first time he gets a good look at the "canopy" they're on.

Marion and Steve have inflicted enough American football on him that he thinks he can safely judge the "canopy" to be about two football fields wide in every direction. In one spot, it wraps around one of the weird columny things. Here and there, it rises in sharp peaks a few meters high, and then falls into shallow valleys. White and very bright, the canopy looks like pictures he's seen of the arctic. Occasionally, irregular shapes like giant cocoons pock the surface.

He squints. About half a football field away, long silvery sticks are popping out of the canopy floor, followed by a round sort of ball with six red lights set into it, and then a body and more sticks and...

Amy's rather weird suggestion that he have sex with large arachnids and her continued reference to webbing suddenly clicks in his brain. "Giant spiders!" Bohdi shouts.

Amy, now a few paces in front of him, turns back and grimaces. "I knew they would come back! Hurry, this way!"

Bohdi scrambles after her. It doesn't take long to catch up. Despite having eight legs, Mr. Squeakers isn't particularly fast; they're barely at a jog. Bohdi turns to look behind and instantly regrets it. The giant spider is zig-zagging across the canopy, but even with its uneven path, it's rapidly gaining on them. His eyes go wide as two more spiders pop their heads out of the canopy a little further back from the first.

"Do you think we should maybe carry Squeakers?" Bohdi says—and promptly runs into Amy.

"Oompf!" she grunts. "I don't know how to tell the difference between sticky and non-sticky web." She says. "Squeakers?"

The little creature darts to the left toward one of the oblong shapes. Amy and Bohdi follow.

"Where's Thor?" he says.

"More archaeopteryx came," Amy says, a little breathlessly. "They went…" She gestures westward with an arm. "That way."

Bohdi looks back again. "Um…the spiders are getting closer!" The creatures are almost at their landing point.

"I know! I know!" says Amy.

Bohdi turns to see the oblong cocoon shapes they're rapidly approaching. They're probably twice his height, and six times his height in length.

Most of the web on it is so smooth it's like fabric. As they close in, he realizes it's slightly transparent. Bohdi stops in his tracks.

"Uh-oh," Amy pants, taking the words right out of Bohdi's mouth.

Under the layers of silk, he can just barely make out the shiny wings and long lizard-like neck, head, and jaws of one of the dragon creatures. He swallows. It's not a cocoon…it's a coffin.

"So that's why…the archaeopteryxes…left us alone," Amy whispers, between pants.

"Do you think being eaten by a spider is less painful than being eaten by an Arche…dragon?" Bohdi says. He's not even winded. If he survives, he's thanking Steve for all those boring workout sessions.

"Probably," pants Amy. "Some creatures that suck blood

have an analgesic in their saliva. In a dragon's stomach, you'd be burned by acid before you asphyxiated."

Bohdi's lips purse, and then Amy stops so suddenly, Bohdi bumps into her again. Eyes wide and worried, she says, "Or was that a rhetorical question?"

"Rhetorical." Giving her a gentle shove, he says, "Still, that was fascinating."

Mr. Squeakers skitters to the top of the cocoon-tomb-spider-burrito-thing. Amy might be muttering something as she tries to follow him. Bohdi can't really pay attention…all of his attention is on the new giant spiders poking their long spindly legs and glowing eyes out of the canopy up at nine and three o'clock. He turns his head around to see the ones directly behind them. They're only about ten meters away, so close he can hear them chittering. "Oh…" *fuck.*

The expletive dies on his tongue. All but one of the spiders turn around and tilt their butts at them. "Are they going to shit on us?" Bohdi mutters.

Just pulling herself up the cocoon, Amy turns her head. Eyes going wide, she screams. "Hurry! Over the bump!"

Bohdi doesn't have a chance to ask why. A bolt of spider silk as wide as his arm thunks against the cocoon beside him.

"Climb!" says Amy.

Bohdi jumps up beside her, hoping he doesn't land in anything sticky. He doesn't. But most of the web is too fine to find a toe hold; he has to support himself by holding onto thick bands of silk that run vertically along the cocoon at regular intervals. He blinks…which is a lot easier than he expected. Wow. Steve's insistence that he work out is actually proving useful. He'll have to buy the guy a drink when—

Thunk.

Something sticky splatters Bohdi on the cheek. His eyes dart to the side. A large bolt of silk has just hit the cocoon an inch from Bohdi's elbow. With a grunt, he frantically pulls himself up and swings a leg over the top of the dragon's silk tomb.

Several bolts of silk hit the cocoon, Mr. Squeakers starts squeaking frantically somewhere near Bohdi's head, and Amy gives a cry from below. Bohdi looks down to see her only half way up. Her forearms are trembling, a bolt of spider silk attached to the back of her jeans. He hears himself curse. His heart pounds in his ears. Grabbing hold of a thick strand of silk, he lowers himself upside down. His eyes light on his knife in Amy's back pocket. "Hold on!" he hears himself say. More silken bolts land on either side of him, and one lands on his back with such force it knocks the wind out of him. In an odd, sort of half-conscious way, it registers that he isn't stopping even though he's close to petrified, his fingers feel stiff and cold even though the day is relatively warm.

Amy nods, just barely, her whole body shaking. Bohdi grabs the knife out of her back pocket. He blinks. The silk bolt has hit her precisely on the other rear pocket. With a flick of the wrist, he cuts the pocket away and then pulls her up as much as he can, the bolt of spider silk attached to his sport coat keeping him from completely retreating.

He hears Amy beside him, panting as she throws a leg up over the top of the cocoon. "You're stuck!" she says.

Frantically trying to wiggle himself out of his sports coat, Bohdi can only nod. A loud chittering catches his attention. He glances toward the sound. The spiders that had been shooting bolts are turning toward him. Closing his eyes he wiggles more frantically. "Run!" he shouts to Amy.

She slips down the side, finally deciding to pay attention to him. It doesn't feel as good as he thought it would.

And then he hears her yell, "Hold on! I'm pulling you!" He feels pressure around his knees and he looks up to see spiders charging through horizontal beams of silk. Each has a body the size of a grizzly bear with limbs as long as boa constrictors. They're so close, he can see their carapaces are shiny and slightly reflective. Each spider has six crimson eyes…and they have eyelids. He watches in sick fascination as they blink one eyelid at a time. Below their eyes are mandible things that remind him of the sharp prongs of an earwig. The mandibles click together rapidly as the spiders chatter. One of the spiders darts forward.

Bohdi shrinks as far as he can into his coat, and then Amy gives a mighty yank on his legs. His jacket goes flying off, he feels a cool rush of air, and he goes slipping backward. He lands on top of Amy, in a tangle of limbs.

"Thanks," he mutters.

He hears Amy gulp. "Don't thank me yet," she whispers.

He lifts his head. Coming straight toward them are six more spiders, a few turning, obviously preparing to aim their own silken bonds.

Above his head, he hears chittering. Looking up, he sees the eighteen eyes of their original three pursuers.

"There's a hole in the canopy," Amy whispers.

Bohdi's eyes shift downward. Just a meter in front of them are several layers of canopy billowing in the breeze. Ripped by the dragon in its death struggles, maybe? The layers' flutters reveal a hole, just barely big enough for a human to fit though.

"Mr. Squeakers, can we go that way?"

The eight-legged mouse hops forward into the hole and

cheeps.

"Down the rabbit hole?" Amy says.

Whistling sounds in his ears. In the periphery of his vision, Bohdi sees a bolt of silk shooting at his head.

Without a word, he and Amy dive toward the hole as silken strands streak past where their heads had been just moments before.

Amy hesitates. Bohdi doesn't. Grabbing the edge of the gaping hole, Bohdi somersaults through without even looking. His feet connect with something solid and then slip apart. Still holding on to the webbing above his head, he looks down and blinks. He's surrounded on all sides by spider silk of different weights and textures. A braided, cylindrical beam of silk, broad as a tree trunk, is beneath him. He lowers himself down until he's straddling it. Amy looks through the hole above him, still sitting on what he now realizes is the roof of a giant spider nest.

Bohdi hears whistling from outside. Grabbing Amy by the arms, he pulls her down. Silken strands crisscross in the sky where her body had been. She lands in a heap right between his legs, and he wraps his arms around her before she teeters off the beam they sit on. Above them, silken strands pelt the loose fraying pieces of silk they escaped through, sealing the exit through the roof.

Looking up, Amy whispers "Did they just trap us?" Her chest is heaving, and Bohdi swears he can hear her heart pounding.

Maybe it's his heart. "Uhm…"

"It's not over until it's over," Amy whispers—or maybe chants. Bohdi can feel her body shivering even through the thick winter coat she's still wearing.

"We have to think," he murmurs. Bohdi was never the strongest in Boot Camp, or the fastest, or the most experienced with guns when he arrived. Whenever he was assigned a challenge, the way he always succeeded was by using his brain.

He quickly surveys their surroundings. The light filtering through the roof above is actually quite bright and sparkles and glints in the web. It reminds Bohdi a little of sunlight underwater…or the world after an ice storm. Above, the web had been like a sheet, but here the thinnest strands of net are as thick as sapling trunks. They spin outward at forty-five-degree angles from the thick strand Amy and Bohdi are sitting on. More such thick beams and supports crisscross beneath the roof. Bohdi tilts his head. "We're in the rafters…"

"I think you're right," whispers Amy. "And this space is too small for the spiders… We may be able to make it if there are more nooks like this."

"Make it where?" says Bohdi.

Gesturing down with a hand, Amy says, "Down. When Loki was almost caught by spiders, he was on the ground—it was a wide-open plain. We could run there. Here if we get cornered…"

"Down it is," says Bohdi, mostly because he has no other ideas.

Mr. Squeakers, who had been sitting just in front of them, gives a cheep and jumps off the beam, a little bungee cord of his own silk trailing behind.

"Did he understand us?" says Bohdi, gaze riveted to the path the spidermouse took.

"Yes," says Amy.

He blinks. "That's one smart mouse."

She nods her head, and her ponytail tickles his nose. She's sitting between his thighs, and very close. "Yes," she whispers. "I've discovered magical creatures are generally smarter than you would expect based on the relative size of their prefrontal cortex. I think it has something to do with the magical matter in their nervous systems."

The circuits in Bohdi's brain immediately light up. Magic has strange relationships with space and time. "So, do magical animals have extra capacity stored in another dimension of space...or is it stored in a different place in time?" he asks, and then nearly groans. Wrong time, wrong task, brain...

In front of him, Amy twists in his direction, her gaze connecting with his. "I know," she says, excitedly. "That's the big mystery, isn't it?"

Oh. Her brain is inconveniently wired, too. His hands tighten on her waist, and his eyes move to her lips...

From below comes a "Cheep?" and from above comes skittering thumps.

Amy's face goes pink. "We, ummm...better go." She pulls herself forward on the beam out of his grasp and looks down. "Think I can do that..."

Following her gaze, Bohdi sees below them is a eight or ten foot drop to a sort of hammocky gangway about three feet wide. "I'll go first," he says. Swinging over the beam, he lowers himself as far as he can with his arms and then drops down, letting his legs bend to absorb the impact. He needn't have bothered; the floor gives like a trampoline. He tests it with a few bounces.

"That looks easy enough," Amy says. She tries repeating his moves, but when she lowers herself, her arms shake and give out. She drops like a stone and bounces with such force she nearly flies off the gangway. Bohdi catches her and steadies her without comment, but inside he feels a cold wash of worry. Women have less upper body strength, and she's already over-taxed herself trying to climb the cocoon—and trying to save him from falling.

"Thanks," Amy says, pulling out of his arms and ducking her head. "Look at the railings," she says.

Bohdi inspects the lines of silk that line the gangway. Instead of being at right angles, the "railings" are set at four, five, seven, and eight o'clock relative to the walkway.

"To accommodate eight giant legs…" says Amy, her eyes widening.

Mr. Squeakers suddenly pops up from the railing at eight o'clock and gives a hiss. A chittering behind them makes the hairs on Bohdi's neck stand on end.

"Down!" says Amy, her eyes trained over Bohdi's shoulder, very wide with alarm. Mr. Squeakers vanishes on a line of silk, and Amy slips beneath the railings. More chittering rises down the gangway. Bohdi doesn't even bother to look, he just squeezes himself between the silk railings—and finds himself in a layer of more support beams. Amy is sitting on a large tree-trunk-wide beam. "Seems to be alternating layers of walkways and supports," she says.

Sliding to sit beside her, Bohdi blinks down and verifies her analysis. Above, he hears loud chittering. "I'll go first again," he says. He lowers himself, bounces, and calls up to her, "Now!"

Amy lands beside him with about as much grace as before, and Bohdi catches her without comment. "Thanks," she mumbles.

They pass through three more alternating layers like this.

Occasionally, they see cocoon-tombs of strange creatures suspended in the web, but no more spiders.

Bohdi feels the chill leaving his bones. And actually, without threat of imminent death…

Bouncing on a gangway, he looks up at Amy sitting on a beam of silk and can't help himself. He grins. "This place is fun."

CHAPTER 8

Sitting astride a beam of spider silk, Amy looks down at Bohdi bouncing cheerfully on a gangway. He's wearing a pink dress shirt. It strikes her that she's only seen ADUO agents wear white or blue beneath their coats. It suits his brown skin, and the warmth of the color is in striking contrast to the muted grays of the spider silk.

"Don't you think this place is fun?" he says.

She gives him a tight smile and steels herself for the drop below. Her arms and fingers are shaking, even when she isn't exerting them. Swinging a leg over, she tries to lower herself and falls—again. She hits the gangway, bounces hard, and almost soars over the railings, but once again, Bohdi catches her without comment, complaint, or even a scowl. She feels her face heating as she mumbles her thanks.

She can't meet his eyes. She's slowing him down and she hates it. With a deep breath she looks around. There's still enough light to see by, but now, instead of like being outside on a bright snowy day, at this level of the nest, it's like being outside on an overcast snowy day. At least there are no spiders. But how much further is it to the ground...and how much longer will they be alone?

"Ready?" Bohdi says, snapping her from her thoughts.

"Right," says Amy. She and Bohdi slide between the railings to another level of scaffold. Before Amy's even braced herself on the large beam, Bohdi's sitting comfortably, peeking down below. "Hmmm. This is different," he whispers.

Amy peeks down. Below them, instead of a gangway is a sort of room. Instead of being at right angles, it's ovoid, with walls the same texture of web as the roof had been.

Beside her Bohdi whispers, "Should we try and clamber through the supports or drop down and—"

Right above their heads comes the skittering of feet, and loud chittering. Amy's and Bohdi's eyes lock. Amy looks down, and she nods at Bohdi. He nods back, black hair flopping over his dark eyes. His darker features are indistinct in the low light, but the sharp angle of his jaw stands out, and is oddly familiar.

Amy looks away, something in her chest tightening. The chittering above them gets louder; a silvery limb pokes the air in front of them. Without a word, Amy and Bohdi drop into the space below.

The drop is farther than the others, but the floor is springy, and it doesn't hurt. As usual, Bohdi's fall is graceful, and Amy almost bounces off her feet. Taking her hand, he silently steadies her.

The room is fairly small—only about the size of Amy's bedroom. There are round doorways in front and behind them. Toward one side poking out of the floor, slightly to the side is a bush crowned with dead leaves. Amy's jaw drops. Not a bush.

"A tree top," she whispers.

Bohdi's eyebrows hitch up. He gives her a nod and then puts his fingers to his lips. She watches his eyes slide to the walls and his brows constrict. The walls are about eight or nine feet high and solid. Bohdi could probably jump up and swing himself over. Amy's hand tightens on his and she swallows. She's not sure if she could. If he wants to go that way...

From behind them, she hears skittering footsteps. Mr. Squeakers, suspended on a line of silk, drops down to the floor and starts hopping in the opposite direction. Bohdi follows the mouse, pulling Amy along. Right before they enter the next room, he tugs her so she's leaning against the wall and pokes his nose cautiously around the door. Amy looks in the direction they just came from. She hears chittering and footsteps getting louder, but sees no spiders.

Before she knows what's happening, Bohdi pulls her into the next room. It's a lot like the first, but longer, and with multiple doors. Dead tree tops poke through the floor and the walls. More chittering rises outside the door they just entered, and Amy looks over her shoulder as Bohdi pulls her along.

There's still no sign of spiders, but she swears she hears more of them.

Bohdi gasps, and she snaps her head forward. She's relieved to see there isn't a spider in front of them.

But that relief only lasts a moment.

Bound to a wall with fine spider silk is a hominid figure with dragonfly wings. Obviously long dead, it's still terrifying. Through the silk, Amy can see its skin is sunken to its bones. Its mouth is open in a silent scream—revealing fangs nearly as long as Amy's pinky fingers.

"Adze," she whispers.

"Oh," says Bohdi. His Adam's apple bobs. And his eyes

slide down the creature, its shape still visible beneath the nearly translucent silk.

"So um…did the spiders take some parts off of him, or do adze…" He winces.

Amy follows his gaze to the adze's sexless groin. "They come like that."

"Ahhh…" he says. "Still disturbing."

And it is. The creature's body is smooth like a Ken doll, and there's something about it that makes Amy feel like her hair is being brushed the wrong way.

"Which way?" Bohdi whispers. Mr. Squeakers hops over to one of the doorways and disappears. From the way they just came, the chittering increases in volume.

Without further conversation, Amy and Bohdi bolt after her mouse and find themselves in a narrow hallway. Instead of loft-like scaffolding above them, there is a smooth roof. Mr. Squeakers darts down a side hallway, and then another. At one point, he slips through a narrow space in the floor, just large enough for Amy and Bohdi to slip through one at a time. They work their way through another jungle-gym-like obstacle course of silken support beams and then pop out another tiny hole into a narrow, twisting hallway.

As they follow Mr. Squeakers down the corridors, Amy notices they're slowly going downward. It's getting progressively gloomier, and the sound of spider chittering seems to be rising around them everywhere—from the walls, ceiling, even the floor.

Amy gulps. They're in the spiders' living quarters…which explains the seeming lack of stickiness in the web.

Ahead of them, Mr. Squeakers makes a sudden break right. Bohdi and Amy follow him down a narrow hallway that drops abruptly about eight feet or so into a cavernous room. Mr. Squeakers keeps hopping forward, extending out a bolt of silk to lower himself. Bohdi and Amy come to a skidding halt.

The room is slightly larger than an Olympic swimming pool, and the chattering of spiders echoes through it, though Amy can't see any of the web's inhabitants about. But then, it's impossible to see very far. The room is filled with treetops that rise at least twenty feet from the floor. The branches are adorned with their own dead leaves, brown withered ivy with dark black fronds, wispy cobwebs, and odd bits of spider silk.

"Weird," whispers Bohdi. And Amy knows what he means; everywhere else the spiders' webs have been spun with engineering precision. Here it looks like cheap Halloween decorations.

Mr. Squeakers bolts between some of the tree limbs. Amy feels herself tremble, and Bohdi meets her eyes. Without a word, they slip down the drop and follow Mr. Squeakers, trying not to step on dried husks of plant matter that litter the floor.

They've only gone a few feet when Bohdi gives a low hiss. He veers away from the path Mr. Squeakers is weaving and goes to a wide, loose, pile of spider silk, barely visible in the gloom.

Amy looks at where Mr. Squeakers sits patiently, and then back to Bohdi, now kneeling by the silk.

What is he doing? Why is he stopping?

Biting her lip, Amy walks over to him. She is about to put her hand on his shoulder, to remind him that they are in a nest of giant, human-eating spiders, when he grabs hold of the silk and pulls it away.

Amy's jaw drops. Beneath the layers of silk is an airplane.

Well, not an airplane. At about eighteen inches high, four feet long, and maybe eight feet wide it is obviously not for passengers.

Kneeling on the ground, Bohdi looks up at her and whispers, "RQ-487 Albatross. Spy drone." He shakes his head. "These things were only prototypes when I was in the Corps."

Amy swallows. So Steve and company—or someone on Earth—is looking for them. She wishes she could feel more relieved, but all she wants to do is get out of here now. The spider chitters are making the hairs on the back of her neck stand on end.

Unfortunately, Bohdi doesn't seem to share her urgency. Still kneeling, he runs a hand down its frame and whispers, "Looks like the electronics are out... If I can get it out of here, I might be able to turn it on, maybe re-launch it, and get a message to Steve."

"We have to get out of here first!" Amy whispers. And how he will carry that ungainly thing, she has no idea.

Bohdi blinks at her, and then his eyes snap back to the drone. "Right."

Instead of getting a move on, he picks up the drone. It must be lighter than it looks because he lifts it with one hand. Raising it to eye level, he studies it and then pulls a lever beneath its body. The wings and tail finny-things fold inward and collapse until they are flush with the body of the plane. Suddenly Bohdi is holding something that looks more like a very long baseball bat than an airplane, although, where there would be a handle on a baseball bat, there is a rather sharp, pointy tail end.

Her face must show some surprise because Bohdi whispers, "Know why they call it the albatross?"

Amy's brain does a little blinky-away-from-reality thing. "Because it doesn't look like it can fly?"

Bohdi's jaw sags. "Yeah.

Bouncing on her feet, Amy whispers, "Can we just go?"

Somewhere nearby something crunches in the leaves. "Right," he whispers.

Together they follow Mr. Squeakers, Amy's heart dropping as they do. The chittering echoes in the room are getting louder.

Beside her Bohdi whispers, "Do you think he knows where he's going?"

Amy can only shrug.

Mr. Squeakers hops up to a wispy curtain of spider silk adorned with dry leaves, and stops. A faint breeze stirs, and the silk rustles.

Bohdi goes forward and glances through the cobweb. Inhaling sharply, he whispers, "Uh-oh."

Slipping to stand beside him, Amy peeks past him. Her legs immediately go weak. Beyond the curtain is a break in the trees. About thirty feet in front of them there are two massive spiders, plucking at something on the far wall, concealed by their bodies. Writhing between their legs are smaller spiders chattering madly. They range from the size of miniature poodles to golden retrievers. Where the large spiders have legs that are long and spindly in comparison to their body size, the little spiders have short stubby legs. Instead of smooth, silvery carapaces, the little ones have soft downy white fur. One turns its head briefly, and Amy notices its six red eyes are very large in its little head, and its mandible is proportionally very tiny.

All of the spiders have their backs turned to them—the better to shoot them with web. She blinks. Whatever the large

spiders are doing has the little ones very excited. Their chittering is becoming deafening. A few shoot wispy bits of webbing
from their butts. It doesn't look strong or go very far.

"Spider babies?" Bohdi whispers.

"Yes," Amy whispers back, not really afraid of being overheard over the deluge of chatter. They're kind of cute, and
if she was watching a Natural Geographic special, she's sure
she'd be utterly besotted.

She wonders what has them so excited. And then one of
the large spiders steps sideways, and Amy sees what it was
plucking at.

No. Not plucking. Stabbing. The adult has a forelimb protruding from the chest of an adze—and although the adze's
head is lolling downward, its wings are still trembling. Blood
is gushing from the wound. Little spiders are hopping up and
down trying to catch the geyser in their mouths.

She hears Bohdi take a sharp intake at the same time she
does. She hopes with all her might the adze is unconscious. As
soon as the thought crosses her mind, the adze raises its head,
hisses, and then begins lunging against the spider's forelimb,
driving it further through its chest. Seemingly oblivious to
the pain, the adze roars, clawing and gnashing its fangs at its
captors. At the adze's feet, the little spiders make a sound that
sounds like a baby's coo.

Bohdi and Amy both jerk their heads away.

Amy scrunches her eyes shut.

"Mr. Squeakers," Bohdi whispers. Amy opens her eyes.
Bohdi points through a little hole in the curtain.

Amy hears a hiss from the adze, and despite herself, her
eyes go in its direction. The other adult spider has jammed
a forelimb through its chest. The creature is pinned against

the wall, its head is rolling from side to side, and its teeth are bared. At its feet the little spiders begin hopping excitedly again. On their short legs they don't hop very high.

Tearing her eyes away, Amy follows Bohdi's gesture. Mr. Squeakers is skittering across the floor, almost invisible among the dried leaves and cobwebs. As she watches, her mouse goes to a wall to the left of the spiders and climbs up to an opening roughly eight feet above the ground. Her eyes follow the wall and she sees other similar openings, all set above ten feet. She looks at the little spiders and their tiny hops. The openings are baby spider proof. They're in the spider nursery, and apparently it was designed to keep the babies from getting out.

How touching. Unfortunately…Amy swallows as she looks at the opening. "I don't think I can jump that high."

Bohdi pulls away from the curtain. Looking her up and down, he puts a hand to his chin. "I can and you don't have to." He doesn't sound at all afraid, or angry, and it's such a relief she could kiss him.

"How?" she says, instead.

Leaning close, Bohdi says. "We make a break for it. I go first. I reach the wall first." He interlocks his fingers and raises his hands. "I throw you up in the air."

Amy's jaw drops, about to protest. She won't make it… and then he won't make it and then…

Cocking an eyebrow he says, "We don't have time to argue, and I'm not going anywhere without you."

She bites her lip.

He looks cautiously through the hole in the curtain. She follows the direction of his gaze. The adult spiders have lowered the adze to the ground, and the little spiders are crawling all over it, making sounds that sound eerily like the laughter of small children. They seem focused, but she can't imagine the feeding frenzy will last long.

"Ready?" he says.

"No."

Bohdi's teeth flash white in the gloom as he grimaces—or maybe smiles. "Me, either." He shrugs. "Shall we?"

Amy nods. "Yes."

"On three," Bohdi says. "One."

Amy takes a deep breath, her hands trembling.

"Two."

She exhales slowly, trying to stay calm. Bohdi drops to a sprinter's crouch, still holding onto the drone. Amy does the same.

Pushing the curtain of cobwebs aside with the drone nose, he whispers, "Three," and bolts. Amy follows.

Bohdi is terribly fast. It seems like she is instantly several paces behind him. Out of the corner of her eye, she sees the baby spiders lift their heads. They make a sound like, "Ooooooooooooo."

A loud deeper chittering fills her ears. The adults. She doesn't turn, she just pumps her legs faster. In front of her, Bohdi has already dropped the drone, fallen to a crouch by the wall, and entwined his fingers. "Now!" he shouts.

Her heart is beating in time with her feet. One, two... there. Her foot connects with his hands, miraculously on the first try. She jumps, and he lifts, and she is soaring through the air. Her gut catches on the lip of the opening, knocking the wind out of her. Mr. Squeakers gives a squeal somewhere beside her, and she yanks herself up and into the tunnel. She turns. Below her Bohdi shouts. "Catch!"

He has the drone in his hands and is about to throw it, but

Amy's eyes are riveted behind him—an adult spider is closing in, mandibles clacking.

Amy screams.

Bohdi turns, just in time for the spider to lunge at his midriff, mandibles open wide. In a motion too fast for Amy to see, Bohdi twists his body around with a snarl, stabbing the pointy tail end of the drone right into the spider's largest bottom eye. He pulls the drone out of the spider's eye with an angry shout. Ochre liquid splashes from the gaping wound. The spider's mandibles clack in a rapid staccato, and then the whole beast drops to the ground. With a shout of triumph or anger or both, Bohdi springs onto the fallen spider's head and then leaps into the tunnel opening, with so much impossible grace, it's like he's being lifted by invisible strings. An instant later, he is on his hands and knees on the tunnel floor, panting at Amy's feet.

In the nursery, the other adult spider lets loose a shriek that is nearly ear-splitting. Amy's eyes rise to a point beyond the spider's head. She gasps. "More adults!"

Adult spiders are spilling through the other openings; a few are already on the ground, preparing to fire silk. "Run!" Amy shouts.

At a crouch at her feet, Bohdi snarls. "No!"

She looks down to see him jamming the drone's sharp tail, now ochre and sticky with fluid, into the tunnel floor. He pulls on it, gives a grunt, and releases a lever beneath the drone's core. The drone's wings fly outward and pierce the tunnel's walls and lights flash along its sides.

"Huh," Bohdi says, eyes shining in the electronic glow. "Impact must have reconnected a wire." Bohdi gives it a yank, and she sees the glint of his teeth in a vicious smile when it doesn't move.

She hears a whistling in the chamber, and on instinct pulls him back. He falls on his butt just before bolts of sticky silk land on the drone's tail end, sticking it to the floor.

Bohdi laughs. "Heh, they're sealing the exit for us."

In the nursery, all the adult spiders come to a halt. Mr. Squeakers cheeps from the floor, hops up onto Amy's arm, and crawls to her shoulder.

All the baby spiders stop chittering. And then seemingly at some unheard command, they surge forward, their tiny bodies swarming over the body of the adult spider Bohdi downed. With excited squeals, they try to hurl themselves into the tunnel, even as the adults rush forward and try to pull them away from the exit.

With a gasp, Amy takes a step backward. The juveniles are small enough they can fit beneath the spider silk and the drone wings.

"Run!" she says.

"Yep," says Bohdi, clambering to his feet. Even though Amy's got a head start, he is instantly beside her. He grabs her wrist, and pulls her along. She doesn't think she's ever run so fast, it feels like she's flying. And the next thing she knows, she is flying, suspended in midair as the tunnel floor drops out from beneath her feet. Before she can process what is happening, she falls with Bohdi, her wrist still in his grip. They land an instant later in a slide as the tunnel drops at an incline too steep for human feet. Bohdi shouts, Squeakers squeaks, and Amy bites her tongue, blood welling in her mouth. But even as they fall, her heart leaps... She smells fresh air!

They tumble, Squeakers frantically clinging to the front of her coat, her hand sliding to link with Bohdi's. And then the tunnel opens to the outside, and they crash downward into a clump of undergrowth that breaks their fall. It's so dry beneath the nest that dust rises up around the brush in a small whirlwind.

Beside her, Bohdi coughs. It must be near noon, but the light around them is dark and gray. She lifts her head. The spider nest is a looming gray cloud, not eight feet above their heads. They are surrounded by a dead forest of tree trunks and undergrowth.

Bohdi laughs. "Did we make it?"

Amy's mouth drops. She almost laughs, too, but the laughter dies before it's left her mouth. Beyond the copse of dead vegetation they've landed in, she hears angry chittering noises. She lifts her eyes above a clump of brown grasses that is nearly the height of her head. Leaning sideways, she looks between two trees whose trunks are choked with the same dead ivy they'd seen in the spider nursery. Closing in, less than fifty feet away, are more spiders than she can count.

"No," she whispers. "We haven't made it yet."

The spiders move more slowly than they had on the roof or in the nest. Because Bohdi killed one of them? Do the spiders think they're dangerous?

Climbing to his feet, Bohdi turns around, surveying the distance beyond their protective little wall of trees and dead plant life. "Fuck," he says.

Scrambling up, Amy slowly turns around. Outside of the trees, it's mostly underbrush. Spiders are everywhere.

A few bolts of silk streak toward them, but the silken bolts catch harmlessly in the trees and brush. Dipping his chin, voice low, Bohdi says, "So Loki got out last time by dashing beneath the nest…"

Amy nods. "But he had fire…"

A gentle breeze stirs. Bohdi drops to his knees and pulls out his lighter

"I know it won't work," he mutters.

Dropping down, she squeezes his hand holding the lighter. "Do it," she says. She hears an edge in her voice that sounds like hopelessness or hysteria. She remembers the adze, the sharp forelimbs of spiders thrust through its chest. She will try anything to escape that fate. Bohdi's lighter sparks, and he holds it at the base of a high clump of undergrowth. The tall spikes of grass begin to smolder.

From above them comes a sound like a child's gleeful, "Whee!"

Amy lifts her head to see two small spiders falling from the tunnel just above them. Before she knows what's happening, Bohdi is on his feet. His right foot connects with a small spider body before it even hits the ground. There is a sickening crunch and the spider's body flies through the dead trees. There is a collective clicking beyond the small patch of forest they're in.

The second spider scurries at Amy's feet, mandibles twitching. Is it poisonous? She wants to kick it, but somehow she winds up only hopping backward, like her legs are bound together. Before she can regain herself, Bohdi's already giving the spiderling a smooth roundhouse kick with his left foot. There is another crunch as his foot connects, and then the small creature goes flying between the trees.

Amy shivers. There is something so effortless and natural in the way Bohdi fights. As though he does this all the time…

She twists around to look at him, expecting a cocky grin and glinting eyes. Instead Bohdi just looks befuddled. "Wow," he says. "I must have played soccer in my past life."

In the periphery of her vision, Amy sees two of the adults rush forward.

She falls with Bohdi into a defensive crouch—as though they have some defense. But the two spiders merely grab the semi-crushed baby spiders and scurry backward. As they do, the mob of spiders chittering becomes so loud and fast it becomes a furious roar.

Amy blinks. For a heartbeat nothing happens. And then the spiders surge forward from all sides with such force the ground actually shakes.

Another high-pitched cry sounds above. Lifting her head, maybe to avoid looking at her fate, she sees a small spider falling right toward her.

"Amy," Bohdi shouts.

He reaches for her, but it's too late. The spiderling is just inches from the crown of her head. She should run, or hit it, or kick it…Instead she catches it. Her hands connect with its fuzzy, round, middle, just at the level above where its stubby little legs begin. Its fur is incredibly soft beneath her fingers, and its body is warm.

The roaring clatter of the spiders instantly goes silent, the wave of their momentum coming to a halt just a few paces from the trees.

The small spider in her hands gives a cheep. Its six eyes open and close rapidly, its little legs pump the empty air, and its mandibles quiver.

"I can't…I can't kill it!" Amy cries, knowing she's being ridiculous. It's probably poisonous. It would suck her blood in a heartbeat.

Bohdi puts a hand on her shoulder and the little spider

squeals in terror, its legs helplessly churning backward in the air.

"Maybe you won't have to," he whispers, but he might as well be shouting, the spiders beyond the trees are so eerily silent.

Amy lifts her head. The adult spiders have drawn back, their mandibles opening and closing—but so softly they make almost no sound.

"We have a hostage," Bohdi says.

Amy's heart stops. One little spider's life…has made the whole hive retreat.

"Don't drop him," Bohdi says. He pushes Amy forward a step. In front of them, the spiders draw back.

"I don't want to hurt him," Amy says, her voice ringing with despair. As they advance toward the spiders, some of the adults drop their abdomens low to the ground. Amy's not sure if she imagines it, but there's something sinister in the movement. Bohdi spins beside her, jaw hard. Flicking open his knife, he shouts, "You don't have to hurt it, honey, 'cause I will."

He sounds so much more confident than Amy; she shifts nervously on her feet. The spiders crawling on their bellies skitter backward with nervous, light clicks of their mandibles.

The little spider in Amy's hands squeals, a line of silk shooting out its rear end. Bohdi's eyes drop to it, and he whispers through clinched teeth. "I don't want to hurt you, little guy…but I don't want to be eaten."

There's a sort of frantic desperation in his voice, and it's like a spell has been broken. He's just as human as she is, just as afraid and conflicted.

Bohdi licks his lips nervously. Rolling his head, he flips his bangs back and whispers, "We're in a stalemate. In the trees they can't shoot us with silk, and while we've got the little guy, they can't advance. But as soon as we leave the trees…"

Amy swallows. As soon as they leave the trees and underbrush, they'll be surrounded by spiders. It will be easy enough for the spiders to trap them both in bonds of silk before Bohdi can threaten their "hostage."

For a moment, they both stand paralyzed. A gust of gentle wind sweeps beneath the nest, ruffling dead leaves.

Amy takes a deep breath and catches a whiff of…campfire.

A twig snaps very close in the underbrush to their right. Expecting to see a spider, Amy turns her head, and Bohdi raises his knife.

But there is no giant arachnid about to pounce, just a bright dancing flame, crackling in the brush. There is another crackle, another gust of wind, and a tiny spark floats gently from the burning undergrowth to the trunk of a tree. It disappears among the blackened dead fronds of ivy. And then, with a sound like a soft sigh, a warm orange flame blossoms along the tree trunk.

More sparks rise from the first bit of brush Bohdi set to smoldering. Some land in the ivy embrace of another tree. Another tiny fire starts with frightening swiftness.

"Uh-oh," says Bohdi. "Errrr…"

A patch of grass erupts into a blaze. The tiny flickers of flame dancing in the ivy fronds suddenly flare—and the tree trunks rapidly becoming engulfed in fire so dense it is like flaming bark. Spreading up into the tree limbs, the fire begins stretching orange tendrils of flame into the spider nest.

Amy lifts her head and gasps. Where the flame touches the nest, the web melts like cotton candy.

A whoosh sounds behind them, and another tree trunk bursts into flames, tongues of fire flicking up quickly into its branches and into the web...Amy turns in place, the fire is spreading everywhere around them. In a few minutes, they'll be trapped.

Beyond the flames, Amy hears the rise of more spider chitters.

There is a loud crack, and a branch longer than Amy's arm and twice as thick tumbles down behind them, one end of it lit like the butt end of a cigarette.

"Death by spider or by fire?" Bohdi mutters.

"I don't know..." Amy says, turning to face their captors beyond the flaming brush. As she turns, a shrill shriek fills the air, followed by another, and another. It sounds like a baby's cry, and makes the hair on the back of her neck stand on end.

"What?" says Bohdi.

And then the spider in Amy's arms raises its voice in the same eerily human shriek of terror. Above them, more wails rise up in a horrible chorus of pain and fear Amy knows she'll never be able to forget it as long as she lives.

Eyes widening, Amy looks upward. Above them spider silk is melting away from the flames as the fire leaps from branch to branch.

"The nursery..." Amy whispers, but her voice is drowned out by the cries of the adult spiders beyond the trees. Their chittering rises in another roar; however, this time, it is higher in pitch, almost frantic.

Beside her, even in the warm light of the growing flames, Bohdi looks vaguely green. But then gritting his teeth, he surveys the distance beyond Amy's shoulder. Putting his knife away, he grabs her shoulder. "Come on." Pushing her forward, he pauses just long enough to pick up the branch that had fallen, and begins steering Amy out of the trees that are rapidly becoming giant torches.

Death by spider then, she thinks. That thought dies almost instantly. The ranks of adult spiders surrounding Amy and Bohdi have thinned. All around them, the spiders are jumping into the air, and disappearing into half hidden tunnels in the floor of the rapidly disintegrating nest.

The shrill cry of baby spiders is still rising in the air. Amy's own spiderling's shriek is fading to a near incessant whimper. Flipping the little guy around in her arms so its back is to her stomach, she clutches it like a stuffed animal.

Bohdi steers them beneath the nest, between clumps of smoldering grasses and trees, brandishing the branch at any spider that looks like it'll get close…but there aren't many. One does send a bolt of silk at them—but Bohdi catches it with an angry snarl with the end of the branch and it disintegrates without smoke or even a sizzle. After that, the spiders mostly skitter away as they approach.

Without any spoken agreement, Bohdi's and Amy's feet begin picking up speed, they're both running as they approach the edge of the nest. The fire is spreading behind and above them, Amy feels heat against her back, and the smoke is making them cough and gasp.

The little spider she carries cries again as they reach open air. Bohdi and Amy come to a skidding halt. Amy looks up through the branches of the forest they find themselves in, slightly disoriented. Where before the sky had been a beautiful blue, now it is dark and overcast. Her heart lifts. Thor?

"Smoke," Bohdi whispers.

A hot wind licks against her back. Flames jump from

beneath the nest to the undergrowth in the forest around them. The forest isn't as dry as the vegetation choked beneath the nest... Still, Amy hears the crackle of twigs snapping in the fire's heat.

In her arms, the little spider lets loose one of those too human shrieks, and Amy pulls it tighter on impulse.

Behind her comes a soft clicking. Amy and Bohdi both turn slowly to see a single spider standing about twenty paces behind them, the nest melting away over its head.

The spider in her arms wails, and its little legs pump the air. Amy feels tears welling in her eyes and it's not just from soot. In the back of her mind, she knows this is just some primitive part of her brain responding to a baby's cry, an evolutionary impulse—that really isn't suited to this situation.

The baby's cries become whimpers. Amy bites her lip, and lowers her small hostage to the ground.

"What are you..." Bohdi stammers.

The large spider darts forward before Amy can answer.

Bohdi grabs her hand, yanks her back with such force she spins around, and then pulls her into a dead run through the trees. For an instant, Amy thinks the spider is letting them go, and she feels a weird sort of kindred with the creature. And then she hears whistling behind her, and then something hits her back with enough force to knock her to the ground. Turning her head in the dirt, she watches as Bohdi shouts and sinks the end of the smoldering branch into a band of silk that's attached to her coat.

As the silk melts away, Amy scrambles to her feet, and Bohdi charges the spider with a yell. Hoisting the baby on its back, the spider skitters away, chittering angrily. Without a word, Bohdi grabs Amy's arm, and they take off again. They don't stop running until they reach an open bluff. By that time, even Bohdi's gasping for air.

Releasing her hand, he walks a few paces away and bends over, panting hard. She expects him to say something about her being an idiot—for not kicking the spider and then for letting it go. She's been holding him back and putting him in more danger the whole time.

But Bohdi only stands there. Wiping his face, now smudged with soot, he looks back the way they came. Still panting, Amy looks, too. Clouds of smoke are obscuring the sky. She can't see the nest at all. Wind is carrying the flames into the forest they're now standing in.

Jaw tightening, Bohdi says, "The drone turned on back there. Steve will keep looking for us."

It's at that moment Amy realizes that besides losing Thor, they don't have any Promethean wire…or any supplies at all, really.

She can't bring herself to answer.

Bohdi closes his eyes and his body sags. He looks…beaten. And it's so strange, after all they just went through.

Trying to be encouraging, she says, "You did really great back there. I mean…it's like you just knew how to…" Kill spiders. Take hostages.

Looking down, Bohdi's lips tighten. "I did get some combat training in the Marines." He doesn't meet her eyes, and she can't read his mood.

Amy tilts her head. "I didn't realize the Marines taught you how to fight giant spiders."

Looking up, Bohdi says, "They didn't…maybe I should suggest it be part of the standard training?"

His lips curl up, just a little; and Amy smiles, just a little.

Bohdi's jaw goes tight, and he looks away. "Those baby spider screams…" With jerky movements, he runs a hand through his hair. "That sucked."

Amy bites her lip. She wants to console him, to tell him she's glad she doesn't have a forelimb pinning her to a wall, and mandibles piercing her skin. Opening her mouth, she inhales a lungful of soot.

"Looks like I started a forest fire," Bohdi says. "We better move before Smokey the Bear catches me." He doesn't smile at his joke, and Amy just coughs on the smoke.

CHAPTER 9

Leaning against the wall in Macy's, Steve clutches Claire's ice skates and his own skates under one arm, pondering the oddly accusatory text on his phone.

You lost Amy Lewis.

The text is from Prometheus.

He wasn't aware that the mysterious source that the FBI has for all things magical knows Lewis. That Prometheus is concerned with her fate is more than interesting, but Steve has had enough interaction with the elusive contact to know a direct question will get him nowhere.

Instead, Steve taps out a quickly: *Can u help?*

There is a moment's pause and then the screen lights with another message. *No one can see cle*arly into Nornheim. And my doors to the realm are closed.

Doors closed? Steve closes his eyes trying to remember. Skírnir had said something like that about the gates in Asgard, hadn't he?

Another message pops onto the screen. *Your drones our only intel.*

Steve's brows knit. Not comforting.

Another message from Prometheus blinks on the screen. *Keep me informed.*

Typing fast, Steve taps out: *Wait. We need more wire.* Bohdi had "borrowed" most of their reserves of Promethean wire.

There is a long pause and then a reply: *I have none on hand.*

Steve runs his tongue over his teeth.

But then another text appears. *It will take time. Goodbye.*

Scowling, Steve checks the time on his phone—again. It's still another three hours before they check in on the drones. He shifts the skates under his arm. If their sources can tell them nothing helpful about the realm, they're at the mercy of human tech. He scratches his chin…and perhaps human myth? Haven't both Amy and Loki said that mythology is a skewed reflection of actual events?

He shakes his head. He can't do anything now. It's after five o'clock on a Saturday. He needs to give it a rest. Slipping the phone back into his pocket, he lifts his head and scans the crowd at Macy's. Where is Claire?

Steve and his daughter had come to the department store to buy Claire a new pair of mittens and to get a snack before going skating in Millennium Park. She'd just gone to the bathroom. He turns to look down the hallway toward the restrooms. A little Chinese guy is pacing nearby, too. Also waiting for a lost female relative?

A voice, elegant and contralto, comes from beside him. "Are you looking for someone?"

Steve turns his head, and has a bit of a disconnect. The tall woman, in knee-high black suede boots is a dead ringer for the '80s pop-singer, Sade. She has full lips, nearly Asian eyes, skin a little darker than copper, and a strong nose that verges on being Arabic. Her rich contralto voice almost makes him think she is Sade, but this woman is a little younger, maybe late thirties.

He always had a thing for Sade. Steve opens his mouth, but it takes a little while for words to come out. "Ah...yes... my daughter is in the bathroom."

"Oh!" says the woman. "I was just in there, and I think I saw her! She looks exactly like you, right? But small and pretty." She smiles.

Steve nods, and the woman waves a hand. "Don't worry, it's just a bit crowded...a lot of skaters coming in for hot chocolate, I think."

Is that a hint of a Nigerian accent? It's...sexy. "Oh..." Steve suffers through his speechless moment, then his face melts into a smile. She is so beautiful, he can't help it. Trying to reclaim some dignity, he says, "Do you skate?" And then mentally kicks himself. Steve only skates for Claire. She loves skating, and years of ballet training and a few skating lessons have given her the speed and grace of a snowflake. Steve is just barely capable of not embarrassing himself. If this woman is good at skating...

She smiles again. "No, but I've always wanted to learn. I had no idea there was skating nearby. I'm new in town, and by myself."

"New in town?" Steve manages to say. And by herself?

The woman nods. "I have just taken a position at Northwestern University."

Steve lifts his chin, impressed. "A scholar?" Smart and beautiful? Is manna raining from heaven?

She nods. "Of myths and folklore."

"Oh...," says Steve. "That is..." very interesting, and strangely apropos. The hairs on the back of Steve's neck tickle, and he almost reaches into his pocket for his magic detector. But it's silent...and that would be ridiculous...and...He straightens. Claire will be out in a minute. He needs to act fast.

Holding out his hand, he says, "I'm Steve Rogers."

She smiles and proffers a hand adorned with elegant gold bracelets in his direction. "My name is—"

From behind Steve, someone starts speaking fast in Chinese, and Claire's voice cracks through the din of the department store. "You!"

Steve turns around to see Claire coming slowly down the hallway, a frail, elderly Asian woman leaning on his daughter's left arm. The other arm is pointing just past Steve. Claire's chin is high, and her eyes are flashing. The small Chinese man who had been pacing down the hallway is scurrying to the old woman.

"What?" says Steve, breaking into a jog toward his daughter.

Claire blinks. "She's gone..."

"Who?" says Steve.

Standing on her tip toes, Claire scans the large room. "The woman you were talking to—"

Steve looks and sees empty air where Sade had stood. Damn.

Claire puts a hand on her hip. "She was checking her makeup in the mirror, turned around too quickly, and knocked this lady over!" The little old lady is still hanging on to Claire's arm for dear life. The man, maybe her son, is trying to pull her away.

Addressing the Chinese man, Claire says, "I think maybe she should see a doctor…"

The elderly woman pats Claire's arm and says something in Chinese. The man looks at Claire and says, "Thank you, thank you."

Steve appraises the elderly woman. She does look a little wobbly on her feet. Bending down, Steve looks into her eyes. Her pupils are too small. Pulling out his phone, he turns to the man, "Your mother has a concussion. She needs a doctor, I'm calling nine-one-one."

"Oh…thank you," says the man. He turns to the old woman and starts talking in rapid Chinese. The old woman responds and pats Claire's arm.

A few minutes later, Steve, the man, and the department store staff have gotten the elderly woman to lie down while they wait for the paramedics to arrive. They sit quietly, and it's uncomfortable, mostly because it gives Steve time to think.

Why does Prometheus care about Amy? Ratatoskr, the squirrel messenger of the Norns, had told Steve to keep an eye on her, because "there is something not quite right about her." He rubs his jaw in irritation. There is something not quite right about so many things: Amy visiting other universes— one where Steve was killed by Odin, one where Bohdi was killed by Loki; Bohdi's memories in this universe; Beatrice being sharp as a tack and one-hell-of a shot; trolls still popping up downtown…

Hernandez would say the common denominator is magic.

Steve runs a hand along the back of his neck. But there's more than that. He feels like he has all the pieces of the puzzle, but without the final picture, he doesn't know how to put them together.

As a reviled politician once said, too many "known unknowns, and unknown unknowns."

Interrupting his thoughts, the Chinese guy says, "You have a very good daughter."

A headache that had been brewing behind Steve's eyes is suddenly gone. Steve hears rapidly approaching footsteps. The paramedics are arriving.

He puts an arm around Claire's shoulders. She's ten years old, nearly as tall as the man, but thin as a bean pole. He kisses the top of her head. "That, I know."

"Dad!" says Claire, but she doesn't pull away. Steve doesn't let her go, but he doesn't look at her for fear of getting misty eyed. He has one thing in his life he knows is perfect.

As the paramedics come rushing in, Claire and Steve leave the scene, Steve's arm still around his daughter's shoulders. He gives her a squeeze, as his eyes sweep over the spot where he had been speaking to the Sade impersonator.

Beside him, Claire says, "Who was that woman talking to you?"

Steve stops for a second, something tickling the back of his mind. "I don't know…"

CHAPTER 10

"I don't know…" Amy says, from above Bohdi, nervously scuffing the toe of her sneaker in the dirt.

He glares up at her from where he squats at the riverbank, cool, enticing, water cupped in his hands.

Amy is silhouetted by Nornheim's pinkish sun. Filtered through clouds of smoke, the sun's light has taken on a foreboding red hue. Her winter coat is tied around her hips; a fleece sweater is drooping in her arms. She's stripped down to an over-sized, unflattering boxy tee shirt with a picture of a cat on it. Above the cat, in an Old West font, are the words: Wanted Dead & Alive, Schrodinger's Cat. And okay, it's funny, but he'd think the God of Mischief's girlfriend would have a little more body confidence. The tee shirt might as well be a muumuu. Why is she trying to hide? Even if her waist is thick, why not wear something that shows she at least has a waist?

Amy presses her lips together. "Amoebic dysentery is a pretty bad way to die."

"So is dehydration," Bohdi counters.

"We don't have any iodine tablets to treat the water

with…" Amy says.

Bohdi closes his eyes. "We don't have anything." Besides his knife and lighter, they have their phones—powered down now, possibly of use for light later, Amy's protein bar, some tissues (a few slightly used), a couple of hairpins, some condoms Amy snorted at when Bohdi pulled them out of his wallet, and the branch Bohdi picked up when the fire first started—slightly shorter now than it was then. They also have two Archaeopteryx feathers that Amy found in her hair and is ridiculously giddy about—they're not even pretty feathers. They're tiny little white things that could have been pulled out of any duck's butt.

Bohdi looks down at his makeshift club. He's not sure what kind of wood the branch is, but it is still smoking at one end. Bohdi's heard wild animals are afraid of fire, and he's hopeful the smell of smoke will keep predators at bay.

As if to punctuate that thought, something, somewhere, gives a blood-curdling howl.

Bohdi almost snorts in exasperation. His tongue is parched, his lips are cracked, and his eyes are burning from soot and exhaustion. "I'm drinking," he says. "Didn't you tell me that Thor has healing powers? If we don't find him, we'll die anyway, with or without amoebic dysentery."

With that, he lifts the water to his lips and slurps it down. It is just as delicious as he imagined. With a squeak, Mr. Squeakers hops off Amy's shoulder, settles himself beside Bohdi, and dips his whiskers into the water.

Bohdi smiles smugly at Amy. He slurps down a couple more handfuls before she grudgingly squats down beside him. As she drinks, Bohdi picks up the branch and looks northward in the direction they came from. Smoke is pouring from the trees into dark clouds. If Thor is up there, Bohdi can't see him.

A brisk wind from the east ruffles his hair. So far, the fire's path has been mostly westward, but it's spreading southward along the river's path, too, just at a slower pace. They have to keep moving. As long as they keep following the river to the Norns, their path and Thor's should intersect.

Bohdi scans the river. Framed on both sides by high boulders, right now it is about as wide as a four-lane highway and so slow moving, it mirrors the sky. As he watches, a reflection of a dark cloud slips across the river's surface from the south up toward where Amy is drinking.

Bohdi blinks. The wind is from the east... "Amy! Get back!" he shouts, raising the branch with both hands.

Amy skitters backward on her hands like a crab, just as something lurches out of the shallows, making angry slurping noises.

The creature comes up to about Bohdi's chest. It's roughly hominid but has a face like a snapping turtle and a carapace on its back. The crown of its head is inverted, like a dinner plate. With a gurgly growl, it snaps its jaws and flexes spindly claws at the ends of its too-long arms. With a yell, Bohdi whips the branch around and knocks the creature in the side of the head. It staggers back a half step and then comes forward with an angry snap. Bohdi jams the end of the branch in its face. The smoldering end hits the creature's skin with a long hiss and a cloud of steam. The creature gives an anguished cry and plunges into the water, just as another pops out of the river.

Springing to her feet, Amy says, "There are at least two more along the bank."

With a snarl, Bohdi jams the tree limb into the second creature's jaw. It screams and dives back into the shallows and streaks away. Bohdi smirks. The bastards don't like fire.

A shape streaking toward them from the left catches his eye. Twirling the hot end of the branch in his hand, he jams it into the approaching creature. Crying in agony, it veers into the water.

Bohdi almost laughs. He has an odd sensation—the same adrenaline rush he gets when he's at the end of a run, when he feels like he's flying. His mouth tastes like metal. He'd swear his vision has become sharper, his hearing more acute.

From the boulders around them, angry gurgles sound. Bohdi raises his eyes. Peeking out of the rocks are at least twelve more of the creatures.

"Run for it?" Amy suggests.

Frowning, Bohdi pauses. "Thinking about it…" Running will leave their backs exposed. Taking a step forward, he swings the branch experimentally. As it whistles through the air, the creatures draw back.

He might smile at them. Or maybe he sneers.

A gust of wind ruffles the back of his head, bringing with it the smell of burning trees and vegetation. The creatures give a few nervous clicks with their snapping-turtle jaws. One breaks away and dives into the river. The others stare at Bohdi and Amy, and then—almost in unison—turn and bolt from the boulders to the river, disappearing into the slow moving current, leaving only a few angry waves in their wake.

Spinning the branch around, Bohdi exclaims, "What were those?"

"Kappa," says Amy. Her voice takes on a slightly distant air. "They were in Japan back in the days of the Heian

Empire…Loki and Thor helped clean them out…"

Bohdi frowns as he looks out at the water. One more nasty to look out for. "The smell of fire scared them away," Bohdi says, almost absentmindedly. He feels loose and a little strung out, as though he's spent some time out of his body and is just coming back to it.

"You're really good at this," Amy says softly, from behind him.

Flushing at what must be a compliment, Bohdi ducks his head. Good at what? Staying alive? "You saved me from being a spider snack," he says. And she had refused to let him go when he was falling… He still feels weird about that.

As he turns to her, Mr. Squeakers runs up her arm to sit on her shoulder. Face flat and unreadable, she says, "You're better with a stick."

Bohdi looks down at the branch in his hand. Is he? "In boot camp, we trained with pugil sticks." Bohdi had been decent at it, but had gotten verbally reamed for cracking jokes… How did you not joke about giant Q-tips?

Idly scratching, Mr. Squeakers' head, Amy's eyes on him don't waver. "Huh."

He gets the disturbing feeling like she's looking through him, not at him. The wind whips around them, settling into a southwest direction. Running a hand through his unruly bangs, Bohdi says, "We better move."

Nodding, Amy turns from the bank. Shifting the branch in his hand, Bohdi follows.

They make their way to a trail they'd found earlier. It follows the river and is wide enough to walk side by side. What sort of creature makes a path wide enough to walk side-by-side? Bohdi's stomach flutters and he glances up. Still no happy hammer-toting alien in a physics-defying chariot in the sky…

A crash in the underbrush makes them both stop in their tracks. They turn toward the forest to their right. Bohdi's eyes go wide. A cat-like thing the size of a tiger is slinking through the forest not twenty feet away. It has huge canines protruding from its jaw. His hand tightens on the branch. "Is that…"

"A saber-toothed tiger," Amy whispers.

The cat lifts its head briefly in their direction, flicks its ears, and then continues on its way.

Bohdi stands slack-jawed. A creature that doesn't think they'd make a tasty snack?

Beside him, Amy says, "It's running from the fire. I've heard of predators and prey animals taking shelter together during natural disasters."

Above their heads come eerie calls. Bohdi looks up to see a flock of large crane-like birds flapping above the trees, heading south.

Without a word, Amy and Bohdi start walking again, but at a slightly faster pace. The thin fern-like trees still predominate in the forest. But they begin to see trees with trunks as thick as a small car, soft, velvety-red bark, and tree tops with dark green leaves that spread out like giant mushroom caps. In the next hour, they see more animals: a bear, some deer, and even a unicorn. At one point, a pack of large slender wolf-like things with spikey lizard-like tails lopes onto the path in front of them; they barely glance at Bohdi and Amy before trotting away.

Bohdi's stomach is growling for food; he's sore and tired, and he feels…amazing. He's walking side-by-side with fierce and magical creatures in an exotic alien landscape. Bohdi feels like he's connected to something larger than himself—something that is everything, the animals, and the alien world they inhabit. He steals a sidelong glance at Amy. Her chest is heaving, and she has streaks of soot on her face. Her eyes are wide, her full lips slightly parted—not in fear, but a look of wonderment. He feels a connection to her, too. He reaches out and almost takes her hand. And then he realizes it's all a lie in his head, probably brought on by lack of sleep and adrenaline. He has to kill it.

"So," he says, feeling a wave of bitterness he can almost taste, "I know why you are trying to find Loki, and why Thor's trying to find Loki, but why is Odin trying to find Loki?"

Not meeting his eyes, Amy huffs. "You don't know why I'm looking for Loki."

He's broken the spell and made her angry already. "Sure I do," he says, lifting his chin. "He's your boyfriend."

Casting him a glare, she says, "As you pointed out, he may be a she." Looking away she adds, "And possibly not even hominid."

Bohdi gives her a knowing grin. "But you hope he's a he."

Her cheeks redden. Bingo. She's here looking for a ghost. He frowns.

Quickening her steps, she says, "What I want, what I hope, doesn't matter. I have to find him...her...it..."

"Why?" Bohdi needles.

Slowing, Amy exhales. Jaw tight, she says, "He has to know the truth."

"Which is?"

Amy stops, and turns to him. "Are you Hindu?"

Bohdi shrugs. "Who knows what I was? But cow is delicious." He grins.

Rolling her eyes, Amy says, "In Hinduism, there is a trinity: Krishna, the preserver; Brahma, the creator; and Shiva—"

"The Destroyer," Bohdi supplies. He gives her a tight smile. "Hoping it would help me remember anything, I went through a phase where I investigated Indian religions."

Leaning closer, Amy says, "Then you know Shiva is also the transformer. Destruction isn't necessarily evil... The Hindu tradition isn't black and white like Christianity."

Bohdi's lips quirk. He loves poking holes in blanket statements like that. Clearing his throat, he says, "To everything there is a season...A time to kill, and a time to heal; a time to break down, and a time to build up."

Amy blinks.

His lips slip into a smile. "Ecclesiastes, King James Version." He looks at the smoky sky. "I did paraphrase a bit..."

Amy gives up a sigh and then starts walking. "Fine. The point is, the concepts of creation, preservation, and destruction are all equal, all necessary, and in balance, all good."

Falling into step beside her, Bohdi says, "I'm not going to argue about that, but what does this have to do with finding Loki?"

Not looking at him, Amy says, "He needs to know that he's not evil, that he isn't just a destroyer...Odin won't tell him." She stops again and looks at Bohdi. "The next Loki has three choices." She holds up a finger. "He can be a tool of Odin." Raising a second finger she says, "He can be an agent of pure chaos, bringing about senseless destruction without meaning or purpose." Holding up a third finger she says, "Or he can be a transformer—like he was for us when he transformed Cera and saved our universe."

Scratching the stubble on his chin, Bohdi mulls her words.

And then he snorts. "He killed himself transforming Cera…" Shaking his head, he says, "Those are all shitty choices, Amy."

Amy exhales. "I know…but being a tool is the worst…"

Quirking an eyebrow, Bohdi says, "I guess it would depend on what you were being used to do. I mean, technically, we're all tools. I'm a tool for the FBI, I hack into their systems to make them more secure—" He grins wickedly. "Well, no I hack into their systems because it makes the tech guys in D.C. go ballistic, but the end result is the same."

Amy huffs. "Odin used Loki to destroy his problems."

Bohdi remembers pictures of bodies strewn about Loki's apartment after Steve's old boss sent in a SWAT team. "Like an assassin?" he says, his voice becoming hushed. Steve's old boss was an ass, but the guys on the SWAT team probably thought they were doing the right thing.

Amy shivers. "Sometimes. But sometimes it was more mental…Loki was, is…" she blinks. "…probably every time, very clever. When there were problems that Odin couldn't solve, he'd call in Loki."

"Problems like?" Bohdi probes.

Amy smiles tightly. "Like any change that was a threat to Odin's power."

Loki peers from behind Odin's shoulder as the Allfather sits upon his throne. He hasn't been here since before the incident with Rind, before he went to Aegir's feast and was implicated in the death of a servant, and before he went to the cave as punishment for two hundred years.

Loki's life before the cave seems like a dream. Sometimes he wonders how much of what he remembers is real, what is imagined, and what he hopes he imagined. Maybe it is time that has softened Loki's memories of Odin and Rind. Maybe it is that Odin showed him mercy during his imprisonment, giving Sigyn a magic bowl that caught the snake venom bathing the cavern. Or maybe it is that Odin has been kind and attentive, since Loki's punishment ended—perhaps time, and Loki's penance in the cave allowed the Allfather to forgive Loki for Baldur's death.

Whatever, Loki doesn't feel the same anger he did to the Allfather. But he doesn't feel the same love, the same reverence he always hid with irreverence, either. He feels hollow as he stands behind the Allfather. An actor just playing his part.

Freyja, the Vanir princess humans call the Goddess of Love, Beauty, and War, is kneeling before Odin's throne. Long ago, she came to live among Asgardians, and long ago, Asgard accepted her as one of their own. As always, she is surrounded by her magic's pink glow. After two hundred years with nothing to do but practice magic, Loki doesn't have to concentrate to see auras.

Odin, in his own aura of black, holds up a scroll given to him by Freyja. The Allfather is flanked on either side by the twelve members of the Diar, the judges that help him rule the Nine Realms. The hall is lined with his Einherjar warriors.

Freyja is flanked by her husband, Ord, twelve of her own Einherjar warriors, and twelve Valkyries, all unarmed.

While Loki was locked up, Freyja's influence grew exponentially. Even Sigyn and his sons seem to be in her thrall now. Loki thinks Freyja is vain and violent, and if she were in Odin's place, it wouldn't be an improvement. Sigyn says that any change in Asgard is an improvement. Loki likes to counter by saying, "Really? Shall I invite His Majesty Sutr, King of the Fire Giants through the front gates?"

To which Sigyn usually replies by throwing inanimate objects at him.

As he stands behind the throne, Loki remembers the last time he fought with Sigyn. It ended with Loki on his knees—literally. He sighs happily.

A member of the Diar clears his throat and raises an eyebrow in Loki's direction.

On the throne, Odin rolls the parchment back into a scroll. Loki had a brief glimpse at its contents. Freyja would like to see the Diar expanded to include Einherjar, Valkyrie, and Vanir members. "We will consider your suggestions—"

"They are demands!" *one of the Diar snaps. And it's true. Freyja's entourage is unarmed, but if Odin were to arrest them, it could trigger wide-scale riots among the populace, and incite rebellion among the Valkyries, at least half the Einherjar, and the Vanir that live in Asgard.*

"Suggestions," *Freyja corrects with a smile that is just the perfect amount of confidence without being cocky. It is a beautiful, artful bit of politics. Loki doesn't remember Freyja being this subtle before his time in prison.*

"Precisely," *says Odin, without raising an eyebrow.*

"As you can see, these changes do not benefit me directly; they are for Asgard's benefit," *Freyja says.*

Loki rolls his eyes. Freyja's primary interest has always been Freyja.

Giving a tight smile, Odin says, "Then I thank you for them." *Loki feels a shiver down his spine at the lie, but he does grudgingly admire Odin for his diplomacy.*

"When shall we convene again, Allfather?" *Freyja asks with an incline of her head.*

Dipping his chin, Odin says, "Give us one week to consider your…suggestions…"

Angry murmurs rise from the Diar, and hopeful smiles flit across the faces of Freyja's entourage.

The smiles remain on the faces of her supporters as Freyja leaves Odin's audience. As soon as she is gone, there is a lot of shouting among the old men who make up Odin's judges. The Diar argue her plans are just the first step—she'll see herself elected as the leader of the council, and then who knows?

Looking bored, Odin hears them out, and then dismisses everyone but Loki.

Bohdi has to lean in to hear Amy as she recites the story. Her voice is hushed—and sometimes she stops and blushes.

"...Instead, he invited Loki back to his library," says Amy, her voice drifting off. Amy stops and lifts her head to look at Bohdi. "Did you hear that?"

"No. Are we getting to the interesting part, yet?"

Amy looks into the forest beyond the trail but then begins to walk and resume her story. "Odin knew that Freyja's ultimate aim was to make herself elected leader of the Diar—and to see the Diar's influence increase so that its power would rival his own. He wanted to put an end to her plans...but he couldn't confront her directly because she was so well loved."

"Why?"

Amy huffs. "I'm getting to that. So, during Loki's time in the cave, there had been three dwarf goldsmiths who'd come to Asgard and offered Freyja a magical necklace that would make everyone fall in love with her and make her the most beautiful woman in the world—yadda yadda. But they'd only give it to her if she slept with them."

Bohdi perks up. "Sleep with them all at once—or one at a time?"

Amy's mouth falls open. "Loki didn't know." Dropping her head, she mutters. "But that is the first question he asked…"

Bohdi snickers. "And are dwarves proportional or—"

Amy's face goes beet red. "Oh God, dwarves have a saying about that."

Heh. Bohdi bites his lip and grins. "Which is?"

Smacking a hand to her face she says in a sing-song-recital voice. "Like in their stature, what dwarves lack in height they made up in girth."

Bohdi guffaws. Amy meets his eyes and laughs, too. There's something so adorable about the way she's a little embarrassed but divulged that bit of info anyway. She's curious, like he is, just maybe a little more discreet. His laughter dwindles. What did he expect? A prude, the God of Mischief's girlfriend? Of course not. He almost sighs aloud.

"Anyway, Freyja said no to the dwarves…"

Bohdi frowns. "Wait…no… Now the story is boring again!"

Rolling her eyes, Amy says, "No, you see, Odin knew she had to have been lying, that she must have said yes—that's why everyone was so smitten with her."

"How did he know?" Bohdi asks.

"I don't know… He just did. Anyway, he needed proof though, and he couldn't find the necklace—not with Heimdall, or with his ravens, or from maids he bribed into spying on her, so he needed Loki to find it and prove to all of Asgard, that Freyja—" she waves a hand, and her jaw goes tight.

Bohdi lifts an eyebrow. "So was extramarital sex such a

big deal or—"

Amy sighs. "Not so much, not for warriors anyway, even if they were women. But an Asgardian with a dwarf…yeah. Big no, no."

Bohdi looks to the side of the trail. In the forest, a few dozen feet away is one of the columny things; it makes his chest tighten a bit. Somewhere in the distance he hears a crash, like a tree falling.

Trying not to think of the columns and what he saw before, Bohdi says, "Loki never had sex with dwarves?"

"Um…" says Amy.

"I mean he wasn't exactly known for being…" Bohdi catches his mouth too late.

Giving him a tight smile, Amy supplies. "Discriminating?"

"Well…" Bohdi clears his throat. "Not all the time."

Narrowing her eyes, she says, "Don't you dare bring up the story about the horse."

"Errrr…" Well, damn. Throwing up his hands, Bohdi says, "No! I would never do that!"

"Did you hear something?" Amy says, turning away from him.

"No I—"

The sound of laughter, high pitched and light like a small child's, rolls along the trail. It rings above the rustle of the wind in the tree leaves. The hairs on the back of Bohdi's neck rise.

"Where's it coming from?" Amy says, looking into the forest.

Eyeing the forest nervously, Bohdi's voice drops to a whisper. "You know, so far, we've run into giant spiders, dragons—"

"Archaeopteryxes," says Amy, standing on her tiptoes and peering over Bohdi's shoulder.

"—and crazy mutant ninja turtles. I don't care what it sounds like; whoever is making that noise is trouble."

Falling back to her heels, Amy bites her lip. The laughter rings again. She swallows and looks down. "You're probably right."

Gripping the branch more firmly, he whispers, "Come on." Leading the way, he moves carefully down the trail, trying not to think of the columns that spin their way into the sky on either side of them. Although they are set back from the trail, even at a distance, they cast tiny rainbows of light here and there in front of them. He swears the child's voice is getting louder, though the words are garbled and indistinct.

They pass beyond the columns, and he feels tension draining from him, the strange voice is getting fainter. He looks back at Amy.

…and sees empty trail.

The child's voice rings, light and happy. And then comes another voice, not in English, but definitely adult and male. It sounds vaguely familiar.

Bohdi darts back down the trail until he stands between the columns. To his right, he hears the man's voice, the child's, and then Amy's voice. "Hello?" With a gulp, he tears into the underbrush, following the voices. He hears Amy and the child. Amy seems to be speaking another language. The child sounds like it's laughing.

Twigs and leaves whipping at his body, he lunges into a clearing in front of one of the columns. Amy is standing with her hand pressed against the column's milky white surface. Bohdi doesn't see an expansive street scene in India. Instead, he's looking into an oval window—a tiny toddler in a green dress has her hand pressed against the window's glass. The little girl has bright red hair, deep blue eyes, and full lips. Except for the red hair, she's the spitting image of Amy.

Oh, no.

Bohdi runs forward. "No, Amy, she's not real."

Amy turns her head to Bohdi. Her eyes are wide. "You can see her? I couldn't see what you saw in the column."

"It doesn't matter," Bohdi says. "We have to go."

Taking her arm, Bohdi tries to pull her away. The toddler starts to cry.

Twitching her wrist out of his grasp, Amy says, "No, no, this is her magical ability, to cross universes. She must be using the magic in the column to amplify her own magic!"

"Actually," says a man's voice, American and East Coast-ish, "she's using the magic in the mirror to amplify her ability to see across universes."

The little girl sniffles. Bohdi's eyes flick up to the mirror. Kneeling behind the little girl is a man.

Reaching forward, the man flicks the mirror with a finger. Tall and thin, with rumpled ginger hair, pale skin, and gray eyes he could be anyone. But of course he's not.

Bohdi's heart sinks in his chest, and the hand that he'd unconsciously put on Amy's shoulder sinks to his side.

Laying her hands against the column, Amy whispers, "Loki!"

CHAPTER 11

Loki tilts his head, one eyebrow rising. It's an expression Amy associates with bemusement. "Where is your Eisa?" he says in English.

Amy's legs are shaking; she's vaguely aware of Mr. Squeakers crawling up onto her shoulder. "Eisa?" Her eyes drop to the little girl with red hair and big blue eyes. A beautiful little stranger. But she isn't a stranger...is she?

The little girl points in Squeakers' direction and giggles.

Amy's breath catches. Of course. There aren't just three universes. There are an infinite number. And surely, somewhere in that infinite number of possibilities, Loki didn't come into possession of Cera... He must have realized Amy was pregnant, and taken her someplace where she could get the type of medical care she'd need to carry a magical child.

"Eisa..." Amy whispers. "That is what we named her." Her fingers tremble against the column's surface.

In the Frost Giant language, the little girl says, "Mommy." And it's like being punched in the gut. Amy feels light-headed. Her hand reaches to stroke the child's cheek, but connects with only the cold, hard, surface of the column.

Loki flicks the mirror again. "There's no television in Jotunheim. But Eisa's ability and this mirror have worked well." A hint of the bemusement returns to his voice. "Go get your little girl. They'll entertain each other for hours... We can both have some time to relax."

Amy's mouth falls open. From behind her Bohdi's voice cracks. "Her little girl is dead."

Loki's eyes go wide; he draws his head back. "No..." His hands go to either side of the mirror and his face crumples. "No, no, that's not right. There is always another Eisa at the end of the line... It can't work any other way...I thought..."

"Is this some sort of sick entertainment to you?" Bohdi demands.

In the mirror, Eisa smiles and puts her hands over eyes. Opening her tiny fingers, Eisa giggles. "Peek-a-boo."

"Who are you?" Loki demands.

"Why don't you tell me?" Bohdi retorts.

Amy's eyes rise to Loki's. "Where are you?"

There is no smile on Loki's face now. "The land of King Utgard in Jotunheim. I destroyed the main gate from his realm to Asgard in exchange for sanctuary... Right now, you're off exploring his library." Voice hushed, he says, "In your universe?"

Amy shakes her head. "What happened to Cera?"

"Still on Earth," says Loki with a bitter smile. Laying a hand on Eisa's shoulder, he says, "I've put aside my plans to burn Asgard to the ground...for now." He leans close to the mirror, his eyes too bright. "What happened to Cera in your universe?"

Amy can't answer.

Bohdi does. "You destroyed Cera and yourself, saved all

our lives, and now we're trying to find your ass before Odin finds you first." His hand falls on Amy's shoulder, and she rises instinctively. When had she fallen to her knees?

"We have to go now, Amy," Bohdi says.

In the mirror, Eisa makes a whining noise. As though pulled by an invisible string, Amy leans down again, puts her hand to the glass, and the little girl smiles and covers her eyes.

"Where are you, Amy?" Loki asks.

"Nornheim," Amy whispers.

"Are you mad?" Loki shouts.

Amy lifts her gaze to his. Loki's scanning the world above her shoulder. "It's dark—you have to find shelter before nightfall, when the adze rise."

Eisa opens her hands and smiles at Amy. "I see you!" Eisa says in a sing-song voice, her cheeks making dimples as she smiles.

"Yes, you do," says Amy, her vision blurring with tears.

"Go!" says Loki.

Eisa giggles and hops, her red curls bouncing. "Peek-a-boo!"

"Come on, Amy," says Bohdi.

Shaking her head, Amy says, "It's only the smoke of the fire...we have time..."

"Amy," Loki says.

She lifts her eyes. A wry smile is on Loki's face. He touches the mirror. "You—the you in this universe—told me this was a bad idea." Shrugging, he sighs. "I'm not the so-called-god of well-thought-out choices."

Bohdi snorts.

"You must go," Loki says, his chin dipping, his voice low.

Amy reaches again for the column. "No...not yet. It's so

good to see you again." Even if her vision is swimming with unshed tears and she barely sees him at all.

"No, it's not. Not for you," Loki says. He picks up Eisa and deposits her behind him, even as the child squeals in fury.

Holding up a hand, Amy begs. "No, wait!"

But Loki is already pulling back his fist, and in another heartbeat his knuckles are connecting with the mirror's surface. The picture shatters into shards that slip to the ground. And then Amy is staring at the milky white surface of the column. It shimmers and she sees herself and Loki tangled beneath sheets and—

Suddenly, she is spun around. She's staring at wide brown eyes that are tinged red in Nornheim's pink light. "We. Have. To. Go."

Amy's heart is racing. She can feel her pulse pounding in her neck. In the distance, she hears what sounds like a tree crashing to the ground. Even through her tear-blurred eyes, she can see smoke rising beyond Bohdi. She knows it's warm, but her skin feels cold, she feels so empty...

"Amy?" Bohdi says.

Tears slide down her cheeks. Something she's learned over and over again, when your world falls apart, the only thing you can do is keep going.

Nodding, she says, "Yes, I..." She puts a foot forward, and her legs give out, but there's a hand already on her arm.

She's barely aware of Bohdi as he leads her from the underbrush and back onto the trail. Her body is shaking. Her mind is spinning. How had it happened? How had Loki lived?

She bites her lip—they'd almost gone to Vanaheim together. If only in her universe, Amy had been more enthusiastic about that plan, if they'd gone, and Loki had discovered

she was pregnant, he never would have abandoned her. She
sucks on her lip. No matter what he felt about her, he would
never abandon his own child.

Inhaling a sharp scent of burning ash, Amy closes her
eyes, relying on Bohdi to guide her, methodically willing her
feet to go forward.

There is no guarantee that the Loki she just saw loved
her—or if she was happy—or loved him, or...

She squeezes her eyes tighter. Of course she loved him,
she'd probably always love him a little bit. Once you loved
someone, could you ever stop? She takes a shaky step. Up
ahead there is a break in the clouds of smoke, a little pink
sunlight filters through.

Something in Amy's chest unwinds. But would she have
liked being with Loki? Would she have been happy? He never
saw her as an equal—how could he? He was ancient, and
magical. But more than that, could she respect him? Amy
thinks of Rind. Loki had felt betrayed, let down by Odin—
but he'd watched rape before and hadn't interfered. It was
something he found distasteful; but it was also something he
took for granted as just happening. Like torture. Even after
being tortured himself in Geirod's castle, he didn't think it
was wrong.

She searches her mind for the Frost Giant or Asgardian
equivalent for the phrase "human rights." It doesn't exit. Biting her lip, she lifts her head. Her eyes still prickle, but she is
feeling lighter, and her steps becoming surer.

...And then Amy thinks of Eisa's red curls bouncing, her
tiny fingers covering her eyes, and her legs almost give out
again. If not for Bohdi's arm in hers, she'd probably have
landed in the dirt. Putting a hand to her face, she wipes her

tears away and stumbles on the trail. "I'm sorry," Amy stammers, to Bohdi, or the Eisa in this universe that might have been, she's not sure. "I'm sorry..."

Voice tight, Bohdi says, "It's all right."

He's quiet for a few minutes. The only sounds the rushing of the wind through the trees and the falling timber in the distance.

And then out of the blue, Bohdi says, "What you saw... That was fucking awful."

Amy laughs. Well, it's more of a sob. "That is..." The perfect description of what just happened.

"Yeah," she manages to say. She begins to regain her feet. She doesn't let go of Bohdi's arm. For a few minutes, she forgot he was with her, but now she remembers, and she's grateful...for the arm, for his understanding. And she feels a little guilty. "Bohdi, what you saw in the column when we first got here..."

He shakes his head. "It wasn't as bad," he says, and says no more.

If he elaborated, Amy might have believed him. Beatrice says that each person has his or her own way of coping. Beatrice survived the Holodomor famine instigated by Stalin in the Ukraine, and would know. So Amy doesn't press. But she squeezes his arm.

She feels the wind rising behind her back. As if by some unspoken agreement, Bohdi's and her steps quicken. Bohdi briefly turns to look behind them. "We've got to put some distance between us and the fire...otherwise we're going to get smoked out of any shelter we find tonight."

Amy nods her head, and releases his arm. Without speaking, they half-jog half-walk down the trail.

Sitting on a boulder, Bohdi eats his portion of the protein bar Amy stowed in her pocket. At his feet is a tiny stream that intersects with the river just a few yards down the trail. The stream is too small to hide kappa.

He stares down at the last bit of the protein bar in his hand, but in his mind, he sees Loki putting his fist through the mirror. Up until that moment, Bohdi hadn't really believed Thor and Amy's story about Loki destroying Cera out of an act of supreme self-sacrifice. He's still not sure... still, the mirror...How dumb is it, to put your hand through a piece of glass? But it's also understandable on a gut level. In the mirror, Loki had seen Amy—his girl, in trouble—not even his girl, really, but close enough. He'd reacted, in a way that was kind of noble, if stupid...which makes Amy's quest to find him not quite as crazy as he thought...and that doesn't exactly make him happy.

"Sheesh, I thought I was the one who hated protein bars," Amy says.

Bohdi blinks at her. Sitting on a boulder beside him, she's licking the last bits of her ration off her fingers. Her eyes are dry, but they're still red rimmed.

"You've been glaring at it for the past three minutes," she says.

Standing up, he pops the last bite in his mouth and gives her a grin. "Aren't you glad I bought them now?"

"Aren't you glad I didn't eat it on the roof?" Amy counters, her lips curling into the barest hint of a smile.

He's glad she's not crying, but her mention of the roof

makes the smile drop from his face. That seems like a world away. He swallows the bit of food. It is a world away. The enormity of what he's done, where they are, suddenly catches up with him. He feels dizzy and short of breath. Or maybe that's the smoke in the air.

"Hey, you okay?" Amy says, coming to his side and putting a hand on his arm. Mr. Squeakers twitches his whiskers on her shoulder.

Shrugging her hand away he says, "We should probably get a move on."

Two creases appear on her brow, but she says, "Yes, right."

They set off down the trail in silence. The wind has picked up, and Bohdi's certain that the sound of trees falling in the fire's wake is louder. As they start to walk, Amy says, "Thank you...for the protein bar."

Not looking at her, Bohdi shrugs again.

"And thanks...for everything," she says softly. Bohdi hears a sniff beside him.

His eyes slide to the side, and he feels an uncomfortable lump form in his throat. Amy's wiping tears from her eyes again. A hopelessness he hadn't felt when facing giant spiders slips into his limbs.

"Ugh..." she groans, shaking her hand as though trying to shake away her tears. "This isn't the time for this." She swallows and her face crumples. "Whenever I think of Eisa..." Her voice trails off, and she turns her head away.

The little girl. Her little girl. Bohdi's never thought of himself as particularly sensitive, but he's seen how even Steve gets worked up about his kid. And Amy getting worked up over Eisa, well, maybe he likes to hope someone gets that worked up about him. He clears his throat. "Yeah, must have been like being hit with a brick." A painful collision with what might have been. Eisa might not be Bohdi's, but she was a kid, and as Steve would say, "cute, perfect, and oblivious in the way kids are."

Amy sniffles again and wipes her face.

What to do about this? Bohdi bites his lip. His hand seeks out his lighter in his pocket, and instead connects with a tissue. What an idiot he is! He has tissues, rumpled, possibly slightly used—but probably better than her sleeve.

"Hey," he says, pulling one out without looking.

Amy turns, looks down at his hand, and then groans. "Just when I think you're kind of okay…"

Rolling her eyes, she quickens her pace and steps ahead of him.

He looks down at his hand—and his eyes go wide. He just offered her Frieda's thong. He chuckles. "Whoops, that's probably unsanitary." He considers tossing it aside, but decides that would be littering. Nornheim is kinda pristine and it seems wrong to spoil its one redeeming feature.

Ahead of him, Amy spins around. "It's not just unsanitary, it's wrong!"

"Huh?" says Bohdi breaking into a jog to catch up with her. "I thought it was a tissue—"

"You don't get it, do you?" Amy says, turning her head to glare at him.

Get what? Bohdi's eyes slide to the side, and his mind draws a blank. "Errr…no?"

Beside him, feet thumping loudly along the path, Amy mutters, "Throwing trophies of your conquest around."

"Trophies of my conquest?" Bohdi says.

"The. Thong," Amy spits out, eyes focused too deliberately

straight ahead.

Pulling the thong out of his pocket again, Bohdi dangles the slip of pink satin on a finger. "This isn't a trophy."

Amy harumpfs. "Then why did you take it?"

Bohdi bites his lip. Should he...or shouldn't he... Oh hell, he's a United States Marine, he's allowed to be secure in his masculinity. He cackles. "I couldn't find my underwear so I borrowed hers!" He'd been in a bit of a rush. Frieda had gone off to the shower alluding to another round, and Bohdi had needed to make a quick escape.

Amy stops dead in her tracks.

Bohdi smiles and waggles his eyebrows. Bouncing the tiny piece of pink on his finger he says, "Girly satin is comfy." He sighs dramatically. "But unfortunately, this little bit of ribbon wouldn't provide even a lesser endowed male with support."

Amy's eyes go wide. Her gaze drops from his face to the waistband of his jeans. "So what are you—"

"Nothin'," Bohdi says, biting back a smirk.

Groaning, she turns and begins walking again.

Bohdi skips a step to catch up. "I didn't mean to take it after I realized how small it was, but when I left the hotel room, it was wrapped around my wrist, so I shoved it in my pocket—and then I forgot about it."

His skin heats. "Until Bryant accused me of lying."

Jaw clenched, Amy grinds out, "Throwing it was still wrong."

Perplexed, Bohdi scratches his head. "Why?"

Amy lets out a heavy sigh. "How would you like it if someone threw your underwear at work?"

Bohdi's smile drops. That's a big question. "Why are they throwing it?"

"Because they had sex with you, and you forgot and left it at their place...I don't know." The last words come out in a huff.

How would Bohdi feel about that?

"Well?" Amy says, hopping over a large root on the trail.

Bohdi taps his chin. "So everyone in the office would know I had sex?"

"Yes," Amy snips.

Bohdi laughs. "Awesome! You know, some people have strange ideas about Asian men."

Amy groans. "Okay, don't think how it would make you feel, think about how it would make the woman feel."

Bohdi purses her lips. There is a right answer to this question, if he thinks hard...

"Humiliated!" Amy says. "It's not fair, but there's a double standard, and yes she would feel utterly humiliated."

Bohdi's eyes widen, and then narrow as he recalls his night with Frieda. "Then she might actually like it."

"What?" says Amy, her nose wrinkling.

Bohdi shrugs. "Frieda, the owner of this..." He holds up the tiny slip of fabric. "...was totally into the humiliation thing."

Amy draws to a stop. Her hands go to her hips, and she glares up at him.

Stopping only long enough to give her a curt nod, Bohdi continues down the trail. "The only reason she was with me was because she got off on me being Steve's lowly minion."

Amy scampers as she catches up with him. "Did she call you his lowly minion?"

Bohdi nods again. "Yep."

"And you were okay with that?"

Bohdi shrugs. "She was hot."

"Who uses the words lowly minion?"

Bohdi stops short. That was a little weird. Shaking his head, he starts walking again. "Look, some people like a lot weirder stuff, I'm not here to judge. As long as there are no clown outfits, or scat, or…"

"Stop, I get the idea!" Amy says.

Bodhi stuffs the thong back into his pocket and readjusts the branch he's carrying in his hand. "So anyway, yeah. Frieda was totally into the humiliation thing. She made me tell her over and over again what a bad girl she was, and then she flung herself across my lap and made me spank her." Grimacing, he adds, "It was kind of a lot of work. I dunno if the payoff was worth it…even though she was hot. I hurt my hand, my arm got tired, and I had to use my belt, and then…"

"I don't believe this," Amy mutters.

"That some people enjoy being humiliated? It's just a game, it's not how they are in real life…"

"No!" says Amy.

Bohdi scowls, disappointed. "That's very closed-minded of you, Amy. It's true. Humiliation turns some people on, and judging…" He tsks.

"I'm not being judgmental! I just can't believe you're telling me how you spanked her with your belt!" Amy cries, putting both hands to her face. She groans. "Believe me, I know some people like to be humiliated."

Bohdi's feet slow. It would probably be in bad form to ask how she knows. He bites his tongue. Literally. It's the only way he can keep his mouth shut.

In front of him, Amy sighs. "Freyja…Loki had to find a way to get into her home to find the necklace…"

The morning in Asgard is misty and cool. Loki snaps his fingers. In the cave, he'd learned how to split water molecules into hydrogen and oxygen. A small flame sputters to life at the tip of his thumb, fed by the humid air. He hasn't learned how to control his temper.

His jaw clenches. If he didn't love his sons so much, he'd kill them. Apparently, Heimdall has overheard Nari and Valli discuss much more radical changes than expansion of the Diar. Unlike Freyja, Nari and Valli don't pose a credible threat to Odin's power, but Odin could have them tried for treason.

Odin has offered Loki a bargain—find Freyja's necklace, destroy her reputation—and Nari's and Valli's crimes will be forgotten and forgiven.

Snapping his fingers again, Loki feels the bite of flame on his skin. Scowling, he remembers asking the Allfather how exactly he was supposed to sneak into Freyja's chambers. Freyja has cats. Two of them. The humans speculate that they pull her chariot. That is ludicrous, of course. Convincing even just two cats to work as a team is beyond even Freyja's considerable magical skills. They do, however, have keen noses for enchantment. If Loki were to try and sneak into her chambers invisibly, they'd be all over him, alerting her guards to his presence.

The only solution is to be invited into Freyja's hall. When Loki reminded Odin of that fact, the Allfather replied, "Get yourself invited the same way you have always gotten yourself invited."

Loki felt his skin heat in rage.

Odin cocked an eyebrow. "What, are you worried about Sigyn finding out?"

Loki's jaw tensed. Odin snorted.

Sigyn had changed during Loki's time in the cave. She'd taken up with the Valkyries as soon as the boys were able to fend for themselves, learning for herself the art of combat. She'd also begun studying the rapidly evolving cultures and happenings on Earth. She regularly advised Freyja on where to find new candidates for the Einherjar. And although the Aesir rarely heard prayers from humans anymore, when they did, they went to Sigyn to learn how to walk among the mortals without drawing undue attention.

The woman who had so tenderly and loyally cared for Loki for two hundred years had become ferocious—mentally and physically. How could Loki not adore her? How could he not fall in love with her all over again?

Also, with the boys out of the house, the sex that had been good before had become fantastic.

"Just make sure Sigyn doesn't find out," Odin suggested. Leaning closer to Loki, with a slight sneer on his face, he added, "Believe me, Freyja isn't likely to croon about your activities now that she has Ord." Odin's expression had gone dark. "Her relationship with him and the birth of their daughters has only increased her respectability. Now people see her as having more important concerns than laying men or slaying them."

Loki snaps his fingers once again. Flames bite his skin again, jolting him from the memory. In front of him, Ord himself comes striding through the mist. Ord was only half grown when Loki went to the cave, but he's grown into a man who is generically handsome—tall, broad of shoulder, blond, blue eyed, with a square jaw. He is fierce and respected on the battlefield, earning the respect of all the warriors. Off the battlefield, he is humble, funny without being offensive, genial, kind to children, courtly with women, and overall quite popular.

Loki dislikes him on principle. With a nod in Ord's direction, he graces the soon-to-be-cuckolded man with a smirk.

Ord stops short. But instead of hurling the expected insult, he offers his hand in Loki's direction. Dipping his chin, Ord says almost shyly, "Loki, Thor has told me about your quest to find Gungnir, and of the humans you saved from trolls and kappa." He shakes his head almost apologetically. "I am sorry to have been too young to join you."

Somewhat in shock, Loki takes the proffered hand. Ord shakes it warmly and puts his other hand on Loki's shoulder. "I look forward to fighting beside you someday. Thor has told me many times of your cunning."

Surprisingly, Loki detects no lie.

Odin has said that, besides the magic necklace, Ord is Freyja's greatest asset in her quest for political power. For the first time, Loki understands why. Ord's likeability is infuriating.

Loki smiles as genuinely as he can. Smiling back as though Loki has just bestowed upon him a great honor, Ord gives Loki a thump on the shoulder, and with a reverent nod, walks away.

Loki's nostrils flare in annoyance as soon as Ord is out of sight. For all his niceness, the other man has made Loki's quest too easy. When he approaches Freyja, shooting arrows with machine-like precision into a distant target, Loki knows exactly what to say.

As she nocks an arrow in her bow, Loki smiles. "I just met your husband. He is quite charming."

Freyja is rarely the same woman twice. She changes her appearance to suit her and her lovers' fancies—it's a skill she had even before coming into the possession of the dwarven magical necklace. Today she is wearing the guise of a blonde, blue-eyed

Aesir beauty. At Loki's words, she smiles triumphantly and lets her arrow fly into the target.

As she nocks another arrow, Loki slips up behind her and whispers in her ear. "But such a shame that he doesn't know how depraved you can be. He doesn't know how to punish you, does he?"

Freyja trembles, and the arrow flies wide.

"What do you want, Loki?" Freyja whispers.

"To help you, of course," Loki says.

Turning to face him, Freyja licks her wide pink lips, and Loki knows he's won, and he hates her for it. He hates the whole situation—Nari and Valli at Odin's mercy, Odin's machinations, the jeopardy he's putting his relationship with Sigyn in.

He doesn't really want to have sex with Freyja, but he finds he really wants to hurt her, more than he ever had in any of their games before.

For a few heartbeats, she says nothing, and then she whispers. "Meet me at my home in an hour." Pulling another arrow from her quiver with shaky hands, she returns her gaze to the target. She lets the arrow fly...and her aim once more is true.

"So," Bohdi says, walking down the trail beside Amy. "Freyja, the kick-ass Goddess of War—"

"And Love and Beauty," Amy supplies, scowling a little at him for interrupting.

"—was a bit of a masochist and maybe into a bit of humiliation?" Bohdi says. Waving the branch in his hand, he says, "Kind of fits my theory that the high-powered people like that sort of thing." Pulling the thong out of his pocket, he swings it around his finger. "Frieda was a beautiful, high-powered, lawyer type. She'd be extra humiliated if she knew everyone knew that she slept with lowly minion me."

"You still shouldn't be throwing underwear around!" Amy snaps.

Bohdi blinks at her. His face is the picture of befuddlement. Amy feels her skin heat.

"It creates a hostile work environment!"

Bohdi purses his lips and looks to the side. "Technically, I wasn't at work when I—"

Ignoring the semantics, Amy puts her hands on her hips. "Even if you didn't take it as a trophy—even if you just stole it—"

Drawing his head back, Bohdi holds up the slip of fabric. "It wasn't stealing, I worked for this. Smacking a woman's ass until you think your hand will bleed is—"

Skin heating, Amy shouts, "The perception will be that you see women as objects, as conquests, as less than human!"

Bohdi's eyes widen. "Really?" He slips the underwear hastily back into his pocket.

Amy vaguely registers the look of obliviousness on his face. But she's furious. And maybe Loki's flashbacks are gnawing at her. "It is threatening! You don't get it. You don't know what it's like to be surrounded by people who are stronger than you, who see you as a sexual object, as not one of them, as a lesser being…" She remembers Odin, This is what women are made for. In the United States, they've moved so far from that, but she feels like maybe there is a precipice, and with one wrong step, society could fall back over the edge.

Stopping in his tracks, Bohdi's jaw goes hard, and he pulls his lighter out of his pocket. "Yes, as a skinny underrepresented minority in the Marine Corps, I wouldn't know anything about that."

Amy's feet and her thoughts stumble to a stop. She feels the sickening sensation of being in the wrong; it wraps around her insides and cuts off her ability to breathe. Hadn't she once read that most victims of sexual assault in the military are male? Before she's recovered herself, Bohdi is already walking away.

Running to catch up, Amy stammers, "I'm sorry."

He waves the hand with the lighter and doesn't meet her eyes. "It's okay."

Half jogging to keep up, Amy says, "No, really, I'm…"

Swiveling to face her, Bohdi says, "Just drop it…" His hands fist and his lips curl dangerously. She opens her mouth to speak, but Bohdi cuts her off again. "It's okay. I beat the living shit out of them. And that's all I want to say about it."

With a dismissive shake of his head, he turns and begins to walk again.

Limbs heavy, Amy, looks up at the sky. It's getting darker. She squints. And the darkness is not because of smoke. Night is coming.

CHAPTER 12

The alley is lit by dull orange streetlights. The dive bar Nat brought Bohdi to has cheap beer, and amazing mojitos, but the bathroom makes him gag before he's even entered... so he slips out the back door—the alley it is. He's just finished up when he hears familiar voices. A group of three guys turns around the corner. He hears someone say something about, "You sure that shit you got will keep this from showing up on a piss test?"

There's a laugh, and a "Yeah, man. Trust me. It's taken care of."

Not acknowledging them, Bohdi turns to the door. His hand finds the doorknob, he turns it, pulls—and it doesn't budge. Bohdi turns his head. That is a mistake.

"Hey," says one of the silhouetted shadows at the mouth of the alley. "Don't I know you?"

Bohdi reaches into his pocket for his knife, hoping to jimmy the lock. His pocket is empty.

Three silhouetted forms come closer, floating in a cloud of strange, acrid-smelling smoke. "Bohdi Patel," says the largest, and then laughs. The laugh is familiar. What isn't familiar is the way Gonzalez is tapping his hand on his thigh in an uneven staccato rhythm, head bobbing not quite in sync. Every muscle in Bohdi's body tenses.

Bohdi's met a few men in the Corps who prefer men. They've come out to him quietly, maybe hopefully. But when he'd expressed no interest they hadn't pressed. Tyrone Gonzalez isn't one of those men.

Tyrone Gonzalez will tell you he "Ain't no fag." He'll also tell you, that if there aren't any women around, fucking a man up the ass is "acceptable." He's said Bohdi has "pretty eyes," and "skinny little girl hips."

Straightening his shoulders, Bohdi gives a curt nod and tries to maneuver between Tyrone and his buddies. Tyrone's hand shoots out and stops him. "What's your hurry? I haven't seen you in a while...What's your MOS?" says Tyrone, using the slang for the schooling all Marines get after infantry training.

Throwing Tyrone's hand off of his shoulder, Bohdi says, "EOD."

Tyrone laughs and briefly turns to his friends. "See, *smart* and pretty."

Bohdi takes the opportunity to try and walk away again. But Tyrone physically steps between him and the exit to the alley. One of Tyrone's buddies steps forward, the other hangs back.

Bohdi holds his ground, afraid if he takes a step back, he'll literally wind up against the wall. Tyrone's hand comes back to his shoulder. He squeezes hard enough for it to hurt. Bohdi's mind spins. Tyrone's about his height, but he's broader and it's all lean meat. They were in boot camp together. Bohdi's seen him fight. His eyes slide to Tyrone's companions. The one cornering him is only slightly leaner.

Tyrone snaps Bohdi's attention back to him with a laugh. "You're still as pretty as I remember. Look at those eyes!" He brings his hand up to briefly touch Bohdi's cheek.

Bohdi's lip curls. Not flinching away, he bats his eyelashes. "Really, you think so?"

Tyrone's eyes widen. Turning to his buddy, he says, "See, I knew it."

Bohdi leans back, and Tyrone turns his head again—

And Bohdi is frozen in place. He can't move. He feels like his lungs are choked. Tyrone laughs and...

Bohdi wakes up to darkness and coughs out a lungful of smoke. For a moment, he has no idea where he is. He's back in the alley unable to move.

He brings a hand to his face. Something hard and rough bites through the back of his shirt. The ground is uneven, and slightly soft. No, he's in Nornheim, sitting with his back to a tree. And back in that alley, he hadn't been frozen. He'd head-butted Tyrone hard enough to break his nose, then stepped back and dropped into a crouch just in time to dodge the fist that Tyrone had aimed at his head. Tyrone had driven his hand into a brick wall. On the ground, Bohdi had found a glass bottle.

Bohdi's breathing comes fast and quick, smoke tickling on the way down.

He doesn't remember the sequence of events after that. He remembers the third guy screaming, "I don't want no trouble, I don't want no trouble!" He remembers the glass bottle shattering and driving the sharp end of it into the face of Tyrone's buddy. He doesn't remember when he knocked Tyrone to the ground. He doesn't remember if his foot connected with

Tyrone's head, but he remembers winding up to kick it. He remembers Nat screaming, light streaming from the bar's back door, and then Nat, her girlfriend, and some other guys dragging Bohdi off Tyrone.

Bohdi shakes in the darkness and stifles a cough. It's the first time he's had a nightmare about the actual attack. He's only had nightmares about being convicted and sent to prison.

He puts his head between his hands. Steve is the only person who knows about it. He feels a flare of indignation in his gut. He hates Amy for making him bring it up—making him remember. Lifting his eyes, he watches a glowing ember waft by. He hears a snapping sound, like flags in a strong breeze. He sits up straighter, the nightmare of the dream giving way to the nightmare of reality. He was supposed to be on watch. He looks through the brush and can see the forest fire's orange light. It's much too close.

Turning, he finds Amy leaning on the tree trunk beside him. "Amy, wake up!" he whispers.

She sits up with a start.

"We have to go," he says, finding his branch in the darkness.

She doesn't ask questions.

Nornheim's three moons are obscured by tree limbs and smoke. The light from the fire is behind them, and they stumble together in their own shadows and the shadows of the trees. When they'd chosen a spot to rest and hide, they'd moved off the main trail away from the river.

Leaning close, Amy whispers, "Do you think we should use our—"

A screech rises above the crackling of the fire and the rush of leaves; it makes every hair on Bohdi's body stand on end.

He feels Amy's hand on his side. "Adze," she whispers.

Shivering, Bohdi remembers the murderous, sexless creature that seemed incapable of feeling pain.

And then another sound reverberates through the darkness. Deep and hoarse, it sounds a little like the lowing of a cow. Without seeing the animal, or even knowing what it is, Bohdi knows it is a cry of anguish. The screams of the adze intensify; the sound of hooves, and more cries of pain and fear, rise in the night.

Above their heads, Bohdi hears branches crack. There are furious snarls, and a writhing thing with two sets of wings, four arms and four legs, tumbles through the branches, lands about twenty feet from them, and rolls, hissing and spitting through the underbrush.

Bohdi's suddenly gripped by the shoulder and yanked behind a tree.

"What…?" says Bohdi, craning his head to look around the tree.

The hissing, spitting, rolling thing comes to a halt. A gust of wind whips through the trees, and there is a sudden bright burst of moonlight on the ground where two adze, hands at each others throats, wings ripped liked tattered sails, lie motionless, staring up at Amy and Bohdi with glowing eyes.

"Oops," says Bohdi.

The adze slip from their murderous embrace, and clamber to their feet with hair-raising screeches.

"Run!" says Amy, tugging again on his shoulder.

Bohdi hesitates, hand tightening on his club, considering the odds of beating two adze in a fight.

From the air come more screams.

"Running's good," says Bohdi, turning in Amy's direction.

He outpaces her in only a few strides. He wants to speed up, but that would mean leaving Amy, and some instinct as strong as the will to survive makes him slow down. Cursing, he grabs Amy's wrist and pulls her faster through the trees.

Twisting roots and rocks jut from the ground as it rises beneath their feet. Bohdi feels the muscles in the front of his legs start to burn as they stumble and crash uphill. He hears snarls behind them. Turning his head, he sees an adze twisting and hissing, its enormous wings caught in some low hanging branches.

Looking ahead, Bohdi sees some smaller trees growing very close together. He drags Amy in that direction, just managing to dodge an adze swerving out of nowhere inches from their heels.

Bohdi yanks Amy sideways through a narrow gap in the trunks, and pulls her into a sprint. A few seconds later, he hears a frustrated screech, and then a snarl. Glancing back, he sees two adze, one pinned between the tree trunks, another trying to claw its way over the first.

If he wasn't so busy being terrified for his life, he'd have laughed. Beside him, Amy looks too. Their eyes meet. Amy points to a narrow gap between two bushes, and they dart in that direction. Seconds after passing through the gap, they hear more frustrated snarls and hisses. They keep running without looking back.

When the only sound Bohdi can hear is the mad thumping of his heart and his own panting, they finally slow. Dropping Amy's hand, Bohdi bends over. "I think we lost them," he pants and looks eastward. Is that his imagination, or is it getting lighter?

Amy puts her hands on her knees and gasps. "I think I

hear the river."

He's about to say no, when he hears the sound of water on rocks. Before Bohdi can answer, she moves toward a gap in the trees. "Oh…" he hears her say.

Bohdi catches up to her and gazes over her shoulder. "Oh," he echoes, looking over her shoulder. In front of them there is a patch of barren rock leading to empty air. A few scraggly bushes grow in a shallow indentation right near the edge.

Amy goes forward in a crouch. And Bohdi follows. They kneel down together at the rock's gravelly edge and look down.

The outcropping they're on marks a bend in the river. Beneath them is a sheer slope that turns into a cliff just a few meters below. From there, it is a fifty-foot drop to where the river seethes and churns.

He looks eastward. The sky is definitely getting lighter. He feels a flush of relief that dies instantly when a distant scream echoes in his ears. He's just about to suggest they head back to the trees, when Amy says, "Look!"

He follows her gaze upriver. At first, Bohdi thinks he is seeing a giant wave with a dark cloud floating above it and fanning out in a wide circle over the banks.

"Adze must not be able to swim," Amy says.

Squinting, Bohdi peers at the approaching cloud. And then every muscle in his body tenses. What he took for a wave are elk-like animals, with four long, twisted horns, swimming downstream. The black cloud is the adze hovering above them. Here and there, one of the elk-creatures stumbles onto the bank and is immediately set upon by the swarm—they sink their teeth into the animals while they're still thrashing…but other times, an adze drops into the water and doesn't emerge.

"The herd jumped into the water to escape the swarm…" Amy says, voice drifting off.

Bohdi blinks at the fast approaching cloud of adze, haloed by the glow of the forest fire. Grabbing Amy's shoulder, he says, "Get back."

They start toward the forest, but the swarm is closing in too fast. "Under the bushes!" Amy whispers. Bohdi doesn't answer, just turns with her and dives beneath the low hanging branches, brambles biting his skin and tugging at his hair and clothes. Moments later, the cries of adze ring above their heads and the frantic lowing of the elk creatures echoes from the canyon below. Pressing his face and the smoldering head of the branch into the dirt, Bohdi swears the flapping of the adze wings stirs the branches above their heads.

They lie there for what seems like hours but is probably only minutes. At last, the sound of the adze cries grow fainter.

"I don't think they saw us," Amy says.

A breeze from the north ruffles Bohdi's hair. It smells like smoke. Lifting his head, he follows the swarm's path. They're now downwind. "We better go," he whispers.

"Yeah."

They've just clambered out when Bohdi hears a hiss from the trees. Looking behind them, he sees a single adze emerging from the forest, moonlight glinting on its bald head, ripped wings, and long, glinting teeth.

Raising his branch, much smaller than it was before, Bohdi shouts to Amy. "Stand back."

The adze bares razor-sharp teeth and snarls.

There is a sound of rocks sliding behind Bohdi, and Amy screams.

Bohdi turns his head…to see empty air. "Amy!" he shouts. "I'm here!" she calls.

The sound of claws on rock behind him is all the warning Bohdi gets. With a cry, he swings his body and the branch around. The adze is charging him, head lowered. With a snarl, Bohdi bludgeons it neatly on the side of the head. The creature drops sideways with the sound of crushing bone. Without another look, Bohdi runs in the direction where Amy stood moments before. Gazing down, Bohdi feels his heart sink. Amy is a few meters down the incline, Mr. Squeakers clinging to her hair. She's grabbed hold of a twisted little sapling growing on the steep slope. As he watches, her weight is causing the sapling's roots to slowly tear loose from their tenuous hold in the rock face.

"Hang on!" He cries, seeing a barely-there path winding down to where she is. "I'm coming."

She stammers. "I don't know if…"

Bohdi is already scampering down the slope, rocks and dirt sliding in his wake.

"The swarm!" she says.

Bohdi doesn't answer. He's almost to her…

The twisted tree she clings to drops lower, its roots jutting out of the slope face. The path Bohdi is taking melts in a small avalanche before his eyes. Amy gives a yelp and drops a few feet with the sapling. Her feet dangle in open air.

Casting aside the branch he's carrying, Bohdi flops down on his stomach. Slithering forward, he puts his weight on the tree's roots, hoping he can keep it from slipping further.

"They're coming this way!" Amy shouts.

Bohdi reaches forward and grabs her wrist.

Above his head, he hears a gurgling snarl.

Bohdi looks up to see an adze, one side of its face covered in dirt, the other side weird and lopsided, leering down at him. The one he hit? Shit. That had seemed too easy. Another adze's face emerges by the first. Oh fuck.

The sapling slips, its roots coming further upended, and digging into his ribs. Amy's hand slips, he grabs her wrist more firmly. And then the sapling, almost like a living thing, slithers from beneath him, slipping through the soft earth and into the river below. Grabbing hold of what is left of its root system, Bohdi just manages to keep Amy from sliding down with it.

"Let go!" she screams.

"No!" he snarls. She wouldn't let him go, how dare she ask him to?

"We have to fall!" Amy screams. "The swarm is coming!"

Bohdi gasps and looks in the direction the adze had flown. The cloud of adze is coming back in their direction fast; their blood curdling cries suddenly a chorus in his ears. They're so close he thinks he can see the whites of their eyes... How had he not heard?

Rocks slide down from above him. He looks up to see the hissing adze above begin to make their way down the slope, teeth bared and glowing dimly in the early morning light.

"Let go!" Amy screams again.

One of the adze above them lifts its wings and takes to the air, circling in a wide loop just a few meters above their heads.

Bohdi looks down at the turbulent river.

Amy shouts. "It's the only way!"

She's right. They might even survive the fall. Bohdi lets go of the roots he's clinging to. But not Amy's wrist. There is an angry shout from the adze above them, and louder screams from the swarm.

His eyes meet Amy's. He's falling with her, again. He feels the air whip around him, stirred by adze wings, and then there is the shock of hitting water, and he sinks into cold and darkness.

CHAPTER 13

Amy's mind is blank, all thoughts stolen from her by the shock of plunging beneath the river's cold dark surface. And then she is carried away in the blackness. Her eardrums feel like they will burst, and she can't decide what way is up. Panic rises in her as turbulent as the tide. Just as she thinks her lungs will explode, her feet connect with something solid, and she kicks. A moment later, she explodes through the surface, gasping, sinking, spinning around, and rising again with the current. Coughing and sputtering, Amy treads water. Her clothes are dragging her down, but she's afraid to stop the furious pumping of her limbs even for a moment. The shore-line is sweeping past her fast, and rushing water deafens her. Upriver, where she fell, adze are swooping down to the river's surface and pulling up, she can't hear their cries, but the looks on their faces are furious.

From behind her comes a frightened cheeping. Spinning with the current, she sees Mr. Squeakers on the roots of an enormous log only a few feet away. But where is Bohdi? Something dark catches her eye, bobbing on the surface. She reaches forward and her hands connect with smooth skin. She slips her arms underneath what she hopes are armpits, pulls, and finds herself staring at an armload of adze—its limbs unmoving, eyes open to the sky, mouth slack. With a gasp, she pushes the creature away. It quickly disappears beneath the surface.

Struggling to stay afloat herself, she hears a gasp and a sputter, spins again, and sees Bohdi just a few inches from Squeakers' log. A rush of gratitude to God or the universe or *something* shoots through her. She kicks in the direction of the log just in time to see Bohdi sink beneath the surface.

"Bohdi!" she screams, plunging her hand down. Her fingers connect with the collar of his shirt, and she feels herself going under. Throwing out her other hand, her fingers find a part of the log, slick, but firm. Pulling herself to the log with one hand, she yanks on Bohdi with the other, despairing that they're both already lost—she's too weak, she hadn't been strong enough in the chariot—but then Bohdi's head pops above the surface.

Mr. Squeakers cheeps in alarm. Amy's gaze is glued to Bohdi. His eyes aren't open. Pulling him toward her, she wraps her arm around his waist and spins him so he's in front of her. She tries to press him against the tree trunk but finds herself pressing him into the maze of the tree's root system instead. His body must be caught on a part of the tree beneath the surface, because she suddenly can't move him anymore. Sputtering, Amy slides beside him and nudges him deeper into the roots until his chin is resting on another root, just barely above water. His mouth is open, but she's not sure if he's breathing.

Mr. Squeakers' cheeping becomes frantic, and then suddenly the mouse is in her hair, his tiny feet scraping against her scalp. She looks up and sees the adze swarming above her.

One tries to land in the roots above her head. The tree must hit something, because a tremendous shock ripples through the log, and the adze slips off as the makeshift raft spins in the current. Instinctively, Amy squeezes Bohdi's stomach, and he heaves and coughs. She gasps in relief, but it's short lived. Three adze alight on the trunk of the log, the wind in their dragonfly wings making them list dangerously to the side—one topples into the water, but the other two drop to all fours and begin crawling forward, hanging on with the long, catlike claws of their feet and hands.

Amy pulls herself tighter to Bohdi with one arm. She can hear his breathing, ragged and strained. She feels his heart beating in his chest, and the warmth of his body through his thin clothes. Her other arm is trembling, and her fingers are burning, as she clings tightly to a root above, trying to hold them both just high enough to breathe.

Mr. Squeakers gives a cheep; Amy hears a hiss and sees an adze just a few feet away, its head pressed between two thick roots. Its skin is gray, its eyes are wide and unblinking, and they glow in the low light. It's completely hairless. It opens its mouth and Amy can smell decay in its long razor-like teeth. Hissing, it leans back and shoots an arm forward through the gap.

With a cry, Amy presses her face against Bohdi's head. She feels the air stir above her and the adze releases a furious snarl. Amy's whole body quakes. She wants to let go, take her chances with the current. But she finds she can't. Bohdi would die, and it's a relief and agony to know she can't let that happen. She hears a cry and realizes she's sobbing. The sky is almost black with adze, and their screams and the flapping of their wings is as loud as the river. Occasionally there is a splash and snarling as the adzes knock one of their own into the river.

There is a snap of wood, and pain races through the fingers holding to the root above. She hears a snarl that sounds almost like a chuckle. Fury wracks through her body; looking up between the roots she sees the adze licking its claws. She can't fight it; her hands are tied. Lips curling, tears streaming down her cheeks, she starts to shout. "Fuck you! Fuck you! Go to hell!" It's a hopeless waste of what little strength she has left, but it feels good somehow. Like she's telling off fate. The adze leans forward, sniffing the air. Amy spits at it and hits it squarely in the eye. She almost laughs as it draws back with a startled hiss.

Between the wings of the swarm, a bolt of pink light suddenly shines. The adze's cries of fury begin to change to cries of fear. The second adze on the log leaps into the air. The one sitting in front of Amy sits back on its haunches and stares at her. Amy squeezes Bohdi tighter reflexively, preparing for the creature to strike. But then it raises its wings and takes to the sky.

Amy drops her head to Bohdi's. She's suddenly aware how cold the river is. After a few minutes, she begins to carefully untangle herself and Bohdi from the tree roots.

CHAPTER 14

The log drifts and spins slowly with the increasingly lazy current. The forest fire rages on. By Amy's guess, it's less than half a mile north from them.

Even with all the smoke in the air, the sun is hot on Amy's back as she kneels over Bohdi's prone form. She has one knee between Bohdi's legs, and the other precariously perched on the sloping side of the log. They're very lucky it's one of the big trees they found. At some point, they'll have to worry about getting stuck in shallow water, but for now...

Amy takes a breath and runs her hand between Bohdi's shoulder blades and down his spine. Lying on his stomach, head draped over the side, he coughs. It's a horrible, wet choking sound. Some water spews from his mouth into the river.

Where he's tucked in her shirt, Mr. Squeakers gives a worried cheep.

Keeping her voice calm, patient, clinical, and steady, Amy rubs Bohdi's back and whispers, "That's it. Let it out."

Inside she's screaming, *Please, please, please, don't die.* Her hand stills on his spine. Beneath her fingers she can feel his muscles and bones drawn taught by the coughing spasm. She lifts her eyes. He's looking at a distant point in the water. His face is drawn, a day's worth of beard growth a shadow across his cheeks and chin. Weak and helpless, he doesn't look like the ghost of Loki that he did in the spider's nest.

She bites her lip. If they were on Earth, she'd have called an ambulance and insisted they administer oxygen. Bohdi inhaled a lot of liquid. Dry drowning is a real possibility.

At a loss for anything to do, she leans over and presses her ear to his back. Her fingers instinctively clench against his sides...as though she can hold his life in the shell of his body if she squeezes tight enough. "Breathe for me," she says, "as deep as you can."

Bohdi obliges. Without a stethoscope, Amy's not sure if she can trust her ears. She tells herself she's imagining a slight crackle. She bites her lip. She doesn't know the incidence of pneumonia after drowning, but it has to be pretty small...unless of course, you're on a foreign planet with bugs you've never encountered before and have no resistance to. She glances down at her hand. She'd left the cut over her knuckles free to bleed, hoping to purge any foreign bacteria. It must have worked, her knuckle is scabbing over beautifully.

On the log, Bohdi begins hacking water out of his lungs, again. He's stronger than she is, and it seems a strange twist of fate that he should be the one who's hurt and sick.

Sitting up, Amy resumes rubbing his back.

As the spasm comes to an end, Bohdi whispers, "Amy... still have...your phone?

"Yes," says Amy.

"Is my phone...still in..." He rasps and stammers. "... back...left...pocket?"

It's the most he's said since she pulled him onto the log.

And a good sign. Amy looks down. "Yes."

"Take it out," Bohdi whispers.

Amy slips her hand into his pocket. Her mind is immediately filled with the very inappropriate realization that Bohdi has a *well-conditioned gluteus maximus.* She flushes. Wrapping her hand around the phone, she pulls it out as fast as she can.

"What do you want me to do with it?" she asks.

"Nothing..." His eyes slide shut, and he smiles. "Just wanted...you to...feel me up."

Amy's skin goes hot. She gives him a hard thump on the back. He immediately spits out a little more water.

"Thanks," he mumbles.

Amy sits back on the log with a harrumph.

He gasps. "Need to take...them...apart."

Amy blinks.

Before she can ask, he says, "If parts dry out...may be able to use them later."

It's a good idea. Amy starts to back away, but Bohdi whines. "Please don't go." He coughs.

Her chest constricts. Does he know what bad shape he's in? She remembers him grabbing her wrist and dragging her through the trees—she couldn't have run so fast without his help. And she remembers him beating back the spider, leaping onto its body as light as a flame. He hasn't moved since she helped him lie down on the log. There's a good chance he knows.

"Don't worry, I know you'll be fine," she says, as much for herself as for him.

Bohdi's muscles tense beneath her. Instead of coughing, he sneezes.

Amy silently wills Bohdi to not be getting a viral infection.

Without a word, she takes off her winter coat, lays it over his lower thighs, and scoots back so she can sit between his calves. Silently shifting, he reaches into his front pocket, pulls out his knife, and hands it back to her. As she takes it, he begins hacking again.

"Amy?" Bohdi whispers, after the coughing subsides.

"Hmmm?" she says, using the knife to undo a few screws.

"Talk to me," Bohdi says, his voice faint.

Amy lifts her head. "About what?"

"Anything…" he rasps.

Amy bites her lip. She's never been a good storyteller. Detailed anecdotes about operating on cats fall flat at cocktail parties. She winces. She knows.

Perking up, she says, "I didn't finish telling you about Loki and Freyja's necklace."

Groaning, Bohdi rasps out, "I only want to hear that…if you tell me the dirty parts."

Amy gives his leg a smack. "There aren't any dirty parts."

Bohdi lifts his head. "But he was…" He coughs. "On his way to her house?"

Slipping the casing off the phone in her hand, Amy frowns. "No, he was on his way to get a drink…"

It is just Loki's luck that Freyja's husband, Ord, is at the pub he goes to. Even more his luck when Ord buys him a drink and invites him to sit down with him and his friends. The friends cast suspicious glances in Loki's direction, but Ord is oblivious.

Sitting next to the man Loki is about to prove was cuckolded when Freyja traded sexual favors with three dwarves for a magical necklace leaves Loki feeling too sick to do more than sip his ale. Pointing out the sexual peccadilloes of Asgardians has gotten Loki in trouble before—it certainly didn't help his sentence when he was sent to the cave.

His hand tightens on his knife. He is risking everything on this errand for Odin. Not just his marriage, but his relationship with his boys. They'll be even less likely than Sigyn to forgive him if they find out Loki's cheated on their mother. Sigyn might believe him if he tells her he did it under duress. Sigyn knows Loki isn't interested in Freyja. Loki's inherently lazy. Sex with Freyja is a lot of work, and then afterward, she forces her lovers to engage in her favorite topic of conversation: herself.

Maybe if he just gives Freyja a spanking and calls her a few naughty names, he can tie her up and use the time to find the necklace. If he's clever about it, she'll be none the wiser. And if he leaves her unsated she'll be happily furious…and maybe Sigyn won't see that as infidelity per se…

Jamming his knife into the tabletop, Loki drops his head into his hands. Sigyn will be furious either way. She is enthusiastic about the reforms Freyja is petitioning for. And when Loki casually mentioned the "rumor" of Freyja and the dwarves, Sigyn snapped, "I don't care if she slept with dwarves, I care what she can do for Asgard. Just like I don't care about you sleeping with dwarves, I care what you do for our family!"

Loki had blinked. "Who told you I slept with dwarves?" That had been before they were together, he hadn't thought she'd known—quite frankly, he's shocked that she married him if she did know. Even for a man, sex with dwarves was decidedly… unsavory.

Sigyn had just rolled her eyes. "Who haven't you slept with, Loki?"

Ord's hand falls on Loki's shoulder. "Loki, are you all right?"

Loki silently curses him for being so kind.

At just that moment, one of Odin's ravens flies in an open window. Landing on the table it bobs its head and says, "Hi ya, Loki! Just saw Valli and Nari with Odin."

Sitting up straight, Loki meets its beady eyes. Odin never has audiences with Valli and Nari. This is just a not-so-subtle reminder that Odin holds the fate of Loki's family in his hands.

Cocking its head, the raven rawks. "Don't you have an errand to do?"

Loki's hands curl into fists at the implicit threat. "Right," he says. Wishing he'd tried harder to get drunk, he stands and says his goodbyes.

When he arrives at Freyja's home, he is greeted by Valkyries and Einherjar guards at the front door, and one very nervous servant girl. With a tip of her head, the servant says, "Right this way."

Following the girl, Loki scowls. He had expected the servants to be dismissed so that this bit of business could be kept as quiet as possible. His skin heats, and his fist clenches at his side. At least he won't have to fake wanting to smack Freyja.

The servant turns down a corridor Loki has never been down before. Halting before a set of double doors, she throws them open, and beckons Loki to enter.

Stunned by what he sees, Loki enters, his ire momentarily forgotten. He is in a library. Shelves stretch upward at least three stories on all sides. They are overflowing with clay tablets, books, and scrolls of parchment, silk, and papyrus. Light streams from a circular skylight overhead. The light falls in a golden curtain upon Freyja, bent over a desk, her cats on either side of her.

She wants help clearing her desk? Well, at least this is slightly different…

Looking up from where she is sitting, Freyja gently lays down an enormous quill pen. "Ah, Loki..."

Her voice is faint, unusually uncertain. Even when she requests to be humiliated, or thrown over a knee, Freyja is demanding.

Immediately on alert, Loki scans the room, almost expecting to see her Einherjar or Valkyries slip from the shadows.

Freyja waves her hand, and the servant disappears, closing the doors behind her.

"We are alone," says Freyja, stepping around the desk. Her movements are unusually hesitant.

Smirking, Loki takes a step forward. "A new game, Freyja?"

Grecian garments are the style of the day, and her dress is open in a deep V at the neck. Trailing her fingers down the bare slope of her skin, she says, "I'm not playing a game, Loki—but you are."

Her voice isn't accusatory. It's soft, as are her eyes. Tilting her head, she says, "The only question...is why?"

Taking a step forward, Loki grabs her wrist. Freyja's mouth opens, and her pupils dilate. She trembles under his hand and swallows. "I want this..."

"Well, then—"

Twisting her wrist, and pulling back with her considerable magical strength, Freyja frees herself with frustrating ease. Quickly putting her other hand on Loki's chest, she pushes him back, gently, but firmly. "But you don't, Loki. So why are you here?" The warm pink of her magic rises in the room.

If she were angry, Loki might fight. But her voice is soft and soothing.

Freyja licks her lips. "I've always been able to see who a man's in love with..." she looks Loki up and down. "And right now, you are in love...with your wife..." She huffs, a gentle laugh, that is somehow empathetic and not mocking. Loki's fists unclench.

Shaking her head, almost sadly, Freyja says, "Being in love won't stop a person from taking a lover. But we both know Sigyn would have your head if she found out." Meeting Loki's eyes, she reaches up and touches his cheek. "And you wouldn't risk it," she whispers, her eyes wide, as though seeing something for the first time.

She pulls back, and her mouth drops. "Loki, you're not here for yourself..." Her voice trails off. "Odin...he wants something."

Loki takes a step back and stumbles on a cat, threading its way between his feet.

"Whatever he is offering," Freyja says, as Loki regains his balance, "I can match it."

Loki raises an eyebrow. There is nothing she can offer more valuable than the lives of his sons.

Freyja steps forward, putting her hand on his arm. Her magic rises around them again, and something else twists with the pink of her aura, darker and warmer. He cannot and doesn't want to move.

"It's not riches, or power, you want..." She draws her head back, as though surprised. "Those things don't mean much to you..."

Pulling his knuckles to her lips, she kisses them. It's oddly not erotic; it's maternal. Loki stands transfixed, unable to move or even think.

Freyja's eyes widen a fraction. "I can help you take care of them, Loki. I can help you take care of your family."

Gasping, Loki drops his head. Overwhelmed. Freyja can be loving... How had he not known?

Still stroking his cheek, Freyja whispers, "I have the hearts of the people of Asgard, and the swords of all the Valkyries and half the Einherjar. I can protect you, and them."

Loki wants to fall to his knees, lean into her, and beg her for her help. His chest is filled with warmth, with love ignited by her caring. He almost does fall...but then something dark and wicked whispers in the back of his mind. When has Freyja ever asked him what he wants? And how is it that now she just knows?

"I will rule all of Asgard," Freyja whispers. "And if you tell me what he's after, you will have a powerful friend."

Loki's suddenly aware of Freyja's magic glowing around them, but he can feel reason, like an icy snake, crawling up his spine. When has Freyja ever been his friend? Where was she when he was in the cave?

And even if she were his friend...Odin was his friend once, as well.

Loki takes a small step back, a rueful smile coming to his lips. "And then you can blackmail me, too?"

Freyja's brow tightens. Her mouth opens, and she looks like she is going to refute him—but then she steps back. She reaches her hand to her neck and brushes the bare skin of her throat and shoulders, and sighs. "I will do what is best for Asgard. And what is best for Asgard will be good for your family, too."

Loki looks into her eyes. She's not lying...at least from her perspective. Loki takes another step back. The shift from emotional appeal to logic is sudden... If she had continued on her path of emotional manipulation, it would not have worked. When did she become so sensitive?

His jaw clenches. He still needs to find the necklace...Maybe he can trick her into revealing it.

"And what do you offer Asgard that Odin does not?" Loki asks.

Freyja straightens. Her voice becomes cool and professional. "*Asgard is stagnating under the weight of Odin's magic.*" *Taking a step forward, she says,* "*Our young take centuries to mature… and there are so few of them…*"

Loki's lip twitches. Her words ring true. There are a dwindling number of children. The task of raising them over centuries is something that few want to undertake more than once or twice in a lifetime.

"*And you think this is Odin's magic?*" *Loki asks, trying to look like he's bored as he covertly scans her desk.*

"*I know it is,*" *says Freyja.* "*The same thing happened under the rule of my grandfather.*"

Loki's head jerks toward her. He had not known that. Freyja's Vanir grandfather had ruled Asgard, before Odin slayed him…

Stepping closer, Freyja says, "*And the young who mature in body never mature in mind. They play games of war and think that it makes them warriors. They are idle, lazy, and weak.*"

Giving her a too brittle smile, Loki says, "*I prefer my boys lazy and alive.*" *He looks down. One child is enough to lose in a lifetime.*

Freyja takes a tiny step forward.

Loki looks up to see her stroking her neck. A tiny frown slips across her lips and then disappears. Hand still on her neck, she says, "*I'm sure we can work something out…*"

A frantic pounding sounds at the door.

"*Come in,*" *Freyja says.*

The servant bursts into the room. "*My Lady,*" *she gasps.* "*Master Ord is here, and the Allfather is approaching.*"

At that moment, Ord's voice echoes down the hall. "*Wife! Where are you? Something is…*"

Ord is suddenly in the library. He sees Loki and Freyja

standing together. Frowning, he says, "...amiss." Eyes shifting to Loki, face hard, he says, "I thought you had an errand to do for Odin?"

Loki smiles tightly at him.

From down the hall comes the sound of boot steps. The Einherjar who'd been guarding the door comes into library and bows. "The Allfather is here." His eyes go to Loki. "He is accompanied by your sons—among others."

"Show the Allfather and his companions in," says Freyja with a tight smile.

Loki finds himself backing toward the bookshelves as Odin enters the room with two members of the Diar, and four of his own Einherjar warriors. Standing between the warriors are Nari and Valli. They're both golden haired like their mother. They're as tall as Loki, but broader. They have Loki's features, but they have Asgardian coloring—they're tanned; they don't sport Loki's Frost Giant pallor.

Freyja's own guards stand nervously just behind Odin's entourage. Ord's hand casually drops to the pommel of his sword.

"Father?" says Nari. Loki hazards a look at his son. Nari looks distinctly nervous. He is unarmed and wearing not a shred of armor. Valli is similarly dressed, but his face shows only curiosity.

Turning to Freyja, Odin says, "We were just on our way to go hunting and wondering if you'd like to join us?"

It's an obvious lie and a threat. Loki grinds his teeth...It would be very easy for Odin's warriors to kill Valli and Nari in a hunting excursion.

Freyja laughs. Sounding a little tired, she says, "Loki failed, Odin."

Loki turns to her, shocked she'd call Odin at his game.

One side of Odin's lip curls up. "Did you fail to find the necklace, Loki?" he asks.

"What are you talking about?" Ord says.

Freyja sighs and strokes her neck. "Finding the necklace would be impossible, even for Loki, because the dwarves have it. You've lost, Odin..."

"This is ridiculous!" Ord shouts. "Freyja turned the dwarves down. All of Asgard knows it!"

The Einherjar on either side of Loki's sons step closer. Have they been instructed to kill Loki's sons right here? He stiffens. How dare Freyja call Odin on his game and put Valli's and Nari's lives at stake.

Stepping forward, pink magic rising around her, Freyja says, "Do not take it out on Nari and Valli."

Loki's anger washes away at her words. She's not playing with his sons...she wants to save them. Loki turns his eyes to the so-called Goddess of Love, Beauty, and War. For the first time, he thinks even he might love her. Sunlight is streaming down on Freyja, as though Asgard's star is in love with her, too. For a fragile moment, Loki sees Freyja as a queen, proud, wise, firm, and caring. He sees all of Asgard basking in her reflected glow.

Dropping her hand, she inclines her head in Loki's direction. "Your faith in this fool is just a symptom of your decline."

The spell shatters. Loki takes a step back and hits the bookshelf behind him. A scroll falls to his feet.

Odin chuckles. He looks to Loki and says, "My faith is not misplaced. Loki, where is it?"

Loki's mouth opens.

"It's with the dwarves," Freyja says, the lie sending shivers down Loki's spine.

"Loki?" says Odin.

Loki looks between Freyja and Odin. One, at least, has some faith in him…And also has his sons nearly at sword point.

"I'm done with this," says Freyja, taking a step toward the door—and the Allfather.

"Where is it, Loki?" says Odin. Loki looks toward his sons, and swallows.

"I don't have it," says Freyja, the lie prickling Loki's skin.

He doesn't know and…

Loki's jaw drops. Freyja is a master of illusions, she's always been adept at appearing as what a man—or woman—wants to see. Her spell is so strong, she fools her lovers' minds into believing they feel what they want to feel: softness, strength, or taut skin on bone. She's always been able to do that…but love is deeper than a beautiful shell. Love is an accident that comes from being what a person needs at the right time.

"Loki," says Odin. His voice is deep, rich, almost fatherly.

"I know where it is," Loki says.

Freyja's hands go to her neck. With eyes almost pleading, she says, "Loki, I'm sorry, I…"

The gesture, the sudden empathy she's never had before. All doubts are erased from Loki's mind. "She's wearing it," he says.

"Liar!" says Ord.

Loki closes his eyes, concentrates, and wills the magic swirling around Freyja to still, the tiny photons passing through the chain he knows is there to show themselves and reveal the necklace.

Ord makes a choking noise.

"It's a trick," says Freyja.

Opening his eyes, he sees Ord ripping a golden necklace from Freyja's throat. Ord lifts the tiny slip of gold, so fine it might be silk, to his eyes. Then he drops it to the floor, spins on his heels, and leaves the room.

"Ord!" says Freyja, trying to rush after him.

Odin raps his spear, Gungir, on the floor. "Stay, Freyja. We need to talk."

"We're not going hunting?" says Valli, sounding distinctly disappointed. Wide-eyed, doubtlessly aware of the danger they were just in, Nari turns to his brother, mouth gaping.

Loki massages the bridge of his nose. Love for children has nothing to do with them being the right person at the right time.

Amy looks down at the phone pieces spread out on her coat.

Despite the smoke, the sun is making sweat prickle on the back of her neck.

Bohdi is still lying with his head hanging over the side of the log. His eyes are open, but he's very quiet.

She's just about to ask him if he's all right, when he says, "So…what happened to Freyja?"

She lets out a relieved sigh. "Odin made her part of the Diar…and ordered everyone in the room to keep quiet about the necklace. But he didn't open the Diar to anyone else, like Freyja had originally suggested. And anytime she stepped out of line, he threatened to reveal the necklace to all of Asgard."

She blinks and idly studies the blank surface of her phone. "It was kind of brilliant actually…Just enough carrot and stick to keep her in line."

She shakes her head. "Sometimes Odin would use Freyja's abilities to seduce his enemies. She could look like anyone… and with the necklace's power to see into hearts…she could be anyone… Odin used her to blackmail them, sway them, or sometimes even kill them…"

Bohdi coughs. Amy looks upriver. She swears the fire is getting closer.

"Frieda was kind of Steve's type…" Bohdi whispers. He pushes himself up on his arms and Amy quickly moves the coat out of the way.

Pulling himself into a sitting position, he says, "Super tall, with long legs, and they were talking law and shit for hours…"

Despite the heat, goose bumps rise on Amy's skin.

Looking up to the sky, he says, "Up until the point when she invited me back to her hotel…I thought…that there might be something there between them."

Amy feels her body relax.

Bohdi runs a hand through his hair. "Ah…my brain is just on the crazy train. I mean Steve's not that important…He's just a mid-level bureaucrat, right?"

Amy starts to reassure him, to say that Steve isn't in any danger. But she can't. In another universe, Steve Rogers was one of the first people a nearly omnipotent Odin put to death.

Bohdi wraps his arms around himself. His clothing is dry, but he shivers. He's not quite looking at her eyes when he says, "Aren't you cold?" He shivers so violently his teeth chatter and doesn't so much lie back down, as fall.

…And Amy knows she has more immediate concerns than Steve and Freyja.

CHAPTER 15

Garbage blows through the underpass beneath Congress Parkway and Des Plaines Avenue. Beside Steve, Beatrice says, "This isn't a gate to Nornheim. We're wasting our time."

Steve can't look at her. His attention is riveted to Gerðr. She's not wearing any magic-blocking helmet or cuffs. In her heavy down jacket, borrowed boots, and ill-fitting jeans, she shouldn't be so alluring.

Standing facing him, Gerðr's eyes are closed and she's whispering words he can't hear. Steve can almost imagine her… He turns around and finds himself staring at the backs of Brett and Bryant. Besides Beatrice, Stodgill, Brett, and Bryant are the only members of ADUO Steve trusts for this little assignment. They all have the dubious distinction of believing that Loki was being controlled by Cera when he attacked Chicago. Stodgill because, "If he was so intent on conquering the world, why would he disappear right when he was about to win?" Beatrice, Brett, and Bryant because, "Loki was an ass, just not that kind of ass."

"Is she done yet?" says Brett, snapping Steve from his reverie.

"Can she put the hat back on?" says Bryant.

"Mmmm…" is all Steve can manage to say. Forcing himself not to turn around, Steve looks up Des Plaines Avenue. There are no ravens in sight; they'd managed to give Steve's minders the slip. It's close to dusk and lights are coming on in the homes of the high-rise condo buildings. Most of the homes will stay dark. Magic is still in this town, and it brings only destruction; they haven't learned to harness it. Hell, the scientists he's talked to say they don't even know what it is.

From behind them, Laura Stodgill says, "She's back!"

Steve turns around. Gerðr is standing exactly where she was a moment before. But her light blue eyes are wide, and her lashes are thick with snow. More flakes dust her hair and shoulders. Trails of ice sparkle down her cheeks. She looks exactly like the illustration of a snow fairy that Claire has in one of her picture books, a magical vision that steals Steve's breath away.

Beatrice comes forward and puts a pink crocheted cap on Gerðr's head. Steve blinks. The pink crocheted cap hides Promethean Wire. Ice still sparkles on Gerðr's cheeks, but he finds he can speak again…and he realizes the ice trails are from tears.

Clearing his throat he says, "Gerðr?"

Gerðr looks down. "It is a path to Jotunheim."

She puts her hand to her mouth. Laura puts a hand on her shoulder, and Gerðr chokes out, "But…leads to South Wastes."

Steve stands at a safe distance, waiting to hear more.

Sounding like she's biting back a sob, Gerðr says, "Cannot go home this way. Even in summer, I don't know way…and there is South Sea to cross."

"Well, we'll keep looking," Steve says. He has to make magic, and magical World Gates, an advantage for this town. Trade with creatures that might want human technology and can clean up the messes human technology causes could help with that. But first, they need to make contact.

Gerðr thinks that Odin is already interfering in the US, cutting humans off from the Allfather's magical enemies.

But Steve has a plan.

"There is…gate…I came from," says Gerðr, referring to the first gate she took from Jotunheim to Earth.

Steve shakes his head. "Under several tons of rocks in hostile territory in Afghanistan."

"We should be looking for more gates to Nornheim!" says Beatrice.

Steve rubs his eyes. "We are, Beatrice."

"You said the drones picked up evidence that Bohdi and my granddaughter are still alive!"

Steve walks over and opens the doors to the windowless van they've brought with them. "That I did," he says, gesturing with his head for the others to climb in. He left out the part about the giant spiders.

"We should be sending in troops—"

Steve snaps. "Amy and Bohdi were hundreds of miles from the World Gate when they made contact with the drone. Even if I parachuted troops in, there would be no way for us to get to them—let alone get them out if we did reach them. The gate is thousands of feet above the ground and too small for a chopper!"

He feels a little sick thinking about Bohdi and Amy. He wants to help…but won't send a team to certain death.

Beatrice averts her eyes and climbs into the van.

Steve waits for the rest of the team to enter, images the drone picked up replaying in his mind.

His hands clench at his sides. He's not going to mourn Amy or Bohdi yet. Amy is resourceful, Bohdi has survival training, and Thor won't leave comrades-in-arms behind.

He looks at the spot where Gerðr had just made a million-or-more light-year journey to Jotunheim. Maybe he's just pushing away uncomfortable truths by finding a new project? That would be his ex-wife's analysis. Steve bows his head and tries not to think of that first terrible year with Claire, the hole in her heart, how he destroyed his marriage, and almost lost his little girl.

The van starts and Steve's body sags. He has lost his little girl. She's in the Ukraine now.

Ducking his head, he climbs into the van and shuts the door just in time to hear a newscaster over the radio say, "And there have been allegations that Associate Director Steve Rogers, who many hope will run for mayor, took advantage of a prisoner in the FBI's custody. Human rights watch groups are pushing for—"

In the driver's seat, Laura hurriedly turns off the radio.

Steve rolls his eyes. Skírnir's allegations at the meeting have been made public. Perfect.

From the front of the van, Laura says, "I'm already on it."

As Steve crouches his too large frame into a seat, Gerðr says, "You...are...in problem?"

Steve waves a hand. "Doesn't matter."

Scowling, Gerðr sits up straighter. "I will..." She bites her lip, and gives a tight nod. "Speak against you."

Steve's mouth falls open.

"What!" says Bryant. Brett grunts.

"I don't think you said what you think you said, dear," says Beatrice.

Gerðr's lower lip trembles. "I...you." With a frustrated growl, she rips the crocheted hat from her head, then smiles, and says in perfect English, "Testify on your behalf." Before Brett, Bryant, or Steve can drool, she puts the hat back on and then gives a little nod.

Steve's eyebrows go up. Well...that is...oddly touching. Of course, his enemies would claim she was under duress. Shaking his head, he says, "It won't come to that. We have plenty of witness testimony."

He's not sure if he is imagining it, but he thinks Gerðr's face falls slightly.

They're almost at the office when Steve's cell phone starts playing *Green River.*

Brett and Bryant perk up like bird dogs on a scent. "You like Creedence?" says Brett.

"Sure," says Steve. Not really. Bohdi set up that ring tone—the thought makes his throat tighten up a bit, but Steve thinks he knows who the tone is for, and that's a bit of good news. He glances down. Sure enough...It's Dale Meechum, his CIA contact in Eastern Europe, and best friend from Officers Training School.

"Let me out," Steve says.

"The ravens will see you," says Beatrice as Laura pulls the van over to the curb.

"Don't care," says Steve.

A moment later, he's walking down Van Buren beneath the "L" tracks. A train's wheels screech and sparks fly above his head.

Making sure no one's around to hear, Steve presses the

phone to his ear and says, "Hey, Cracker, got anything for me about fairy lights in your neck of the woods?"

"No," says Dale. Dale and Steve have a code. If Dale had finished with a joke or mild insult, Steve would have believed him. Dale's answer stops Steve in his tracks. Regaining himself, he turns and steps into an open courtyard with black stone fountains, dry for winter and filled with evergreen fronds.

"Then why—" Steve starts to say.

"But I do have other news for you, Hommie," Dale says, Texan accent loud and clear, even though the connection has static.

"Lay it on me, *Bak Guiy,*" Steve says, using a derogatory Mandarin word for white man.

Dale chuckles. Dale's a polyglut, and undoubtedly knows that one. There's a crackle at the other end of the line, and a familiar voice shouts, "Daddy!"

Steve's mouth drops open, and he forgets all about fairy lights over Chernobyl.

Dale laughs. "Guess who's temporarily assigned to the embassy in Kiev?"

Instead of answering the question, Steve blurts out, "Claire!"

"Putting her on speaker," says Dale.

"Dad! Uncle Dale is here!" shouts Claire.

Steve grins, vaguely aware of two dark shadows swirling overhead but not caring.

"Just for a while," says Dale. "Thought you'd like it if I just checked in on things here."

Steve does like it, a lot, but can't make himself say it. His voice might crack.

"Uncle Dale's coming with us when we visit the Kiev Ballet school tomorrow!" says Claire. Steve winces. That's an assignment Steve's friend is probably looking forward to about as much as a root canal.

"No, that's a few days from now, String Bean," says Dale, and Steve can hear him smiling.

Sounding like she's jumping up and down, Claire says, "And then we're going to some fancy party with the President of the Ukraine."

"That sounds great, honey," Steve says, trying to sound happy for her.

"Dana's real happy I'm here, too," says Dale. To his credit, his voice holds no hint of sarcasm. Steve's ex and Dale never got along.

Steve's mom gets along with Dale. But Dale, is, in her words, "unvarnished." Dale doesn't possess Steve's tact, and some of his notions of the world he inherited from his family...and Dale comes from a long line of people who wear white sheets and light bonfires on weekends.

...But Dale wants to be better than where he came from and wants to think beyond the boundaries his heritage placed on him. Steve's a poor black kid from the west side of Chicago. He and Dale have an unusual sort of kinship.

"And you should see my room!" Claire says. "It's huge! And it has princess furniture!"

"Oh...that's nice, honey," Steve says, feeling distinctly small.

"And Uncle Dale's teaching me Ukrainian!" says Claire.

"Well, that's good!" Steve says, glad he can be enthusiastic about something.

"And—" Claire starts to say. Steve is vaguely aware of a

soft beep—from the magic detector in his pocket, or from his phone, he's not sure.

"And?" says Steve.

There is no answer. Pulling the phone away from his ear, he sees the screen is completely blank. With a curse, he pushes the power button.

Nothing happens.

Above his head he hears the ravens cackling.

"Goddamn it," Steve mutters, flipping the phone over. Maybe if he takes the battery out and puts it back in…

"Is something wrong?" says a smooth feminine voice.

Steve raises his eyes to see a businesswoman standing just a few feet away. Her skin is a deep mocha; her hair is pulled back in a neat bun. The pencil skirt she wears and her fitted wool coat outline an elegant silhouette.

How had Steve not noticed *her?* Shaking himself out of his stupor, he holds up his phone. "My phone died. I was talking to my daughter." He hadn't even had a chance to say goodbye.

"Oh," she says, with a bright smile. "I have one of those!"

Steve blinks, transfixed by her smile.

"Do you want to borrow mine?" she says, with a glint in her eye. Steve's eyes fall on her generous lips, tinted just the right shade of wine red.

He doesn't remember she's asked him a question until she pulls out her phone.

Waving a hand, he says, "Oh, I can't—she's in the Ukraine."

The woman blinks her wide, doe-like eyes—they have just a hint of fine lines at the corners. "But they have mobile phones in *Ukrayina*, don't they?"

She pushes the phone closer to Steve.

"Yes, but—" He stalls, something tickling the back of his mind.

"Go ahead, it's your daughter," says the woman.

His eyes fall to the phone. It's very pink...He wants to take it, but something in him seizes up. Who offers a cell phone to a complete stranger for a call to the *Ukrainya?* And why does she sound so *excited* about having a cell phone?

Steve's eyes snap to hers. Maybe she's not quite right in the head?

She takes a step back, and her jaw falls, and then her lips form a small "o," like she's just been found out.

Cocking his head, Steve says, "I don't think I caught your name?"

From behind him, he hears Hernandez. "Agent Rogers?"

The woman scowls and with a *humpf* spins on her heel and walks away.

The ravens alight on the evergreen branches in the fountain. Bobbing its head, one of them says, "You suck with women, Rogers!"

Doesn't he know it.

Hunkering down, the raven takes a crap, and then takes off with its partner into the air.

"You want us to shoot it?" says Hernandez.

Steve turns to see Hernandez walk up with Agent Marion Martinez. Blonde, brown-eyed, in her mid twenties, Marion has girl-next-door easy, good looks. She's a solid team player and has a passion for all things football and baseball.

Most of the guys in the office have a soft spot for her. As far as Steve knows, Bohdi's the only one who's gotten anywhere with that. Bohdi hadn't talked about it...Steve just happened to call Bohdi one Saturday when the kid was "helping

Marion with her computer." Bohdi hadn't hung up his cell after the call, Steve was on his landline and it didn't disconnect when he set it on the base—Steve had gotten an earful. Steve's not sure what happened between Bohdi and Marion after that, but they're professional in the office.

Hernandez clears his throat. "We were on our way to get some coffee and wondered if you wanted to come along."

Steve shakes his head. "I better get back to the office."

Hernandez backs up, but Marion doesn't move. "Do you have any news about Bohdi?" she asks.

Hernandez shoots Marion a look that's so transparently jealous, Steve has to restrain a snort.

Shoving her hands in her pockets, Marion says, "He's kind of a friend...I'm worried about him." She looks very young.

It hits Steve that this is the first time she's lost someone like this. He doesn't say, me, too. All he says is, "We believe he is alive. More than that I can't say."

CHAPTER 16

Bohdi is dead. It's the only explanation for the river of fire he is drifting on. Above his head flames and smoke are at war for control of the sky, below him, the river glows orange. Putting his hand to his forehead, he finds a wet cloth. Who put it there? Why does it matter? Any minute, he'll be face to face with an eight-headed dog, or is it a two-headed dog? He's mostly okay with being dead, except all his muscles ache, and he's so hot he's shivering—and that seems unfair. When you are dead, there is supposed to be nothing, or heaven…or maybe he's in hell, but when was his trial, who spoke for him?

He closes his eyes. And there is blackness, and that's much better, until he hears Amy calling to him. "Bohdi, Bohdi, Bohdi, wake up!"

He screws his eyes tighter, trying to get back to the peaceful black, but it doesn't work. He's hot again, and shivering.

He opens his eyes. His head is lying on something soft, and Amy's eyes are upside down directly above his, smoke and flames above her head.

Someone with Bohdi's voice whispers, "You're dead, too?"

"You're not—" she lifts her eyes and lets out a frightened

gasp.

Bohdi barely manages to lift his head. A long coil of smoke is writhing its way onto Bohdi's boat to the underworld. It opens its mouth and releases an angry hiss like a serpent.

Somehow, Bohdi's knife is in his hands. He throws it at the ghost-smoke-serpent. Falling back down onto the pillow, he says, "Fucking hate snake venom." He's vaguely aware of Amy's eyes, wide and startled, on his again. He shivers right before everything goes black and peaceful.

"Bohdi, you're going to get better. I know you will." The words pierce the blackness and set Bohdi's teeth on edge, making every inch of his skin itch.

A sneeze rips through him and his eyes flutter open to see Amy's upside down gaze on him once more. It could be his imagination, but the sky above her head seems lighter. Maybe he is going to heaven? But she is going to hell.

"You're lying," he hisses. And how dare she fuck with a dying person? "You're just trying to make me feel better."

She shakes her head. "No, I'm telling you, so that you can make it happen."

Her fingers trail through his hair, and Bohdi's eyes slip closed. "Placebo...not going to work," he mumbles.

"Let me tell you a secret about placebos," she says. Her voice is very soft, and she must be close to his ear because he can hear it over the sound of fire and crashing trees. "Placebos work just as well when patients know they're getting placebos. The trick is in the doctor's care and the patient's belief."

Something cool and soft brushes his lips. Did she just kiss him? Obviously, he is dreaming, not dying.

"Get better, Bohdi," Amy says. "Don't leave me alone with the snakes."

Some addled thoughts slither together in his brain. Opening his eyes, Bohdi smiles up at Amy. The light above her head is brighter.

"I'm just doing this to lie in your lap," he says. He thinks she might sigh. But his eyes are already slipping closed.

Every muscle in Bohdi's back aches, and his stomach is so empty he feels like he might throw up. He sits up with a start. His vision immediately goes blurry, and he sways dangerously. As blood makes its way to his head, his vision clears and he finds himself sitting alone, water lapping against a motionless log. The world is no longer on fire. Although…he turns and sees clouds of smoke upriver and downriver—but no flames. The fire must have passed over them in the night and burned itself out. Around him are the charred remains of trees. Here and there are more of Nornheim's crystalline columns, their bases blackened by soot.

"You're awake!" The voice comes from behind him. He turns to see Amy, waist deep in water. She's holding a long thick branch in her hand. Walking to the end of the log, she wedges the branch underneath the root end, grunts, and lifts. The log begins to drift with the current. Sloshing quickly through the water, Amy grabs hold of the trunk, and pulls herself awkwardly aboard, still holding onto the long branch.

"Yeah…" says Bohdi, wanting to help but feeling strangely lightheaded.

The terrain is different. Flat. The trees look like they might have been different, too. It's hot and humid. He looks to the sky. It looks like it's afternoon. He wasn't out that long then. Rubbing the back of his neck, he mumbles, "Strangest dreams," and turns his head. Tied to the tree roots jutting above the water is a pink bundle. He squints—the bundle is his pink shirt. Next to the bundle, Mr. Squeakers is hanging from a line of silk. And next to Squeakers it looks like something coiled, as thick as Bohdi's thigh, three times as long, and burnt to a crisp... He blinks. "Is that a dead snake?"

"Biggest water moccasin I've ever seen," says Amy.

"You killed a giant snake?" says Bohdi.

"No," says Amy.

He looks to her. "Then how...?"

"You killed it," says Amy, straddling the log, balancing the long branch on her thighs, bare toes just barely skimming the water. Her skin looks like she's acquired a tan, but the healthy look is undercut by dark circles under her eyes. The bottom of the enormous tee shirt she's wearing is wet and clings to her body in a way that hints that there may be some curves hidden beneath; the thought doesn't evoke the warm feeling in him that it should... He feels like shit. Even breathing doesn't feel good.

Inclining her head, Amy says softly, "You threw your knife and hit it dead in the center of its head. You don't remember?"

Bohdi looks back at the snake.

"So did they teach knife throwing in boot camp?" Her voice is so flat it almost doesn't come out a question. She's looking at him, but Bohdi has that weird idea that she's looking through him, again.

Still eyeing the dead snake, Bohdi purses his lips and taps his chin. "No... Where is its head, and why is it all black?"

"I cut off the head and venom sacks, skinned it, and cooked it," Amy says.

Bohdi jerks around and faces her, making his head spin a bit.

She sighs. "I'm hungry. Aren't you?"

"Maybe not that hungry," he says, eyeing the blackened snake. In fact, he thinks he just lost his appetite. He looks to the bank. "Is the river narrower here?"

"It split into tributaries a while back," Amy says. "Which means that it will be harder for Thor to find us. Night is coming, but we don't have fire to protect us from the adze this time, and with all the ground cover burned away, we'll have nowhere to hide. But I'm not worried."

Bohdi sniffs, tries to hold back a sneeze, and fails. His spit and snot sprinkles in the water. Wiping his nose, he doesn't look at her, feeling all of three years old.

"Do you sneeze when people lie to you, Bohdi?" Amy's face and voice are unreadable. And for some reason, it's creeping him out.

Bohdi snorts. Maybe he isn't the only person who's been hallucinating. Sounding more defensive than he means to, he snaps. "What are you talking about? I have allergies. I forgot my Zyrtec." Not that meds had ever helped. He shivers, despite the heat and humidity.

Amy starts—maybe at the harshness of his tone. "Why did you come to Nornheim, Bohdi?"

"I'm…" Bohdi stops, his whole body going cold. "My wallet!" He frantically pats his back right pocket. His fingers close on the familiar shape…and then his heart sinks when he realizes it's damp. Pulling it out with shaking fingers, he opens it and all the air in his lungs rushes out of him. The picture of his parents is smeared, the colors bleeding together, their faces hopelessly distorted.

Bohdi's hands start to shake. The wallet falls open on his lap, his elbows fall onto his knees, and his head drops to his hands.

"Bohdi?" says Amy. He's vaguely aware of her coming closer.

He feels tears form in his eyes and blinks hard to keep them from falling.

"Who are they?" Amy says, so close she can drag a finger over the useless slip of plastic covering the photograph.

Too choked up to speak, Bohdi barely grinds out, "No one." He's managed to destroy the one thing he had, the one connection to his past.

Amy's hand closes on one of his. "Liar." But there is only tenderness in her tone.

Bohdi can't respond. His mouth is suddenly too dry. He licks his lips. Without looking at her, he says, "The phones?"

"Tied up in your pink shirt," says Amy.

Unable to meet her eyes, Bohdi scrambles unsteadily to his feet. He has a picture of his parents on his phone, and he suddenly has to see them, to know they're real. He is just unknotting the shirt from the root, when Mr. Squeakers gives a cheep. Bohdi looks to the shore. When had the current picked up?

Mr. Squeakers cheeps again. A movement downriver catches Bohdi's eye. Two dark logs, suspended in the current.

"Amy?" he says.

Amy turns to look in the direction of his gaze. The dark shapes are getting very close very fast...in fact...they have to be swimming.

Cocking her head, Amy says, "Oh, it's only alligators."

Bohdi coughs. "We're on a floating island, virtually

unarmed, with no where to run, and you say it's only alligators?"

Amy looks at him, eyes wide and hurt. "Well, it's better than archaeopteryxes, giant spiders, or adze."

Bohdi stares at her. And then he nearly falls over as laughter and coughs wrack through him. Amy starts laughing, too.

Wiping away a tear, Bohdi eyes a loose branch floating by. "Hey," he says, "Can you knock that log over here?"

Amy swings her own branch around and knocks the floating branch toward them.

A few seconds later, Bohdi is armed with a new, slippery, wet pugil stick, and Mr. Squeakers has taken a position on top of Amy's head—just in time for a giant green scaly to crawl onto the log close to Amy. It's twice as wide as Bohdi at the shoulder, and its toothy snout is as long as his leg. As it tries to trundle aboard, the log rolls, and then gets stuck below.

The alligator opens its mouth and Amy pokes at it...rather half-heartedly in Bohdi's mind.

"Harder!" he shouts, as another alligator gets closer. Bohdi wallops it on the nose and it disappears under the water.

"I'm trying!" Amy shouts. The alligator darts forward and bites down hard on her branch. The end snaps off, and Amy backs up into Bohdi. Reaching around her, Bohdi pokes it hard in the eye. With a snap of its jaws it backs up and slips below the surface.

He starts to see other shapes rising around them. "Get us unstuck, Amy."

"Right," she says, slinking past him and sticking the remains of her branch in the water.

Bohdi hits another alligator in the eye as it lifts its head out of the water. It disappears under the surface. Bohdi jams the end of the stick into another's nose, just as the log breaks free and starts to head down river.

"Definitely better than dragons!" Bohdi says.

"Archaeopteryx," Amy says, sounding mildly vexed.

Another alligator raises its head, Bohdi pokes its eye, and it disappears and joins his comrades below the surface.

Bohdi pants. "It's like whack-a-mole!" It's easy, which is a good thing. He's kind of lightheaded with hunger, and his breathing feels shallow and strangely ineffective.

Amy gives a little yelp as another one raises its head beside the log and snaps its jaws. With a gasp, she pokes the air in the alligator's direction.

"Don't be afraid to hurt it!" Bohdi says, ramming his stick down its throat. It makes a strange gurgling sound, and Amy says, "Ooooo...you hit it right in the palatal valve." The wonder in her voice makes Bohdi burst into laughter and coughing again.

The log bobs in the current as they wind around a wide bend in the river, passing through a smoldering stretch of forest. Bohdi and Amy stand armed with their branches. The alligators swim beside them, but, other than snapping their jaws occasionally, don't do anything dangerous.

After a half an hour or so, the alligators dip below the surface.

Bohdi tenses up but then he sees them resurface upriver from them and swim in the opposite direction.

"Huh," he says. "Guess they got bored."

"Do you hear that?" says Amy, looking down toward the bend in the river.

"Hear what?" says Bohdi. But then he does hear it. The distant rush of water. "Rapids," says Bohdi. "Let's try to get to shore."

"Right," says Amy, already bending over, branch in hand. "Ugh," she groans. "I can't reach the bottom."

Bohdi dips his branch in, too. He doesn't connect with anything solid until he's down on his knees, and has the branch almost completely submerged.

"There," he says, giving a shove off the river bottom. "We'll get to shore before we reach the rapids."

"Not rapids," Amy says.

Bohdi lifts his head. His jaw drops. Just a few meters ahead of them the forest ends. And so does the river. In fact, the whole world seems to end.

"Waterfall," says Amy, falling down to her stomach, and jabbing her branch back into the water.

Bohdi does the same, but only half of his frantic thrusts seem to connect with anything solid. The sound of rushing water is getting louder too fast. He turns to Amy and shouts, "We have to swim for it!"

She meets his eyes and nods, Mr. Squeakers bobbing on her head.

Grabbing the pink bundle that holds their phones and wrapping it around his wrist, Bohdi says, "Count of three..."

Before he can say another word, the log connects with something hard and rolls. They both fall off. He sees Amy's head bobbing in the water just a few feet away, and the shore speeding by. His head slips under the water. He makes it up for air once more and hears Amy scream his name, and then he's sucked along with the current over the edge of the waterfall.

Bohdi's heart leaps to his throat, and just as he prepares for bone-shattering impact, his back and legs connect with something springy. For a few moments, he bobs up and down, completely disoriented, as water continues to pound on his chest and head, splashing into his mouth and pinning him in place. Rolling over onto his stomach, he opens his eyes and looks down…and sees he's suspended in a net with palm-sized spaces between the fibers.

Fibers that look familiar. "Argh! More spider web!" He hears Amy shout, but the spray of the waterfall is so thick he can't see her. He feels in front and behind him. The web seems to rise in both directions, like a giant hammock. But why would spiders hang a hammock in a waterfall?

There's a loud plunk beside him. Bohdi turns to see a human-sized fish lying next to him. Bohdi screams. The fish begins thrashing madly, its tail and fins pummeling his side. And then it all comes together. Spiders are using this web as a giant fishing net.

Bohdi's throat tightens. He crawls as fast as he can away from the dying fish, stopping a few times to tug at the bundle of their phone parts, still wrapped around his wrist. As he goes forward, the pounding of water on his back and neck subsides and he starts to see pinkish light ahead.

From behind him, he hears Amy shout, "Bohdi!"

He squints into the pounding spray. "Over here!" he shouts. "Are you stuck?"

There's a pause, and then he hears her voice. "No! Just wet! I can't see anything!"

Bohdi looks in the direction he was crawling. "I think we can crawl out of the spray," he says. "Follow my voice!"

"Okay!"

Bohdi crawls forward up the sloped side of the web. There is plenty of room between the web fibers for his feet and hands.

"Amy," he shouts, turning to look behind him.

"Here," she says, crawling up beside him in the webbing. Mr. Squeakers is plastered to her wet head. As he waits for her to catch up, Bohdi looks from side to side. The spray is too thick to see what the web is suspended on.

When Amy reaches his side, they crawl together up the web's sloped side. "Oh," says Amy.

"Wow," says Bohdi.

The waterfall continues to plunge for at least one hundred feet below them. It falls into the great well of an ocean that stretches as far as Bohdi can see.

"Thor said all rivers lead to the Norns…" says Amy.

A shadow falls over their heads. Bohdi looks up and squints…and then his eyes go wide. A dark shape with bat wings is diving from the sky in their direction.

"But how will we find the Norns in all of that ocean?" she says.

"Dragon!" Bohdi manages to grit out.

"Archaeop…" Amy starts to say, as she lifts her head beside Bohdi.

Bohdi hears her swallow as the large bat-winged creature becomes larger—a neck longer than a giraffe's, and a whip-like tail coming into view, too.

"Nope, that's definitely a dragon," she squeaks.

CHAPTER 17

They both stare upward. Impossibly, the dragon keeps getting bigger. As it draws closer, its scales become distinctly dark maroon.

Shivering, Bohdi says, "Duck back into the spray!"

"Right," says Amy.

They start crawling back down the side of the net, but not before they see the dragon veer slightly to their right. Bohdi has a brief glimpse of forelimbs with long clawed hands at the base of its bat wings, and a body he's sure is the size of a school bus with wings too large to calculate…and yet still seem too small. And then the dragon disappears into the mist at the side of the falls.

Amy and Bohdi both freeze in place. Nothing happens. Turning to Amy, Bohdi whispers, "Maybe we're too small to eat?"

"Maybe," whispers Amy, her side pressed to his, her lips almost at his ear. "Did you see? He had forelimbs and *fore-wings*! I'd love to see his scapula!"

A chuckle rises in the mist, so deep it makes the spider web vibrate.

"Uh-oh," whispers Amy.

An enormous shadow glides below them from the right, and hot humid air tickles Bohdi's stomach.

Mr. Squeakers gives a cheep.

Before Bohdi can say or do anything, a maroon snout attached to a head as big as a VW bug rises in the space directly in front of them. The end of the snout has a slight beak; the base of the snout has two garbage-lid-sized green eyes that seem to glow from within. Tentacles that might be whiskers dangle from the snout and adorn the top of the dragon's head.

The snout opens to reveal teeth as long as Bohdi's arm. Amy and Bohdi both gasp and draw back. Squeakers gives a very unhappy squeal.

There is another deep reverberating chuckle, and the dragon rumbles. "And I would love to see your scapula, too." Its accent is unmistakably Queens English, and for an odd moment, Bohdi thinks the creature's interest might be as clinical as Amy's. And then the dragon licks its lips, pushes its snout closer, and its eyes shimmer.

Beside him, Bohdi hears Amy swallow. "I feel I should warn you," she says, "that humans are very dirty, disease-ridden animals and some carnivores develop chronic and sometimes fatal conditions after devouring our flesh."

The dragon's head whips back and it roars.

Bohdi jerks back. And then his eyes widen… The dragon is laughing.

"What you just told him, is that true?" he whispers to Amy.

"Happens to tigers," she whispers back, eyes on the laughing dragon. Her gaze comes back to Bohdi, and she shrugs. "I thought it was worth a shot."

Before Bohdi can answer, the dragon's chortles subside. Lowering its head back down so its eyes are level with them, it says, "If I can eat adze, I can eat anything. However—"

"He's not here to eat you!" shouts a tiny voice from the top of the dragon's head.

Beside Bohdi, Amy sits up and beams "Ratatoskr!" she shouts.

Two of the whisker-tentacles on the top of the dragon's head part, and a squirrel comes scampering out. Standing up on two legs, it stamps a tiny foot on the dragon's forehead. The squirrel lets loose a flurry of chittering that ends with "Chit-a-chit-chit Nidhogg! You almost threw me off!"

Rolling its eyes, the dragon says, "There's no need for obscenities."

Amy puts her hand to her mouth and goes red. "Oh my God, I know what that last swear means."

On top of the dragon's head, the squirrel gives a small bow. "My language has the best swears," he says.

Straightening, the squirrel lifts his nose to the air. "Babe, how is it that whenever I run into you, you manage to look like chat-a-chit-chat."

Bohdi opens his mouth, a little offended on Amy's behalf at the obvious derogatory comment. Not that she looks great at the moment, but neither does he, and there have been alligators, adze, and—

"Ratatoskr!" the dragon bellows, cutting off Bohdi's words. "That is no way to speak to a lady!"

"Oh," says Amy, perking up as the wind simultaneously leaves Bohdi's sails.

Ratatoskr chitters. "Like you aren't thinking about what

she tastes like."

"Oh," says Amy, drawing back a little. Bohdi's hand goes to his pocket and finds his knife. Maybe dragons have a palatal valve, too?

The dragon bobs and tilts its head in a sort of shrug. "Habit," he says, eyes on Amy. "I can eat adze, but they're all lean meat, gristle and—"

"Nidhogg!" says Ratatoskr. "Stay on task."

"Oh," says Amy. "You're *the* Nidhogg?"

"At your service," says the dragon, bowing his head slightly.

Amy giggles. Which makes Bohdi's skin heat for some reason. "Would someone tell me what's going on?" he shouts.

Amy turns to him, all wide-eyed and happy like a puppy. "This is Nidhogg. In Norse myths, he's a wyrm, but obviously, he's a dragon, and—"

Ratatoskr lets loose a squeak. "We're here to take your sorry asses to the Norns."

Bohdi and Amy both turn to the dragon and squirrel duo. Nidhogg nods. "Normally the Norns let adventurers navigate the Sea of Sadness on their own, but given that you've already caused so much mis—"

The dragon stiffens and its eyes go wide. A puff of smoke comes from his nostrils.

Bohdi blinks. Ratatoskr has his front teeth buried in one of Nidhogg's forehead tentacles. Nidhogg's mouth drops open, and a giant tear comes to his eye.

Releasing his bite, Ratatoskr scampers down to the end of Nidhogg's snout. "Being that you've already been through so much, the ladies have decided to help you out the rest of the way." Giving another little bow, Ratatoskr adds, "Out of the kindness of their hearts."

Bohdi sneezes so hard it ruffles the squirrel's fur.

Lifting its head, the squirrel stares at Bohdi, tufted ears drawn back. "God bless you," it says, voice dry.

Bohdi sniffs.

Nidhogg sniffles. "You bit me. I need a snack after that."

"We don't have time," Ratatoskr says.

Nidhogg's head lunges past Bohdi so fast Ratatoskr goes somersaulting through the air. The squirrel lands on Amy's back with an indignant squeak.

Before Bohdi can even blink, Nidhogg's head jerks back with two fish in its jaws. The fish are about Bohdi and Amy's size, but they look small in Nidhogg's enormous mouth. Nidhogg lifts his head back, and the fish vanish down his maw.

Licking his lips, Nidhogg looks back at Amy and Bohdi. "Now how to get you across the sea," he puffs. "Perhaps you could ride in my mouth…"

"Erm," says Amy.

"No," says Bohdi.

"No chit-chit-a-chit-chitting way!" says Ratatoskr.

Sitting in the ocean shallows, just to the right of the waterfall, Nidhogg tilts his head down at Amy and Bohdi. "Are you comfortable?"

Bohdi isn't sure what to say. He and Amy are lying in an actual hammock of spider web. Nidhogg snipped it off the web waterfall with his claws. The hammock is suspended between those same claws at the end of Nidhogg's enormous and powerful-looking forearms. As typically happens with hammocks, Amy and Bohdi have slid to the center. They're almost, but not quite, lying on top of each other.

Bohdi generally likes cute girls on top of him—but usually he's won them over with his wit and charm. Being thrown together kind of takes the fun out of it….Also, Amy keeps looking at him strangely. Maybe she really isn't comfortable so close to him? But she has to know the whole thing with the thong was an accident. He didn't mean it like that and…

"It's fine," Amy says.

Bohdi feels himself relax. Laying the arm with the pink bundle on his stomach, he takes a wheezy breath.

Amy looks down at him, concern etched clearly in the lines between her brows. Mr. Squeakers cheeps from her shoulder.

"You look a chit-a-chat lot more comfortable than me," says Ratatoskr from atop the dragon's head. "Sure I can't join you?"

Mr. Squeakers' fur puffs up so he looks about twice his normal size. He hisses up at the squirrel.

Raising a tiny fist, Ratatoskr says, "Hey? Rodent power, right brother?"

Mr. Squeakers' hiss increases in volume.

With a few chitters, Ratatoskr disappears behind Nidhogg's tentacles.

Clearing his throat, Nidhogg lifts his enormous bat-like wings, completely blocking out the sky. "Shall we be off? The longer I sit here, the more likely it is I will attract the attention of a giant eel."

Bohdi's eyes go wide. Nidhogg is, if anything, bigger than he'd anticipated. Brontosaurus sized…if brontosauruses were real. But Nidhogg's head is bigger than a dinosaur's, and of course, there are the wings…

"Ready to go!" says Amy.

Her side is pressed tightly to Bohdi's, and he can't bring himself to look at her.

"Excellent," Nidhogg says, lifting his giant head. His wings beat the water making waves crash on either side of them. There is a sensation of weightlessness, and then Bohdi feels wind whip around them, and gravity pressing him into the hammock. Seconds later, the ocean waves are crashing beneath them, and the hammock is rocking in time with Nidhogg's wings.

"How are you feeling?" Amy says, taking his hand.

Bohdi shivers at the unexpected touch. "Fine," he lies.

"Hmmmm…" says Amy.

He wants to squeeze her hand, he wants to look at her, but keeps his eyes on Nidhogg. Her affection is too easy… and somehow that isn't right. Neither of them says anything for moments that stretch too long. Bohdi carefully studies Nidhogg's wings to avoid looking at Amy. Her head lolls into the space between his head and shoulder. It's kind of a weird time for her to suddenly like him.

Carefully looking elsewhere, Bohdi clears his throat. "So, you know, I don't really think Nidhogg's wings are physically large enough to support his weight. That he can fly has to be defying some of the laws of physics."

Amy huffs a soft laugh. "Hmmm…you think there might *possibly* be some *magic* involved?"

Bohdi opens his mouth to reply, and then he realizes she's teasing him.

And suddenly the moment is perfect. He turns his head, a grin on his face, a flirtatious quip at the tip of his tongue…

and finds Amy's eyes closed. Her hand slips from his, her body shivers, and her breathing deepens as she falls into sleep.

Bohdi stares at the so-called God of Mischief's *former* girlfriend. The moment is still perfect. His heart feels bigger, and the sensation of want that had eluded him when he first woke from his fever is back. Even if it won't be sated, even if he still feels off, wanting feels good.

He almost kisses Amy's forehead. But he doesn't. He shuts his eyes and immediately feels himself falling again, this time into sleep.

CHAPTER 18

When Bohdi's eyes open, he's still lying in the spider web hammock, but instead of it being slung to the forelimbs of the dragon, it is now suspended between what looks a lot like palm trees—only with branches. Pink sunlight is filtering through fronds above him. Mr. Squeakers is making snoring sounds as he swings at the end of a bungee line of spider silk. The breeze smells like water and fishy things. He hears the sounds of waves close by and cries that might be from birds above his head.

He inhales…and feels a twinge of pain as air enters his lungs. His stomach is clenched in hunger, and his left arm is tingling uncomfortably.

He glances down. Amy's head is pillowed on his shoulder. One of her legs is tangled with his.

Even with tangled hair and no makeup, she looks really cute, and where her body presses against his, he's warm. She's soft, and it's…nice. He's not sure he wants to wake her, even if his arm hurts.

Every muscle in his body tenses. Maybe he should wake her. He has no idea where they are, and every near-idyllic moment on Nornheim seems to turn bad fast. He turns his head, and sees a beach with sparkling pinkish sand, tiny birds darting through the waves. Looking the other way, he sees a shorter stretch of sand punctuated by ankle-high, succulent plants with purple flowers. A path winds through the succulents to a palm forest with thin underbrush.

No dragons, kappa, adze, alligators, or spiders... Something is obviously amiss.

Amy stirs against his shoulder and then sits up with a gasp, the hammock swaying with her motion. Not moving, she stares at him wide-eyed.

There is something to say in this situation, something funny and flirty—or maybe something suave and suggestive—but all words leave him. Amy straddling his thigh brings the strangest sense of déjà vu.

"Hi," she says quietly.

Bohdi licks his lips, about to reply, when there is a whoosh of air, the sound of footsteps in sand, and a cheery feminine voice says, "Oh, you are awake!"

Bodhi looks up. Standing among the purple flowers is the most beautiful woman he has ever seen. She has caramel skin, huge brown eyes, a tiny perky nose, and lips like a bow that stretch into a radiant smile at his gaze. Her glistening black hair is pulled back from her face. Her clothing resembles traditional Indian attire. Her smooth, curved, belly peeks from between a low-slung orange silk skirt, and a short, sleeveless, yellow silk top. The very sheer orange sari she wears draped over her shoulder does nothing to hide...anything. Bohdi lifts his eyes so as not to stare at her belly button—and finds himself staring at the neckline of the top instead. It reveals a lot more than is traditional—partly because the top is small, partly because there is a lot to reveal. His mouth waters; he feels his eyes growing larger against his will. Steve says Bohdi's "type" is breathing. It is true that Bohdi sees beauty in a wide range of ages, shapes, and sizes. That said, he does like voluptuous and this woman…

Flushing, he drops his eyes again, this time to her feet. Tiny toes bedecked with gold rings poke from beneath the skirt, and staring at them feels just as wrong, right, and good as staring at her breasts and hips.

The woman laughs, light and musical, and claps her hands together below her chin—snapping Bohdi's attention back to her face. And then another set of hands comes from behind her back and rises to her ears. Bohdi's jaw drops…just as a third set of hands clasps in front of her breasts.

Bohdi's eyes widen. Six arms. Huh. Actually…his mind starts wandering down a path where he imagines what all six of those arms could do at once. He licks his lips and swallows.

Bouncing on her heels, the woman says, "It's so wonderful to meet you both."

Both?

Bohdi's eyes slide to Amy. She's sitting at the edge of the hammock, legs slung over the side. He hadn't noticed that she had moved. But her eyes are still on him. Is he imagining her shoulders slumping just slightly? It's hard to tell in that damnable shapeless tee shirt.

"Errr…" says Bohdi.

Biting her lip, Amy turns quickly away.

Taking hold of her skirt with a delicate brown hand, the woman gives a deep curtsy…revealing more of her ample assets. Bohdi's skin goes hot.

"My name is Chloe." Standing, she gestures with two

arms toward the trees. "My sisters and I have prepared something for you to eat. Won't you follow me?"

Amy slips off the hammock a little hesitantly.

Bohdi sits up...too fast apparently. His vision goes black, the world spins, and he feels his pulse pounding in his ears. When light and gravity return, Chloe's head is cocked to the side. Four hands are on her hips. Her other two arms are crossed over her chest, and she is tapping her chin with an elegant finger.

"Are you all right?" Amy says.

Bohdi sits up straighter, remembering she is there. Throwing his legs over the side, he says, "Never better," even though every time he inhales, he can feel the path of air burning its way into his lungs.

Crawling out of the hammock, Bohdi steps out from beneath the palm fronds with Amy. They both stop, look up, and gasp. About a quarter of a mile away, the biggest silvery column they've yet to see rises from the trees. There is an enormous cavern in its base. Bohdi can see daylight through it. There are also small steps that lead up to what looks like a dwelling carved into the column itself.

"Our home," says Chloe. "But for now, this way." With that, she turns and vanishes into the trees.

Amy and Bohdi follow her. They've barely stepped away from the beach when Chloe stops in a small clearing. Behind her a gentle waterfall gurgles into a crystal pool. Holding up all her arms she says, "And now you will eat."

Before Bohdi can even process her words, there is another gust of wind from behind him, and then there are two other women standing in the clearing. Both of them have six arms like Chloe, and both are wearing clothing that could be described as vaguely East Indian. But one woman is African in appearance, her skin darker than Bohdi's ever seen on anyone, her eyes Asian, her hair orange-red and tied in braids that fall halfway down her back. Where Chloe's frame is soft, hers is taller, lean and athletic, but still gorgeous. It would be impossible to turn his eyes away from her if her companion wasn't equally beautiful, and just as different. The last woman is pale and Caucasian in appearance. She has youthful, finely chiseled features, and bright blue eyes, but her hair is silvery white. Her frame is as thin as any runway model.

"My sisters," says Chloe.

The tall, African-looking woman bows her head. "I am Lache." Her voice is deep and rich, and a small smile pulls at her lips. Gesturing with three arms, she says, "And this is Addie."

Addie dips her chin slightly, but otherwise her face has no expression.

Beside Bohdi, Amy says, "Errr...nice to meet you."

Addie's lip curls in Amy's direction, and her expression turns so openly hostile both Amy and Bohdi take a step back.

"I cannot say the same," Addie hisses, her eyes locked with Amy's.

"Addie," Lache snaps. "She is our guest, as is Bohdi. Behave."

Addie scowls and crosses all six of her arms over her front.

Bohdi looks between the three women, and takes a wild stab in the dark. "Wait...are you the Norns?"

Addie's eyes narrow, Lache smiles, and Chloe laughs. "Of course!"

Bohdi suddenly feels as though a weight has been lifted from his shoulders. "Well, I have a question for you—"

Lache steps forward, her hips swaying mesmerizingly. "And we will give you an answer…if you fulfill the task we have chosen for you." Chloe giggles. Addie smiles, and all the hairs on the back of Bohdi's neck stand on end.

Lifting her hands, Lache says, "But for now, eat." At those words, she steps aside. There is a gust of wind and where she stood a table and chairs appears. The table is laden with a riot of shapes and colors that can only be fruit. There is also something that might have been a bird, but is now cooked to a golden brown. There is a plate with small slightly charred fishes, and a basket with loaves of breads of every sort.

"Oh," says Amy, taking a step forward.

Bohdi's mouth waters.

"One more thing," says Addie. The thin woman waves her hand and a centerpiece appears on the table: an elevated platter with a dead snake coiled into a pillar. Stuffed in the snake's fanged maw is an apple.

"Since you enjoy destroying my creatures!" Addie hisses at Amy.

Amy takes a step back, right into Bohdi. He puts a hand on her shoulder. Addie's eyes follow the motion and her nostrils flare.

"Addie!" Chloe says. "That isn't nice!" With a wave of her hand, the snake centerpiece disappears. Rolling her eyes, Addie disappears, too.

"I'm sorry," Chloe says, stepping toward Amy, eyes soft, and leaning forward just slightly, giving Bohdi a rather nice view. His fingers tighten on Amy's shoulder, and he squeezes his eyes shut. It's not like he's getting anywhere with six-armed, gorgeous goddesses, and something about all this just feels wrong. Lifting his head, he opens his eyes and focuses on a seagull-like creature skimming above the trees.

"She's not happy with you right now," Chloe says. "But of course, it's understandable, isn't it?"

Bohdi's eyes snap down to the Norn.

Drawing closer to Bohdi, Amy says, "No, not, really…"

Bending further at the waist, revealing even more, Chloe reaches forward with two hands to touch Amy's cheeks, her other hands come forward to stroke her sides. "But I like you."

Bohdi's brain disengages from the conversation almost completely at that point. But he's vaguely aware of Chloe saying, "Have you ever thought of being a boy?"

Bohdi tilts his head. Chloe appears to have a birthmark just above her left…

"Errrrr…" says Amy.

"Enough, Chloe!" says Lache.

Bohdi's gaze slips to the tall woman. She meets his eyes and smiles, showing all her teeth. "Eat now. You'll need your strength."

Bohdi swallows. His hand tightens involuntarily on Amy's shoulder. Reaching up, she takes her fingers in his.

Chloe giggles. "So cute!" And then she and Lache disappear in a gust of wind.

One of the gull-like creatures cries above their heads. Amy says. "Well, I guess we should eat…"

There is a swirl of wind, and Addie's voice comes from behind them. "Yes, fatten up!"

Bohdi and Amy turn just in time to see Addie's smirking form disappear.

"That was…" Bohdi starts to murmur.

"Oh!" says Chloe.

Bohdi and Amy turn again to see Chloe standing by the

table, a large basket in her hands. "Soap and towels," she says with a smile, setting the basket down.

Lache appears beside her sister, another basket in her arms. Looking Bohdi up and down, the dark woman says, "You really need to bathe." Setting her own basket down she says, "And I've brought clean clothes." She gives Bohdi a broad, gleaming white smile. "Don't worry, there are no kappa, alligators, or snakes in the water."

"Bon appetite!" says Chloe.

"āp kā khānā svādiṣṭa ho," says Lache, in the Hindu equivalent.

Chloe looks at her sister and giggles. "Getting in the mood?"

"Shhhhhh…" Lache says with a smirk in her sister's direction. And then both women disappear.

"Well…" says Amy, her hand still in his.

"That was different," says Bohdi. Getting in the mood? He knows what he'd like to think that means.

They look at each other, and then on some unspoken agreement, they cautiously approach the table and sit down. With trembling hands they reach toward the food, Bohdi for something that looks comfortingly like Ruth's Sunday biscuits, and Amy for an orange, triangular-ish, shaped fruit.

As they start eating, all hesitation vanishes. Amy seems to know every fruit on the table. Bohdi doesn't ask how. He doesn't want to start her on the subject of her ex.

It's not until Bohdi's hands stop shaking that he realizes that his pink shirt is still tied around his wrist. As soon as he notices it, he has to see if his phone is working and has to see the picture of his parents. Still chewing a Svartheimer root pear, Bohdi lifts the bundle, unwraps it on the table, and gingerly touches the components. Everything feels dry. Hands shaking again, he hastily puts his phone back together, Amy watching quietly from the side.

Pressing the power button, he closes his eyes, mentally preparing himself for it not to work.

"It's on!" Amy says.

Sighing in relief, Bohdi enters his passcode and navigates to his photos. The touch screen must be damaged, because it seems too responsive. Biting his lip, he still is able to pull the picture up.

He stares at the smiling man, woman, and baby that maybe is him, and an odd sort of emptiness overcomes him. He's on an alien world with six-armed women, eating fruit from yet another realm, and it's the picture in front of him that feels unreal. He stares at it for a few more minutes and then passes the phone to Amy.

"That's why I came to Nornheim," he says.

"Is that your girlfriend?" Amy says, staring down at the phone.

Bohdi's brain sputters. "What—"

Amy holds up his phone revealing a picture of Bohdi on leave during MOS. He's with Nat at a bar. They're kissing. It's on the lips, but their bodies are far apart.

He shakes his head and smiles. "Oh, no. That's my friend Nat from MOS. She's a lesbian." She was Bohdi's best friend in MOS.

Amy's eyebrow hikes up.

Laughing, Bohdi says, "There might have been alcohol involved." Leaning close to Amy, he whispers conspiratorially, "But she tells me, if I were a girl, she'd totally do me." Giving Amy a wink, he says, "If I were a girl I'd totally do her, too."

He's not sure if it's his imagination, but he thinks Amy's cheeks have gone a little pink.

Waggling his eyebrows, Bohdi snatches the phone from Amy. And then scowling at the wonky scroll feature, he tries to navigate back to the photo of his parents. Almost to himself he says, "I don't know why every man doesn't have a lesbian friend. They're the most underutilized source of priceless information." And Nat was just plain cool. He looks up at Amy and says wistfully, "She's how I know women's underwear is so comfortable."

Amy's cheeks do go very red at that—which makes Bohdi snicker.

Narrowing her eyes, she says, "If she is a lesbian. How—"

Bohdi nods. "Had to borrow hers. I woke up in the back of her car with my underwear draped over a potted cactus." Seeing Amy aghast at the visual, Bohdi waves a hand and says, "There's a long story behind it…"

"Do tell," says Amy.

"That, I'm sure, would be very interesting if I could remember it," Bohdi says. Finding the picture of his parents again, Bohdi hands the phone back to Amy.

She takes it and her eyebrows go up. "This is your girl-friend? She looks familiar…"

Bohdi snatches the phone from her again. It's a picture of Marion and him at a Cubs game. She's beaming, perky, and cute—as usual. He shakes his head. "This is Marion, you probably saw her at headquarters. We're just friends."

Actually, the polite term for it might be friends with benefits. But Marion asked him to keep it quiet, and he likes Marion, even if out of the sack he finds her as exciting as well… baseball… He's sure Marion's feelings about him are pretty much the same, even if baseball isn't the metaphor she'd use.

"Are you drunk in this picture, too?" Amy says, leaning over to take another look at the photo. Bohdi snorts. His eyes are half closed in the picture and he has a beer in his hand. "I wish," he says. "I was just half asleep. I don't know how anyone stands baseball. It's a lot of foul balls, time outs, and crotch grabbing."

Amy groans. "I know!"

Bohdi sighs and shakes his head. It isn't that Marion isn't clever, or interesting... It's just that they don't have any interests in common.

Bohdi scrolls to the picture of the happy Indian family. Handing the phone to her, he says, "I came here to find them."

"Oh," says Amy taking the phone from him.

Bohdi swallows. "I think they're my parents."

Amy's eyes meet him over the phone. "You don't remember anything...before?"

Bohdi looks down at the ground. "No. Not about them. Not about my culture—I'm a blank slate." He rubs his jaw. Even his accent has faded. And he has a low tolerance for spicy food. Asha, an Indian girl he'd dated for a time, thought that was the saddest thing ever.

"They look like such nice people," she says as she looks back down at the photo.

The honest response would be, I know. But the conversation is getting too heavy. He gives his best cheeky grin and says, "You say that like you're surprised."

Amy lifts her eyes to meet his.

Putting his hand over his chest, he gives her his best hurt puppy dog look and says, "You think I'm not nice?"

Amy's eyes narrow. "Nice isn't the first word I'd choose,"

she says.

Bohdi sits up straighter. "Hey!" But he feels the affront melting away.

Handing the phone back to him, she says, "Still, you're all right." She gets up and walks over to the baskets the Norns left. Popping a top off a vial tucked between some towels, she says, "I am so tired of smelling like water moccasin."

"You don't smell like water moccasin," says Bohdi.

Smiling, she says, "You just don't notice because you smell like dead fish."

"I…" Bohdi lifts his shirt, inhales, and winces. "Thought that was the surf…" he mumbles.

Joining Amy, he begins picking through the contents of the other basket. Pulling out what looks like a bunch of bright purple silk fabric, he says, "I think this is for you."

Regarding it a moment, Amy says, "No, it's too long. I think it's for you."

"But it's a skirt," says Bohdi, blinking a little as his vision goes blurry for a moment.

"Nope, just poofy pants," says Amy.

Bohdi holds the fabric up in front of him. They are pant-like, but… Turning his head and lifting his nose, he sniffs dismissively. "I refuse to dress like a giant grape."

Amy giggles and he can't contain his grin of triumph. Dropping the pants to hold them against his waist, he whispers to Amy, "Maybe they think I'm Aladdin…you know, 'cause I'm brown."

Amy puts a hand to her mouth and laughs. She has a cute smile and a cute laugh…and he wants more. Bohdi begins to sashay his hips and sing. "Daaa-da…Dot-dot-da-da-daaaa… Daaa-da…Dot-dot-da-da-daaaa…"

Amy laughs, "That's the *I Dream of Jeannie* theme song!"

Flicking a wrist, giving a Bollywood-worthy hip shake, Bohdi says, "I don't know the Aladdin theme! Da-da... Dot-dot-da-da-daaaa..."

Amy laughs so hard she looks like she's about to fall over. Bohdi's laughing, too, somehow able to ignore the pain in his lungs. And then there is crack from the sky behind him, a boom, and the whole world shakes. Bohdi falls face first to the ground, coughing and spitting dirt from his mouth.

Thor's voice rages through the trees. "What is the meaning of this?" Rolling over, Bohdi lifts his head. Amy is immediately at his side. Thor's hammer lies in the sandy loam just beyond his feet. Bohdi raises his eyes. Thor's chariot hangs in the sky. It's coated with black soot and bloodstains and is missing a wheel. Lashed to the front of it is a military drone.

Bohdi swallows, and exhales in a raspy wheeze.

The chariot starts to descend. Bohdi meets Thor's eyes. The space Viking lifts a hand and the hammer flies up into it. Swinging the hammer in the air, Thor roars. "I have searched for you—through fire and in forests! I have fought winged dinosaurs, and giant spiders, and I find you here—making jests!"

Thor leaps from the chariot before it's even met the ground. Lips curling into a snarl, he strides toward Amy and Bohdi, hammer raised.

Amy's hand tightens on Bohdi's shoulder. There is a whoosh of air. Bohdi blinks and finds himself staring up at the back of the silvered-haired Addie. "Easy there, Gilgamesh," she purrs. "No one dies on this island except by my command."

Thor stops in his tracks. His nostrils flare. His gaze locks on the Norn.

From beside Bohdi, Amy shouts at the now very red-faced warrior. "Oh, yeah? We fell into a nest of giant spiders! We fought big spiders, baby spiders, fire, kappa, alligators, adze, and snakes! Bohdi caught a fever and nearly died!"

Bohdi blinks. Nearly died?

Thor's eyes slide to Amy. He snorts. "You embellish."

There is another rush of air, and Lache is suddenly beside Thor, idly stroking his hammer. "No, Beowulf, they don't."

From behind Amy and Bohdi comes a giggle. Bohdi turns to see Chloe pressing four hands to her mouth. "Sorry, Master Skywalker, but it's true. They had a more exciting adventure than you."

Lache tsks. "Chloe, this isn't Skywalker, you are getting your heroes confused."

"Indeed, I am not," rumbles Thor, pulling his hammer away from Lache. "Skywalker is…was…one of Loki's names." He eyes the other two Norns. "Nor am I Beowulf, or Gilgamesh."

Giving a light laugh, Addie says, "Forgive us. You heroes are all alike…" Turning her head to Chloe, Addie says, "This is obviously Hercules…Loki's sidekick."

"Loki's what?" shouts Thor, lightning whipping from his hammer.

All three of the Norns break into laughter.

"I am Thor!" the space Viking bellows.

Waving a hand, Lache says, "Whatever. When you're ready to talk in a civilized manner, you may walk up to our home and ask your question, Hiawatha."

Walking over to Thor's chariot, Chloe says, "Don't bring this thing." She sniffs. "It's filthy."

And then all three of the women disappear.

Thor spins in place with a growl. He looks up at the towering column, his eyes narrow, and then he starts beating a path through the trees in that direction. Growling to himself, he reaches out with his hammer and knocks down a few trees— apparently just out of spite.

Still sprawled out on the ground, Bohdi watches him go. When Thor's disappeared from view, Amy sits down on the sand beside him.

"Are you all right?"

"Sure," Bohdi lies. He rubs his forehead and gets slowly to his feet. "Why don't you take the first dip?" He mumbles, tipping his head toward the pool of water. "I think I need a nap."

He stumbles in the direction of the hammock, and Amy follows, just behind him.

"I'm too tired to sneak a peek if that's what you're worried about," Bohdi says snippily.

"That isn't what I'm worried about," Amy says, but Bohdi's only half aware.

He falls into the hammock a few moments later and closes his eyes. He's dimly aware of Amy's hand on his forehead. What seems like just a few minutes later, she's shaking him. "Hey, Sleeping Beauty, wake up."

Bohdi swats in the general direction of her voice. "Go away!"

Amy catches his hands. "Bohdi, wake up! You're scaring me!"

Something in her voice makes him shiver, even though it feels like the day has gotten much warmer.

He opens his eyes and sees Amy sitting sideways beside him. She swallows. "Your fever is back." She bites her lip.

"This happened when Beatrice caught pneumonia, too. Her fever would go away, and then come back…"

She motions toward the trees. "The pool is cool. It will help keep your temperature down." She raises an eyebrow. With what sounds like forced cheeriness, she says, "You don't need anymore brain damage."

Bohdi snorts at the joke. And then for the first time, he realizes that Amy's hair is wet, combed back, and pulled into a neat ponytail again. She doesn't look beautiful like Addie, Chloe, or Lache, but she looks real and human. She's wearing her jeans and a too large linen shirt. The shirt wouldn't be flattering, except it's almost sheer, and from this angle, he thinks he can see the outline of her form beneath it. It might be the cut of the shirt, but her breasts look fuller, her waist finer, and the slope between her hips and belly button the perfect place to rest his hands, pull her in and just…snuggle.

Oh hell. He's dying.

He sits up so quickly his vision goes black. Before she can say anything, he stands and heads back in the direction of the pool.

"What do you think?" Bohdi says, buttoning a small navy vest over his bare chest. He's sitting on a towel, with his back against a boulder. On his bottom half, he's wearing his pants from work.

Sitting in front of him, Amy studies his appearance. "Well…"

Bohdi waggles his eyebrows. He'd like to stand up and strike a pose, but even though the dip in the water made him feel better, he still feels…off. Light headed. A little too warm.

"It's flattering…" she says.

Bohdi adopts a bored expression, and casually flexes his biceps. When he turns and sneaks a peek at Amy, she's blushing.

His lungs are burning and he feels like falling over—but he can't help grinning. It's true, he's not precisely huge, but Steve's forcing him to work out has definitely kept him toned. Amy's blush is worth every boring moment at the gym. He is so buying Steve a beer when he gets back.

Amy regains her composure and says, "But it's kind of Chippendale-ish, isn't it?"

Bohdi's watched Chip and Dale with Claire. He blinks. "Chipmunks?" He looks down at the vest. It isn't striped like a chipmunk.

Amy snickers into her hand. "How is this the one cultural reference you've missed?"

Bohdi snips. "What? When it comes to cultural references, I'm only two years old. I haven't watched every Disney cartoon…"

Amy laughs aloud. "No!"

"Well, what then?" Bohdi says, skin prickling.

"Strippers, Bohdi," Amy says, face almost straight. "Male strippers." She puts a hand over her mouth, obviously stifling another laugh.

Bohdi just stares at her. He hates it when he doesn't know stuff like that. Lifting his chin defiantly, he bats his eyelashes. "Are you saying I could be a male stripper?"

Amy's mouth makes a small "o."

Breaking into a grin, Bohdi says, "Because if you are, I think I…"

Love you. A cough wracks through him, cutting off the last words. And maybe it's good, even if he was just fooling.

"Bohdi!" Amy says, crawling over to his side.

And he doesn't mean to, but he's suddenly leaning on her. Holding a hand to his mouth, tears coming to his eyes— because of the force of the cough, or because he's furious at his body for being so weak, he's not sure. How the hell is he supposed to climb up to the Norns like this? He came all this way, and he can barely sit up.

The fit seems to last forever.

When he finally regains himself, he feels hotter, less lucid. It takes him the span of a few wheezy gasps to realize a shadow has fallen over them.

Lungs rasping, Bohdi lifts his head

…and finds himself staring into the face of Thor.

The space Viking is staring down at him. He doesn't look angry. Just confused. Maybe even concerned.

Thor's fingers flex on his hammer. "I…" The large man takes a deep breath. "…Overreacted earlier."

Amy exhales softly.

"You must understand…" Thor says. "I thought I had failed to protect two weaker beings in my charge. I mourned your deaths…" Thor swallows, his eyes flit between Amy and Bohdi. "I apologize for my outburst."

Bohdi feels Amy shift beside him.

Thor falls to one knee before them. "You are dying," he says to Bohdi.

Bohdi sinks against the boulder he's leaning on. Amy grabs his hand. "No, if we get him home, and get him a round of antibiotics, he'll be fine."

Thor shakes his head. "The pneumonia is not what's

killing him...It is his own body's over-reaction to it."

"Oh..." says Amy. Bohdi hears her swallow.

"How do you know that?" Bohdi wheezes, leaning into Amy. He would much rather believe her assessment...and yet...

Thor bows his head. "The Lord of Chaos can feel lies... I can feel sickness...and injury." Raising his head, looking a little bashful, he shrugs. "It is not a particularly manly ability. But it is so."

Little alarm bells go off in Bohdi's mind. The Lord of Chaos can sense lies... Why is that important?

Amy squeezes Bohdi's hand. "It's true..." she whispers. "Thor can help you. I remember..."

Thor stretches a hand toward Bohdi's chest. Bohdi scrambles backward in the sand, and presses himself against Amy, instinctively.

"Let me help you," Thor says.

Amy squeezes Bohdi's hand again. "Let him."

Bohdi coughs. "If I let you...will I owe you something?" He doesn't know why he asks. The words just come out.

Thor's shoulders slump, as though Bohdi's wounded him. "No. This I offer in friendship."

Bohdi blinks. When did he and Thor become friends? He almost wants to say he'll wait for the antibiotics. Something is wrong here, and yet... He looks up at the column. He won't be able to walk those steps if he keeps feeling like this. So he nods and coughs out, "Sure, do your worst."

Thor presses his hand against Bohdi's chest, just above the V of the vest. His fingers are cool and calloused. He says nothing. Just holds his hand there.

Bohdi is starting to feel silly...and then Thor's fingers start to warm. The warmth spreads to Bohdi's skin, and then inside to his lungs. At first, it's comfortable…and then it's not. His lungs feel like they're burning and he gasps.

Pushing hard on Bohdi's chest, Thor says, "Exhale!"

Bohdi does. The air that rushes out of him is a heavy cloud of moisture and blurs the world around him.

"Again!" barks Thor.

Bohdi gulps down some air and then exhales. The same thing happens—though the moisture in the cloud is lighter this time.

"He's clearing the water from your lungs," Amy whispers.

The big man nods. He presses his hand more firmly against Bohdi's chest and closes his eyes. "And now to still his immune system…"

The heat in his chest dissipates. Bohdi feels only warmth. He inhales…and smiles in awe and relief. "There is no more pain." And he feels like he can stand up.

Nodding again, Thor pulls his hand away. Standing, he gestures at the still blinking drone attached to the chariot. "Although we've lost the magical wire that helps you open gates, it appears your allies are opening them anyway. Perhaps we can use the metal bird to contact them somehow?"

Bohdi tries not to look surprised at Thor's foresightedness.

"They must be periodically checking in…" Amy says.

Bohdi meets her eyes. "We could probably give them a time when we'll be at the gate…"

"Or…" says Thor.

Amy and Bohdi turn to him.

Putting a hand on his chin, Thor says, "It is true this realm is dark in Heimdall's eyes. However, if there is a magical event large enough, it can act like a beacon… He would be able to see where we are…and my father could create a new gate to Asgard."

"Uh…" says Bohdi. Amy draws closer to his side, if that were possible.

"As my faithful companions, you'd both be my honored guests," Thor says.

Bohdi's brow furrows. They hadn't been companions that long…

"And able to stay as long as you like…" Thor says. "It is a beautiful realm, filled with wonders of magic and science."

"No," says Amy, her voice quavering.

Thor's eyes slide to Amy. Her gaze is traveling between Bohdi and the space Viking. Standing up, she clears her throat. "And won't you be off right away to find the new Loki anyway?"

Thor's eyes don't stray from her face. After a long moment, he says, "Aye, my father's first orders upon my return will be to bring the new Destroyer to Asgard…for good." His voice is almost a whisper.

Amy licks her lips nervously. "I don't suppose you'd like to tell me where he is?" She shrugs. "Obviously there'd be no way for me to get to him before you…"

A long moment of silence stretches after her words. Bohdi swears he can hear every insect on the island cheeping. The tension is a little too much. Clearing his throat, he says, "The Destroyer…that's one of Loki's names, right? Doesn't exactly sound like the guy you'd want to invite to the party…"

Both Amy's and Thor's eyes swing to where Bohdi sits against the rock.

"Errrrr…" says Bohdi. He pats his pockets frantically. Scrambling to his feet he mutters. "Where is my lighter?"

Did he leave it at the table?

As he walks over to the table, he hears Amy say quietly, "You gave us your oath, Thor."

His lighter is with Amy's phone guts. He picks it up, gives it a flick, and is rewarded with a small burst of flame. "Hey, it still works!" He tries to sound cheerful, because obviously, something weird, tense, and unhappy is going on. Someone has to be the glass half-full guy.

Thor rumbles. "What about you, Son of Patel... Do you wish to return to Earth?"

Surprised by the question, Bohdi takes a tiny step back. Is Thor serious? The giant hammer-toting alien is leaning forward slightly, his eyes on Bohdi. Bohdi blinks at his seeming earnestness. He considers the offer... Asgardian culture seems kind of shitty. However, there are lots of shitty places on Earth he wouldn't mind going to. The Congo, North Korea, to name two—just to say he'd done it.

Flicking his lighter, Bohdi looks between the space Viking and his companion of the last few days. Thor looks extra large standing so close to Amy—or she looks extra small. She's brave and smart and cute...but there are a lot of cute girls in the world. Or worlds...and it's not like they're a thing...

Thor's armor is blackened by soot—but it's still impressive, in its video game, cool way. To go to a whole new world—with cool armor, weapons, and tech...without creatures trying to eat him at every turn.

Amy sucks in a breath. Bohdi meets her eyes. She looks afraid. More afraid than when they'd been chased by spiders, or a swarm of adze had been about to attack them. She could have left him with the spiders. Or let him drown. And he's pretty sure she kissed him when they were on the log, trying to wish him better. Which is sweet. Even if it didn't work. Or maybe only worked for a while.

He almost sighs. He's so going to regret this. Clearing his throat, he says, "Ummm…if it's all the same, I'd rather head back to Earth…"

Thor's shoulders slump. "As you wish."

Mouthing the words, "thank you," Amy closes her eyes.

Bowing his head, Thor says, "We can be off at once."

"No!" say Bohdi and Amy.

Lifting his big head, Thor blinks.

"I have a question to ask the Norns," Bohdi says. He rolls his shoulders, and smiles. "I feel up to climbing the stairs." He looks up at the dimming sky. "I'll make it before it gets too dark."

"You have a question for the Norns?" Thor asks sounding a bit incredulous.

Bohdi's smile drops. "Errr…I thought they'd answer anyone's questions in exchange for a task…"

Thor gives a hearty laugh. "Indeed they will, Son of Patel! And whatever task they ask of you, you can count on my aid."

"And—" Amy starts to say, but Thor claps a hand on her shoulder so hard she almost falls over.

"And what, pray tell us, is your question? Do you seek a magical weapon? A map of the known worlds? The source of magic, perhaps?"

Bohdi shifts on his feet. Amy is rubbing her shoulder scowling at Thor.

"I uh, actually just want to find my parents," Bohdi says.

"Your parents?" Thor says.

Bohdi shrugs. "I don't remember anything before Loki—" He points a finger to his head, and gives a rueful smile. "Not even my real name."

"Nothing…" says Thor. His shoulders slump and he looks like a kicked puppy.

Going to the table, Amy says, "Maybe you'd like some fruit for the climb?"

"Yeah," says Bohdi, turning quickly away from Thor's hurt. "That would be great."

"You can take my flask," says Thor, as Amy wraps up some food in Bohdi's pink shirt.

"Thanks, man," says Bohdi.

Thor beams, and presses it into Bohdi's hand.

Since he has Thor's attention, Bohdi asks, "So, if I don't like the task the Norns give to me…do I have to do it?"

Frowning, Thor scratches his head. "Why would you come all this way and not accept the task?"

Bohdi shrugs.

Rubbing his chin, Thor looks up at the sky. "Aye, I suppose you could. But it might be unwise."

For some reason, Thor's words make Bohdi shiver.

CHAPTER 19

Flask belted to his hip, pink shirt with snacks wrapped around his wrist, lucky lighter and knife in his pocket, Bohdi sets off through the sparse forest. He follows the path Thor took. It's not hard to follow felled trees.

As he walks away, he hears Amy's voice carrying on the breeze. Her words are indistinct, but Thor's response rumbles loud and clear. "Being a human would be ridiculous."

Bohdi wonders what that's about but doesn't turn from his path; the first part of his quest is nearly done. His steps feel light. The air tastes sweet.

He does have a flash of apprehension as he gets close to the column. The stairs to the Norn's abode are hewn directly into the pearlescent surface. In some places, the steps appear wide and steep, at other places low and narrow. If he tries to avoid looking at the surface, he'll probably fall. Taking out his lighter, he approaches. To his relief, and sadness, the images sparkling there have nothing to do with him. They look interesting—people he's never met, places he's never been—but he doesn't feel the same gut-wrenching need to watch.

Putting his lighter away, Bohdi takes the first step. And

he's suddenly hit with a sense of wonder and accomplishment. He's made it to another world. He's battled monsters with nothing more than improvised clubs and a knife. He's somehow managed to win the affection of Thor—and maybe even Amy. Whatever the Norns task him with will be easy in comparison.

With a happy whistle, he begins to climb in earnest, taking two and three steps at a time. The column is about the width of a city block. Not perfectly round, the base undulates, like that of a tree. The stairs loop all the way around the column on their upward journey, allowing Bohdi to see the lay of the land. The island is shaped roughly like a bow tie, with the column as the knot in the center. The sound of waves from the opposite sides of the island crashing in the caverns at the column's base reverberate through the air and in the steps.

The waves are still louder than Bohdi's slightly labored breathing when he reaches the first landing. A few hundred feet above the sea, it is on the side of the column opposite Amy and Thor. The landing features a lip about seven feet wide, and a cave entrance blackened by soot that is about fourteen feet across and nearly as high. Bohdi slows his steps and cautiously approaches. Somehow he thinks the cavern maw looks much too dirty to be home to the Norns—

A giant maroon head shoots out of the cavern. Jumping back just in time, Bohdi nearly falls off the stairs.

The head turns on its enormous serpentine neck, and Bohdi finds himself face to face with Nidhogg.

"Bohdi!" Nidhogg roars, a tiny ball of fire forming at the back of the dragon's tongue and escaping past his lips. Bohdi drops and rolls to avoid the flame and finds himself hanging on the edge of the steps. He looks down. It's only about six feet from his feet to the loop of stairs below him, but he'd rather not have to walk up again.

"Oh, I am so embarrassed!" Nidhogg declares. "I could try and pick you up." A shadow flows over Bohdi, and he feels a gust of heat at his back.

"No! Got it," Bohdi says, hastily pulling himself up, and swings a leg over the steps. Climbing to his feet, he says, "I'm fine."

Blinking his enormous eyes, Nidhogg seems genuinely embarrassed. Or at least, his facial scales seem a deeper shade of red.

"I am so sorry," Nidhogg rumbles. Leaning the side of his head very close to Bohdi he whispers, "Truly, it was an accident."

Bohdi blinks. He is talking…to a talking dragon. And how cool is that?

Patting Nidhogg's head, Bohdi says, "No problem, big guy."

Nidhogg's head whips back, and the dragon gives Bohdi a toothy smile that is as friendly as it is terrifying. "Would you like to stop for a bite?"

Bohdi swallows, but he tries to give a cheeky grin. "I hope you don't mean that the way I think you could mean that."

Laughing, Nidhogg pokes Bohdi with his snout, and then pulls back, shaking his head. "Oh, no, no, no! Not that you don't look delicious, mind you, but I'm on strict orders not to eat you."

Bohdi gulps and tries not to look as discomfited as he feels.

Seemingly oblivious, Nidhogg smiles again and the little tentacles above his eyes waggle. "I'm smoking adze." As if for emphasis, he lets out a puff of smoke from his nostrils.

Bohdi sniffs. The air smells slightly of pork. Trying to sound grateful he says, "Ah, thanks, but I'm getting really close to the Norns."

The dragon nods. "Oh, right, right, of course!" He sounds very understanding, but his huge head still stays on the landing, blocking Bohdi's way forward.

"Um, may I pass?" says Bohdi.

Nidhogg's head jerks, and then head and neck slink back into the cave so that only his beaked snout peeks out. Rolling his eyes, the dragon says, "I am so sorry. I forget how you don't have wings. Please don't think me speciesist."

"Nah," says Bohdi. "Wouldn't think you speciesist for that." The desire to eat him on the other hand...Trying to appear nonchalant, he continues across the landing but can't help stopping and peering into the cave. "How do you get in there? It's too narrow for your body." In fact, it seems barely wide enough for the dragon's head.

Nidhogg's head bobs and the column reverberates with his chuckles. "Oh, I enter at sea level. This is just a little window I like to peek out now and then. You never know what sort of errant adventurer will stop by for dinner."

Bohdi tries to keep his eyes from getting too wide.

Nidhogg's head bobs inside the cave. His eyes narrow. "But the Norns seem to have a thing for you. So I wouldn't worry."

Smoke puffs from the dragon's nostrils and floods from the entrance. Raising an arm to his mouth, Bohdi chokes and coughs. When the smoke clears the dragon has vanished into the darkness of the cave.

"Why worry?" Bohdi mutters.

From the cave mouth, he hears a laugh and the stairs tremble beneath his feet. Turning on his heels, Bohdi starts quickly on his way. It's only a half loop more, when Bohdi comes to another, wider, landing. This landing has a door set into the column. Nearly twice Bohdi's height, it is made out of whitewashed wood. Emerald inlays with twisting leaves and dancing figures seem to move along its surface. It doesn't appear to have a doorknob...but that isn't what immediately concerns Bohdi. Sitting on a stunted branch jutting out just above the door is an eagle. The bird appears to be nearly as large as Bohdi himself—even with its wings tucked in. The bird is cocking its head in Bohdi's direction. The feathers on the back of its neck are ruffled.

Bohdi's heard about eagles on Earth occasionally killing sheep, and as it is, he's fighting the urge to bleat.

What had Nidhogg said? The dragon was under strict orders not to eat Bohdi...maybe the eagle will be friendly-ish too?

Stepping forward, Bohdi tries to give his friendliest, most winning smile. "Hi!" He says.

The feathers on the back of the eagle's neck rise higher.

Gesturing toward the door, Bohdi says, "I don't suppose you'd mind if I just walked underneath you and—"

The eagle issues an ear-splitting shriek.

Bohdi nearly falls off the stairs. A low grinding noise sounds from the direction of the door, and it slowly begins to open inward.

Bohdi blinks. "Uhhhh...thanks..." he says to the eagle.

From the doorway comes an indignant huff. "It wasn't his feathered chittta-chatt. It was me."

Bohdi looks down to see Ratatoskr standing on two legs

in the doorway.

"Well, don't just stand there!" Ratatoskr chitters, ears back. "Come in!"

With a nervous glance at the eagle, Bohdi darts through the door. He finds himself in a windowless hallway, lit from the glow of the column's pearly surface. Here and there, he sees more ornate doors, all as heavy and imposing as the first.

A low grinding reverberates through the hallway. Bohdi looks behind him just in time to see the front door slam shut.

At his feet, Ratatoskr clears his throat. "This way."

Bohdi blinks down at the squirrel. "Are you sort of their butler?"

Ratatoskr's eyes narrow. "No, I am not—"

Bohdi puts a hand to his lip, feeling the onslaught of an approaching sneeze.

Clearing his throat, the squirrel says hastily, "—not *just* their butler. I do other important things."

Bohdi sniffs. His urge to sneeze recedes. He looks down at the squirrel. "Cool," he says, trying not to sound like he almost just gave the squirrel another snotty shower.

Ears still back, Ratatoskr begins to walk down the hallway. "I've never liked you," he grumbles.

Bohdi sniffs again, oddly hurt. "But we've only just met."

Ratatoskr lets loose a cackle. "That's what you think."

Bohdi starts to protest, but then he hears laughter, light and feminine, rising around him, from everywhere and nowhere. He hears a voice say lightly in Hindi, "*…a child that could carry us between universes.*"

It takes Bohdi a moment, but he realizes it's Chloe talking about Eisa.

"*…If we knew how different events played out in different*

timelines, we wouldn't just be watchers of history, we could shape it!"

"Chloe!" Lache's voice snaps. What follows is an almost shout that Bohdi hears as, something-something-something-in-a-harsh-guttural-tongue, "…Hindi!"

He stops in place. Did Lache just tell Chloe off for speaking in Hindi?

He hears Chloe giggle, and a raspy laugh from Addie.

The hairs on the back of his neck stand on end, and he can't say why. This is hardly the weirdest thing he's encountered since coming to Nornheim.

As if to punctuate that point, Ratatoskr grumbles a few words about apples, the In-Between, and broken ribs. The squirrel is still walking on two legs.

Bohdi jogs a few steps to catch up with the disgruntled animal. Flicking the flint wheel of his lighter, he feels the comforting burn of flame on his thumb. He doesn't remember when he took it out of his pocket.

They approach a final door at the end of the hallway; it's ever so slightly ajar.

"Hold on a chitta-chat-chat minute," Ratatoskr says. "I'll announce you—"

Before the squirrel has even finished, the door swings inward, and Bohdi finds himself face to face with Addie. The clothing she'd worn before hadn't been precisely modest, but what she wears now is even less so. It's still vaguely East Indian, but it is impossibly sheer. Bohdi can see every outline of her body, and the blush of the tips of her breasts—which, while they aren't as full as he prefers, are still amazingly perky. He suddenly feels warm and lightheaded and knows it has nothing to do with a fever.

"Don't you look delicious," Addie says.

Bohdi's eyes snap back to her face. She's smiling, and ordinarily the smile and the comment would be an open invitation. But considering who she is and what she is...

"I could just take a bite out of you," she adds with a laugh.

As Bohdi wavers in the doorway, he's vaguely aware of Ratatoskr mumbling at his feet. "I am so chitting out of here."

Bohdi forces himself to smile at the Norn. "Should I be afraid you mean that literally?"

Addie leans closer and whispers, "Is that the question you came here to ask?"

Eyes widening, Bohdi takes a step back. "No!"

Addie laughs, and Chloe and Lache are suddenly at her side. "We know what you want to ask," says Chloe. "Addie was just teasing."

Reaching out a soft brown hand, Chloe takes Bohdi's arm. "We're really so happy to see you." Sidling up beside him, she pulls Bohdi through the door. Despite the tempting female flesh around him, he can't keep his eyes from wandering around the room. It is shaped like an enormous half circle. Beyond nine looms, he sees nine enormous windows, open to the Nornheim breeze. He blinks. No, only the one directly in front of him is open to Nornheim, the others open to other places. He sees a landscape of ice and snow in one. In another there is a smoldering volcano. One window overlooks a castle that looks like it was stolen from the set of a Disney movie. He sees rice paddies in another, and people who look vaguely like him—and yet...

Lache snaps her fingers, and all the windows shift so he is seeing only the Nornheim sunset. "Too distracting for the poor dear," she says.

"Mmmm…yes…" says Chloe.

Bohdi blinks and his gaze drops to the looms. Eight show weavings that are near identical, but the ninth is a riot of color. He steps toward it. Addie snaps her fingers and all the looms disappear. "That will be too distracting as well."

Arm still in his, Chloe leans close and whispers in his ear. "Don't worry, you're not missing anything. That weaving was only Earth, where you most recently came from. It's the most exciting of the Nine Realms—for now."

Stepping around and in front of him, Chloe brushes his cheek with her fingers. Lache and Addie sidle up on either side.

"We expected you'd be drawn to it…" Chloe says. Bohdi's eyes slide to her lower lip, it's so close, and kissable, and this is so strange. He's not afraid…and he doesn't feel awkward or out of his league.

Lache comes to his side and whispers, "Your disguise is so good, even we weren't sure it was you; that's why we had so many tests."

On the other side of him, Addie says, "I told them it wouldn't matter what form you took, you would be yourself—and if we made the odds of your success impossible, you were bound to succeed."

Bohdi's body is warm…and so are theirs. He wants to reach out, he wants to touch, and it feels like he should, and like he shouldn't. Their words are only slowly filtering through to his brain. Disguise? Form?

His eyes fall again to Chloe's lips. He has this strange idea that he should bite her bottom lip, hard…

Two of Chloe's hands slide feather light down his arms. Taking his hands in two of hers, she rests them upon her hips and steps ever so slightly closer, two more of her hands go to stroke his face, and the last pair go to his waist. Maybe they are three very powerful, beautiful, ancient, six-armed women, and maybe he is only a too-skinny amnesiac from Earth, but if that isn't an invitation, nothing is. Bohdi pulls her to him, and though it isn't really his thing, he bites her lip so forcefully he tastes iron in his mouth.

Chloe moans. And that moan is his thing. The sound jolts through his system like an electric shock. He barely keeps his hands from pulling up her skirt, instead he just pulls her closer and kisses her, licking the blood away with his tongue.

She is so soft beneath his hands and where her breasts brush his chest, and he should be startled by what's happening and yet he's not. And that is startling. Bohdi pulls back, his mouth suddenly dry, the beginnings of a shiver at the base of his spine.

Chloe opens her eyes and smiles at him. "You remember," she whispers.

He's suddenly aware of two of Lache's hands in his hair, and on his back, and Addie's hands sliding down his stomach. The shiver he'd felt turns to heat.

"You and I are most alike," Addie whispers. "But you're always drawn to Chloe first."

Bohdi's eyes slide to hers. Their words should be disturbing to him, but his brain is a cold fog, and his body is alight. He has this idea that Addie would like it if he kissed her softly. He lifts a thumb to gently brush her lips. Addie's blue eyes slide shut, and the heat of the non-kiss goes right to his core. Chloe leans against him, and Lache whispers, "Bohdi, we can tell you about your parents, but first we need to discuss our terms."

Addie and Chloe both sigh. Bohdi turns to Lache. She's as tall as he is. She's smirking at him, one arm on his shoulder, her face very close. He tries to dart in and steal a kiss, but she pulls back laughing. "First our terms." She winks. "I think you'll like them." With that she turns her back and sashays to the far side of the room.

Chloe slips back to his right side, and his arm finds its way around her waist. On the other side his arm slinks around Addie, but his eyes are on Lache. The same way he knew Chloe would want him to bite her, and Addie would want him to be gentle, he knows sex with Lache will be a battle. His skin heats, his lips twist into a smile. Pulling Chloe and Addie along, he follows Lache like he is being drawn on a string.

Glancing over her shoulder, Lache grins, and her tongue darts between her teeth. She waves an arm and a circular table appears, a single chalice filled with grass-green liquid at its center. Another flick of her wrist and four upholstered backless chairs appear.

"Sit," says Lache, gesturing at the nearest chair. Quirking an eyebrow, Bohdi obeys. Chloe and Addie peel away from him, and the shock of their warm bodies leaving starts his brain spinning. Is he skipping right over the vaunted three-some right to a foursome—with three six-armed goddesses? Because that's awesome…

…and also, very odd. His nose twitches. They're not out of his league—they're out of his whole stratosphere, solar system, and possibly galaxy.

His eyes fall on Chloe's breasts, and he remembers how soft they'd felt. Then he remembers the small birthmark he'd seen earlier. Chloe's eyes meet his and she giggles.

Maybe they're just slumming it? Hey, it's happened before.

And who is he to deprive them?

As if in answer to that thought, Addie says, "We've never had sex with you as a human before."

There's something about that answer that makes the circuits in his brain short. But before he can figure out what it is, Addie and Chloe both drop hands to his knees beneath the table. Their fingers start creeping upward. Bohdi's jaw drops, and he closes his eyes and struggles to stay upright.

Bohdi's eyes bolt open. Did she say she'd never had sex with him as a human before? Maybe it was just a slip of the tongue… But then hadn't Chloe said something about him remembering how to kiss her. And more bizarrely…he does remember, doesn't he?

Sitting across from Bohdi, Lache says, "So have you guessed what task we're going to require of you?"

Cockily as he can manage, he says, "I think I have an idea." He doesn't feel cocky though. All of this weirdness is leading in one direction—but it's a leap in logic Bohdi doesn't want to take.

Lache chuckles, low and rich, and someone's hand skims over a very sensitive bit of anatomy under the table. Bohdi feels warm and dizzy again.

"Spend the night with us. Know us carnally," Lache says with a wide predatory smile. "That is all we ask. Do you accept?"

Bohdi stares at her a moment. It's exactly what he expected, and even if it's weird that he expected it, why question the best thing that's ever happened to him?

Bohdi grins. "When do we start?" As soon as the words slip out, he feels his smile slip away. Something else washes over him. Dread? Suspicion? He can't name it. Addie licks her lips, Chloe purrs, and Lache pushes the chalice toward him. "First, drink this."

Bohdi looks into the chalice and the hairs on the back of his neck prickle as his nerves begin to light up in a not helpful way.

When he's nervous, he tends to talk. "And Amy thought I wouldn't need my condoms," he says. A harmless joke. But mentioning Amy is a mistake. He feels a twinge of…something…even if he shouldn't. He thinks of his head pillowed on Amy's knees and fights a scowl. There's nothing between them, he has nothing to be ashamed of, and three birds in hand is definitely better than…he doesn't remember the rest.

Not quite ready to take the first sip, he pats his back pocket. "But I left them in my wallet." Which he forgot. Not that he cares…Even if wearing a condom is the one thing Steve is constantly badgering him about. He glances around the table. This is the one time he should just throw caution to the wind.

He hesitates anyway. "But I guess you've magically taken care of that…" Why is he even asking? Why is he suddenly a hopeless puddle of indecision?

Lache sits back in her chair. "Drink."

Bohdi stares at her perfect face. His mouth is wet, his body is hot, but his brain is screaming…something. He can't really hear the words. Addie, or maybe Chloe is running her hands right up to the bulge in his pants and Bohdi thinks his eyes are about to cross. Reaching down he catches the straying hands.

Addie and Chloe giggle and more hands light upon his legs. Even though he's practically swaying in his seat, Bohdi's brain is becoming increasingly pesky. Staring at the green liquid, words begin slipping out of his mouth. "Is this like a liquid condom? Because that would be great. Condoms suck." Bohdi bites his lip. Stupid, stupid, stupid brain.

No one answers his question.

Bohdi lifts his eyes to the Norns.

"It's not an issue," Lache says, a bit too casually.

Dropping Addie's and Chloe's hands, Bohdi just manages to pull his arm up in time to catch the sneeze.

Addie, Chloe, and Lache all lean back, eyes wide. Chloe's mouth drops in a small "o."

Addie snaps something at Lache, and Lache glares at her sister.

Sniffing, feeling like an idiot, Bohdi searches his pockets for a tissue. "Here," says Chloe, passing him a bit of silk. He's distantly aware of Lache saying something snippily to Addie.

Bohdi takes the handkerchief from her hands. Pressing it to his nose, he is unable to meet her eyes. He remembers Amy's question. *"Do you sneeze when people lie to you, Bohdi?"*

He sniffs into the tissue and recalls Thor's words, *"The Lord of Chaos can sense lies…"*

He blinks. A shiver running through him, he raises his eyes. Addie and Lache are still arguing in another language, but Chloe's eyes are on him, soft and sad.

"Am I…?" Bohdi whispers. He can't even finish the sentence, it's too ridiculous. Lord of Chaos? Destroyer? Him?

"Do you have a different question for us?" Lache says, turning away from her sister. "The price would still be the same."

For a moment, he wants to ask. His hands clench at his sides. But he needs to find his parents.

He shakes his head and looks at the green liquid. It smells

vaguely like cough syrup—but worse. He doesn't think he'd want to drink it if smelled like chocolate chip cookies. Pushing it away, he says, "You know, if this is an aphrodisiac, I don't need it. I may be only human, but I am in my twenties, I can go a few rounds without it." Even if he's rapidly finding himself not in the mood.

He blinks. He'd asked if birth control was covered…and then he'd sneezed.

Addie picks up the chalice. "It's not poison, it will not incapacitate you. It is a gift. You're practically infertile. Without help you're likely never to have any children."

Lache and Chloe both inhale audibly.

Addie turns defensively to them. "He was already suspicious."

That's true, but having his suspicions confirmed is another matter. Bohdi feels like he's just been thrown into a cold shower. Actually, no, cold showers don't really work. This works.

It's not that he doesn't like kids. Kids are cool. Even good kids like Claire are natural little mischief makers. But he's not ready to be shackled to that sort of responsibility right now, especially to three women he's just met, even if they are saying that it may be his only shot. Or three shots. Or something.

A little lump forms in his throat. And what a way to learn all your little swimmers are floating belly up.

Addie pats him gently on the shoulder. "Even with this rather potent brew, it will probably only work for one of us."

"Errrrrr…" he says.

Chloe's eyes widen. "You've frightened him!" Putting a hand on Bohdi's opposite shoulder, she says, "Remember, in the United States if a man fathers a child, even unknowingly, he is bound to support it."

"Ohhhhhhh," say Lache and Addie in unison, nodding their heads knowingly.

Looking suddenly understanding, Addie puts a hand on his. "We really don't require anything else from you."

Bohdi doesn't feel the faintest desire to sneeze. Nor to drink the "medicinal" fluid in front of him.

Shaking her head, Lache says, "We don't want you to stick around."

Bohdi sits up straighter. That doesn't make him want to sneeze either. Or feel better.

"Don't get us wrong, we like you," says Lache.

"Your visit has already been very exciting!" says Chloe, with an emphatic nod.

"But you and the girl have brought a lot of trouble with you," says Addie. Shaking her head, she says, "You've killed, displaced, and ruined so many of our guardians." She sighs. "We can't allow Nornheim to be a nice place for hominids to visit."

Lache shrugs. "Most of you are useless to us."

Chloe leans in toward Bohdi and says, "And humans are like chocolate for Nidhogg."

Bohdi raises an eyebrow at that.

Lache sighs. "He loves you, but if he eats too many, he gets horribly sick."

Bohdi looks down at the green chalice. "Well, that's a shame," he says, more to stall than anything else.

The three women laugh.

Reaching out a hand, Bohdi lifts the chalice. The room and the Norns are reflected in the liquid and the chalice's crystal surface. The women are beautiful—even in the fractured reflections. They're also ancient, powerful, and supposedly they know all that has happened.

He pulls the chalice closer. Making a baby and leaving, that would be an act of chaos, wouldn't it? And chaos is what they're implying Bohdi is. He scowls. That thought is too big for his brain; he can't believe it.

And he can't abandon even a theoretical child on purpose. Maybe it's because Steve has infected Bohdi with his morality. Maybe it's because Bohdi saw Steve's depression when he found out Claire would be moving away, or because he saw Amy fall apart at the sight of her almost child. Or maybe it's an echo of the life he forgot—Hindi has a ridiculous number of words for family relationships. He swallows. Does Hindi have a word for child of a past life? He can't remember…but he does remember the little redheaded girl. "Eisa," he murmurs. That's what the Norns want.

Chloe scoots closer to him. "You heard me earlier when I spoke about her." She puts a hand on Bohdi's knee. Instead of going warm, his muscles tense.

Chloe's face is painfully lovely. And now her eyes are wide and earnest. "Yes, we would love a child like Eisa, but we would love any child you gave us. Like we loved Jörmungandr…"

"And little Heimdall," says Lache.

"My first little adze," sniffs Addie.

Bohdi exhales and watches the ripples it causes in the surface of the green medicine. Jörmungandr…the world serpent, and in myths one of Loki's children. He blinks. Not his. Not him. No way.

Tipping the chalice slightly toward his mouth, he winks at the Norns. "How could I say no?"

The three women lean closer. Addie's and Chloe's hands

are still on his thighs. Raising an eyebrow, Lache says, "You really can't."

He feels a rueful smile on his lips. And he thought spiders were bad. He thinks of the man and woman in the picture on his phone. He may never know them, but leaving another orphan, even a half orphan, would be dishonoring their memory…or the memories he doesn't have.

He sniffs at the contents of the chalice again. It smells revolting. Swirling the chalice like a glass of wine, he lets his eyes rove the room. The enormous heavy door he entered has no knob. There's only one way out.

Holding the chalice loosely in one hand, Bohdi puts it to his mouth. Eyes on Addie, he says, "So does this stuff taste good?"

She waves a hand. "It's palatable."

Bohdi's eyes screw shut. A sneeze rips through him, splashing liquid, and knocking the chalice from his hands.

The Norns gasp. Bohdi opens his eyes to see the chalice on its side, liquid spreading across the table.

Ripping off the vest he's wearing, he throws it on the spill, edging around the table toward the window as he does. "I'm so-so-so sorry!" he says.

"Addie, you shouldn't have lied to him!" says Chloe. "You knew what would happen!"

Bohdi backs toward the window, feeling a fresh breeze buffeting his back.

Lache stands up and spins toward Bohdi, eyes narrowed. "Did you spill the potion on purpose?"

Bohdi's back hits the window ledge. If he remembers right, the staircase is just over seven feet down. "Why would I do that?" he says, spreading his hands.

Chloe and Addie both rush to their sister's side.

Narrowing her eyes, Addie says, "You already gave us your word to cooperate. You're bound to us."

Bohdi starts at that. And then remembering his words when he first sat down at the table, he can't help the shit-eating grin that crosses his face. "Nope. I only asked when we would start."

Chloe makes a little sound of "Ahhhhh!" which causes her curves to expand in wonderful resolve-breaking ways.

He winces away from the sight. And then, biting his lip, he turns and vaults through the window into the Nornheim evening.

From behind him he hears a screech of "Nidhogg!"

Before Bohdi knows what is happening, a shadow darts out below his feet.

The dragon roars. "What—"

Which is the exact moment Bohdi's feet connect with the dragon's head, his hands reaching instinctively for its tentacle eyebrows.

"—is it my mistresses?" finishes the dragon.

"Catch him!" roar the Norns.

"Errrrr…Hi, Nidhogg," says Bohdi, looking into one of Nidhogg's enormous green orbs.

"Mmmmm…chocolate," chuckles Nidhogg. His tongue slips out of his mouth, it's long and black, and it looks like it will be able to reach Bohdi's perch.

Bohdi doesn't have time to pull out his knife. He bites down hard on one of the tentacles he's holding. It tastes better than the potion smelled.

The tongue retreats, and Nidhogg squeaks. A bit of smoke puffs from his nostrils.

Releasing the tentacle, Bohdi slides down Nidhogg's neck and jumps to the staircase. Above him he hears the Norns screaming and the eagle give a shriek.

Feet connecting with the steps, Bohdi executes the next part of his escape plan. At the top of his lungs he screams. "Thorrrrrrrrrrr!!!!"

"You'll pay for that!" Nidhogg roars. Bohdi hears the rush of wind behind him, and the shriek of an eagle above him.

Putting a hand on the column surface, he looks behind him to see Nidhogg's maw, open, pulsing with fire, and rushing toward him. Bohdi skids down the steps. He hears an abrupt, "Urrrrffffffff."

Turning again, he sees Nidhogg's snout snapped closed, his eyes wide and watery. The dragon's head pulls a little further forward and then snaps back. He's stuck.

Bohdi's about to cheer when Nidhogg opens his mouth again, and a little ball of flame starts to dance on his tongue.

Taking off down the stairs again, Bohdi again shouts, "Thooorrrrrrr!" He feels heat on his back just as he reaches a bend in the undulating shape of the column. He turns the corner and a bolt of fire shoots past his left elbow. "Thooorrrrrrrrr!" he screams.

There is no answering lightning, just the screech of an eagle above his head. Bohdi resumes his mad dash down the stairs. The steps are lit by the sparkling lights within the column, but still, it's getting dark. He hasn't gone five more paces when he slips, tumbles, and rolls right over the side of the stairs, barely catching the edge in time.

An eagle screech rips through the night. Bohdi screams as a feather lands right next to his hand. Dangling from the stairs, he looks down. It's hard to judge at night, but the next set of steps is at least eight feet below. He looks up, sees a shadow of the eagle descending, and feels the wind of its wings on his back. His body seizes up in indecision. He can let go or pull himself up. Closing his eyes, he presses his head to the column surface, arms beginning to tire from the hang. Does it matter which way he goes? It's a friggin' eagle, it's flying and…

A light flickers beyond Bohdi's eyelids, a boom fills the night, followed by the scream of the giant bird.

Bohdi opens his eyes and sees an enormous dark shadow falling in the periphery of his vision. And then he feels a hand hauling him up from the waistband of his pants. Before he's even aware of what's happening, he's in Thor's chariot, across from Amy. She's cowering against the far wall, clasping his pink shirt. And then they're streaking off into the darkness. Behind him, he hears the Norns shout, "Nidhogg!"

Releasing Bohdi, Thor shouts, "Chariot, up and away!"

Without Thor to hold him upright, Bohdi sinks to the floor across from Amy.

Arms tucked around her knees she says, "Where is your vest?"

Bohdi looks down at his naked chest. His mouth drops open, but instead of a pithy response, all that comes out is, "….errrrrrr."

Thor's snort is audible even above the rush of the wind.

Mr. Squeakers pokes his head out of the V in Amy's tunic, and then disappears.

"Oh," Amy says, eyes wide. Her shoulders slump slightly.

Bohdi bites his lip, preparing to say It's not what you think, even if it almost was. But he's interrupted by a roar from below, so mighty it shakes the chariot.

Amy and Bohdi both look over the edge. Amy gasps.

Spreading his enormous wings, Nidhogg is launching himself up from the base of the column.

Bohdi exhales. They're ascending rapidly, and they're already miles from the base of the column. Below them, the Sea of Sorrows is sparkling beneath Nornheim's moons. "We should be okay," he says.

At his words the chariot shakes.

"Uh-oh," says Thor.

Amy's and Bohdi's eyes meet, and then they both look up at Thor. "Uh-oh?" says Bohdi.

Thor looks down at them. "I think the Midgardian expression is, we're running out of gas."

"Uh-oh," says Amy.

"What?" says Bohdi.

Thor's nostrils flare. "Did you think my magical chariot could just replenish its magic…magically?"

Bohdi snips. "It doesn't seem like a ridiculous assumption."

Looking down at Amy and Bohdi, Thor says, "I need to summon my father. We won't make it to the Earth World Gate."

Amy inhales sharply. The chariot trembles beneath them.

Meeting her eyes, Thor says, "But you have my word, I will return you to Earth, if that is where you wish to go."

Amy looks over the side of the chariot and her eyes widen. "I don't think we have a choice."

Bohdi's gaze follows hers. Nidhogg is below and to the east of them, but closing in fast. "Can we just not be dragon kibble?" he says.

"Hmmm…" says Thor. He looks Bohdi up and down and narrows his eyes. "I have an idea…but it is so outrageous it cannot possibly work."

Before Bohdi can ask what that is about, Thor roars, "Get back."

Amy and Bohdi scoot toward the front wall of the chariot, just as Thor spins it around.

Dropping his visor and raising his hammer high, Thor shouts, "Down chariot!" At the same time, sparks start leaping off the hammer, making the world around them as bright as day.

The chariot plunges. Nidhogg roars, and with an easy flick of his wings, adjusts his flight to intercept them. Bohdi looks up at the sparking hammer. It may be a beacon for Odin, but it is also a beacon for everything else.

"Chariot, halt now!" Thor says. They are so close to the sea, Bohdi can hear the crash of waves beneath them.

"Don't look over the edge," Thor shouts, voice nearly drowned out by the sound of waves, thunder, and the fizzing of electricity.

…Which of course makes Bohdi peek. In the hammer's light he sees what looks like a river of inky black surrounded by deep blue.

"What?" he hears Amy whisper. He looks to the side and sees her eyes glued on the water. It makes him feel good to know he isn't the only one who can't obey basic instructions. Her gaze meets his. "An undersea chasm?" she whispers.

As soon as she says it, the inky black river shrinks and vanishes. Bohdi shrugs, and then the sound of flapping wings above makes him lift his eyes. Nidhogg is dropping toward them, opening his maw, a bright ball of fire dancing on his tongue.

Holding the still-sparking hammer aloft, Thor drapes

himself over Amy and Bohdi, crushing their bodies together. Bohdi hears Amy hiss in pain, but Thor ignores it and shouts, "Chariot, face incoming fire!"

Bohdi hears Nidhogg roar, but the sound is lost in the rush of air. The bluish light of Thor's hammer is replaced by the orange of dragon flame. The smell of burning hair rises in the air and Bohdi's skin heats to the point where it is painful. Just when he thinks he will be cooked, the heat begins to abate and Thor shouts, "Chariot, level, forward, full-speed twenty paces." The chariot darts forward and stops abruptly, air whipping around them as they just miss being buffeted by Nidhogg's wings.

The dragon's body skims the sea, and it lifts its head and screams, "You're mine!"

"Chariot, forward!" Thor shouts, lifting his hammer. Lightning makes the scene as bright as day.

The chariot trembles forward, slowly this time. Nidhogg flaps his wings so fast that waves fan out from his body.

"Thor, turn off your hammer!" Amy screams.

Her warning is just in time. An enormous wave crashes into the chariot and Thor, Bohdi, and Amy are thrown together against the far wall. For a moment, they lie there motionless in darkness—Bohdi swears he can feel his ribs groaning with the space Viking's weight, and then Thor bolts upright, leaving Bohdi and Amy wet and gasping for air.

The chariot is moving, but too slowly. Bohdi can see Nidhogg, silhouetted by Nornheim's moons, stirring up waves on either side of him as he rushes across the sea. The dragon opens its maw and a flame starts to leap again. This time, the flame will come into the open back side of the chariot. Amy presses herself against Bohdi—or maybe he presses against her. Either way, somehow his arm is around her, his head ducked against hers.

Above them, Thor starts whipping his hammer in an arc. And then the big man shouts, "Hammer!" And once more, the world is lit bright as day by the hammer's blue light.

…Which means Bohdi can better see the saliva glistening on the dragon's teeth, the gleam of his enormous eyes, and the shimmer of spittle falling from its jaws.

Bohdi snaps, "You wanted us to better see ourselves as we get eaten?" But then Amy gasps, and he sees the inky black below the surface is getting larger. In fact it's huge. The size of a four-lane highway and rising up below Nidhogg.

"What?" Amy whispers.

"Chariot! Up!" roars Thor.

The chariot lifts. Nidhogg roars, the flame on his tongue barreling beneath the chariot. The dragon flicks his wings, his great body rises, and the hammer flickers out and all goes dark.

Bohdi hears a sound like a thousand tiny teeth smacking together, and then the mighty blast of a wave. Another sound pierces the night, a snarl, and then a scream. It takes Bohdi a moment to realize the scream is Nidhogg's.

The chariot trembles. Bohdi hears the distant sound of waves below, and Thor says, "Chariot, level."

The scream below continues, and so does the sound of the clacking tiny teeth.

Shaking his great head, Thor says, "Sea eels." His gaze shifts to Bohdi, and he says, "That should not have worked."

Amy shifts against Bohdi, and they both creep forward on their knees to look down over the edge. There isn't much to see. A deep stain spills out over the water. Bohdi thinks he sees a wing floating in the waves, but then something darts up, a black tunnel ringed by sharp white knives, and the wing disappears.

Amy inhales sharply. Bohdi sits back against the front wall of the chariot, hands fisting at his thighs.

Above him, Thor says, "They come! Chariot forward!" Smacking Bohdi on the shoulder, Thor says, "Stand up, my friends!"

Bohdi climbs shakily to his feet, Amy beside him. Just about thirty-five feet in front of them, a circle of light is forming. In it he sees the form of a man standing with arms spread...and then more shapes appear beneath the man's arms. Bohdi blinks; the shapes become winged-human shadows—and then the shadows dart out of the circle. Bohdi lets out a breath in wonder. Sixteen angels are hurtling through the night toward them—female angels with spears and armor.

"Valkyries!" Amy whispers.

One of the Valkyries shouts something and Thor answers, a smile on his lips. The angels circle the tottering chariot protectively, spears at the ready, shouting words in a strange language. It may be relief, but Bohdi would swear they are all gorgeous. Or maybe it is just that chicks with spears are extra hot.

They are just a few feet from the circle of light when a gust of wind sweeps from behind them. Thor curses, the angels hiss, and suddenly Chloe, Lache, and Addie are suspended in midair, ends of their saris swirling like wings, blocking their path to the beckoning light.

...And okay, if you can pop in and out of existence seemingly without effort, it makes sense that being able to fly like superman—or supergirl—probably shouldn't come as a shock. But it is a shock. And Bohdi's knees go weak at the same time his blood goes cold.

Chloe's scream rips through the night. "You killed our dragon!" Is it his imagination, or is she now sporting a pair of fangs?

"You will pay for that!" Addie hisses. He thinks he sees fangs again.

"Back off!" roars Thor, a lightning bolt tearing from his hammer. Lache catches the bolt as though it was a coil of rope and flings it down toward the water. Eyes flicking between Amy and Bohdi, she smiles. And yes, there are definitely fangs, and her smile is really scary.

"Give us back the man-whore," Lache says.

Addie laughs and hisses, "Yes, he insulted us."

"Little slut," Chloe sniffs. And Bohdi winces. Even Chloe is against him?

Every one of the Valkyries' eyes lands on Bohdi. Their gaze feels like a physical weight... He darts a glance at Amy and instantly regrets it. She looks shocked. And a little hurt. Which she shouldn't be, since they weren't a thing. He wishes she was angry, because that would just be annoying and he could be righteously angry back, and then he wouldn't feel like a heel.

Amy drops her gaze.

"It wasn't..." Bohdi starts to say, but just then Thor roars, "Never!" The Valkyries' voices rise in a scream, and a dozen of them break off toward the three Norns.

As the chariot dips below the raging women, Bohdi hears the shriek of steel, and crack of bone. "Rise, Chariot!" Thor commands, but the craft just shakes in the air. The remaining Valkyries grab hold of either side of the chariot and pull it upward.

A moment later, Bohdi hears the Norns scream behind them. Light flashes before his eyes, heat flashes behind his back, and then the circle of light is right in front of him. The chariot begins to disappear and then there are all the swirling colors of the rainbow.

…and then the rainbow is gone, and the screams, too.

Nornheim's night is replaced by blinding light. Lifting a hand to shield his eyes, Bohdi finds they're in an enormous room, with soaring golden beams and walls of windows letting in bright sunlight.

The chariot and its angelic bearers fall a few feet and skid to a halt in front of an enormous throne. On the throne sits a man decked out from head to toe in golden armor. He has a short snow-white beard. A raised visor reveals one eye that is eerily blue, and one eye covered by a gold eye patch. Gripping the armrests of the throne, as though if he were to let go he would fall, the man barks something to someone behind the chariot.

Turning around, Bohdi sees four men in reddish brown robes. They hold staffs pointed at the circle of light. The circle is flickering madly on this side, with tiny bursts that look like lightning erupting from its core. The four men with staffs are shaking and sweat shines on their brows. Whatever is snaking out of the circle seems to be drawing them into it.

A moment later, the circle goes dark, and Bohdi is staring through an empty archway. Beside him, Thor bows his head. "The Norns closed the gate."

A hush falls. Bohdi looks around. There are male warriors of every ethnicity lining every side of the hall. Their heads are bowed, too.

The man on the throne closes his single eye and wipes his brow, his movements slow and weary.

"Odin," Amy whispers, her voice quavering slightly.

For some reason Bohdi shivers.

The four Valkyries holding the chariot go forward— miraculously, though it is missing a wheel, the chariot doesn't keel over. But it trembles slightly. Heads bowed, the women fall to one knee in front of Odin, bringing their right fists up to touch their chests. Up close, Bohdi can see their wings are actually attached to elaborate vests they wear. Stepping from the chariot, Thor goes forward and kneels, too.

Bohdi's eyes widen. Are he and Amy supposed to kneel, or stay in the chariot? Should they kneel in the chariot? The neurons in his brain fire unhelpfully. Does he want to kneel? Before he can ponder more, Odin says, "Rise."

Thor and the Valkyries stand.

Beside him, Bohdi hears Amy release a breath.

Odin speaks in English, his voice a low rumble. "Thor, the Norns and I had an agreement… They would give my messengers safe passage on their world. And yet they attacked…"

Thor grunts and takes a half step forward. Before he speaks, one of the winged women opens her wings and points at Bohdi with her spear. "It wasn't Thor they were chasing—it was that boy."

Every eye in the hall is suddenly on Bohdi. His mouth goes dry, and he swears he can hear his heart beating in his chest. He's also suddenly aware he isn't wearing anything above the waist.

Striding toward Odin, the warrior woman shouts, "They called him a man-whore, a slut, and said he insulted them!"

Two ravens drop from the eaves of the hall. One alights

on the back of the throne, the other lands on Odin's shoulder and whispers in his ear.

Straightening in his seat, Odin sighs. "Bohdi Patel, the amnesiac... You haven't been able to keep it in your pants lately, have you?"

Bohdi's mouth opens to protest. It wasn't like that! But then one of the Valkyries hisses. "Did you think the Norns would be interested in a human boy?"

"Fool," someone mutters.

The Valkyrie turns to Bohdi and snarls. "Because of you, twelve of my sisters, all valiant warriors, are dead."

Twelve dead...because he decided to keep it in his pants for once. Bohdi feels dizzy. Part of him wants to argue. But if he protests, he'll either be branded a liar—or worse, they'll believe him. And then they'll wonder why the Norns would bother with a human boy. Not that it matters. Thor is about to rat him out. His throat constricts. He feels air entering his lungs but doesn't feel like he's breathing.

Odin's eye slides to Thor. "Why didn't you give him to them?"

Thor stands taller. Every muscle in Bohdi's body tightens. Something warm and soft slides into Bohdi's hand. He looks down to see Amy's fingers in his. She squeezes, as though to say I know.

He's too afraid to look at her, instead his eyes slide to Thor. This is it. He'll tell Odin.

Thor's voice rumbles loud and clear through the hall. "I gave these two my oath that I would return them safely to their world."

There is a low murmuring in the great hall. For a moment, Thor's words don't register. And then they sink in, as does the cleverness of Amy forcing the big lug to make that oath.

Bohdi bows his head and squeezes Amy's hand back, trying to say thank you.

Odin raises a hand and the hall goes quiet. To Thor, he says, "And did you discover the location of …" he draws in a breath and licks his lip, "the personage we seek."

Thor bows his head and says, "I discovered better…"

Amy's hand abruptly tightens in Bohdi's.

On his throne, Odin says, "Go on."

Bohdi tries to breathe, and shivers. He swears he can feel an invisible noose tightening.

Raising his eyes to Odin, Thor says, "He travels to Hel and will be there shortly."

He feels Amy's grip slacken slightly.

Bohdi blinks. That wasn't a lie. But…leaning toward Amy, he whispers, "Hel is a place?"

"On Niflheim," Amy whispers. "It's where Loki's daughter was banished." She swallows. "Humans called it Hel and after a while Asgard did, too."

On his throne, Odin raises a hand to his beard. Amy goes silent. And then the one-eyed man nods. "A he…a he… Well done, Thor, for getting that extra information… It's more than I expected." Nodding, he says, "You will prepare a war band and go to Hel at once."

"What?" Amy whispers.

"Father," says Thor, gesturing to Amy and Bohdi. "My oath."

Shaking his head, Odin sinks back in his throne. His single eye falls on Amy. "Miss Lewis…" He reaches up and strokes his beard. "Interesting… Perhaps you should go to Hel with Thor…"

Amy gulps.

Bohdi's free hand clenches and unclenches at his side. The hall is dead silent. Even the ravens don't do as much as ruffle a feather. At last Odin shakes his head. "No, Miss Lewis, you will remain here. Sending you with the war band would be too much of a gamble."

Thor steps forward. "I must return them to Earth."

Odin waves his hand. "After you've completed your task on Nornheim, you will return the boy…"

Bohdi straightens at Odin's words; he feels a weight rise from his shoulders.

And then the one-eyed man says, "…and Miss Lewis."

Pinching his nose, Bohdi just barely catches his sneeze. If he's allergic to lies, then Odin is telling a whopper. With an angry grimace, Bohdi manages to stifle the tickle. But it's as though the discomfort can't be eliminated, only transformed. He feels like every hair on his head has been rubbed the wrong way.

Beside him, Amy has squared her shoulders and is staring directly at Odin. But he can't miss the slight tremble of her lower lip, and her fingers are very limp in his.

Sagging on the throne, Odin says, "Court is dismissed." But he shoots one last look at Amy.

Bohdi squeezes her hand, trying to say, I'm here. I won't let you go.

She doesn't respond.

CHAPTER 20

Leaning against a wall in a secondary corridor outside the throne room, Amy is only half listening to Bohdi and Thor argue. She is surveying the palace. Even though the hallway isn't a main thoroughfare, it is still ornate. The walls and vaulted ceiling are cream-colored marble with deep ochre veins. The supports and accents are gold. The floor is polished obsidian. Amy glances up at a skylight made of leaded crystal. Everything she sees is an exact replica of Vanir architecture from about nine hundred years ago.

…Or that is how it is illusioned to appear. The only things that are real are the Vanir bioluminescent butterflies flitting above their heads. Amy closes her eyes. Beneath her fingers she feels the porous grain of concrete. She slides her hand down and finds the cement seam.

Bohdi shouts. "You need to take us home now!"

Amy's eyes snap open. A few feet away, Bohdi and Thor are glaring at each other. Bohdi's still not wearing a shirt. Fidgeting with the pink bundle on her wrist holding their phones, she looks away, face going hot.

She'd been so certain…the fires on Nornheim. How he

seemed to literally sniff out lies. The easy way he killed things. Even the way he came running shirtless from the Norn's lair with a dragon on his heels—it was such a clear echo of her time in Alfheim and Loki's side adventure with the Elf Queen.

Amy bites her lip. It shouldn't hurt that Bohdi would be interested in the Norns. There was nothing between him and her. Although it had felt like maybe there was. Or could have been. But maybe that was just all in her head, because she thought he might be the new Loki. Or because she'd held his head on her lap for nearly a full day, keeping cool rags on his head, begging him not to die, and she'd kissed him just when she thought he was lost.

Thinking back on the recent events, something about the Norns thing doesn't feel right. Bohdi may be an unrepentant flirt, but he wants to find his parents very badly…and he's not stupid enough to blow it with an insulting comment. She remembers The Thong and purses her lips. Maybe.

Her eyes go to a spark at the end of Bohdi's thumb. And for a moment, the little hamster wheel in her brain spins without a hamster. And then she shakes her head. He's flicking his lighter again.

Raising a hand in Amy's direction, Bohdi snaps. "Odin has no intention of letting Amy go back to Earth! He knows that Loki would never leave Amy here. Your father is using her as bait!"

Suddenly feeling very uncomfortable, Amy whispers. "Actually, Loki probably won't remember me."

Thor and Bohdi both turn to her. For just a moment, she doubts…

But Thor wouldn't lie to Odin… She doesn't think he can. Hugging herself, she looks down the corridor and a memory hits.

Loki was a small child, leaving the throne room. In his hands he held a staff, Mimir was mounted at the top. It was Mimir's favorite way to get around, if a bit gruesome. He liked being "nearly his old height."

"Mimir," Loki said, "how long has it been since Hoenir made you just a head?"

Mimir looked down at Loki. "Why, Hoenir didn't animate my head... Odin did."

"Odin?" Loki said. "He can do that?"

"Why, yes," said Mimir. "Odin can do nearly everything that Hoenir can—though not as well. And like you, he can sense lies—though not as well. And Odin is also a cunning warrior, as you will someday be."

Loki's nose wrinkled. "I don't want to be a mighty warrior. Warrior practice is soooo *borrringggg.*" Being out in the hot sun for hours, repeating endless drills, and then inevitably getting thrown on his back by the drill master was not Loki's idea of fun.

Mimir's eyes narrowed. "Which is why I said *cunning,* not *mighty.*"

"So Odin reanimated your head after it was cut off because you were friends?"

Mimir's face went blank. And then jaw going hard, he looked away. "That is a story for another time," he said.

Amy blinks. It was a story Mimir never told. And...she's almost certain Loki told at least a few lies to Odin and got away with it. Although, he was sometimes called the God of Lies so maybe...

In front of her, Thor raises his hands. It looks like he might grab Bohdi and shake him. But he only growls. "Loki was my friend, my most frequent companion for over a thousand years! What would it say about my honesty…integrity, and my honor if I do not seek him now?"

Bohdi's posture softens.

Thor turns to Amy. "If I pursue Loki in Hel, perhaps that will give you a chance to spend some time with the new Loki?"

Amy steps away from the wall. She hasn't argued with Thor because of that reason. Bohdi shoots Thor a dirty look, and she knows how he feels. This whole situation just stinks, and that's why she hasn't been able to argue with Bohdi, either.

Down the hall, four Einherjar round the corner. One steps forward, bows his head, and says in Asgardian, *"Thor, your chariot has been repaired."*

Coming forward, Thor takes Amy's hand with surprising gentleness. Guiding her to Bohdi's side he says, "If my father plans to use you as bait, then you can be assured he will treat you well."

Bohdi hisses softly.

"Great," says Amy.

Oblivious, or pretending to be, Thor takes Bohdi's hand and says, "I give you my oath, I will take you back to Earth on my return, if that is what you wish."

"Yes!" Bohdi and Amy say in unison.

Thor sighs and puts Bohdi's hand on top of Amy's. Smiling, he says, "In the meantime, enjoy yourselves."

With a curt sort of semi-bow, he backs up, and then turning on his heel thunders away.

Amy stands motionless with Bohdi for a moment, watching Thor disappear around a corner.

And then her eyes meet Bohdi's. They both seem to realize at the same time that they're alone in a hallway, facing each other, and holding hands.

"Um," says Bohdi.

Dropping his hand, Amy looks down. Right at Bohdi's chest. Which is actually rather nice, which makes her blush, and makes her instinctively lower her gaze...where she sees the line of his inguinal ligament trailing down from his also rather nice abdominals to...

Feeling herself go so red she swears her eyes may be tearing up, Amy turns on her heel and stares down the hall at the spot Thor just stood. "If we go to the right, we should reach the main foyer..." she says, in order to say something, and then realizes saying it implies that she has some knowledge of where they are.

"Huh?" says Bohdi.

A black shadow passes above the skylight. Amy scowls. She doesn't want Odin to know she has Loki's memories, and in Asgard spies are everywhere.

She is saved from having to answer by the sound of someone clearing his throat.

Amy and Bohdi turn to see two men and two women bowing and curtseying in their direction. Their clothing is brown, and in the style of Vanir servants from about nine hundred years ago.

Amy smiles tightly. Asgard, the great big dress-up-party in the sky.

The man at the lead bows. "Take you...to rooms. Please."

"Well?" says Bohdi, eye on the servant but leaning toward Amy.

"After you," she says, extending her hand toward their guides.

They fall in step behind what must be the head servant,

the other man and women following behind. Amy recognizes the route—they're being led to the wing of guest quarters. She starts to relax.

And then the servants bringing up the rear of the train start whispering in Asgardian.

"Humans!" says one woman. *"I never thought I'd see one."*

"They're much taller than I'd been led to believe," says the other woman. *"And they seem to have all their teeth."*

Amy can't contain the quirk of her lips at that.

The first woman says, "The boy is kind of handsome… even if he is a little skinny."

Both of the women giggle. Amy's eyes go wide. Her eyes slide to Bohdi; he's giving her a funny look.

Quickly looking away, she stifles a sigh. He isn't romance novel cover material, but he is nice to look at. No wonder he gets around…he can. And if he's like Loki before he met his first wife, Anganboða, he doesn't get emotionally ensnared. Which is, objectively, really convenient. She sort of wishes she could be that way.

The man behind them says, *"I hear the girl was Loki's whore. I wonder if she'll get lonely in her room tonight?"*

The women's silence is ominous. Amy turns her head sharply. The women look slightly afraid. Mr. Squeakers, hiding in the fold of her shirt where he is tucked into her jeans, begins to squirm. Stilling Squeakers with a hand, she turns to face front again. Her gaze briefly meets Bohdi's. His eyes are narrowed.

The man in front abruptly stops at an intersection of two corridors. Bowing, he says in faltering English, "Sir, follow me. Girl, follow girls."

"No," says Bohdi sharply. "We stay together." And then

he turns to Amy, eyes wide, voice uncertain. "Errrr...right?"

"Yes," she says.

Perplexed, the lead servant says, "It is...protect...girl's virtue."

There is a low snort from the male servant behind them.

Amy's jaw tightens and she steps closer to Bohdi. "No," she says.

Looking flustered, the lead servant says, "It is orders from Odin."

"No," Bohdi and Amy say in unison.

The servant raises an eyebrow. "I will call guard."

"Go ahead," says Bohdi, stepping toward the servant.

Amy scans the hall. There is a window that leads to the garden. She blinks. And the whole palace is filled with hidden tunnels—Loki used them to spy on guests for Odin—and his own amusement. But could they hide until Thor got back?

Her mind spins. They need help...but who is brave enough to stand up to Odin? Hoenir...if they got to the gardens, to where his home used to be, that would get his attention, surely...maybe he could open a gate!

She winces and her head ticks to the side. But Hoenir can open a gate anywhere...at anytime...Her vision goes white with a pain behind her eyes.

The lead servant claps his hands. Amy's attention snaps to their immediate danger. She hears fast heavy footfalls, and then four armed Einherjar jog around a bend in the corridor, swords already drawn.

"Ideas?" whispers Bohdi.

Amy looks frantically. "The window?"

In Asgardian, the lead servant says to the guards, *"Seize the boy!"*

"Halt!" shouts a feminine voice from behind Amy and Bohdi.

The lead servant's jaw drops. The guards stop in their tracks.

Amy and Bohdi both spin.

Down the hall, leading a train of six women dressed in beautiful gowns is a woman, head held high. Her skin is tan, her eyes a piercing blue, her wavy brown hair is long and upswept. She wears a dress of ivory and sky blue, gathered by a bodice of gold. At her waist dangles a ring of keys. Loki has many memories of her—for once, none carnal. She looks Amy's age, but the woman was ancient when Loki was a child.

"Queen Frigga," Amy whispers. Mother of Loki's archrival, Prince Baldur the Beautiful. Wife of Odin, Frigga had to know about Rind, and Odin's other extramarital meanderings. Yet she'd stuck with him for over a thousand years.

The servants who had been following Amy and Bohdi drop to their knees and thump their hands to their chests. Glancing behind, Amy sees the guards are still standing.

Beside her, Bohdi whispers. "Whose side is she on?"

Turning, Amy finds the queen's eyes on her.

Swallowing, Amy says, "I don't know."

"Nari did what?" Loki shouts, shaking the walls of his and Sigyn's cottage with the force of his voice.

Putting her hands on her hips, Sigyn says, "He went to fight beside Queen Elizabeth—she is ruler of…"

"I know who she is!" Loki says, wiping his brow.

"It is not so bad, the Spanish Armada wasn't able to land—"

Loki's heart is beating too fast, and he feels lightheaded. "But they haven't been defeated either! They'll regroup in Spain, have a bit of holiday, and then pick up ten thousand or more troops. Spain is the most powerful nation in Midgard! Elizabeth is a queen of a bunch of scraggly pirates!"

"Loki…" says Sigyn.

Starting to pace, Loki says, "England is a tiny, foggy, damp, armpit of a nation—they can't possibly win. Why did Nari hear their prayers?"

Much too calmly, Sigyn says, "He admires their Magna Carta, and their parliament." With a smile, she adds, "He has the scabbard you gave him. It will protect him from harm—"

"Only if he manages to keep it on! What if he is taken prisoner?" Loki snaps.

"It's a cause he believes in, Loki," Sigyn says, much too calmly.

Loki roars. "He could die for his cause!"

Sigyn's shoulders straighten, her fists curl at her sides, and she shouts, "If nothing is worth dying for, what is worth living for?"

Loki draws back. In the fireplace, flames leap. Sigyn's eyes stay fixed on him, her fists rise. He wants to strangle her but knows he couldn't, even if she didn't have a decent left hook.

He wipes his forehead again. A knock sounds at the door.

Neither Sigyn nor he moves. And then magic seeps through the air, wisps of glowing ivory with the faintest tint of sky blue. Loki turns toward the source. It's creeping through the door.

His posture must shift, because Sigyn's voice is quieter when she speaks. "Who is it, Loki?"

"The queen," he whispers.

Sigyn's fists uncurl. Her eyes go to Loki, wide and afraid.

When he was a child, Queen Frigga was like a kind aunt until her son Baldur had been born. The queen became distant, more and more enamored with her "golden" child, and completely blind to his flaws.

After Baldur's death, the queen had often noted that Loki did not cry at her son's funeral. Not that she'd wept for Helen...

There is another knock. To not answer would be treason... But answering may be a ticket to the cave again. Loki's fairly certain Frigga could find something to accuse him of.

"Shall we answer?" says Sigyn. "Or flee?"

Closing his eyes, Loki sends an invisible projection of his consciousness through the door. He expects to see the queen and a host of guards, or at the very least her ladies in waiting. Instead he sees only a lone figure shrouded by a sky blue cloak.

Loki looks to his wife. "Answer."

Together they cautiously approach the door. Odin has come by to the cottage upon occasion—Loki actually acquired it from the Allfather in a wager. But the queen has never visited. Loki finds himself unaccountably nervous. He notices a slight sheen on Sigyn's brow, too.

Biting her lip, Sigyn turns the doorknob, pulls the door open, and then both of them drop to their knees. Loki thumps his chest, but Sigyn can't thump hers; if she does the door will slam in Frigga's face—which would probably be an act of treason in and of itself. Loki restrains a snort at all the ridiculous formalities that have developed in the court.

"You may rise," says Frigga, striding into the cottage.

"Oh, please come in," Loki mutters as he climbs back to his feet.

Raising an eyebrow at him, Sigyn also stands.

They turn to see Frigga has dropped the hood of her cloak. She stands facing them in the foyer, her back stiff, and face pinched. "Loki."

Loki bows his head. "Queen Frigga."

"I need your help," the queen says, in a tone one might use to say, "This fish is off."

Loki does not snort. He thinks it shows an amazing amount of self-restraint.

Casting a nervous glance in his direction, Sigyn says, "How, My Queen?"

Frigga rubs her temple. "I hear the prayers the wives and mothers of England and the Netherlands utter…even though they are offered to their new gods." She closes her eyes. "They pray for their husbands, brothers…and their sons."

She raises her eyes, and Loki is shocked to see they glisten. Except for Baldur, he's never known her to weep for anyone. She puts her hands to her temples and bows her head. "Every night, I hear them."

Loki's lips tighten into a thin line. Prayers are humanity's one magical trick. Magical creatures don't hear every request from humans; Odin says they only hear prayers that relate to their higher purpose. Loki, who isn't particularly selfless or noble has always wanted to respond to the few he's heard. He's always found them a gift—like the prayers from Hothur and Nanna requesting help to slay Baldur. But Frigga seems haunted by her human requests.

The queen brings a hand to her temple. "Odin hears the prayers of Spain. He has already planted Einherjar warriors on the boats that sailed for England, and among the reinforcements the fleet plans to gather."

Loki's eyes meet Sigyn's. He has visions of an Einherjar blade slicing the belt that holds Nari's magic scabbard—and then the blade going to his son's throat.

Loki bows his head. "My Queen…would you like me to stand beside the Englishmen?" Not that he plans on helping the English, *he'll just cast an illusion over his son, and spirit him away. His fists clench at his side. He'll just have to come up with a clever lie to lure Nari away from his misguided convictions...*

"I'm not a fool, Loki," Frigga says, sounding more weary than angry.

Loki lifts his head.

"You seek your son." *Frigga smiles ruefully.* "You'd never save him, he's too foolhardy to abandon the cause." *Her jaw hardens.* "The Spanish must never be allowed to land in England."

Loki almost argues. But then he remembers Frigga sees the present nearly clearly as the Norns, and even though no one sees the future, she sees the possibilities more clearly than most. His fists clench at his sides. For his sons' sakes he needs to hear her out. "How precisely do you expect to accomplish that?"

Frigga stares at him for a moment, as though she doesn't recognize him. And then she says, "With treachery and magic, of course."

Reaching into her cloak, she pulls out a letter sealed with wax. "Njord sits in his boat off the coast of Ireland waiting for Skadi to come to him. The Spanish will pass that way soon."

Njord is a king of the Vanir. He is capable of summoning storms. Skadi is his Frost Giantess ex-wife. Magical beings are only allowed to go to Earth on prayer summons, but Njord would break the rules for Skadi; he is still madly in love with her.

Sigyn voices Loki's unspoken question. "But why would he think that? Skadi has no interest in him—she hasn't in centuries."

Meeting Sigyn's eyes, Frigga says, "Because I told him she would."

"Ah," *says Sigyn.*

Loki's lips purse, and his eyebrows jog up. Sometimes he wonders why, out of all of Asgard, he's the one with the moniker of

"God of Lies."

Frigga hands the letter to Loki. "You will deliver this to him." Loki takes the envelope and opens it. Frigga sniffs and says, "Now I will have to reseal it," but Loki ignores her. Sigyn peeks over his shoulder.

His brow furrows. The letter is from Skadi, saying how she won't be coming to meet Njord after all.

"Why don't you just have Gna deliver it?" Loki says. Gna is Frigga's messenger. Her steed's speed is second only to Sleipnir, and capable of traveling over land and water.

Frigga sighs. "If Gna delivers it, Njord will think it's simply a misunderstanding. He will be hurt, perhaps cry and make a little rain, but that will be the end of it."

Sigyn snorts. "But if Loki delivers it, Njord will think it was a trick perpetrated by my husband from the beginning… He'll try to kill Loki."

"Precisely," says Frigga. "Doubtlessly with storms great enough to destroy an entire armada."

Drawing back slightly, Loki narrows his eyes. "Where will I be during these storms?"

"Probably in the boat you used to meet Njord," says Frigga.

Loki stares at her a moment. Sighing, he says dryly. "I can't imagine how this plan could be any more perfect."

Smiling tightly at him, Frigga says, "Heimdall will have his eyes on the Einherjar aboard the Spanish ships, so he'll see your presence. You'll doubtlessly find yourself on trial."

Loki snaps his fingers, releasing a small burst of flame. He could walk the In-Between as soon as he delivered the message— but he's not sure he wants Heimdall to know of that particular skill.

"But I will say it was on my orders," says Frigga.

Loki's mouth twists in a thin line. It is the best way to help Nari. It will be dangerous, cold, wet, and it will be against Odin's favorites. He opens his mouth, about to agree anyway.

Frigga, seeing his expression, must expect a no, because she says, "You have my oath, I will stand beside you." He detects no lie, but isn't exactly pleased. Frigga and Odin have had spats before, and in a domestic matter, he would expect her to win. But this is about the fate of nations.

Snapping his fingers, he releases another burst of flame. He opens his mouth again, ready to agree.

Again, Frigga must doubt his intent, because she says, "And I will give you this." She pulls a vial from her cloak and presses it into Loki's hand.

Loki immediately feels the thrum of magic on his palm. He stares down at the vial. It is no bigger than his thumb, and where a cap should be it is completely sealed. At the top is a ring with a strip of black leather strung through it. The leather cord is long enough to hang comfortably from Loki's neck.

Loki holds the vial up to the light. The inside is murky, holding something that looks exactly like—

"Clouds," says Frigga. "Break the vial and you'll have enough to cover an entire sea or mountain range with them."

That is farther than the reach of any of Loki's illusions. The gift of the life of his son and this... Loki stares at the vial in wonder. "I accept," he whispers.

Standing next to Bohdi, Amy whispers cryptically. "Loki went to the tower for the Spanish Armada escapade, but Frigga kept her word and got him out..." She gulps. "It only took a little over a year."

The Tower? He has no idea what Amy is talking about, but it doesn't sound good. Bohdi's eyes snap to her in alarm.

She winces and shrugs. Bohdi looks behind them. The asshole who wanted to separate Bohdi and Amy is standing backed by armed guards—now blocking the path to the window.

In front of them, Frigga and the women trailing her are blocking their escape. Bohdi slips his knife from his pocket. "Well?" he whispers.

Before Amy responds, Frigga's voice rings down the corridor in English. "You will sheath your blades!"

The guards start to put their swords away, but then head Asshole says something in Asgardian. The guards stop. Beneath their visors, Bohdi sees them look to one another, eyes wide and confused.

Chin held high, slender body ramrod straight, Frigga says in English. "Who besides my husband may sit on my husband's throne?"

Asshole says something in his language, and Frigga snaps, "Speak so my guests may understand!"

"Yes, My Queen. You, My Queen," says Asshole, his voice starting to tremble.

"And who rules the Nine Realms when my husband is indisposed?" Frigga demands.

Asshole gulps. "You, My Queen."

"And where is my husband now?" Frigga shouts.

"Asleep," Asshole murmurs.

"Then who rules the Nine Realms?" says Frigga, her voice suddenly soft.

"You, My Queen," says Asshole, his voice quivering so much Bohdi might almost feel sorry for him.

"Then why are you still standing?" says Frigga.

Asshole bows his head, drops to one knee, and thumps his hand over his chest. The Other Asshole immediately follows suit, as do the guards.

Frigga's eyes slide to Bohdi and Amy. She raises an imperious eyebrow. The processor in Bohdi's brain must be overwhelmed with other input, because it takes a moment for him to realize it's probably a hint that he and Amy should be kneeling, too.

"Um," he says.

"Oh," says Amy.

The ladies following Frigga narrow their eyes at them.

"Should we?" says Bohdi.

Frigga sighs. Raising her chin, the queen proclaims, "On Earth, customs toward royalty have changed much of late. Since Miss Lewis and Mr. Patel are our guests, I will not insist they kneel."

Offering a slight nod of her head, Amy whispers, "Thank you?"

Not acknowledging her statement, Frigga snaps some commands in Asgardian. Asshole and The Other Asshole thump their chests and then bow and take off down the corridor they had attempted to lead Bohdi down. The guards part and stand at attention, lining the hallway.

Turning toward the opposite corridor, Frigga says, "You will follow me."

With that, she strides past Bohdi and Amy, head held high.

For a moment, Bohdi and Amy stand stock-still. And then, nodding pointedly at Amy and Bohdi, one of the members of Frigga's entourage says, "After you?"

Bohdi exhales. Amy nods. Muscles in his body he hadn't been aware were tight uncoil. Together they follow the queen. Her entourage and the maids of the palace-castle-alien-bed-and-breakfast-whatever trail behind.

CHAPTER 21

Frigga leads them through two double doors nearly as large as the doors in the Norns' lair. But they do have doorknobs, so there's that.

"I hope you find this to your satisfaction."

Bohdi blinks around the room they've just entered. It's enormous—as large as an entire floor of Ruth and Henry's house. The walls are plaster, not marble, painted a nearly gleaming white. Large windows line one wall, tapestries another. Butterflies flutter on the sills and throughout the room. There is a sitting area with a couch and little round ottoman thingies near the other wall, an unlit fireplace with elaborate molding behind it, and a table and chairs a few steps away. A gauzy curtain separates the sitting area and table from two stairs that lead up to an enormous round bed.

That's where Bohdi's mind starts to spin. One bed. And then his shoulders sag, remembering Amy's look of hurt when she'd realized what he'd been up to, or almost up to, with the Norns...Biting his lip, he looks over to her. She'll suggest they split up, and that idea makes his stomach churn. There was something about the tone of The Other Asshole when they were being led here that he didn't like. And he didn't like the way Amy had turned too sharply—or the silence of the maids.

"It's fine," Amy says without missing a beat.

Bohdi's body sags a little with relief. She doesn't think he's that kind of ass… It makes him feel ridiculously grateful.

Frigga nods. Her eyes meet Amy's and then Bohdi's. "You must stick together."

"Why are you helping us?" Amy asks.

Frigga's lips purse ever so slightly. "You are our guests."

Bohdi doesn't feel a desire to sneeze…but…there is a definite tickle on his upper lip.

Dipping her chin, Frigga says, "Enjoy your stay."

"Thank you," says Amy.

One of the other women says something in Asgardian. Amy's eyes go wide, and she bites her lip like she's fighting a smile. Bohdi catches her reaction…but he doesn't feel like asking her any questions until they are alone.

Frigga raises an eyebrow in Amy's direction and says in English, "Miss Lewis and Mr. Patel are acquainted with flushing toilets, Gna."

Amy puts a hand to her mouth as a smile blooms on her face. Bohdi has to stifle a snort.

Frigga motions in the direction of a small door. "It's right through there."

The woman who first voiced the question says, "But they don't have magic on their world?"

Frigga sighs. "And yet they have running water…and…" the queen looks at Amy and Bohdi almost curiously. "Lights at night." Turning to Gna she says, "They use electricity."

"Really?" says Gna, hands coming together in front of her chest. "How charming. I'd love to know more."

"Later, Gna," says Frigga. "Our guests are tired." She looks at Bohdi and her lips quirk. "And they are in need of clothes."

The women behind Frigga titter. Even Amy looks amused.

Bohdi feels his cheeks heat. Even if he's not ashamed of what's exposed, he suddenly feels outnumbered.

With another nod at them, Frigga turns on her heel and strides from the room. Her entourage follows. But the maids stay.

One of them, clutching what looks like clothing, stammers, "Follow."

Bohdi and Amy follow her and the other maid through a pair of ornate double doors into a steaming room with an enormous bathtub.

"Ah," says Bohdi, drawing to a stop. "I'll just wait outside, while you—"

"That's fine," says Amy, eyeing the maids. The two women look slightly frightened.

"If you need me—" Bodhi says.

"I'll scream," says Amy.

Walking back out the doors, Bohdi says, "Right."

As the doors swing shut behind him, The Assholes come through the double doors from the hallway. Slipping his knife from his pocket, he flicks it open and makes a show of wiping it on his pants.

Glaring at him, one of The Assholes sets some clothes and some towels on a chair. And then the two go about fluffing the pillows on the bed and drawing back the sheets.

Bohdi thinks of falling into the bed...and then he thinks of falling into bed with Amy. They'd sleep, but when they woke up maybe...

He bows his head. She'd remember him running like a

fool from the Norns' lair.

Rubbing the back of his neck, he gestures toward the couch. "Yo, guys," he says. "Would you get a pillow and blankets for me over here?"

The two servants freeze in place.

Bohdi smiles, showing all his teeth. "I've got to protect my lady's virtue, after all."

The two men's eyes slide to each other, and then the head Asshole, says, "As man to man, we should warn. No virtue. She was Loki's…"

The Other Asshole finishes for him. "Whore."

Bohdi's vision goes red. For a moment, he stands immobilized. And then spinning in place, he hurls his knife, not seeing or caring where it hits. It lands with a rip and a thunk. He turns back to The Assholes.

Looking beyond Bohdi their eyes are wide. One of them is shaking.

"Get out," Bohdi whispers.

Neither man moves.

"Get out!" Bohdi says again.

Nodding, they scamper from the room, bowing all the way.

Mouth curled in a silent snarl, Bohdi goes to retrieve his knife. And sees why his outburst had such an effect on the two men.

His knife has ripped the tapestry and embedded in the wall. Run through by the blade is a butterfly.

Pulling the knife from the wall, Bohdi catches the dead insect in his hand.

Turning it over, he studies its delicate, shimmering wings. He swallows, backs over to the couch, and falls down into it.

He stares down at the dead insect in his hand and starts to shake.

It's the sort of nightmare where Amy knows she's dreaming. She's only half asleep. She can feel the exquisitely silky fabric of the Asgardian duvet beneath her fingers. Her head is on a soft pillow. She's dry, and warm, and the world smells like spring.

Still, the screams from the baby spiders in the dream make all the hairs on her neck stand on end. Her eyes open fast. She is curled in a fetal position on the bed, a bit of duvet in a death grip in her hand. Her mouth is open and gasping, the world is a blur. The shrieks, so much like those of a human infant, are ringing in her ears.

She closes her eyes. It isn't strange that the spider children sounded so human. They were small and had small trachea, doubtlessly. Rabbits that Fenrir has cornered in the back yard made similar noises before dying. That the sound leaves a chill isn't strange either—hundreds of thousands of years of evolution have made humans easily distraught by the wails of infants.

Which is why it isn't wrong for Amy to hurt remembering the cries of pain of the creatures that tried to kill her.

Amy opens her eyes. The world is a blur. But then shapes within the blur converge and she's staring at Bohdi. He's standing a few steps away from the bed, bent down so his head is level to hers.

"Are you all right?" he asks softly.

Amy nods. "Just a nightmare."

Bohdi's eyes go down. "I heard…I didn't know if I should

wake you." He says it like someone might say, *I'm sorry.*

It's the most he's said since Queen Frigga brought them here.

Amy's eyes clear a little more. She sees the couch where he'd been lying. The blanket is thrown haphazardly over the back. His pillow's on the floor.

"I'm fine," she says. If she says it enough, she knows it will be true.

He ducks his head and walks back to the couch. The new clothes he's wearing are slightly wrinkled after his nap, but otherwise fit him well. Dark blue fitted trousers, with buttons down the outside ankle over brown leather boots. A collarless shirt that's more a tunic, and a gray vest over that—but this vest is more Han Solo than Chippendales. Thankfully.

Amy sits up, and Mr. Squeakers, who'd been sleeping on the headboard, hops on her arm. Across the room, Bohdi flops back down onto the couch. He pulls out his phone from his pocket and powers it on. The screen flickers to life. Amy sees a photo flash on the screen before he powers it down again. She knows which picture it was without asking.

She wants to ask him if *he's* all right.

In Nornheim, as they floated down the river, Bohdi had woken from a fevered dream, looked up at her with surprisingly clear eyes, and said, "It's like the *Life of Pi.*" And then he'd grinned. "If I'm Pi, are you the tiger?" Amy had laughed, equally with relief that he was alive, and at the joke. She was so not a tiger. But summoning up her courage, she lifted a hand, pretended to paw the air, and said, *"Rawr?"* Bohdi had burst out into a guffaw before his head lolled to the side again and he'd fallen back into unconsciousness.

He'd joked while he was dying. Now he's withdrawn and

sullen.

Standing up, she slips on the ballet slippers she was given. She starts to walk over to the couch, but her clothes catch awkwardly under her armpit, and she stops with a huff. The clothes aren't actually that bad—they're modest at least: the thin sleeveless pale green dress she wears is covered by a knee-length fitted coat. The coat is a Vanir linen, cool, and comfortable, but not as wrinkly. It wasn't meant to be slept in, though. The buttons that are supposed to run straight down the front are twisting around toward the back.

Straightening out her clothes and her hair as much she can without a mirror, Amy walks toward Bohdi. She's interrupted by a knock at the door. She's just had time to slip Squeakers into her pocket when it swings open. The maids from earlier stand in the doorway, this time with trays laden with steaming dishes in their hands. Above their heads glowing butterflies flutter, their wings casting light throughout the darkening room. Amy hadn't noticed how close the sun was to setting.

"Dinner?" says one.

Bohdi says nothing.

"Thank you, come in," says Amy.

Without a word, Bohdi walks over to the table and sits down.

He's quiet as the maids deposit the trays and leave, a cloud of butterflies staying behind to light their dinner. It reminds her of the restaurant where Loki created illusions of butterflies to comfort a young girl.

To distract herself, she describes the dishes to Bohdi. Loki probably knew every dish made by anyone anywhere. The man—Frost Giant, incarnation of chaos—ate like, well, not a horse. Loki was very omnivorous—more like a bear. Or several bears.

Bohdi doesn't say more than "Hmmm" and "Mmmmm." In the silence, Amy catches herself mentally measuring how much Bohdi eats. He puts down enough that Amy would feel stuffed to the gills, but nothing like Loki, just like a normal human male in his twenties.

She quietly reprimands herself. She's got to let go of the Bohdi-as-Loki thing. If Bohdi was Loki and sneezed when he heard lies, he would have sneezed when Thor said Loki was in Hel, but he didn't…because it wasn't a lie…and Odin didn't detect a lie either, so Bohdi can't be…

Slipping a hand into her pocket, she runs a finger between Squeakers' ears. She has to open up her mind to the idea of a new Loki, a completely different, unimagined so far, Loki. When Thor brings him back, she has to convince him to come back to Earth with her or this whole trip will be for nothing.

She doesn't know why, but the task isn't just daunting anymore—it makes her sad for some inexplicable reason. Shaking her head, she lets out a sigh to break the silence. Bohdi doesn't comment. And suddenly his quiet, and the butterflies that are like that other time, are sickening and oppressive.

"What are you thinking?" Amy asks.

Pushing the remains of some Vanaheim pink potato around his plate, Bohdi's jaw goes tense. She doesn't think he will answer, but then, head bowed, he says, "I was thinking about Nidhogg, actually."

Remembering the dragon, Amy's shoulders slouch, and she feels a little sick to her stomach. She looks down at her own plate. Nidhogg died so fast. One moment he was there, threatening to eat them, the next he was gone.

"How old was he?" Bohdi says.

Amy can't bring herself to speak. Older than Loki. Probably older than Odin and Frigga. The things he must have seen and known...

Bohdi meets her eyes briefly.

Looking away he says, "In the Marine Corps, they told us it isn't uncommon for guys to fire above the enemy's heads. I used to think that was stupid." He drops his fork with a clang on his plate, and puts his head in his hands. "Now I'm feeling sad about the death of a dragon that wanted to eat me."

Amy stares at him. She's shocked and it takes a moment to realize why. She is still thinking of him as Loki...She can't remember a time when Loki felt sorry for an enemy. Because he'd lost the ability, or because he was raised in a violent culture, she's not sure.

...but Bohdi's not ancient, and he's not from Asgard. And as much as he's better at killing things, he's seen less of death than Amy has.

Biting her lip, she says, "I was having nightmares about spider screams."

He looks up quickly. "That wasn't your fault."

Amy feels her frame soften. "The fire was my suggestion." She reaches across the table but stops short of taking his hand. "And I'm glad I didn't die skewered by a spider leg."

Shifting in his chair, Bohdi says, "Twelve Valkyries are dead. Because of me."

"The Norns killed them, not you," Amy says. She looks down at her plate. Thor, Amy, the Valkyries, they'd all been looking for chaos. In one sense they'd found it. Reaching into the pocket not occupied by Squeakers, she wraps her fingers around the Archaeopteryx feathers. She bites her lip again, overwhelmed by the thought of what may be uncovered by sequencing the DNA in these feathers. That's the thing about chaos—open yourself up to it, and you don't just open your life to danger; you also open your life to wonder.

Leaning forward so fast he shakes the table, Bohdi says, "But it was because I—" He stops.

Releasing the feathers, Amy looks up at Bohdi. "Because you what?"

Bohdi's lip curls. "You heard what the Norns said!"

His tone makes Amy pull back. And then her skin heats. "I heard them say that you are a slut, and a man-whore, and that you insulted them. I didn't hear what happened." She drops a hand on the table with more force than she intends and the silverware rattles. "And maybe you hit on them accidentally, I don't know Norn culture, but you wouldn't have done anything to offend them on purpose and..."

She stops. They said he insulted them...

What had Lache said before she and Bohdi had started eating? "You'll need your strength." And then there was Chloe's comment to Amy about whether she'd ever considered being a boy, and Lache talking in the language that sounded like Hindi, and Chloe's comment about getting in the mood...

Amy's eyes rise to where Bohdi is staring at her across the table, a scowl etched deep in his brow.

"*They* hit on *you*," she whispers.

For a minute, Bohdi's face goes soft, then he smirks and looks at his plate. "What possible reason would the Norns have to want to hit on a *human*?"

Amy blinks and shrugs. "Maybe having sex with one of every sentient species is on their bucket lists?"

Bohdi's eyebrows go up. "Why would creatures who are

next to immortal have a bucket list?"

A memory comes to Amy. She closes her eyes to try and block the images. "Maybe it wasn't so much a bucket list as sort of bingo. You know, where they check off a square for every species they——-"

She can't bring herself to finish.

She opens one eye. Bohdi is staring at her, jaw slack.

She winces. "Between puberty and Anganboða, Loki—"

Again she can't finish.

"Anganboða?" says Bohdi.

A non-distressing question. Finally. "First real love of his life," she says. "They got married and—well lived happily, mostly, until she died." Amy leaves out the committed suicide bit.

"They did have a beautiful little girl named Helen. Hel is where her grave is."

Bohdi stares at her, face expressionless. It's only a few moments, but it's long enough for Amy to start to feel uncomfortable.

Tilting his head, his lips turn up in a tiny sneer. "Loki told you about his sex bingo game?"

"Errrr…" says Amy.

Bohdi shakes his head and shovels up a bit of pink potato stuff. Voice too knowing, he says, "I would never tell my girl-friend something like that."

Amy's ire prickles. "Like you're an authority on relation-ships!" Mr. Alley Cat!

Bohdi's head shoots up. "I had a girlfriend!"

"For how long?" says Amy

Bohdi drops his head, and mumbles. "About six months."

"That's—" *Nothing*, Amy almost says, but then she

realizes, "That's nearly a quarter of your known life."

"Thanks for reminding me," says Bohdi, scraping his fork across the plate.

The words, "What happened?" slip out. Putting a hand over her mouth, she murmurs, "Sorry, you don't have to answer."

Smiling bitterly, Bohdi says, "She was a nice Indian girl, and as you've noticed, I'm not a nice Indian boy."

"That's..." Amy doesn't know what to say. She feels terrible. "I'm sorry."

Bohdi shrugs. "It's no big deal."

Amy's eyebrows go up.

He looks at her and rolls his eyes. "I wasn't in love..." Running a hand through his hair, he sprawls back in his chair. One knee rises and falls as he taps his heel. "I was just trying to regain my heritage, or find a family, or..."

Remembering the picture he'd just been looking at on his phone, Amy swallows. Before she can say anything, outside in the hallway there is the sound of shouts and many footsteps.

"What was that?" says Bohdi.

Amy looks down at their empty plates, and her eyes widen. "Something is wrong. The maids should have stayed to collect our dishes... They must be needed elsewhere."

Her eyes meet Bohdi's. Standing as one they go to the main door. Holding a finger to his lips, Bohdi leans and presses an ear to the door. Shaking his head, he shrugs and whispers. "Just lots of feet."

Amy looks at the doorknob. She reaches out with a trembling hand. Bohdi's knife is instantly out and open. He nods at her.

She opens the door and sees maids and servants dashing

down the halls. There is the clink of metal, and two blurs on either side of her make her turn her head, another blur directly in front of her makes her turn and gasp, and then she's falling backward.

The first thing Bohdi sees when Amy opens the door of their plush prison is two guards in Viking-meets-video game armor. Their backs are to Amy and Bohdi, and their swords are sheathed, but they both hold wicked-looking spears, the metal tips ridged, and gleaming bright. Amy gives a faint sigh, and with the precision of dancers, the two guards swivel on their feet, sweeping their spears around with them.

Bohdi instinctively yanks Amy back. She falls against his chest, and the spears clack together a few inches in front of where her nose would have been. It takes Bohdi a moment to realize they probably weren't trying to hurt her. Still, his hand shakes on her shoulder, and his eyes flit between the two men. One is Caucasian looking. The other looks a lot like Bohdi, but he sports a thicker mustache than Bohdi will ever be able to grow.

White guy nods. "Pardon, Mademoiselle, but we were instructed not to let you leave your chambers. Unfortunately, there has been a bit of an emergency, and there is no one to guard you."

Amy visibly perks. Voice excited, she says, "Wait… You have a French accent, you're actually speaking English, not using magic to translate! You're human!"

A small smile comes to the man's lips. "Yes, I was French, Mademoiselle. Now I am one of Odin's Einherjar."

Thrusting a hand forward, Amy says, "I'm Amy, and this is Bohdi, so nice to meet you!"

The Einherjar looks her up and down—determining her threat level and checking her out. The new clothes confirmed something that Bohdi had been suspecting. Amy isn't thick; the proper description is stacked.

Bowing, Frenchie takes her hand and brings it to his lips.

Bohdi narrows his eyes at the man.

Might-be-an-Indian-guy narrows his eyes, too—at Bohdi.

Gently dropping her hand, Frenchie says, "My name is Pascal." Inclining his head in the direction of his companion, he says, "And this is Gabbar."

Snapping his ankles together, Gabbar bows. "Gabbar Singh Negi. Pleased to meet you, Miss." The name is unmistakably Indian.

"Both of you speak great English," says Amy, a smile in her voice.

Does she have to be so nice to their jailers?

Pascal claps his companion on the shoulder. "Gabbar here fought for the British during Earth's first World War. I learned as a boy."

Putting her hands together, Amy says, "Maybe you could show us around?"

Oh, she's buttering them up. That's a good ploy. Bohdi swallows. And yet he hopes she fails.

Pascal straightens and steps back. He looks to Gabbar.

"We are warriors, not tour guides," Gabbar rumbles.

"I'm sorry, Mademoiselle, but this is our post." Pascal says with a dip of his head.

"Oh," says Amy, hands going to her sides. "That's too bad. I would love to talk to you more…and know when and where you were you recruited, and everything you've seen…" She sounds distressingly enchanted.

Suddenly, unable to take it anymore, Bohdi grabs Amy's arm and pulls her into their room. Barely managing to mumble, "Excuse us a moment," he slams the door shut with his foot.

"What's wrong?" says Amy, eyes wide.

Sucking air through his teeth, Bohdi whispers, "Can we not make friends with our enemies?"

Amy gazes at him. And then she whispers, "Okay."

Bohdi's body sags in relief. His lighter is in his hand. He doesn't remember taking it out.

Stepping around Amy, he goes to the far wall. "Maybe there's another way to poke around." Looking out the window, he scowls. Outside is a small courtyard. They aren't high up, but Einherjar are standing guard on all sides.

Amy whispers in his ear. "All of these guest rooms have secret passages. If we find one…"

Bohdi turns and finds their faces very close. He licks his lips and whispers. "Where?"

Voice hushed, Amy says, "I don't know, but I do know one of these walls is a lie. Sometimes magic wasn't the most efficient way to spy. If we can find it…" Spinning around, she goes to the other side of the room and begins running her hand along the wall. Glowing butterflies follow in her wake.

He doesn't need to ask how she knows. He grinds his jaw and drops his eyes. And then he blinks. One of the walls is a lie? The Lord of Chaos is supposed to sense lies. And if he is… Bohdi hesitates just a moment, but then he joins Amy, lightly trailing his hand over the plaster paneling. His nose almost instantly starts itching, but for once it might only be dust.

The paneling isn't as smooth as it looks. It feels grainy under his fingers, and when he pulls his hand away there is grime on his fingers. Ahead of him, Amy lifts a tapestry, drops it, and then goes over and tips a chair back to peer intently at the space underneath it.

Bohdi keeps running his fingers along the wall. He's just passing the fireplace when he almost sneezes. Wiping his nose, he whispers, "Amy, could it be in the fireplace?"

Dropping the chair back down, she turns toward the fireplace. Rushing over, she exclaims, "Yes!" and begins frantically patting down the molding around the fireplace. The molding is a series of circles, with an elaborate twisting pattern swirling around a central three-pronged shape within. Mumbling cryptically to herself, "Norse knot pattern, probably the only real thing in here." Amy sinks to her knees. She smacks the bottom-most circle right in the center. The plaster jostles slightly.

Bohdi falls to his knees beside her.

"I think this is it," Amy says. She grabs the three-pronged shape and twists. It spins and there is a whisper from the fireplace. Bohdi and Amy both peek. The back wall of the fireplace has slid to the side.

"Wow, you found it," Amy says, her eyes sparkling in the butterfly lights. "How did you know?" Bohdi finds himself unable to speak. He could tell her the truth. She probably wouldn't believe him. He swallows and remembers her hand in his in the throne room. Maybe she would. Maybe she'd even throw her arms around him. He could press their bodies together and tuck his head in the space between her shoulder and her neck. He's cold all of a sudden—and she'd be warm. His legs feel weak, and she could help him stand.

Dipping his chin, evading her gaze, he says instead, "The fireplace arch is shaped like a doorway…"

"Oh," says Amy with a smile. "You're right. That was smart."

Eager to move on, Bohdi says, "You figured out how to open it. You're the smart one."

Something like disappointment flickers across Amy's face. "Right," she says.

Amy waits in the tunnel, just beyond the fireplace archway, Mr. Squeakers in her hand, butterflies swirling above her head. Bohdi stoops and enters behind her. "I told Frenchie and Mr. Judgmental we were going to be asleep and not to let the maids back in."

"Great," says Amy. She's sure that whatever "excitement" is occupying Odin's staff is also keeping Heimdall and his raven spies distracted. But another visit from the maids could be problematic.

Pursing his lips, Bohdi looks around the tunnel. No illusions cover the concrete block here. It could be the utility hallway of any building on Earth. At least it's not dangerous. As soon as she thinks that thought, Squeakers launches himself into the air from her palm. Amy gasps, Bohdi's eyes go wide, and his side is instantly pressed to hers, his knife in his hand.

"Do you think he knows something we don't?" he says, scanning the ceiling above their heads.

"I don't—"

Her words die on her tongue as Squeakers leisurely slips down from the ceiling on a line of spider silk, a butterfly fluttering in his forelimbs. Her spidermouse bites off the butterfly's head with a crunch.

Amy winces. Reaching for her spidermouse, she turns to Bohdi and says apologetically, "Just because Squeakers is dangerous, doesn't make him bad."

Settling into her outstretched palm, Squeakers takes another loud bite from the butterfly's torso. Amy glances up to see Bohdi looking at her, eyes very wide and soft. But maybe that's a trick of the light. His lip curls in a slight smile, and he shrugs. "Well, we could use some danger in here." He looks around the tunnel and sighs dramatically. "No spooky empty suits of armor, no skeletons on the walls." Plucking the line of spider silk Squeakers left behind, he rolls his eyes. "And only *one* cobweb."

Amy smiles, he seems to be himself again. "Come on," she says, starting down the tunnel.

They haven't gone far when they come to an intersection Amy recognizes—or Loki recognized. Bohdi only raises an eyebrow when she says, "I think we should go this way," and leads him toward what she knows are the main rooms of the palace.

They pass by a few doors and then come to a large door that Amy also recognizes. She stops. She bites her lip. On the one hand, they have a *Mission*. On the other hand, whatever is happening isn't likely to be over soon, and who knows if they'll get another chance to go into the room just on the other side of the wall. Her eyes slide to the side. Beside the door, there is a little sort of steering wheel crank thing. There is also a little sliding lever about eye height. Without giving an explanation to Bohdi, Amy slides the lever to the side. She knows that the door is disguised by a bookshelf, and that the little lever opens a window disguised as a book. As the tiny window opens, a butterfly sneaks through, casting a faint light in the space beyond. Amy peeks and sees an empty recessed nook, and beyond that the library proper. Bohdi peers over her shoulder. "Oooo…books," he whispers. He sounds more excited than she would have expected. "It looks empty to me," he says. Pulling away, he adds, "And you know…whatever is going on…it's not like we can stop it, or help, and who knows what magical technology we could discover in a library…even just looking at pictures."

Amy blinks at him. Is she supposed to be the responsible person here? She probably should be…but the library is ordinarily empty this time of night, and she really wants to see the medical section.

Apparently taking her silence for reluctance, Bohdi continues, "And you know the old saying, when in Rome…" He pauses and looks up thoughtfully.

"Plunder the libraries?" Amy supplies with a snicker.

Shrugging, Bohdi smiles like a shark. "Works for me."

A few minutes later, they're trailing through the cavernous expanse of shelves, butterflies lighting their way. Instead of aisles, the shelves extend stories above their heads. Little trellised walkways and sliding ladders provide access here and there. As Amy and Bohdi walk past, the titles and authors on the spines of the tomes flicker and glow.

"Do you think they have a physics section?" Bohdi asks.

"I'm sure they do," says Amy, leading him straight to the medical section. Stopping, she pulls a large tome on troll anatomy from the shelves. The illustrations and neat cursive scrawl light up as her eyes traverse the pages. She sniffs. Magic aside, the pictures aren't as good as *Netter's Atlas of Human Anatomy*.

Bohdi peers over her shoulder and then ducks away. She's

vaguely aware of him climbing up a ladder. She's just review-
ing the troll's anterior cruciate ligament—more human than
orangutan, definitely, when she hazards a glance up at Bohdi.
He's sitting on the highest rung of a ladder, nose buried in a
book. The title on the spine makes her eyebrows hike, *Mating
Rituals Among the Elfish People.*

Stifling a snort, Amy licks her lips and says as innocently
as she can manage, "Whatcha lookin' at there?"

Not looking at her, Bohdi says, "Oh, you know…dry, boring, anatomical…stuff."

"Uh-huh," says Amy, going over to the ladder.

He's so engrossed, he doesn't notice her slinking up below
him until she almost whips the book from his hand.

Lifting the book and snapping it shut, he glares down at
her from between his knees. Raising an eyebrow, he turns it
over and looks at the writing on the spine. Eyes going back to
Amy he says, "So you can read Asgardian, not just speak it?"

He knows. Amy's jaw falls. She should have told him, but
she didn't—at first because she didn't want their guests to
know. And then…because why?

"What else do you know, Amy?" he asks.

Amy takes a step down the ladder. The conversation they
could have plays out in her mind. *You know how Loki wiped
your memories? Well, he gave me all of his. They've been really
convenient. Sorry your amnesia has been a bit more of a bummer.*

She can't speak.

Opening the book again, Bohdi says, "I think I'm going
to keep this." He gives her a leering grin. "For the guys in it."

Amy's mouth falls.

He chuckles. "They're so scrawny they make me feel buff
and masculine."

Amy snatches the book from him and looks down at the pages, purely out of scientific curiosity. The pose on the page looks too painful to be arousing. What's more… "The men make me look buff," she says. And the women look as tiny and delicate as ballerinas. She scowls remembering her trip to Alfheim. "They must have thought I looked like a bloated cow."

"You?" says Bohdi. "No."

The assurance in his voice makes Amy flush. Snapping the book shut, she hands it back up to him. Not wanting to meet his gaze, she instead looks to the side. Her lips purse. "Of all places…how did you wind up in the reproduction section?"

Bohdi looks around at the books. Voice excited, he says, "They're all about sex?" He quickly yanks another book from the shelf and flips it open. His whole body stills. And then he says softly. "This one is about adze."

Amy remembers the dragonfly men and how their sexless, hairless bodies were more discomfiting than nudity. Face expressionless, Bohdi hands the book down to her. "What does it say?"

Amy looks down at the page. There is a tiny line illustration of an adze, and a whole lot of cursive text. Her hands begin to shake a little as she reads.

"What is it?" Bohdi whispers.

"Well…" she says. "Guess it's kind of obvious that they don't reproduce sexually…When they devour a hominid, the bones will sprout muscles and ligaments…nerves…skin…and create a new adze."

"Oh," Bohdi whispers.

Amy's hand starts to shake as she skims the page. "But it doesn't require that the victim be devoured—a single scratch, or bite, is enough to ensure the transformation." At just that moment a butterfly alights on her scabbed knuckle. Bohdi glances down.

Amy looks at the neatly healing cuts.

"Where did you get those, Amy?" Bohdi says.

Clutching her hand to her stomach, Amy says, "When you were unconscious…but it must have been the tree branch." She shivers and glances at the text. "Apparently, if it was an adze scratch, I'd be an adze by now." She lets out a slow breath of air and looks up at him. "Still scary to realize how close I was to…"

"Yeah," says Bohdi. She glances up. His jaw is very tight. He gives her a wan smile.

Looking away, he slips the book of elven mating rituals beneath the front of his tunic. Smacking where it's caught in the fold above his trousers, he says, "So can you find the physics section?" He gazes upward. "Or would that be the magic section here, or are they one and the same?"

Amy's mouth drops. "Yes, but…are you stealing that book?"

Bohdi flutters his long lashes at her. "I am *appropriating* new knowledge for the benefit of all mankind."

Amy's eyes narrow. "You do know that it will be *appropriated* by ADUO as soon as we get back to Earth?"

Bohdi's nostrils flare slightly. "How dare they plunder my plunder!"

Amy sighs. "Believe me. They don't let you keep anything you pick up in another universe…or even just when you disappear from the face of the Earth for an hour." She looks down. "They badger you with questions until you think you're not even allowed to keep your memories, or not-memories. If Squeakers wasn't able to scurry off and hide on his own…"

And if Loki's journal hadn't been so small, so easy to slip into the front of her bra, she wouldn't have that either.

Bohdi shifts above her. "What do you mean *when you disappear for an hour?*"

Amy blinks up at him. "Oh, it's nothing." Bohdi sniffs. She looks past the butterflies into the darkness. No, that's not right. It was something...

"What happened?" Bohdi asks.

Amy looks up at him. "I don't remember."

Bohdi's chin dips. "And that doesn't bother you?"

"No... Maybe it should?" She hardly ever thinks about it.

A crease settles in Bohdi's brow. Leaning closer, he says, "Maybe?"

Amy bites her lip. "But before that time, I was really hurt. There'd been a SWAT raid of Loki's apartment, and they shot me in the neck, and my stomach was a pincushion for shattered glass." She remembers the itch caused by the morphine, and the smell of antiseptic and shivers. "And then when I came back, I was better, and Beatrice was with me, and she was better, and so was Ratatoskr...so it must have been okay?"

The crease in Bohdi's brow grows deeper and his lips part. He looks slightly worried.

Amy shakes her head. "Really, the only thing that bothered me was the interrogation afterward. They kept asking me questions." She winces at the memory. Like they thought she was hiding something.

Her head ticks to the side. Is she hiding something? Yes, Loki's memories...But that's not it, is it?

"Come on," says Bohdi softly. "Let's go check out the physics section."

Grateful for the change of subject, Amy starts climbing

down the ladder. "I didn't know you liked physics," she says.

Following her, Bohdi ducks her gaze. "It's just a hobby. I'm not a Ph. D. candidate or anything. I…" He rubs the back of his neck. "It's not like math, computer languages, Hindi, or English. I like it, but I don't know it…" he huffs softly. "Well, I know it better than Steve does."

Amy hums a small laugh. "Is that hard?"

Bohdi snorts. "Yeah, maybe not." In a perfect imitation of Steve's voice, Bohdi says, "Bohdi, how come World Gates keep popping up in Chicago when the World Seed is gone?"

Amy laughs at the impression and then says, "He just is so stuck on the linearity of time!"

Shaking his head, Bohdi says, "Newtonian physics… Sometimes you just have to let it go."

He gives a small smile and says, "But I shouldn't make too much fun of Steve." Putting his hands in his pockets, he shrugs a bit. "He's kind of my best friend."

Amy's gaze slips sideways. His eyes are on hers and they seem…softer. It's terrifying. Looking away, Amy says, "It's kind of hard to imagine you and Steve as friends. He's so… straight-laced."

"It's true," Bohdi says as they pass a cozy reading nook and enter a section that houses the physics-magic books. "Without me, he might die of boredom—but without him, I'd be in Gitmo, so it all evens out."

Gitmo? Amy opens her mouth to ask and then hears a noise. On her shoulder, Squeakers goes rigid. Bohdi halts at her side. The butterflies continue to swirl in the air above them.

Amy's eyes slide in the direction of the sound. It's foot-steps, coming from around a corner in front of them—an alcove that leads to the main hallway beyond the library. A voice says in Asgardian, "I'm sure I saw lights in here." There is another sound—a clinking noise. Armor?

Amy looks behind them. The door to the tunnels is too far away; they won't make it, even if they run. Mr. Squeakers gives an ill-timed cheep on her shoulder.

"Did you hear that?" says the first voice.

A deeper voice says, *"Yes."* And then there is the sound of fast footsteps.

"Hide!" Bohdi whispers, inclining his head in the direction of the nook.

Amy nods, and they turn into the tiny space just as the footsteps enter the library proper.

"Quick, behind the chairs!" Amy turns and slips into the dusty corner behind an enormous, overstuffed chair. Bohdi slips behind the other.

The butterflies follow, dancing just above the chair backs. From beyond the nook comes the sound of their pursuers. *"Do you see butterfly lights?"*

Amy reaches up and tries to catch the flitting insects. Bohdi does, too…but with much more luck.

The sound of her heart is competing in volume with the footsteps that are only a few feet beyond the nook. Amy bows her head. Maybe if they play dumb…just tell Frigga they happened upon the tunnels. And were bored. And if they apologize profusely…

"Look, the butterflies!" says the first voice. *"What's making them so excited?"*

"I'll check," says the deeper voice.

Amy looks up. Her eyes lock with Bohdi's. This is it.

She hears the sound of a sword being drawn. *"Come out,*

whoever, whatever you are!" says the deeper voice. There is another footstep. She can see the armored boot of its maker around the corner of her chair.

Amy sits paralyzed. So does Bohdi.

Squeakers does not.

Leaping from her shoulder, Squeakers catches a fluttering butterfly midair, and lands on the back of the chair. Settling back on four legs, he bites into the butterfly with a crunch.

The screams that come from the man's mouth sound inhuman. Which Amy guesses, they technically may be, but still, it seems excessive...

"A spidermouse! Kill it!" the first man screeches.

"No! The whole library could be infested with them!" shouts his comrade. There is the sound of thudding retreating footsteps.

"We must get the mages!" says first man, his voice now very far away. Amy and Bohdi creep out from their hiding places. Amy peeks around the corner of the nook. "They're gone," she whispers.

She turns and sees Bohdi holding Squeakers in his palm. Smiling and scratching Squeakers behind the ears, he says, "Who could be afraid of such a cute little mouse?"

Amy's lips purse. Considering that Bohdi is holding Mr. Squeakers in his palm, it seems an inopportune time to point out that in another universe, she'd learned that Squeakers is venomous enough to knock out even a very powerful Frost Giant—and probably could kill a human.

"Errr..." she says instead. "We better go before they get back."

Bohdi nods, and then says, "Can I get a book on physics first?"

Amy blinks at him. Bohdi shrugs and smiles. Rolling her eyes, she runs to where they first heard the footsteps and pulls the first book she sees from the shelf. *The Theory and Practical Application of Magic*, by a Hellbendi so-and-so.

Waving it at Bohdi, she says, "Can we go now?"

"Yep," says Bohdi with a grin, still holding Squeakers in his palm.

They're just slipping into the tunnel, the few remaining butterflies flitting in behind them, when they hear voices rise from the library. Bohdi and Amy twist the crank. There's only a centimeter left to close when Amy hears a man's voice say, *"Are you sure you are up to this task?"*

"I'm sorry, Sir…but with the invasion and skirmishes with the Fire Giants, all the more adept mages are busy."

Amy puts her hand on top of Bohdi's before he can finish closing the door.

He stops and looks at her.

Holding a hand to her lips, she says, "They're talking about an invasion…"

"Invasion? Where?"

Beyond the tunnel, one of the men says, *"How many mages can be needed for an invasion of Earth?"*

Amy looks at Bohdi, her eyes go wide, and she sinks to her knees.

CHAPTER 22

Shrugging his coat against the cold, Steve quickens his steps. He's almost across Jackson when his phone vibrates in his pocket. Stepping onto the curb, he pulls it out and scans the screen. A new text from Prometheus.

Still no news on the whereabouts of Miss Lewis and the other human?

Steve starts walking again, somewhat surprised by the question. They've been assuming that Prometheus was at least located in Asgard part-time. Maybe he isn't. Or maybe he is and this is just a ploy to uncover how much Steve knows. So Steve punts that ball right back at their sometime source.

No, Steve types. It's a lie. From the last transmissions received by the drone, ADUO is almost dead certain that Lewis and Bohdi are in Asgard.

Tapping his thumbs on the screen, he asks, *Do you have intel?*

Three little dots flash on the screen.

For a few seconds, there is nothing. And then a message appears. *I cannot see into Nornheim, but I do not believe that the Norns will harm Lewis. When will you send in a recovery team?*

So much emphasis on Lewis. And certainty that she is still alive. Interesting.

Logistics under review, Steve types back.

A one-word reply appears on the screen: *Understood.* And then Prometheus disconnects.

Steve sighs. Well, at least someone understands that a mission to Nornheim is a little more than a walk in the park—or even a rescue from Somali pirates.

Slipping the phone into his pocket he walks across the courtyard that separates the Board of Trade from the building to the east of it. He spares a look up at the Board of Trade—a hulking, bent shadow against the weak winter sun. His heart sinks. There has been no progress on rehabbing the structure. It's a monument to defeat. He'd almost rather see the damned thing torn down, but it's a national landmark, and that's not going to happen.

Shaking his head, he reaches the east side of the courtyard and ducks into the restaurant there. He's met by a new waitress. She's pretty, in a typical way. Blonde, busty, with a tan that is too expensive for a waitress salary.

"Just one?" she asks. Her accent sounds vaguely Norwegian. There has been a small surge in immigrants from Scandinavia since the appearance of Loki.

"Meeting some people," Steve says.

Picking up a menu, she says, "Oh, you're Steve Rogers. I'm Cindy. Your party is in my section. Right this way."

A few minutes later, Steve is sitting down at a table with three members of Chicago's Democratic Party, "Fats" Mac-Namara, a stout, ruddy-faced man in his fifties, and two young guys. Harrison, an African American with an East Coast accent and Harvard degree who Steve has mentally nicknamed "Two-for," and Richard, a young white kid with stringy, dirty blond hair and a baseball cap. "Two-for" and Richard have convertible tablets open in front of them, every now and then their fingers dance across the keyboards. The conversations of scientists and tourists fill the restaurant. In the corner a TV is tuned to CNN.

"Thing is, Steve," Fats is saying, "you're divorced, and still unmarried. And voters don't like that…"

Richard blinks up over the screen of his tablet. "Oh, come on, unmarried divorcees have become mayors before…"

Two-for shoots a withering glare in Richard's direction. Fats's face goes a little ruddier.

Steve's lips twist into a bitter half-smile.

Looking embarrassed, Fats says, "Steve is black."

Steve rolls his eyes and resists the urge to hold up his hands and say, *What? I am?* If Bohdi were here, he'd make that joke for him. Tapping a finger on the table, he smiles tightly.

"Cory Booker!" Richard says. "Mayor of Newark!"

Two-for shakes his head. "Never married. Not divorced. And everyone thinks he's gay." He turns to Steve. "Are you gay? Because we could work with that. If you're gay, that makes the divorce more excusable. You were finding yourself, your divorce is amicable…"

Steve narrows his eyes. "No."

Richard perks up. Face becoming animated, hands leaving his keyboard, he says excitedly, "No…you're not gay? Or you don't like that plan? Because, dude, being gay would go a long way to easing the younger generation's anxiety about your membership in the Republican Party when you were in college."

"Might also help with the allegations of sexual harassment

of that Frost Giantess," says Two-for.

"Those allegations are *baseless* and I will be found innocent," Steve snaps. Two-for and Richard draw back.

"Steve's not gay," says Fats.

The two younger men turn to Fats, shoulders slumping slightly.

Steve leans back in his seat. "And it wouldn't play with the older generation in this town."

Turning to Steve, Fats says, "But the divorce is an issue. If there was—"

With a brusque wave of his hand, Steve cuts him off. "There are no sordid stories of clandestine affairs, Fats."

Fats leans closer to Steve. "You've given full access to surveillance of the giantess in your custody. Transparency is going to solve your sexual harassment issue... If you gave that same transparency to your divorce, opened up your divorce papers for the press..."

Lowering and shaking his head, Steve says, "No. It would hurt my daughter. And...no. Not happening."

Fats sighs. "Steve...isn't your daughter in the Ukraine now?"

Steve lifts his eyes, his insides turning to lead. Claire is in the Ukraine. This very day going to the Kiev Ballet for a tour, and then to the president's residence for a reception. What had Claire said? Her dress was like a real princess's?

"Think about it, Steve," says Fats. Looking at his empty plate, he says, "Where did our waitress go?"

Steve looks at his own empty coffee cup. He suddenly needs more. And he wants to step away from the table. Scanning the room, he sees the coffee maker at the bar underneath the television. Grabbing his cup, he says, "Anyone else want more?"

The three political gurus shake their heads, and Steve steps away. The only person at the bar is a woman in a neat pantsuit, a tablet in front of her. She looks up at Steve and his breath catches. Her features are very African. She has a wide mouth with full lips, and a flat nose. Her skin looks like it's been cut with cream, though. She is a light tan, her hair slightly darker. But her eyes are stunning, wide and nearly black. Her lips stretch into an easy smile. "Hello."

Steve's brain blinks off for a second. As he gathers himself, his first thought is that this is why marriage is preferred in politicians. If you don't have someone, you're always looking.

His eyes take in the hard hat on the counter beside her. The architectural designs laid out on the tablet, and the black portfolio leaning against the bar between their feet. Someone on the Board of Trade rehab team, maybe?

Almost against his volition his own lips turn into a smile. "Hi," he says, feeling himself lean imperceptibly closer.

From behind the bar, a man's voice says, "Oh my God. Is that real?"

Steve and the woman both turn. Steve's eyes lift to the screen. At first, he thinks he's looking at a trailer for a movie. A winged woman in armor is on the screen, a spear upraised in front of her, a silent scream on her lips. The end of the spear is glowing red. A heartbeat later, a drop of what looks like lava congeals on the tip and blasts toward the camera. The screen goes black. All voices in the room go silent.

The frame switches to a building too engulfed in flame be recognized…but the fire is wrong. Too red, and too bright. Magic.

Steve steps closer to the bar. The bartender turns on the

sound and an announcer's voice fills the room. "This is a shot of the Kremlin… We've also got reports coming in that the residence of the president of Belarus is targeted…and wait, wait…" The screen flashes to another building bathed in the same too-red fire. The announcer says, "And this is a shot of the residence of the president of the Ukraine."

Steve's jaw drops. Someone says, "Are you all right?"

"The parties responsible have not been identified. Some are wondering if it is the work of the elves. However, some reports on the ground are that the attackers look more human than—"

Steve pulls out his phone and frantically goes to check the time in the Ukraine.

Someone is patting his shoulder. It's Fats. He's saying something.

Hands shaking on the phone, Steve can't hear him. His fingers are searching for the time in the Ukraine. His body goes cold.

"She's there," Steve shouts. "She's there for the reception…"

"Who?" says Fats.

"Claire…Claire…" says Steve, now almost a whisper. "And Dana…"

He puts the phone in his pocket. He feels like he's being crushed by an invisible hand. Like the air pressure has suddenly increased. An emergency exit in the corner catches his eye.

"I have to leave," he says, already walking to the door. The office. Someone will know more. And he can't talk here.

"Steve, wait," says Fats.

But Steve is already out the door. Without conscious thought, he breaks into a run and bolts across the street, dodging cars, not caring about the car horns that blare at him, or the cabbies' swears. Once inside ADUO, he passes quickly through security and dashes to the elevator banks. He jams his fingers on the call button. Time seems to stand still. He hasn't run far enough to be winded, but he is panting. Spinning to the stairs, he slams through the fire doors and then takes the steps two at a time.

He's on the third landing when his phone starts to buzz and the tinny sound of *Green River* starts to play. Steve takes a few more steps and then stops, suddenly realizing who it is. Pulling his phone out, he hits accept and says, "What do you know, Dale?"

"Steve, buddy, I want you to sit down…"

"Dale, don't fuck with me!" Steve shouts.

"Sit down. Sit down and get out of traffic right now if you're in your car," says Dale.

Breathing shakily, Steve falls onto the stairs.

"Are you sitting down?" says Dale.

Wiping his head, Steve grinds out. "Yeah, I…"

"I have her," says Dale. "She's here with me."

"What?" says Steve, voice going soft.

"Claire. There was a mistake in the invitations to the dinner, and Claire wasn't invited so we stayed at the ballet school. She's here, Steve, she's okay, but Dana… I'm sorry."

It takes a moment for Dale's words to sink in. And Steve is glad he's sitting down, because as it is, his elbows are on his knees, he thinks he might hyperventilate, and he thinks if he wasn't sitting he might have fallen over. Still, he can't believe it…

And then he hears Claire's voice in the background. "Daddy!"

"Want me to put her on?" says Dale, his voice almost a whisper.

"Yeah," says Steve, biting back a sob of relief more powerful than any grief or terror he's ever felt. "No, wait…give me a minute." He takes a few deep breaths and squeezes his eyes shut to hold back the tears. He can't let Claire hear him like this. She's already hurting. He has to be strong.

"You ready, buddy?" says Dale.

"Yeah," says Steve, wiping his face with the back of his hand. But it's only a half-truth. Something gnaws at him. His daughter has been spared, but this still feels like the end.

CHAPTER 23

"Get up."

Bohdi blinks awake, leaving cluttered, uncertain dreams. He's lying on the couch in Asgard. The wan light coming through the window makes him think it must be early morning. Gabbar, the once-Indian Einherjar looms above him.

Starting slightly, Bohdi scowls.

Gabbar's eyes narrow in a way that clearly says, *I am judging you.*

Jaw tight, the warrior says, "The captain of the guard requests your presence." His voice is firm but not loud. Bohdi looks to the bed. Amy is still asleep.

Gabbar follows Bohdi's gaze. He looks at Amy's sleeping form, and then his attention snaps back to Bohdi. His expression is unclear, and he says nothing.

Bohdi's sure he is going to be dragged away. His hands tighten on the blanket, and his muscles tense. But Gabbar doesn't move.

It occurs to Bohdi this might be a request. "What does the captain want?" Bodhi says.

Gabbar lifts his chin. "We have encountered human

weapons we are unfamiliar with." He sounds almost ashamed.

Bohdi barely keeps his jaw from dropping. Amy and Bohdi discussed the potential for escape last night. Amy suggested they stick around until Thor comes back. She says she has a backup plan if Thor flakes out, but it's risky, and they might be able to gather intel while they're here. Bohdi suspects that she's really just waiting for Loki, but can't bring himself to disabuse her of that notion. Because he's not Loki...and somehow saying he is would feel like he is lying to her, and he can't do it, at least not about that.

And anyway, gathering intel while being a virtual prisoner would be wickedly satisfying. Somehow though, he thought it would be difficult, but right now, intel is about to fall into his lap. However...

Inclining his head to the bed, he says, "Amy comes with me."

Gabbar glares at him. "My orders were to collect only you."

Bohdi smiles at him. "Were your orders not to bring Amy with me?" He says it loud, hoping Amy will wake up.

Gabbar's hand twitches on the pommel of his sword. On the bed Amy stirs.

Bohdi meets the Einherjar's eyes. "I won't leave her alone." Especially now that he knows how easy it would be for someone to enter through the tunnels.

Something in the set of Gabbar's shoulders softens.

"Bohdi?" says Amy, sitting up in her bed and clutching the covers to her chin. Her eyes are sleepy, her hair is mussed, and she's the worst kind of beautiful...Cute in the morning.

Gabbar glances at her and looks quickly back to Bohdi, as though he's done something wrong. With a short bow,

Gabbar says, "I will give you both a few minutes to get ready. And have a maid bring you some tea and breakfast."

Breakfast and tea? Bohdi's too shocked by the civility to ask for coffee. With one more curt almost-bow, Gabbar stiffly leaves the room.

As soon the door shuts behind Gabbar, Amy says, "He doesn't seem judgmental. He seems nice."

Bohdi sits up, eyes on the door. Gabbar *is* judgmental. Last night, when Bohdi asked the guards not to allow any maids in because he and Amy would be "asleep," Gabbar had the nerve to snort at him.

Remembering Gabbar's softening shoulders, he swallows. For once, Bohdi feels like he's been judged and not been found wanting. It's kind of frightening.

"Bohdi?"

He turns to look at Amy; she's still sitting on the bed, covers high. "I'm not great at military-strategy type stuff." A tiny line forms between her brows. "But I thought even allies didn't want their allies to know what they know about each other's weaponry."

Bohdi feels himself go cold.

Amy looks away. Voice flat, she says, "They don't expect either of us to leave."

Bohdi glances around the room he and Amy have been brought to. It's almost as utilitarian as the tunnels they were in last night. The walls are gray block. The floor looks like it might be poured concrete. It's brightly lit by morning light streaming through four large, arched windows. Outside, Bohdi can see men and women marching in formation.

Orders are being shouted in their harsh language. In the room, at least half a dozen armed men are cleaning weapons and talking, their eyes occasionally flitting up to Bohdi and Amy. They shoot sharp smiles when they look at Bohdi and whisper quietly when they look at Amy.

Ignoring the stares, Bohdi tries to commit the room to memory. Against a far wall lean the same wicked spears that Gabbar and Pascal carry. There are also swords, shields, crossbows, and arrows. And a few pieces of armor hang against another wall.

Amy whispers, "Some of the spears shoot a kind of magically generated plasma fire stuff—very hot. Not hot enough to *melt* steel, but hot enough to melt the tissue behind the armor and immobilize the wearer."

Bohdi winces at the gruesome image that conjures.

Amy continues. "The armor is magically shielded—but typically, the armor of the common soldier isn't as well protected." She shakes her head. "Magical shielding can't be mass-produced."

Pascal, who along with Gabbar stands just beside them, turns quickly in Amy's direction.

Doing a decent job of appearing innocent, Amy says, "Loki told me."

Bohdi sniffs and rubs his nose. And then he blinks. If Loki didn't tell her, how does she know?

He shakes his head. Plasma weapons… He wonders how they compare to incendiary rounds or grenades — and if they would be a match for Kevlar. Kevlar doesn't conduct heat, and it *is* mass-produced.

Gabbar and Pascal direct them to a table at the center of the room. Bohdi is trying to figure out just how hot the plasma fire gets, but his thoughts are interrupted when a large man barks an order. Through an enormous door come several Einherjar holding various small arms.

As they lay the weapons on the table, Bohdi picks up an AK-47 that's seen better days. He's fired one before in a Marine Corps course he took on foreign weapons—this one seems much heavier than he remembers. It's loaded and he taps the magazine with his thumb. The magazine is metal, not plastic; it's ancient, heavy and unreliable. Why does that ring a bell?

"Definitely Soviet," Bohdi mumbles.

"Russia!" says the large man. "Sworn enemy of America! Stalin bad!"

Amy and Bohdi both raise their heads.

Pascal directs a hand toward the man. "This is our captain, Farrouk."

"Soviet Union not friend of America," says Farrouk, with a nod. "Help us beat your enemies."

Bohdi's eyebrows hike. Granted, the relations between the former Soviet Union and the US are complicated...but apparently, he and Amy aren't the only ones who need intel.

"Why it fire through armor?" Farrouk says. Is he using magic to translate? Or does he just speak very bad English. Is he even human? He looks vaguely Middle Eastern.

Bohdi blinks back down at the weapon in his hands. "Bullets can cut through steel."

Farrouk's chin rises. "Not our steel." The arrogance in his tone could be read in any language.

Bohdi's hand tightens on the gun.

Eyes on the captain, Amy whispers, "It's easier to create magical shielding for one type of force—momentum, for instance. It's harder to create shielding for a variety of forces, like heat and momentum—like their plasma blasts."

The captain's eyes narrow at her.

"Or so Loki told me," says Amy.

Bohdi manages not to sniff at the lie. To Farrouk, he says, "I don't know." Disengaging the magazine, he pops a round out of the chamber. Holding it up to the light, he scowls. The bullet's shape is right, but there is strange scarring on the surface, and it feels slightly rough under his fingers. He peers closer. He thinks he sees a tiny raised hexagonal pattern on the surface.

He almost smiles. It's Promethean wire. He briefly imagines snapping the magazine back in, pointing it at Farrouk and…

…and thirty bullets later someone would kill him.

Shaking his head, Bohdi says, "I don't know."

Murmurs go up around the room. Bohdi's conscious of Amy's tensing beside him.

Tipping his head toward the gun, Farrouk says, "Tell me more."

Bohdi gives a tight smile. He scans the table, trying to commit everything he sees to memory, and then starts to tell them everything only an idiot couldn't figure out on his own. "So this gun…it's not particularly accurate, but the bullets break apart, which makes them damn deadly and…"

Shouts rise from outside. Farrouk holds up a hand. Bohdi stops. Someone screams and every hair on the back of Bohdi's neck stands on end. There are shouts and then more screams.

Beside him, Amy wraps her arms around herself.

Farrouk barks something at Pascal and Gabbar.

Bohdi swears he sees Pascal swallow.

"Come," says Gabbar.

With a reluctant sigh, Bohdi puts the AK-47 down. He looks at the other weapons on the table. They're mostly old and primitive, but a very pretty Nagent revolver catches his eye.

"Hurry," says Pascal.

A few minutes later, they're walking down a long corridor when, from behind them, comes the sound of a door banging open and more shouts.

Amy and Bohdi both stop and turn.

"Don't…" says Pascal.

But it's too late. Between two Einherjar warriors is a man. His bowed head is covered with shockingly blond hair. His skin is startlingly dark, but a pattern of glowing red highlights track what might be veins beneath his skin.

"A Fire Giant," Amy gasps.

Bohdi swallows. The man doesn't look like a giant. He looks barely taller than Bohdi. A metal collar is fixed to his neck. From it droops a chain that falls to his wrists, cuffed together at his waist. His chest is bare. He wears a pair of trousers that are barely hanging on. They're stained reddish brown at the groin…and the stain is still spreading.

Amy chokes. Bohdi suddenly remembers something Steve told him about Asgardian "rites" of war.

A hand lands roughly on his shoulder. Pushing him away from the prisoner, Gabbar whispers, "The Fire Giants do the same to their enemies."

"So?" snaps Bohdi.

Beside him, Amy struggles and shouts at Gabbar, "You're human! Don't you remember the Geneva Convention?"

Bohdi remembers the dates of Geneva from Marine Corps

classes. Pascal and Gabbar are from the WWI era, a few decades too early. They stare blankly at Amy.

"Come, Mademoiselle" says Pascal. "This is no place for a lady…"

Amy doesn't stop struggling. "He needs medical attention and I can—"

The sound of a whip cuts through the air, and then the sound of chains hitting the floor. Spinning around, Amy stills and a sob comes to her lips. Bohdi turns and sees the Fire Giant hit the floor with a soft thud. One of the guards winds up his leg—

"No!" Amy screams, and Bohdi hisses.

The guard's foot connects with the Fire Giant's head, and there is the sickening sound of breaking bone and squish of flesh. The other guard screams at the kicker, and he shouts something back.

Amy's body sags. "Oh, no…"

Bohdi just stares. It's as though his brain has gone off-line, and he can't think or react or even believe what he's just seen.

Pascal and Gabbar push them down the hallway. Neither protests, but as they cross through a courtyard that leads them back to their rooms, Amy's feet still. Staring hard at the ground, she says, "I need some air…Please…I've heard so much about the gardens. Can we go there?"

Bohdi stifles a sniff at the lie.

Gabbar and Pascal exchange worried glances, and then Gabbar says, "That is fine."

Is it an escape plan? Because Bohdi's ready to leave, with or without Thor, or knowing the melting point of plasma.

…And is Amy ready to leave, with or without the "new Loki"? His heart rate quickens, and he feels a flush of relief.

He doesn't have to tell her... He doesn't have to lie. Bohdi is not Loki. He thinks of the tortured Fire Giant and the arrogant captain of the guard. This place is pretty but shitty, and if Bohdi were Loki, he would have ditched this fucked-up place centuries ago.

Amy's feet crunch along the gravel of the garden path as she tries to lead them in the direction of Hoenir's hut without looking like she's leading them in the direction of Hoenir's hut.

She's vaguely aware of Bohdi beside her, saying, "Hmmm...it's warm out."

...even though it isn't particularly.

"Whatcha think the temperature is?" he asks, wiping his neck. "About twenty-two degrees Celsius?"

"I suppose..." says Pascal.

"But what would that be in Asgardian?" Bohdi asks. "I mean you guys don't use Celsius here."

"About one hundred candles," Gabbar says.

"You use candles as a measurement of heat?" says Bohdi.

"Mmmmm..." grunts Gabbar.

"Yes," says Pascal.

"Huh. Excellent," says Bohdi, and the smile is so clear in his voice, Amy looks over at him. Grinning like a shark, he meets her gaze. She can't even wonder what the joke is. She's ready to leave. She knows everything she needs to know... and the most important among them is that Asgard hasn't found the new Loki. He's gone...whether on his own power, or captured by Fire Giants no one knows.

She shudders, the image of the fallen Fire Giant filling

her mind. The guards' argument afterward in Asgardian makes her blood go cold. *"Why did you kill him—now we can't interrogate him!"* The guard who kicked the Fire Giant had responded, *"He was too weak to withstand torture anyway!"*

They have to get out of here.

She blinks and clears her vision, remembering what Gabbar said. "The Fire Giants do the same to their enemies." And the thing is, it's true.

She shudders.

Just off the path, among some mottled ivy, a gilt statue of Baldur on bended knee before a swooning Nanna catches her attention. She scowls. Baldur's attentions to Nanna hadn't been so courtly. She has the urge to kick some dirt at the statue's face—and then she stops, a dark stain at the bottom catching her attention.

Leaving the path, she crosses through the undergrowth.

"Mademoiselle?" says Pascal.

"Amy?" says Bohdi.

Amy swallows and bends down. The "stain" isn't a stain at all. It's just rough stone. She traces the stone up to where the golden color begins. The texture beneath her fingers doesn't change.

Bohdi's next to her a moment later. He sniffs, maybe at the smell of rotten vegetation. "What is it?" he asks, tracing the same trail with his fingers.

"The illusion is fading," Amy says.

"Ah," says Pascal. "That happens sometimes."

Amy turns. She can see the Vanir-style spires of Asgard beyond the garden's trees towering above her head. If she squints, the spires shimmer like the mirage they are.

Odin is losing control. She ducks her eyes. He has been

for centuries.

Loki is kneeling before Odin in the throne room. They are alone. His heart feels cold in his chest.

"Why—" he starts to say.

Odin says wearily, "Stand up, Loki, and walk with me."

Loki climbs to his feet. Odin pushes himself from the throne and steps down from the raised dais it stands upon.

Pressing a hand to his eye patch, Odin says, "Come." His voice is almost a sigh.

As Loki walks beside him, Odin says, "The ring Andvaranaut has been hidden in the realm of the Black Dwarves for many centuries—so long even they don't know where it is. It poisons their land. Their crops are not as good as they could be. Their children not as strong…"

"Yes, I understand that," says Loki, trying to bite back his frustration.

"To secure more favorable weapons contracts, I need you to find it and destroy it," says Odin. "It shouldn't affect you much, if at all. Its magic is so close to your own—"

"All that I understand," Loki says. "What I don't understand is why Nari and Valli should come with me."

Odin lets loose a long breath. "All the young men of Asgard are being called into service."

Loki lets out a huff of frustration. Not that all were answering the call…

Odin continues. "The Fire Giants' raids at the edges of Vanaheim, Alfheim, and Asgard—"

"I would rather them fight beside Thor, even against Fire Giants, than have them journey with me to the realm of the

Dark Elves!" Loki says. The damn ring has to be dumped into
an even more damnable volcano. It's a suicide mission, but he's
come to realize the more ridiculous a task is, the more likely he'll
succeed. Still, dropping the ring in lava is one thing—keeping
his children alive?

Odin drops his head. "I thought you'd prefer them with you."
There is no lie in his words. Loki turns to the Allfather.
Odin sighs and then says, "I am reinstating War Rites."
Loki's breath catches. Long ago, the Vanir had ruled the Nine
Realms. They raped the enemies they vanquished—men, women,
and children. Men and boys were systematically castrated. When
he marched against the Vanir, Odin ended that last cruel practice
and nearly ended the rape of children, if not their parents.

The Allfather's jaw goes tight. "I know what you think of me,
Loki, but although I may use deception on a woman…I have
never hurt a woman."

Loki's lips tighten into a thin line. Rind, the Frost Giantess
Odin raped, lived only nine days after the birth of their child.
The child himself lived only seven days. Odin mourned them both
and threw them grand funerals…but Rind might disagree that
she'd not been wounded.

Shaking his head, the Allfather says, "And I've never taken a
woman in the heat of battle. In the rage of war, it would be too
easy—" His jaw becomes tight. "Nor have I ever, a child."

Odin isn't lying. It is testament to his disillusionment with
the Allfather that the truth makes Loki reel back a bit in shock.
But hadn't Odin always cared for his children, and their mothers, willing or not, even if they were human? And Odin always
insisted Thor and Loki do the same—not that Loki ever had
unexpected children.

Odin's voice is almost a sigh when he speaks. "I thought you'd *like to keep your sons away from it… It isn't…healthy."*

Loki ducks his head, grateful…but confused. "Why reinstate War Rites? After all this time?" They are logical; keep your enemies from breeding. And compared to what he suffered in Geirod's castle, it's quicker, maybe not even as painful. Still, there's a finality to it that makes his gut clench. And that children aren't spared…

Odin snorts. "Because we don't have enough young men and women willing to go out to the dark corners of their realms to honorably fight a merciless foe they somehow believe will never come to their capitals. The Fire Giants themselves utilize the practice…and the soldiers I do have are asking for the same. I can barely pay my forces, the Fire Giants have nothing we can plunder, and so I must cede to the demands of the least honorable of my men, no matter how I think it spells the end of everything we fight for."

The last comes out in a rush of barked words.

Loki murmurs. "The end?"

Something in his voice makes Odin halt his steps. He turns to face Loki. The mighty Allfather's lip trembles slightly. "It isn't what you want…" Closing his single eye, Odin lays a hand on Loki's shoulder.

Loki's eyes slide to the Allfather's fingers. Once, he would have reached across and clasped Odin's shoulder in return. Now, he feels like a maid with an unwelcome suitor.

Odin's eye flutters open. Barely containing a bitter smile, Loki meets his gaze.

"Fight with me, Loki. Fight for me, and we will hold the end at bay." Odin's hand falls away. He looks older, sadder, and more exhausted than Loki's ever seen him.

Loki can't care. Where there might have once been feeling, there is only emptiness.

Amy reels from the reminiscence, the sadness and fear in Odin's face etched in her mind—and the gratitude and relief when he realized Loki wasn't yet dead set against him.

Behind her, Bohdi is saying, "So plasma fire...hot enough to melt lead?"

"Well, it tends to cool in the air—but it's still hot enough to melt skin at three hundred paces," says Pascal.

"Hmmm..." says Bohdi.

He seems genuinely interested. Maybe he won't mind what the Einherjar are planning for him...too much.

Amy finds a mirthless laugh rising in her throat, Loki's memory still sharp in her mind. Odin didn't rape women in the heat of battle...or children.

Her feet skid across the gravel as she increases her pace. She takes a sharp left, no longer concerned if her path isn't indirect. Behind her, Gabbar says, "Miss—you don't want to go that way."

Amy starts to run deeper into the trees. Her feet fly over roots that seem to writhe beneath her steps. Around her the light is dappled and many colored.

"It's dangerous!" shouts Gabbar.

But Amy keeps going. She plunges through a hedge and comes to a halt.

She stands in a clearing sparsely covered with short, scraggly grass. But where Hoenir's hut used to stand is a roughly rectangular patch of lush, waist high grasses and wildflowers. From it rises the buzz of insects. Sharp chirps of birds fill the air, and she sees insects, birds, and small animals flitting over the tops of the grasses.

But her pathway is not clear. Around the former site of Hoenir's home stand Einherjar in tight rectangular formation. Half of them face inward. Half face outward. All hold spears. None acknowledge her as she walks forward, but a flock of small birds suddenly launches from the long grasses. On their tails rise snakes with butterfly wings.

Hoenir's creatures. Amy bites her lip, in joy, wonder, and relief. The patch of grass may be all that's left of his hut, but in Amy's mind, she sees the home glowing golden, the same color as Hoenir's aura. Once, this place was so alive with magic, Loki had to avert his eyes, as though he was staring at the sun. Magic doesn't exist linearly in time…and Hoenir's hut was a maze of World Gates.

One of the soldiers facing inward hacks in half a snake that flutters in the direction of Amy, Bohdi, and their two guards.

Amy gasps.

Pascal, or maybe Gabbar, grabs her arm, but releases it as another snake hisses and lunges through the air in their direction. Taking advantage of the momentary distraction, Amy grabs Bohdi's arm and pulls him forward. Bless him, he doesn't ask questions, just runs with her, darting toward a space between two Einherjar. The one facing outward drops his sword, holds out his hands, and shouts in Asgardian, *"No, you'll be hurt!"*

Bohdi yanks her right, away from his outstretched arms. Amy lunges forward. Her foot pushes off the ground, she leaps—the Einherjar catches her around the waist and some-how her wrist slips from Bohdi's grasp—but her momentum is already carrying her into the former foundation of Hoenir's home. And suddenly she is wading in the grass and wildflowers, gasping for air because the Einherjar, still holding onto her waist, had knocked the wind out of her. She lifts her head... There is no flash of rainbow.

The Einherjar holding her shouts. She turns with a gasp to see him wincing in pain. He falls forward and Amy catches him, slumping under his weight. A butterfly snake slips from his neck and into the grass. She feels it pass over her feet.

"Amy!" shouts Bohdi, from the edge of the grass. Pascal and another Einherjar are holding him back.

She hears the guards speaking in Asgardian around her. *"Was she attempting suicide?"*

"Think she knows she has the Allfather's eye?"

"She can't have known it would be dangerous—"

"Did the fool just want to pick the pretty flowers?"

Craning her neck, Amy tries frantically to track each voice. And then her shoulders slump, and not just from the weight of the Einherjar she holds barely aloft. She was sure Hoenir would be here—or at least open a gate here—but if he was going to open a gate for her, he would open one anywhere he wished unless...

Pain flashes behind her eyes, so great it almost blinds her. She gasps and winces, nearly falling under the weight of the nearly unconscious guard.

"Get out of there, Mademoiselle," Pascal shouts. "The animals will kill you!"

She doesn't move. She doesn't want to leave this place, even though the brush is so rough it scratches her skin through her clothes and shadows slither and creep at her feet.

"Amy?" says Bohdi.

The man leaning on her groans. One of the Einherjar says, *"Someone should go in and fetch her."*

Stepping forward, Pascal says, "Mademoiselle, I am coming."

"No!" she says. She swallows. Carefully avoiding the shadows slipping among the stalks, she pulls the arm of the Einherjar up and round her neck and leads him to his comrades.

Bohdi casts a worried look in Amy's direction. Several men approach and relieve her of the Einherjar she lugged from the briar patch. Still she walks heavily, staring intently at the ground, feet shuffling over the tiny gravel stones on the garden path. He isn't sure what she was trying back there, but he knows it didn't go as expected, and he's worried.

"This way," says Pascal, guiding them right, a hand on Amy's shoulder. She follows meekly.

Pulling out his lighter, Bohdi spins the thumbwheel and glares at Pascal.

They pass under some enormous trees and then into what looks like maybe an orchard of baby trees. They only come to about his hip. Amy suddenly lifts her head. "What's this?"

"Apple trees," says Pascal.

"Idunn's apple trees?" says Amy.

Pascal smiles. "Oui, Mademoiselle. Odin has ordered that the orchard be expanded."

Amy jerks to a stop, and she spins on her feet. Bohdi follows her gaze. To him, it looks like the orchard extends for about a quarter mile straight ahead, but miles to his left, up to the base of a mountain that shimmers a little in the midmorning light.

Amy bites her lip. And then her face hardens.

"Come," says Gabbar. "Perhaps you would like some tea?"

Amy replies, "Yes, thank you."

Pascal's hand ghosts down her back. "There is a veranda that is—"

"No," says Bohdi, eyes on Pascal's hand. He lifts his head and sees Gabbar's gaze on him, an eyebrow raised. Bohdi feels his skin heat.

"That would be nice," says Amy, voice tired.

The back of Bohdi's neck prickles and his jaw goes tight, but he doesn't protest.

It takes about twenty-five minutes to reach "the veranda." It is nice. But not for the picturesque view of the gardens, or the cool shade of the shadow of the palace-castle-bed-and-breakfast-whatever that they had spent the night in.

It's nice because, after they've sat down, Gabbar abruptly suggests to Pascal, "Let's give them some privacy," and the two guards move to a station out of earshot. With the distance, and the gentle breeze whistling through the building's spires, once the maid-waitressy-people laying out tea and bread-stick thingies leave, they won't be overheard.

As soon as Amy and Bohdi are alone, he leans forward and whispers, "What the hell is happening?"

Amy, whose expression has been carefully blank since the orchard, erupts in a muffled, bitter laugh.

Not meeting his gaze, she says, "From what I gathered back in the guard room, *in Hel,* Asgardian forces are clashing with the forces of Sutr."

Before Bohdi can ask, she says, "King of the Fire Giants. Besides King Utgard of the Frost Giants, the only credible threat to Odin's rule."

"The guns?" says Bohdi.

Amy gives a tight smile. "Supplied by the Dark Elves, who got them from—"

"Former Soviet Block countries," Bohdi says.

Amy nods. "Right. And somewhere in between, the bullets have been reinforced with—"

"Promethean wire," says Bohdi. Leaning forward, he whispers, "If the Fire Giants got their hands on some incendiary weapons and Kevlar armor, the Asgardians would really be fucked… and if Asgard's got forces on Earth, I think they're going to get a little more than they bargained for." He smiles, maybe a touch gleefully.

Amy's face becomes tight. "Maybe…but Asgard attacked the Dark Elves' trading partners on Earth. So I doubt the Fire Giants will be getting Kevlar anytime soon. And from what I've gathered, Russia, Belarus, and the Ukraine won't be able to route Asgard from the new stronghold Asgard's established on Earth."

Bohdi blinks. "How did they manage to attack on Earth? From what I've seen of Asgardian tech…it isn't that great."

Amy shakes her head. "I don't know." She puts her face in her hands. "Bohdi…when I went to another universe, I learned that Odin has had his sights set on Earth for centuries. The only reason he hasn't touched our Earth is because of some deal he has…with someone…" She rubs her forehead and winces. Her head ticks to the side… He's seen that expression before, in the library, when she was talking about the hour she "lost."

"I…I…" she stutters.

Bohdi reaches toward her, but then she abruptly raises her head, and he drops his hand.

"Apparently, that deal is off," Amy says, scanning the trees beyond the veranda. "The Nine Realms are at war, and it's going to be on Earth, too...and I'm guessing that's why Odin is expanding Idunn's orchard."

Bohdi knits his brow in confusion. "Why?"

Amy sighs. "The apples offer immortality—well, sort of. They have to be eaten every year. They also awaken magic in humans. Odin traditionally offers them to his own people and the Einherjar. He also uses them to bribe some Vanir, Frost Giants, Fire Giants, and Dwarves."

The implications of that sink in. "And he wants to bribe humans," says Bohdi.

Amy nods. "I think so...but there are so many of us..."

Bohdi looks out at the orchard. The trees look too small to produce apples, but in another few years... How many apples can a single tree produce? To Bohdi's eyes, it looks like the orchard could produce millions.

"We have to get home," says Bohdi, suddenly finding himself at the edge of his chair. The shade they sit in suddenly feels too cold.

Amy wilts. "Well, my fallback plan didn't work. There was no gate... And no one seems to think that we'll ever go back to Earth. It just isn't done."

Bohdi starts to feel a bit panicked. "But Odin said..."

Amy shrugs and smiles ruefully. "You'll be pleased to know that many of the Einherjar think that your stunt with the Norns should make you an honorary Einherjar—" She waves a hand. "And Thor seems to have told them about your valiant fights with spiders, kappa, and adze..."

"And you?" says Bohdi.

Amy gazes out at the orchard, and then looks down at

her hands.

Bohdi's chest goes tight. "Amy…"

Her lips purse, and then she looks up at him sharply. "You haven't asked if they've found Loki—"

Bohdi's face goes hot. And then he snaps. "Believe me, I really don't want to hear about your ex-boyfriend."

It's not what he meant to say, or how he meant to say it, and to his own ears he sounds like an ass.

Amy's eyes go wide—she looks surprised, confused, and hurt.

His hands find his lighter.

Looking down quickly, Amy says, "He really wasn't my boyfriend."

Bohdi flicks his thumb on the lighter's flint wheel.

Returning her gaze to his, chin a little higher, she says, "They haven't."

"Great," says Bohdi, feeling the burn of flame against his thumb.

Leaning forward, Amy says. "Don't you get it? The Fire Giants are in Hel, too—they have to be there looking for Loki."

Bohdi snorts. "Why is one guy this important?"

Amy's eyes leave his and scan the table as though she's lost something. "I think…Odin always felt as long as Loki was on his side, he couldn't lose."

She blinks and holds her hand to her mouth. "Oh my God—the vial of clouds. He used a magical vial of clouds to create fog and help the British during the evacuation of Dunkirk in WWII!"

Bohdi parses her words. If the German air force hadn't been grounded by fog when the allies evacuated the continent, the war might have gone very differently. Leaning forward, he says, "Loki was on the side of the Allies…?"

Does his voice sound hopeful?

Amy winces. "No, he was just too drunk to use magic, and he'd lost a bet with some Nazis—one of whom was Thor on a recruiting mission—and he had to make a quick retreat."

Flicking his lighter, Bohdi slouches in his seat. "A real hero."

"The point is," Amy continues, ignoring Bohdi's sarcasm, "he is always on the winning side! That's why Sutr must be looking for Loki, too—he probably has spies in the court who were just waiting to hear what Thor found out from the Norns."

Bohdi thinks Sutr and Odin are full of shit. But truth doesn't matter, does it? He flicks his lighter again. "Goody."

Amy meets his eyes again. "This is very important to Odin, so important he's gone to Hel to try and find Loki himself! He even took Heimdall!"

Bohdi blinks. And then another thought occurs to him. "Where exactly in the former Soviet Block did Asgard attack?"

"The capitals of the Ukraine, Russia, and Belarus."

Bohdi's jaw drops. His fingers fumble on his lighter.

"What?" says Amy.

"Claire…Claire is in Kiev. Is she okay?"

Is Steve okay? Bohdi feels his gut constrict, not just in dread for Claire, but for his best friend who must be in his own personal hell.

Amy's face goes slack. "I'm sorry…" She swallows. "I don't know…"

Chapter 24

Steve's eyes blink open, the pain in his back forcing him awake. He's sitting against the metal grate headboard of the bed in his parents' guest bedroom. Even with his sport coat on, the metal is digging into his ribs and spine.

He looks down. He's sitting on top of the covers, legs stretched out. There's a blanket over him that his mom must have scrounged up while he was asleep, but it isn't enough. The old Chicago greystone is drafty. His eyes slide to the side. Claire is tucked under the covers beside him, braids and barrettes spilling out on the pillow. She's under a comforter, and her body is sprawled out. She must be warm.

He almost reaches out to touch her head. Just to make sure she's real. His vision gets a little blurry.

He's never slept in the same room with his kid. He always thought the idea was a little weird; it used to make him vaguely uneasy when Dana used to do it... But he couldn't bring himself to leave Claire alone last night.

Dana. Dipping his chin to his chest, Steve closes his eyes. He didn't love his ex-wife. Maybe never loved her. But she was real, and human, alive, and a better parent than Steve. Claire needed her, and Odin took her away. Behind his lids, he sees a white flash of rage.

Opening his eyes, he runs his tongue over his teeth. This fury… It feels like the anger he's felt a thousand times when he's been privy to casual discrimination, because of his race, or his humble beginnings. He will handle it the same way. He will wait, watch, and scheme.

Steve looks over to the window. It's early morning. He smells coffee and hears three sets of footsteps downstairs.

With one last glance at his daughter, Steve swings his feet over the edge of the bed and goes as quietly as he can in the creaky old house to the hallway.

His parents are downstairs—and Dale's there, too. Of course, Steve's mom invited Dale to spend the night; she always picks up orphans and strays. And of course, Dale accepted. Steve sometimes jokes that Dale might like him, but that he loves Steve's parents. They're all sitting at the kitchen table, looking grave as they stare at a nearly silent television in the corner. As Steve comes in, they stand up. His mother hugs him. Dale touches his shoulder. Henry, Steve's dad, just nods and looks at the screen.

Steve turns to the TV. The news is about the attacks on Moscow, Kiev, and Minsk.

Shaking her head, Steve's mother says, "What does this mean? Will they be coming here?"

As Steve sits down, his eyes meet Dale's. How much can he tell?

"No," Dale says, abruptly looking into his coffee. "I think they've probably gotten what they wanted."

"Yeah," says Steve. He swallows. He remembers something Amy said when he debriefed her about her trip to the alternate universes. *Odin has had his eye on Earth for centuries...but there's a deal...*

In this universe, the deal is evidently off. "But then why haven't they left?" says Henry.

Steve's eyes snap to his dad's.

In that other universe, Odin hadn't stopped until he had all of Earth under his control. Steve rubs his jaw.

The Asgardians have set up base at Chernobyl. They've pitched tents beside the containment arc shielding Reactor Four and the dangerous radioactive material within. From what Steve has been able to glean from Gerðr, the amount of ambient radiation in the area won't hurt magical creatures. From what he's picked up from ballistic experts, firing missiles on the Asgardians would result in destabilization of the reactor's already questionable foundations and would create an environmental catastrophe the likes of which the world has yet to see.

Ground forces are out for similar reasons. Gerðr says a protracted engagement would give the Asgardians time to blow up the foundations themselves before retreating to the safety of Asgard. Which doesn't completely dismiss a quick ground engagement—except US intelligence isn't sure that's possible. There appears to be a World Gate to Asgard right next to the site of the Asgardian camp—meaning virtually limitless reinforcements are possible.

Steve doesn't answer his father, just looks back to the television...and sees himself. It's a shot of him last night entering O'Hare, surrounded by ADUO agents in black suits, followed by his mother and father. For once, he's not playing to the camera. His expression is grave and he turns away whenever a camera points in his direction.

"Oh, turn the channel," his mom says to Dale.

"No, turn it up," says Steve. Might as well see how the press is going to play it.

Dale presses the volume button and a reporter's voice fills the kitchen.

"…As evident in this recent footage from O'Hare, Rogers definitely doesn't look cool under fire."

Another voice interjects, "Alan, the man just lost his ex-wife and is worried about his daughter; of course he doesn't look cool."

Steve fidgets in his seat. The shot is of his back as he walks down a long hallway in O'Hare. It hadn't been far, but it had felt like the longest walk in his life.

The coverage shifts to the studio where the anchor and reporter are seated at the news desk. There's an inset of the burning Kiev building up in one corner.

The reporter continues, "Until recently, Rogers was the hopeful Democratic candidate for mayor of Chicago. However, there have been accusations of sexual harassment—"

Spinning slightly in his chair, the anchor clarifies. "Accusations without material proof."

Pressing a finger to his ear, the reporter nods, looking distinctly disappointed.

The anchor looks smug, taps his own earpiece, and says, "It's just been announced that review of video footage of the incarceration of the Frost Giantess shows no evidence of impropriety on Mr. Rogers' part…"

Leaning back in his seat, Steve narrows his eyes. He'd expected the accusations—he's a black candidate in Chicago—but it still pisses him off.

The screen flashes back to O'Hare. The camera is on

Steve's back, the picture is shaky, but it shows Claire walking toward him. Dale is beside her, arm on her shoulder. Claire looks terribly small next to him. Next to Claire, Dale looks large, slightly sunburnt, and every inch the Texan good old boy he is. Two more CIA operatives trail behind. Claire breaks into a run. On the screen she moves so fast. Yesterday she'd seemed to move in slow motion.

Steve blinks. An instant later, the camera is suddenly zoomed in on just Claire's tear-stained face over Steve's shoulder. Dale is to one side, giving them both a hug, and Steve's mom is on the other side.

"I was technically off duty," Dale says, face going bright red. "It was all right for me to do that."

Steve shakes his head. He doesn't remember Dale doing that.

The screen is suddenly filled with Henry's face.

And then a there's a quick flash of Dale getting a hug from Steve's mom. Just barely audible is his mom saying, "Thank you, thank you… You know you're like my other son," and Dale replying, "Anything for family," in his rough twang.

And then it's Henry again, weathered face, salt and pepper hair and beard. His father's stern voice fills the kitchen. "Excuse us, but this is a time when our family needs some privacy."

The screen flashes back to the news desk, but there is an inset of Steve leaving O'Hare, holding Claire tight by his side, Dale following, this time with an arm around Steve's mom, as Henry holds her hand and scowls at the cameras.

The news changes to the weather, and someone turns down the volume. Standing up, Steve's mom declares, "Would anybody like some breakfast?"

With a look of puppy-dog-like adoration that makes Steve almost embarrassed, Dale says, "Yes, ma'am!"

Steve's phone starts to buzz. Pulling it out, he glances down at the number. Standing up so quickly he shakes the table, he leaves the kitchen.

"I hope you intend to call in today!" Henry calls after him.

Steve doesn't answer, just ducks into the next room, hits accept, and says, "Rogers here."

"Steve," says Fats. "I'm sorry for your loss."

"Thank you," Steve says, not thinking for a minute that is the reason Fats called.

Fats clears his throat. "It may be a bad time to say this… but you've also gone from divorcee to devoted family man overnight."

Steve's eyebrows hike.

"Your family's all over the news. The party would really like to capitalize on the momentum…"

A buzz of triumph shoots through Steve's nervous system. He smiles. He almost says yes, but he doesn't. Henry always said, if you were going to do a job, do it right. And he's not sure he can do right by Chicago…

"Hmmmm…" says Steve instead.

On the other end of the line, Fats says, "Who is the white guy with your family in all the pictures? Can he be part of your campaign? He does well with a demographic you've never done well with."

Steve doesn't have to ask what demographic Fats is talking about. He shakes his head and rubs his eyes. A bitter laugh almost comes to his lips. Dale got him the "good ol' boy" votes.

A knock sounds at the front door, and Steve hears Henry get up with a grumble and go answer it.

"Best friend from the Marines. Works for the Feds. No, he can't be part of my campaign," Steve responds.

"Oh," says Fats, sounding both impressed and disappointed. "Well, maybe we can just get some pictures of you and him? From your time in the Marines. Get people better acquainted with your history…"

Henry walks toward the kitchen grumbling, "Skinny white kid at the door. Probably a drug addict if he's in this neighborhood. I'm calling the police before someone shoots him…"

Steve watches Dale as he heads toward the door, very businesslike. Which in Dale's case could be dangerous.

"I've got to go," Steve says. "I'll get back to you."

"Think about it," is the last thing Steve hears before he disconnects. He almost runs into the foyer. Dale is standing in the open door, staring down at a thin white "kid" with blond hair.

"Yeah?" says Dale. "What do you want?"

"This isn't Steve Rogers' residence?" says the "kid," breath hanging in the frosty air.

The last time Steve saw the "kid," he had pointy ears. His name is Liddell. He is a Dark Elf, the same ones who were trading with the Russians.

"I know him," says Steve, gently pushing Dale out of the doorway.

Liddell looks over to Steve. His ears are rounded again, and Steve's magic detector isn't blinking. Liddell told them the Dark Elves cut the tips off to avoid magical detection.

"Well met, Rogers," he says.

Grabbing a coat off the hook by the door, Steve steps outside.

Raising an eyebrow, Dale says, "You want me along?"

Steve gives him a tight smile. "Nah, got this."

Dale gives him a nod, and shuts the door.

Turning to Liddell, another rush of adrenaline courses through Steve's system. "To what do I owe this pleasure?" he asks.

The day is bright, if cold. The sun gleams on Liddell's straw blond hair. "As I'm sure you've guessed, we lost our trading partners." Liddell looks up at the sky. It's clear, not a cloud or raven in sight. Stepping close to Steve he says, "Perhaps we could work together?"

Steve smiles. The adrenaline coursing through his system feels like it's turned to lightning…in a good way. Yesterday, he thought his world was coming to an end; now he thinks it's just beginning.

"I'm listening," he says.

CHAPTER 25

Amy sits on the couch in their room, the book she "pro-cured" on magic spread open on her lap. She's flipping through the pages, skimming the shimmering text and images, trying to forget the morning. Bohdi is sitting close, eyes over her shoulder.

"Stop," Bohdi says, laying a warm hand on hers. Her hand stops, and so does her brain, heat spreading warm and wel-come from his fingers. It's so incongruous after such a horrible day that it takes her a moment to recognize the flush of heat for what it is. But it feels good. Like an act of rebellion on the part of her body. She still belongs to herself.

Not looking at her, Bohdi leans closer to the book and whispers, "Is that a picture of a hydrogen atom?"

It's light years away from Amy's own thoughts. And for once, more innocent.

Stifling a rueful smile, she focuses on the image he's point-ing to. It looks like a grainy photo negative of the iris of an eye. There is a light band of pixelated color on the outside, a darker cloud of color within, and a dense splotch of shimmer-ing light at the center. A single dot of light wicks in and out of existence at different places in the cloud and rim.

Her eyes go to the text. "You're right!" she says. Her mouth drops. The little orbiting dot of light is an electron orbiting a nucleus.

Bohdi leans back and runs his hand through his hair; the other loosely clasps his lighter. "How can they know what a hydrogen atom looks like and not have electricity? Or Kevlar..."

Amy looks at the book. It's ancient, but in wonderful condition, almost as though...

She looks at Bohdi. "I don't think anyone here reads this book." She looks away. "It's kind of considered unmanly to know magic, and magic is their technology..."

Waving the hand with the lighter in it, Bohdi says, "Unmanly? Why?"

And suddenly Amy's hit by déjà vu. "But why is it considered unmanly, Mimir?" said Loki in Hoenir's sitting room, snapping his thumb by a candle. It burst into flame. He was only a child, but he learned this trick years ago. He doesn't even have to imagine the tiny invisible particles in the wick spinning together with other invisible particles to make flame anymore—it just happens.

He looked to Mimir's severed head. Sitting on the edge of the overstuffed chair, Mimir's eyebrows rose and his eyes slid to the side. "Well, it is considered so among the Frost Giants, and most of Asgard is at least partially of Frost Giant descent... Odin himself is half Frost Giant so..."

"But Odin knows magic! And you once told me the greatest schools of magic were on Jotunheim, where the Frost Giants live!" Loki protested.

"Ah, well..." Mimir's voice stuttered to a halt. Loki turned to see Hoenir glaring at the severed head.

Looking down, Mimir said, "Those schools. It has come to my attention that some of their practices...were immoral... Odin saw that they were shut down."

Loki whispered, "Does Odin not want people to know magic?"

In the present, Bohdi snaps. "Do they want to be stupid?"

Amy blinks. She meets Bohdi's gaze and repeats what Mimir told Loki. "No, not at first...but I think it has been convenient for Odin that there are few people who can rival his power."

And then she realizes that what she said doesn't quite make sense as a response to the question.

Brow furrowing, Bohdi opens his mouth...but before any words come out, there is a knock at the door.

Amy shuts the book and sits on it.

"No!" whispers Bohdi, grabbing the edge of the book and pulling it frantically. "Under the cushions!"

Amy lifts up as Bohdi simultaneously gives a yank. He promptly falls on his butt on the floor, clutching the book to his chest. The doorknob turns, and Amy rushes to stand in front of Bohdi as he fumbles with the book. Fluffing her skirts, she looks up just as the door opens and Pascal and Gabbar stride in. Gabbar's mustache is at a slight angle, like the whiskers of a disgruntled mouse.

Pascal seems his normal, happy self. "Mademoiselle, we have requested permission from the head of staff for you and Mr. Patel to join us at dinner."

"He thought you might be bored," says Gabbar.

Bohdi's head darts out from behind Amy's skirts. "Yes, we are bored. So bored."

Amy looks down at him. The book is no longer in his hands. He looks pointedly under the couch.

Pascal beams at Amy. "Excellent. Right this way."

Bohdi sits with Amy at a long table. The ceiling of the dining hall is high and the room is cool. It's very loud. Einherjar and people he's come to realize are servants are seated across and on either side of them, engrossed in conversations. Bohdi fidgets in his seat. Pascal and Gabbar are chatting at the other end of the table with some of the other Einherjar.

Elbows on either side of his nearly empty plate, he leans close to Amy and whispers, "Are there supposed to be kids here? 'Cause this looks family-style, but there are no kids..." Come to think of it, he hasn't seen a child since he's come to Asgard.

Amy's eyes soften a little. "I don't think they have many children," she says but doesn't elaborate.

He looks to the enormous windows at the far end of the room. They are open to the orchards, now bathed in the shadows of early evening. Turning around, he looks to the double doors behind them. They are unguarded.

No one expects them to bolt. In fact, every time he meets someone's eyes, they smile warmly at him. Sometimes they say words in fractured English. It makes him feel less comfortable instead of more comfortable.

Amy looks as tense and unhappy as he feels. Leaning toward her, he whispers, "Learn anything?"

She smiles grimly. "No one has caught the *personage* Odin seeks."

"Hmmmm..." says Bohdi. He feels pretty caught.

His eyes flick to Pascal, leaning over some men in brown. They nod and pull out what look like instruments from under the table.

Leaning closer to his ear, Amy whispers, "And no one's figured out the person he's looking for is Loki."

Bohdi lifts an eyebrow at her. Across the room some music begins to play.

Eyes on an undecipherable point in the crowd, she says, "Makes sense, not a lot of people liked him."

Bohdi flicks his lighter. Is he likable? Steve likes him. Mostly. Sometimes. He tells Bohdi it would help if he learned when to keep his mouth shut. Marion likes him—well, in bed. Laura, the legal counsel, calls him a pain in the ass. Hernandez is convinced he was a member of Al Queda. Brett and Bryant "tolerate him for comic relief," but most of the techies don't like him. Can he help it if he finds security loopholes in their code?

He sniffs. Why is he thinking about this? He lets out a huff and looks at the band just as they start up a tune. Tapping a finger in time, he tilts his head. It's definitely not hip-hop, but it doesn't sound as alien as he might have expected. The key is Western, although some of the instruments are unfamiliar. Tapping a finger on the table, Bodhi raises his eyebrows. "Is this a waltz?"

Amy perks. "Yes." She puts a hand to her mouth. "Oh, they're playing it for us to make us feel at home."

Some people get up and start to dance in an open space by the windows. To Bohdi's surprise, Gabbar starts dancing with a pretty girl… And he's actually not bad. Bohdi thumbs the wheel on his lighter, again. From what he knows of Indian culture from the WWI era, that doesn't seem culturally appropriate. But then, Indian culture isn't monolithic, and what he knows of it is so fragmented…

A movement in the periphery of his vision catches his eye. Bohdi looks to see Pascal coming across the room, an easy smile on his lips, eyes on Amy.

Bohdi's nostrils flare. Putting a hand on her arm and standing up he says, "Wanna dance?"

Her eyes widen, and she smiles. "You know how to waltz?" Despite the surprise in her voice, she stands with him.

His cheeks heat a little and he looks toward the ceiling, where butterflies are starting to light up. "Normally, I don't like to admit it," he says. "But yeah…" Asha, his ex, had been delighted to discover he could.

Amy's eyes got wide, and her shoulders unslump. "I took ballroom dancing lessons for a friend's wedding—how did you wind up learning?"

Leading her toward the dance floor and away from Pascal, Bohdi shrugs. "I have *no* idea."

And normally he hates that, but right now, he doesn't mind. Amy is smiling, and it's the first time he's seen her smile all day. It lifts his spirits a little. Trying to buoy the mood, he whispers conspiratorially, "I also know the foxtrot, the Charleston, and how to swing…but don't tell the guys at the office." To pull a laugh out of her, he says, "I can even tango…vertically and horizontally."

Amy rolls her eyes, but she laughs, too. Grinning, Bohdi guides her into an open space on the floor, slips his left hand into hers, puts the other around her waist, and pulls her close. This is the best idea he's had all day.

Lifting their hands and adopting a pose of exaggerated dancerly-ness, he says, "Ready?"

Nodding, Amy's shoulders shake in what looks like a stifled giggle. When he raises his chin a little higher and gives an arrogant sniff, he hears a *real* giggle. He takes a step…and there is a bang from the direction of the doors so loud Bohdi can feel the vibrations in the floor. The music stops.

Head snapping toward the doors and Bohdi sees Assholes One and Two pointing in Amy's direction and yelling something. Some maids are bowing and murmuring what sound like apologies; as soon as they're done, they bolt from the room.

"What's happening?" Bohdi whispers.

"Odin's come back," Amy says.

"And Thor?" says Bohdi.

She shakes her head. "No."

Asshole One and Two lead Amy and Bohdi back to their rooms. Gabbar and Pascal follow on their heels. Both Einherjar are quiet and tense as they take their places on either side of Amy and Bohdi's door. Amy enters, as Bohdi follows. Gabbar gives him a tight nod.

Before Bohdi can decipher what that is about, he hears Amy whisper, "Fuck."

Pascal's and Gabbar's eyes widen, Bohdi steps into the room, and immediately sees what's wrong. There is a fire roaring in the fireplace. Asshole Two is slipping another log in before their eyes under the watchful eye of Asshole One.

Turning, Asshole One says to Amy, "It is chilly. Room should be warm after bath. Maids prepare now."

Bohdi turns toward the bathing room. He hears the sound of water, and voices speaking rapid Asgardian.

He glances down at Amy. She's visibly shaking. Turning to Asshole One and Two, Bohdi says, "Get out." He takes his knife out. He doesn't open it, but for good measure, he tosses it once in his hand.

The two men look at each other and then scamper out of the room.

Amy's head is bowed. Walking over to her, he puts his hands on her shoulders and says, "Amy, what's going on?"

She gives a tight smile. "I'm supposed to have an audience with the Allfather."

Bohdi swallows.

Looking down, she trembles. "In another universe, he tried to kill me. The only reason I escaped was because Loki tricked him and whisked me into the In-Between. In this universe…"

Bohdi's jaw tightens. "You have me." It comes out more bitter than he intends.

She is still for a moment, and then she lifts her eyes. He's ready for a snort of derision, or at best a blank stare. Instead, he gets a small smile. "Yeah," she says.

And that's it; he's going to kiss her.

Before he can, she ducks her head and pushes her cheek against his chest. Her hands go tentatively to his sides. "Can't be worse than spiders, adze, kappa, Norns, or dragons," she says.

Bohdi closes his eyes and wraps his arms around her back. She feels just as soft and wonderful as Chloe had. Better. She isn't a mysterious almost goddess; she's human, just like he is.

Giving her a squeeze, he opens his eyes and pulls away so he can meet her eyes. "Don't forget the alligators."

Biting her lower lip, she nods. She's still shaking.

And he is going to kiss her, but the door from the bathroom opens.

"Mademoiselle," says one of the maids.

"I'll go with them… It will buy us time," she whispers. "Get the book."

He nods.

Turning to the maid, Amy says, "Coming."

Before she can break away, Bohdi whispers, "We'll win. You'll see."

Amy turns back to him. She gives him a tentative smile. Voice a whisper, she says, "In that other universe, you outsmarted Loki…*twice*."

Bohdi blinks.

From across the room, the maid says again, "Mademoiselle?"

"Coming," Amy says again, turning away from Bohdi and not seeing the stupid grin that's on his face.

As soon as the door closes, Bohdi rushes to the couch, finds the book, and slips it under his shirt. It's not the thinnest thing, but the shirt is kind of poofy. As long as he stands up straight, it should be okay. He turns toward the roaring fire. They left the book of elf porn in the tunnel behind the fireplace for safekeeping. He sighs. Now they'll never get it back.

The sound of the door swinging open snaps Bohdi back to the present. Spinning in place, he sees a line of maids marching into the room. One carries a dress, another what looks like combs or something, another maid brings what may be jewelry, and the last a pair of sparkly little high-heeled shoes. Bohdi glares, getting a very bad feeling about…everything.

He goes to the front door, opens it just a crack, and finds himself staring into the faces of two new Einherjar in full armor. One of them barks something at him.

"Errr…" says Bohdi.

From beyond his line of sight, he hears Gabbar's voice. "Want do you want, Mr. Patel?"

Bohdi opens the door and smiles. "Just coming out to say hello?"

Voice perfectly flat, Gabbar says, "Hello."

Bohdi looks to the new Einherjar in the hall—in addition to the two directly across from the door, there are four more—and Pascal and Gabbar, of course. All are standing stone faced. Pointing to the new guys Bohdi says, "So ummm…why…"

Pascal clears his throat. "The Allfather has decreed that Ms. Lewis should be treated with all the respect of a visiting princess. A princess deserves an honor guard."

"Ah…" says Bohdi, jaw going tight. "Great." The last word comes out kinda growly.

The Einherjar turn toward him.

Pascal coughs. Gabbar says something in their language; the guards' shoulders soften and they nod. Taking Bohdi's arm, Gabbar directs him back into the room. As the door shuts behind them, Gabbar says, "You are worried about the Allfather's intentions toward your beloved."

Bohdi scowls, his brain snagging on the last word.

"As well you might," says Gabbar. "But you should know, all is not lost. There are many among the Einherjar who would see you as one of us. Odin respects the women of his men."

Bohdi scratches the back of his neck. "Well that's…" off, somehow, and he can't quite wrap his brain around why.

"Good for morale," says Gabbar, with a nod.

"Yeah…" says Bohdi, eyes sliding to the side. "But we're

not…,"

"Married or betrothed, yet," says Gabbar, emphasis heavy on the last word.

Bohdi shivers at the implicit *you will be.* "How do you figure that?" he says.

Gabbar's eyebrows rise. "You sleep on the couch. A man would only do that for his beloved."

Bohdi's eyes go wide. He's going to chalk this up to inter-cultural-and-generational misunderstanding. If Amy were his beloved, they would so be banging.

"Right," says Bohdi.

Gabbar claps him on the shoulder. "Have courage. Proclaim your intent to marry her, and your wish to join the Einherjar, and it will all be well."

"Oh…good," says Bohdi. Prison doors bang shut in his mind. Not that he doesn't like Amy, and he certainly doesn't want anything bad to happen to her. Also, he would have *loved* the sleeping arrangements to have been different…but marriage?

Gabbar nods. "Or Odin may challenge you to a show of your martial prowess and you will die." He claps Bohdi's shoulder again. "But at least it will be with honor."

Bohdi's jaw falls, but he manages not to tremble when he says, "And my life's highest ambition is to die with honor."

"Good," says Gabbar.

From the bathroom door comes Amy's shout. "I will not wear this! This is not a dress! This is barely a slip!"

Gabbar's eyebrows hike.

Bohdi smiles tightly. "That's my princess."

"I will leave you to her," says Gabbar. With a final nod, he steps around Bohdi and heads for the door.

Bohdi stares at the bathroom entrance, rubbing the back of his neck and flicking his lighter. They have to escape.

"No!" Amy shouts. "No, no, no, no!"

He hears a woman's voice say, "But is princess dress in the style of the Vanir—"

"No!"

Bohdi winces. Amy is shouting. Is he supposed to intervene?

From the bathroom come shrill shrieks and screams of fear. Bohdi runs to the bathroom door just in time for it to burst open and maids to come running out, shouting something in Asgardian. Amy comes out last. Her hair is upswept in an elaborate arrangement that looks like it might be painful. She's scowling. One arm is across her chest. In that hand, she is clutching the flats she'd worn during the day. Her other hand hangs at her side, loosely clutching Squeakers in her fist.

Bohdi's eyes widen, and his mouth opens but no sound comes out. The dress she wears is a sheer pale green fabric Bohdi would classify as mosquito net. He can see her belly button and the soft line between her abs. Her underwear is lacey and white. He can't see if she's wearing anything up top because of her arm. There is something that might loosely be described as a belt, but is more a shimmering white-gold cord. It twists around her body starting at just below her breasts, crisscrosses a dozen or more times, accentuating the curve of her waist, and then droops down around her hips, falling low in front, where it's knotted. Atop the knot is a sort of gemstone pendant. About the size of Bohdi's palm, it's shaped like an upside-down triangle. It's so suggestively placed and shaped…Bohdi's jaw drops a little further and his eyebrows kiss his bangs.

She walks up to Bohdi and slips Squeakers into one of the many pockets in his vest as the maids run to the door.

"They think they saw a spidermouse," says Amy. "But I didn't see one."

Bohdi sniffles. "Of course not."

Pascal and Gabbar run into the room. "Quick, Mademoiselle, Mr. Patel! You must evacuate! There is a spidermouse infestation."

Bohdi blinks.

"I don't want to evacuate in this dress," Amy mutters, and then adds, "I hate Odin."

Bohdi forces his eyes away. He thinks he agrees about Odin, but he's suspending judgment on the "dress."

"Hurry!" says Pascal.

"Seems like a lot of fuss for a mouse," Bohdi says.

"Err...yes..." says Amy.

Bohdi's nose itches furiously. Before he can ask, Amy whispers, "But let's just play along."

She begins walking out of the room.

Pointing at Amy's bare feet, one of the maids presses her hands to her mouth. "Your new shoes!"

Voice inflectionless, Amy mutters, "Oops, they must be back in there with the spidermouse."

The maid's eyes go wide, both hands flying back to her mouth. She looks at the bathroom door and quakes.

Amy walks right past her and into the hallway, Bohdi beside her. As soon as they leave their room, the Einherjar snap to attention. Gabbar barks something in Asgardian. He turns to Amy and Bohdi and says, "It is not quite time for your audience. I will see that you get some time...*alone.*"

"Um...thanks?" says Amy, eyes sliding to Bohdi.

He rubs the back of his neck and looks away. "Errrr... yes...." It doesn't come out quite a squeak.

A few minutes after the "spidermouse infestation evacuation," Bohdi and Amy are in a little room with two huge windows with long black curtains and a couple of not very comfortable-looking wooden chairs, and not much else. There are two doors: the one they came in and a second, larger wooden door. Gabbar gives Bohdi a pat on the shoulder and then leaves the way they came in, shutting the door behind him.

Amy spares Bohdi a confused look, and then slips on her shoes and makes a beeline for the second door. She starts yanking on the handle. "Damn, it's locked!" she mutters.

She's trying to escape. Escape is good. Bohdi starts dragging his hands along the walls. "Maybe there's a secret passage in here," he whispers.

"No," Amy says. "But there's one through this door, in Odin's private library."

Bohdi's head jerks up. "How do you know that?"

Giving the door a bang with a small fist, Amy growls.

"Amy?" says Bohdi.

Not looking at him, she says, "The same way I know Asgardian."

"Oh," says Bohdi. Deciding he can ask questions later, he pulls out his knife, flips it open, and goes to the door. "Maybe I can pick the lock."

Amy slides to the side as he slips the blade between the door and the wall. He tries to feel for a weakness, but the bolt feels solid and firmly in the strike plate. Falling to one knee, he keeps trying.

"What's up with Gabbar?" Amy asks.

Not looking at her, Bohdi grunts.

"Bohdi?" says Amy.

He winces. Keeping his blade moving, eyes away from her, Bohdi says, "Well…he mentioned…if Odin's intentions toward you are romantic…"

Amy snorts. Bohdi scowls. He just can't bring himself to describe what Odin's intentions could be. "…there may be an option."

"What's that?" says Amy.

Bohdi slides the blade out. Still on one knee, he turns to Amy. She is wearing a bra…or something that is bra-like beneath the mosquito netting. His eyes grow wide, he licks his lips, time stops…

Amy swallows audibly and crosses her arms over her chest. "Bohdi? Bohdi, up here…"

Bohdi blinks and looks up, feeling his face flush. Even he knows you're supposed to look a girl in the eyes when you speak to her. "Ahhhh…"

She's blushing. She also looks sad. Though why she should be sad with breasts like those…Bohdi opens his mouth to say something to that effect, but then realizes that they may be in a life or death situation here, and he probably won't be able to think if he's staring. So he says, "Would you like my vest?"

Amy smiles. "Oh, thank you, I'm cold."

"I noticed," Bohdi says, slipping off the vest, causing Mr. Squeakers to peek from the pocket.

Amy's eyebrows rise. Snatching the vest from his hands, she puts it on with such speed and force Squeakers gives a surprised sounding cheep from the pocket.

Bohdi goes back to finding a weakness in the lock. There is a large, old-fashioned keyhole below the knob. It's too small for his knife. His brow furrows.

Above him Amy huffs. "They're only mammary glands."

Bohdi tries to focus on the lock, but what he saw moments before rises to the forefront of his mind. "That's like saying the Mona Lisa is only a painting."

She crosses her arms over her chest, even though it's sadly well concealed by his vest. "You've just been culturally sensitized to find mammary glands sexually appealing."

Turning his head, Bohdi looks up at her. "I feel sorry for the man who is culturally desensitized to their appeal." He holds up a hand. "Do you have a hairpin?"

Fishing around in her hair, Amy glares down at him. "Someday, they'll be hanging down to my knees."

Bohdi draws back at the image. "Why did you have to say *that?*" Amy holds out a little golden bobby pin thingy. As he takes it, she says, "Because it's true, and that's why women don't like just being appreciated for their boobs."

Bohdi shrugs and examines the hairpin. "I'm sure there's lingerie to handle that sort of problem...besides you're smart, too." He tries to break the pin in half. With more wiggling than he'd expect, it finally snaps apart. He slips half of it into the lock and applies pressure.

"So, what was up with Gabbar?" says Amy.

The half-pin gives...too much. Bohdi grimaces, pulls it out, and sees it's hopelessly bent. He looks up at Amy. At least she doesn't look mad anymore. "Um, well, he said...that if I was an Einherjar, and we were..."

He stalls. Amy lifts an eyebrow.

Bohdi licks his lips. "Together in a serious sense..."

"In a serious sense?"

Swallowing, Bohdi looks away, "As in married… Odin would probably leave you alone. Bros before…"

He stops and meets her gaze. Oops.

"Hos?" Amy supplies.

"Not that you're a…"

Amy rolls her eyes. "How delightfully patriarchal."

Bohdi bends the hairpin back into shape and pulls out his lighter. "I was going to say just plain sucky."

As he holds the pin over the flame, she says, "At least you get a *little bit* of a choice."

Bohdi turns to face her. "No I don't! I can't…" Abandon her. Spitting on the pin, he mumbles, "You wouldn't let go of me in Nornheim." Slipping the pin into the lock, he releases a hiss of disappointment when it gives too much again.

"I don't want to marry you, either…" he says. And then realizes he might be burning a bridge, to other not-marriage things, that he actually would really like. He turns to her. "Not that you're not…"

"I think you're all right, too," Amy says softly.

"Errrr…right," says Bohdi, although the word on the tip of his tongue was *hot*. "But…"

"We've only just met," says Amy.

Bohdi was going to go with *marriage is fucking scary*, but says, "Yeah, that. But I thought it could be the backup plan… you know…"

"Plan Z, if you will," says Amy.

"Yeah," says Bohdi, glancing up at her. She's smiling. A little. He scowls down at the hairpin. "I don't think this is going to be strong enough, heating and cooling it rapidly was supposed to…"

There's a creak from the door they entered, and the sound of boots on stone. All the hair on the back of Bohdi's neck rises. He's kneeling on the floor by the door to Odin's library with a makeshift lock pick in his hand and he has to—

Amy grabs the hand holding the makeshift pick with both of hers. "I accept!" she says, giving a little bounce, slipping the hairpin covertly into her hand and smiling widely. "I accept your proposal!"

Someone claps. Bohdi glances toward the door and catches Gabbar smiling and nodding. And then he realizes what Amy's done. It's sneaky and wonderful; but as he rises to his feet, his legs feel like limp noodles.

Amy leans closer and smiles up at him in a very good imitation of adoration. Running a hand through his hair, he looks down and forces a smile in return. It's only a trick, a fake acceptance to a non-marriage-proposal. Why is his dinner threatening to make an encore?

In Hindi, Gabbar says, *"It is a glory to die with honor."*

Oh, yeah. Odin might kill him.

As they leave the room, Bohdi feels like his heart might beat out of his chest. The guards lead them down a short hallway. Too quickly, Bohdi finds himself facing double doors nearly twice his height. Swimming before his eyes on the doors' obsidian-black surfaces are gold inlay images of people turning other people into shish kebob. The guards bark in Asgardian and then Gabbar holds out his hand. "Your knife."

Bohdi reaches into his pocket…hesitates…but then hands it over.

He still has his lighter. And Amy has their phones in his vest.

They're so dead.

Gabbar says something to the guards in Asgardian. They nod at him once, and once at Bohdi. The doors swing open and light spills into the hall, so bright it burns Bohdi's eyes. The guards fall to their knees and beat their chests. Bohdi thinks maybe that is what he's supposed to do, but he's paralyzed.

In the dimming light, he sees a long dining table with seats for at least thirty on either side. It's decked out in white and red tablecloths and fruit in golden bowls. Instead of butterflies, the room is lit by candelabras, blazing with flames that are too bright and too orange.

At the far end of the table sits Odin, elbows on the table, hands loosely clasped in front of him. The king wears armor but no helmet. His long gray hair is immaculately groomed. On either side of him stand Asshole One and Two. Asshole One leans in and whispers something. Odin doesn't move, but he speaks, his voice weirdly sounding right next to Bohdi's ear.

"Ms. Lewis, you have brought your...friend."

Amy slips her arm through his. Bohdi feels Amy shiver, but her voice is steady when she answers. "Yes."

Odin raises a finger. Asshole Two leans in and whispers something. Odin does not appear to acknowledge it. He sits perfectly still eyes on Bohdi. Bohdi can hear his heart beating in his ears, all sorts of unpleasant scenarios play out in his mind. But then Odin says, "You may both enter."

Her arm tightening in Bohdi's, Amy steps through the threshold. Bohdi manages to make his feet follow. As they walk toward the far end of the table, he hears the doors shut behind them.

Approaching the Allfather, Bohdi drops his eyes, and

notices a teapot that looks like it's made of solid gold, and delicate white china cups. He smells fresh coffee. He hasn't smelled coffee since they left Earth.

One of the Assholes bows behind a chair right next to Odin. "Ms. Lewis, please sit."

Amy hesitates, her arm tightening in his again, but then goes and allows herself to be seated. The servant goes to the chair next to hers, and says, "Mr. Patel?"

Sliding into the seat, Bohdi realizes with a start that he and Amy never discussed what plans B through Y were. His eyes slip to Amy; it may be a trick of the light, but the healthy tan she picked up in Nornheim appears to be gone. He looks to the Allfather.

Odin is sipping an amber liquid from a shot glass. Up close, he's a lot taller and broader than Bohdi remembers. Bohdi bites back a grimace. On his throne, Odin had looked weary and ancient. Now, the way he sits, the easy movements of his arm—he looks like he could deliver a punch.

One of the servants says, "Coffee, tea, something stronger?"

"Something stronger," Bohdi says. Amy's eyes snap to him, wide and round.

Lifting a finger, Bohdi amends. "…Would be nice. But I'll just have coffee."

"Me, too," says Amy.

Odin raises an eyebrow but is silent as the servants fill cups for Amy and Bohdi, place them on saucers, and then set them in front of them.

Bohdi stares down into the swirling brown and inhales. It smells really good. Too good. It could be drugged; this could be a trap.

"Cream and sugar?" says one of the servant guys.

Bohdi jumps in his chair. "Errr…" And then he has a daring thought. Giving a sort of half shrug and what he hopes is a playful grin, he says, "So is this poisoned or anything?"

One side of Odin's mouth quirks slightly. "You are insolent to insult my hospitality."

Bohdi bites his lip and lifts his hands. "Actually, just completely terrified."

Odin stares at him. And then the other side of his mouth quirks. "As you should be. But there is no poison in the refreshments—magical or otherwise."

Bohdi has no urge to sneeze. He opens his mouth to ask for cream and sugar and then realizes that might look too trusting.

He sits back in his chair and tries to look doubtful.

"I just wish for you both to feel at home," says Odin. He tilts his head. "Which is why I haven't had you flogged for failing to kneel. Twice."

"Ah." Pursing his lips, Bohdi looks hard at the serving ware. "I'll take cream and sugar then." As the servant-guy pours both into his cup, Bohdi says, "This smells really good, by the—"

"It's not our home," says Amy.

Bohdi lifts the coffee to his lips, eyes going from Amy's face to Odin's.

"But it could be, Miss Lewis," Odin says.

"No, it can't," says Amy.

No one says anything for a few heartbeats too long. Bohdi takes a sip of the coffee, slurping a little bit to remind himself that he still exists; Amy's and Odin's eyes are so fixated on each other he's beginning to doubt.

Neither of them spares a glance at the sound. Bohdi thinks he might snap from the tension. And then he does. "They do have good coffee," he says.

Both Odin and Amy turn their heads to him. Odin's lips quirk. Amy's do not.

Bohdi shrinks in his seat. "Just sayin'." He takes another sip and looks pointedly into the cup.

"I'm glad you like it," says Odin. He turns to Assholes One and Two and says. "You're dismissed. We are not to be disturbed."

Bohdi's jaw sags a bit. No servants. No guards. Odin must not think he or Amy is a threat. He gulps. Maybe because they aren't. Beside Bohdi, Amy slumps and slides her hands into the pockets of the vest.

As soon as the Assholes are gone, she says, "We know about your attack on Earth."

Bohdi starts a little. She may be afraid, but she's not playing nice, or dumb, either. He sits a little straighter.

Voice firm, Odin says. "I did not attack Earth."

Bohdi's eyebrows hike. He has no urge to sneeze.

"I attacked a few rogue nations who were supplying Dark Elves with weapons," Odin says.

Bohdi's eyes widen. That's a reasonable interpretation…

"Those elves were in turn trading those weapons with Fire Giants. I attacked the problem at the source—and saved countless lives in the process." Swirling his glass, Odin gives a rueful smile. "You have no experience with Fire Giants and so don't understand. Years ago, I had the gates between the realm of the Fire Giants and Earth destroyed… If they go on the warpath in the Nine Realms, with human weapons, the devastation to elves, Vanir, Asgardians, dwarves, and Frost

Giants would be on a scale not seen since Earth's last great war."

The Allfather tilts his graying head. "But perhaps, Miss Lewis, you think the lives of humans are more valuable than the lives of the other races of the Nine Realms?"

Amy sags in her seat. Her cheeks flush.

Odin raises an eyebrow. "Of course, you do not. You are a moral creature, and kind."

Dropping her head, Amy's eyes rapidly scan the table, as though she seeks to read some secret in the linens. "But...you want to control everything."

"WANT TO CONTROL?" Odin says, his voice gentle. He huffs softly. "I want peace, Miss Lewis. I am a child of war. I have seen horrors far worse than were inflicted on the Fire Giant you briefly met today."

Bohdi inhales. His nose doesn't itch. At all. This isn't right. This is the point where Odin is supposed to be having an evil monologue. Bohdi grips his coffee cup in two hands to warm them; they suddenly feel cold.

Shaking her head, Amy does not meet Odin's eyes. "No. You controlled Loki, you deceived him, used him... You never let Loki know what he was and—"

"Yes, I used Loki. Like I use everyone," Odin says. "For the higher good. And I kept the truth from him, for his own good."

Again there is no lie. Bohdi's gaze flicks from the Allfather to Amy. Her head is still bowed.

Leaning toward Amy, Odin says, "Do you think, Miss Lewis, that you are the only person who has loved Loki? He has been my friend, my companion, my right hand, and my brother for lifetimes." Odin shakes his head. "It is true, in his last lifetime, I did not let him know what he was, but it was an act of kindness."

Amy finally lifts her head. "You didn't want him to know he was your equal."

Bohdi lifts his cup to his lips, but pauses before sipping, eyes flicking between Amy and the Allfather.

Odin's jaw goes tight. "By hiding his identity, I protected him. Do you know how many enemies he has made over his lifetimes? How many would like to see him die slowly and painfully while they watch?"

Bohdi goes very still.

"You could have told him at least what he was!" Amy says.

Odin inclines his head. "Really? You think it would be better for him to know the truth? The incarnation of chaos is destined to live a life of struggle. He destroys everything and everyone he loves and brings them despair, strife, conflict, and pain. You think it better that he know he is destined to die in agony and fire?"

Amy sucks in a gulp of air too fast, and stammers. "There is no destiny."

Bohdi feels no desire to sneeze. His hands start to shake.

Odin leans forward. "His first wife killed herself. His first child was so twisted by the strength of her own magic it warped her body. His second wife divorced him, and still wound up taking an arrow to the chest and found herself engulfed in fire. His sons by her—" He shakes his head.

Coffee sloshes over the edge of Bohdi's cup and onto his hand. Shakily, he tries to gently place it down, but his trembling hands make it clatter against the saucer. His eyes snap to Odin and then to Amy. Neither of them seems to have noticed.

"He destroyed Cera...with his life!" says Amy, and in the same heartbeat, Odin's words echo in Bohdi's mind, *destined to die in agony and fire.*

"Yes," Odin roars. "Because I *let* him." He leans across the table again. "As soon as I realized how dangerous Cera was, I knew the Destroyer was the Nine Realms' only hope. And I let him do what needed to be done. Do you think I couldn't have swooped down with a legion of Valkyries and Einherjar and brought him back to Asgard at any time if I truly wished?"

Amy draws back. Voice quavering, she says, "You only did it because you couldn't use Cera for yourself. I've seen—" She stops, her eyes go wide.

It might be Bohdi's imagination, but he swears Odin's eye glitters. Sitting back in his chair, Odin says, "Do you refer to your weeks out of my sight?"

Amy doesn't answer.

"Hmmmm..." says Odin. "A pity you did not see a universe without me...under Loki's control."

Amy trembles so violently her chair shakes. Bohdi feels all the air leave him. That...is not a great reaction.

Odin sighs. Kindly, fatherly, he says, "Or perhaps you did. The trick, between Loki and me, is to find the right balance." He gives a small smile. "I do not always succeed in that. But I endeavor to try."

Bohdi's nose doesn't itch. Amy's head droops. For minutes that stretch too long, there is more silence...allowing Bohdi to think a little harder on the whole "bringing despair, strife, conflict, and pain to everyone he knows and loves" thing. He remembers Steve fighting with Hernandez about sending him to Gitmo, and then defending him after he hacked into the personnel files. He thinks of Amy, bleeding in the snow...

No...that wasn't his doing... But the twelve Valkyries that died on Nornheim, that was. And Nidhogg, the baby spiders, and the butterfly...

"What about Hoenir?" Amy says. Bohdi snaps back to the present. Pushing his bangs back from his forehead, he shivers.

"Have you met him?" says Odin, his eye glittering again. "Do you know where he is?"

Amy's mouth opens, and then she swallows and brings her hand to her forehead. "No..."

Odin stares hard at her, his single eye narrowing. And then he waves a hand. "It is of no matter. When I find Loki, and I will, Hoenir will come. They are always drawn together." He levels his gaze on Amy. "I think you would like him."

Bohdi shifts in his seat. "Who is this Hoenir guy?"

Odin and Amy both turn to look at him. Bohdi's hand slips into his pocket, he takes out his lighter.

"My gardener," says Odin, eye narrowed.

"The Creator," says Amy, turning to Odin. "The third in your trinity. The other most powerful being in the universe!"

"Powerful? Maybe, in some ways. But not dangerous," says Odin. He raises an eyebrow at Amy. "And I heard that you visited the site of his former house. How did you know it was there?"

Bohdi's eyes slide to Amy. How did she know it was there? His fingers flick his lighter. Does she have another god-like boyfriend? If she does, should he care? Apparently, he is just destined to fuck up her life anyway. Like he does everything. Squeezing his eyes shut, he thinks of the pictures of his parents, their faces smeared beyond recognition. He'd gone to Nornheim with only one goal, and he'd fucked it up. He is a failure, he is…

"Mr. Patel, are you trying to set my tablecloth on fire?" Odin says.

Bohdi's eyes snap open. He looks down at the flame in his hand. He hadn't even felt the heat on his thumb. "No…I'm…"

Dangerous.

"Just scared…" he mutters, putting his hand on top of the table. He can't meet Amy's eyes. He keeps thinking of her lying in her own blood, dying in the snow.

He'd almost gotten her killed in Nornheim, too.

Odin's lips quirk, then he turns back to Amy. "What are you hiding, Miss Lewis?"

She lets go a light, fearful-sounding laugh. "I don't know where Loki is, if that's what you're asking."

"No," says Odin, eye narrowing. "I see you do not. But you are still too interesting to let go."

And oh, fuck, now Bohdi's trapped her here. In another universe, Odin had tried to kill her. In this one…

"Don't worry," Odin says. "I am not a man that fears what he doesn't understand… I don't want to hurt you. You're too valuable."

The Allfather leans closer to Amy. She draws closer to Bohdi.

"Twice you've escaped my sight. You've seen universes and possibilities even I have not seen…"

The Allfather lifts a hand toward her. The edges of Bohdi's vision go red. He feels his face heat.

"And then there was the pregnancy, that shouldn't have happened." Odin says. "What are you, Miss Lewis?"

Odin's hand stretches toward Amy's cheek and the whole world looks like Bohdi is staring through blood-colored glasses.

This is all his fault. And so is Thor being in Hel fighting the Fire Giants... If Bohdi just had admitted who he was... but he can't...

His hand tightens on his lighter. He flicks the wheel. "Don't touch her." The words come out of his mouth in a hiss.

"Pardon?" says Odin, his voice silky. Somewhere in Bohdi's mind, it registers as a warning. But heat is rushing through his body, and it's like he belongs to someone else. He's standing up, pushing the table, shaking silverware, and tipping over china. He's blind to everything but red and Odin; and he's screaming. "Don't. Fucking. Touch her!"

And then he sees Amy standing, jumping back and out of her chair bringing her hands to her mouth as though terrified of him. His nose itches at the sight... His eyes snap to Odin, his body tenses, he wants to hurt him. His muscles coil.

Raising a hand in Bohdi's direction, the Allfather commands, "Stop."

And Bohdi does.

He can't breathe. Or blink. Or even twitch. His thoughts feel like they are riding a slow wave, and his vision is a film in slow motion with frames missing.

Just beyond Odin, Amy's hands open in front of her mouth, as though she's going to blow the Allfather a kiss. In her hands is Mr. Squeakers.

And then Mr. Squeakers is suspended in midair behind Odin, as though caught in a freeze frame. And then he's gone and Odin's hand is on the back of his neck.

Air rushes into Bohdi's lungs. His pulse races in his ears, his eyes are dry and burning, and he's careening face first into the table. He blinks and his eyes feel like sandpaper. He hears a sob.

Looking up, he sees Odin, keeled over on the table, his hands inches from Bohdi's own. Looking up, he sees Amy. She's standing behind Odin's chair, Mr. Squeakers on her shoulder. Her face is contorted in a grimace, her hands are balled in fists, and tears are in her eyes. "I can't kill him! I can't kill him!"

Still gasping for air, Bohdi's eyes fall on the Allfather. "What happened?"

Amy shakes her head and bites her lip. "He stopped you— he froze you in time—but not me."

Which is half an answer. Bohdi's eyes fall to Odin. "He's…"

"Unconscious," says Amy. "Squeakers is venomous and he bit him…"

Bohdi looks up to the tiny spidermouse twitching his whiskers on Amy's shoulder. Back on Earth, he'd sneezed when Amy told him Squeakers was harmless. He bites back a nervous laugh. It wasn't the mouse he was allergic to.

She curls her hands into fists. "I want to kill Odin, but when I try… I…" Holding her fists before her face, she lets loose a frustrated scream.

Bohdi's eyes snap back to Odin's prone form on the table. His long gray hair is spilling out over the red tablecloth. His glass is knocked over. He looks frail. Human. Ordinary. Like a man playing dress up as a king.

Bohdi takes a shaky breath. But he's a real king, and Bohdi's pretty sure kings don't let people humiliate them and just walk away. Amy and Bohdi will be on the run forever.

They should kill him. Bohdi knows all sorts of ways to do it: lift his head and twist his neck, crush his windpipe, even just yanking Odin back by the hair with sufficient force could break a vertebrae.

Bohdi can do it. He's the Destroyer.

He stumbles back from the table. "I can't kill him, either."

On the table, Odin groans.

Amy skitters toward Bohdi. Grabbing his arm, she gives him a yank toward the far wall. "We have to get out of here."

Bohdi meekly obliges. Amy goes to a corner of the room, drops his arm, runs her fingers along the smooth stone, bites her lip, and says, "It's here."

She presses against the wall and it shimmers. Where before there'd been the smooth white stone with golden veins, there are cement blocks and a drab wooden door. Amy jams her hand into one of the blocks and the door swings silently open.

"Come on," says Amy stepping into the darkness beyond. Bohdi follows, setting his lighter ablaze. "Thanks," she says. She pushes a loose block in the wall and the door closes behind them.

The flame of the lighter dies, and Amy says, "This way." Bohdi follows her voice, and a moment later, the wan light of a phone in Amy's hand lights a fork in the tunnel. Without hesitation Amy goes right. A few steps later, there is another fork and she goes right again.

"Do you know where we're going?" Bohdi asks.

"To the stables," Amy pants, walking in front of him, very fast. "Odin is here, which means Sleipnir, his horse, is here. We can steal Sleipnir. He can open World Gates. We can ride him home."

Bohdi shivers. Convenient to have a horse that can world-walk if they're going to be on the run…forever. He squeezes his eyes shut and rubs his eyes. "Sleipnir…"

"World-walking, time-slipping, magical eight-legged horse, child of Loki's mare incarnation. No, Loki didn't have sex with a horse as a mare on purpose so don't even go there," Amy says.

Bohdi's brain short circuits at the words. Another, sort-of-almost child?

For a few minutes, there is nothing but the darkness of the tunnel broken only by the cell phone's light and the sound of their feet scuffling over the floor. A squeak from Amy's shoulder breaks the near silence.

"I'm so sorry, Squeakers," Amy says. "No butterflies for you to eat now."

"Just a harmless mouse," Bohdi says, his voice a little bitter.

Amy stops in her tracks. Pulling Squeakers from her shoulder and clutching him to her chest, she says, "Please, don't tell Steve! Steve would put him in a cage, and ADUO might do experiments on him, and...*please* don't tell Steve?"

Mr. Squeakers gives a little cheep. He is really cute. And Bohdi owes him his life. But...

Bohdi's jaw tightens. "I won't, but when we're out of here, you're going to tell me what else you're hiding."

Amy draws back, eyes wide.

There is a noise, the whisper of soft shoes on stone from the direction they've just come. Amy slips her phone back into her pocket, and they are in complete darkness.

Bohdi looks behind them and sees a pale blue and ivory light. His heart beats in his ears, and his ire dissolves. He feels Amy's hand on his wrist. She silently pulls him forward and he doesn't protest.

They move as quietly as they can through the tunnels,

hands on the walls, to keep from banging into them. Bohdi begins to hear other noises, groaning wood and heavy thumps.

Beside him, Amy whispers, "The stables."

She stops. A phone flickers to life in her hand, and on the wall Bohdi sees a round ring beside a wooden door. She gives it a yank, and the door opens just enough to let a tiny bar of light into the tunnel. Amy peeks through the crack.

"Tack room's empty," she says, pushing the door slightly more ajar. They step out into a room only about as wide as he is long, dimly lit by a little green ball suspended from the ceiling. There is the smell of leather, grassy stuff, and an animal smell Bohdi guesses might be horse. Amy closes the "door" behind them—which is actually the back wall of the room. Hanging from it are harnesses, saddles, and things he can't quite identify. A few bales of hay are stacked neatly on the floor. Amy bites her lip. "There will be at least two guards in front of Sleipnir's stall," she whispers. "I think Squeakers can handle at least one, but…"

Bohdi stares at her. And then he gets what she's saying. He looks around the room and notices all the wood paneling. "Maybe we can set a fire," he says pulling out his lighter. He flicks it. "That would…"

No flame leaps at his fingers. There's not even a spark.

Amy looks around them. "I think this place may be enchanted against fire."

Still spinning the flint wheel, Bohdi rubs his chin and looks around the room. A whip catches his eye. He moves toward it. As he lays his hand on it, a deep lowing fills the stables. Bohdi can feel the whip tremble under his fingers at the sound.

"A hadrosaur!" says Amy, shuffling toward the wall beside

Bohdi. "That means…"

She pulls something off the wall. "Would this work for you?" she asks.

Bohdi turns his head. She's holding a shovel. It looks like the type Henry uses in his garden, pointy and sharp at the trough end and highly polished. But the long handle looks weathered and gray.

Amy runs her hand over the handle. "Elven merwood. It won't break—even if it's hit by a sword." She looks up at him and nods shrewdly. "You need something unbreakable for shoveling hadrosaur dung."

Bohdi looks between the elegant whip and the humble dung shovel. The shovel is at least kind of sword like, and he has gone to a Kumdo class with Steve. Sighing, he takes it from her and turns it over in his hands. It does have a nice heft to it.

"Bohdi."

He looks up.

Amy is standing in front of him, a woolly strappy thing in her hands. "You're a good person to have in these sorts of situations." Looking down she whispers, "I'm glad you're here."

He hears her swallow. He feels like he might throw up. If he weren't here, she wouldn't be here. Turning toward the door, he mumbles. "Let's go."

Amy is still for a moment, but then without meeting his eyes, she turns, opens the door, peeks through, and nods. Together they leave the tack room and enter a short hallway, dimly lit by the same small green glowy lights suspended from the ceiling. There are a few doors off to the side, and a wheelbarrow filled with some goopy white and purpley-blue stuff. Up ahead is another hallway, with half doors that are about the height of Bohdi's chest. He hears shuffling and what sounds like horses to him. Putting a finger to her lips, Amy looks at the intersection and points right.

They creep up to the intersection and peek around the corner. There are two guards about twenty feet away. They wear full armor, and they carry plasma-shooting spears. Bohdi looks down at his weapon. Their armor has helmets with visors. And apparently it's all impact resistant. His eyes slide to the goop. Hefting the shovel in his hands, he goes over and scoops up a load of it, grimacing at the ammonia-like smell. Amy's eyes go wide, but she doesn't say anything.

Approaching the intersection again, he gives Amy a nod and mouths the words, "Lead the way."

A horse is making a noise that sounds like a horse raspberry, and the two guys are looking into the stall, talking to each other.

They turn into the hallway, but the lighting's dim and the guards are immersed in their conversation and don't turn immediately. Amy casually deposits Squeakers on the wall. Bohdi watches the mouse race up to the ceiling and then dart toward the guards, hugging the shadows.

A heartbeat later, one of the guards turns and says, "You there! How did ye get in here?" His voice isn't loud. It's conversational, unworried...and maybe Scottish or Irish. Apparently, word hasn't gotten out about what happened. But it's the middle of the night; they should be suspicious at least. Unless it never occurs to them anyone would ever want to leave, or betray Odin...

Amy speaks. "We wanted to see Sleipnir."

The guard looks behind them. "The watch out front let ye in?"

Amy doesn't answer, and the guard says, "I'm sorry, lass, but ye'll have to come back in the morning. Sleipnir's asleep right now."

Bohdi stifles a sniffle and from the stall comes a loud trumpet-like horse noise.

The other says something in Asgardian and the first man sighs. "Should be sleeping."

Bohdi scowls. Why can't they be suspicious and angry?

Amy bites her lip. "We have to go home… Please, let us go."

Bohdi's heart constricts and he looks at her in alarm, furious, and bizarrely grateful that she's giving these guys a chance.

"What?" says the man stepping forward. The other man tenses. "Oh, no, lass, ye'll be doing no such thing. I know it can be a bit to get used to, but ye'll like it here… I'll call a guard, he'll take you back…"

In his mind, Bohdi sees Odin reaching for Amy, and the Fire Giant collapsing on the floor in a bloody heap.

"No," Bohdi says, gritting his teeth. And he doesn't care about the guards, he just has to survive, and Amy has to survive.

"What?" says the guard. And this time there is tension in his voice. His companion steps forward. Neither yells though. The guard's eyes fall on Bohdi's shovel. "What are ye doing with dino dung?'

So that's what the goop is.

Turning his head to Amy, Bohdi smiles and says, "But then again, maybe he's right, maybe we should go back." At the same time he pulls the shovel back.

Huffing, the man says, "Of course I'm right—"

Bohdi flicks the shovel forward in a wide ark. Clumps of dung go flying, sticking to the walls and the guards' visors. A shadow drops from the ceiling onto the second guard. Both men's spears droop…and it's like Bohdi's body is possessed by someone else again. He grabs the spear of the first man by the shaft, braces it under his arm, simultaneously readjusting his makeshift weapon in his other hand. The man flips open his visor—and Bohdi drives the shovel into his face.

As the man Squeakers has bitten starts to stumble, Amy rushes forward and catches him. He shouts something, loud enough to be heard outside. As he falls, he manages to let off another shout and a few choice words before she takes the wool girth she stole from the tack room and ties it around his head. As it muffles his moans and he slips into unconsciousness, Squeakers leaps from his helmet, licking his tiny chops.

Beside her the other man crumbles and lands with a thump. Bohdi stands above him, chest heaving, hair in front of his eyes. From down the hallway comes the sound of guards talking outside the stables, but she can't make out the words.

Bohdi looks to the man Amy's gagged, and his eyes widen. "That's a good idea. Shut them up, yeah, we need something for this guy." He starts rummaging through his pockets.

Amy looks at the man he's downed. His face is a bloody mess, his nose seems to have disappeared. On instinct, she slips a hand beneath the armor around his neck and presses a hand to his pulse. There's nothing. She swallows, and looks again at his face—she can see bits of brain and bone where his nose had been.

"He's dead," Amy says.

"No, he's not," Bohdi says. "No, see, he can't be...because he's hundreds of years older than me, and has a lot more combat experience, and he has a spear, and a sword, and I had a shovel."

He holds up a colorful slip of fabric. Eyes very wide he says, "It's the thong, but I'm not trying to intimidate you, it's just somehow I still have it and it will make a good gag." He nods frantically.

Amy's mouth falls open. "Okay, Bohdi, okay, you gag him, I'll get Sleipnir."

Jumping to her feet, she rushes to the stable door, throws the bolt, and swings the door open. The only light is the glow of Gleipnir, the magical halter that keeps the stallion obedient. The glow makes the white horse appear ghost-like, but she can see he is awake and alert. His ears prick forward and he gives a friendly whicker. Amy can't help stepping back in shock. Not only does he have eight legs—he's also the biggest horse she's ever seen.

Down the hall she hears a door swing open, and footsteps.

"Bohdi, get in here," she says, stepping into Sleipnir's stall.

In an instant, he's by her side. "Amy, there are guards, lots of them, they're coming—" Sleipnir steps forward, and butts his nose lightly against Bohdi's stomach. Holding up his hands, Bohdi chants. "Horse, horse, horse..."

"I don't think we can mount him," Amy says, frantically scanning the room. "If we just grab his mane—"

With another whicker, the huge animal drops forward so its foremost legs are straight out, and its second forward pair is curled beneath it. Loki's memories tumble through her mind. She remembers Sleipnir doing this for Loki when he was very small.

She grabs Bohdi's arm, pulls him around, and scrambles onto the bowing animal. The sounds of footsteps and shouts are heartbeats away. Bohdi slides awkwardly on behind her. "How do you drive—"

Sleipnir climbs up onto all eight feet as gracefully as an eight-legged horse can. Bohdi's hands cinch around her waist, and Amy nearly falls off from the unfamiliar motion and Bohdi's extra weight. Clinging to Sleipnir's mane so hard her nails bite into her palms, she gives a sharp tap with her heels. With Loki's memories, she steers Sleipnir into the hallway and to the left using just her knees—and nearly collides with at least a dozen guards racing toward them.

Bohdi's head drops to the space between her shoulder and her neck. "I'm sorry, I'm sorry, I'm sorry—" His words are drowned by the shouting of the guards, and swords being drawn from scabbards.

Amy gives Sleipnir a sharp tap on his sides and holds her breath. The horse steps forward...and out of time. All sound stops...Einherjar and a few stable hands stand around her—some suspended mid-stride. Amy's body lightens and her heart does, too. They're free now.

Squeakers scurries into her pocket. Behind her, Bohdi raises his chin, but his hands are still wrapped viselike around her waist.

Sleipnir trots to the barn door, neatly sidestepping the statues of his former keepers. They step into the night and into a curtain of magically suspended raindrops.

Amy wipes droplets from her eyes. A natural storm? Or Thor?

She and Bohdi can't stick around to find out. Bohdi insulted Odin, and she poisoned him. Together they've also managed to steal Sleipnir, one of his prized possessions. Biting her lip, she looks toward the center of Asgard. Even from here she can see the glow of thousands of magical torches that light the largest World Gates in the Nine Realms. There's one to every realm there, even Earth. But it will take her to a place in Northern Europe. She looks into the darkness of the gardens. There is a lesser-known gate that leads to the middle of North America. Leaning in the direction of the shadows, she gives Sleipnir a gentle kick.

Shaking his head as though he's laughing, the horse trots toward the trees.

CHAPTER 26

Lewis and Bohdi sit across from Steve on a couch dragged into the magic-shielded conference room. Thirty minutes ago, Steve's phone had started playing a Bollywood tune. He had stared at it a full three rings before answering. Bohdi's voice was on the other end of the line, sounding shaky and tired. "Steve? It's us… We're in Iowa… It's freakin' cold and we're dressed for summer."

"I can send a team to pick you up, we have an office in Des Moines—"

"S' okay, we stole a horse."

There was a sound like horse noises on the other end of the line, and then Bohdi said, "Nice horse…nice horse… I gotta go."

Beatrice had burst into his office a minute later shouting that Lewis was back. Thinking Bohdi was out of his mind more than usual, Steve had ordered Brett and Bryant to put a trace on Bohdi's phone. Before he'd even finished sending the request, someone shouted, "There's an eight-legged horse outside!"

Now Lewis and Bohdi are both wrapped in blankets.

Mugs of fresh coffee sit on the short file cabinet doubling as a table in front of them. Apparently, a commute from Iowa to Chicago on an eight-legged horse that walks through time only takes about five minutes.

Beside Steve sit Hernandez, Brett, and Bryant. There's a window behind the couch, covered up by shades and lined with Promethean wire—but the sound of rain from outside is still audible. Bohdi keeps looking over his shoulder and at the ceiling…as though he's expecting someone. Which maybe he is.

Steve leans forward and says in as soothing a voice as he can manage, "Bohdi, yes, it's Thor. He's coming, but all our intel says he's alone. Nothing bad is going to happen to you."

And if it does…Lewis says Sleipnir is one of Odin's greatest treasures. Steve thinks the horse will make a lot of glue, and fuck it, if Thor or Odin tries any shit with anymore of Steve's people, that's what the eight-legged pony will be. Damn scientific interest and intergalactic diplomacy.

Flicking his lighter, Bohdi faces forward but doesn't meet Steve's eyes.

"Now," Steve says, "Bohdi you were telling us about going to the Norns to ask about your parents…"

"Ah, yeah, well…" Bohdi's head bobs nervously. "They… they wanted me to…ah…with them…and I said no…"

"Wanted to what?" said Hernandez.

Bohdi swallows, his head droops to one side. He doesn't look at anyone.

"Have sex," Lewis says.

"And you said no?" says Bryant, sounding genuinely puzzled.

And true, for Bohdi, that's kind of startling, even if the

women in question had six arms. But the kid is so distraught…

"Why did you say no?" says Hernandez, his tone too tight.

Hernandez had wanted to interrogate Lewis and Bohdi separately. He doesn't believe they were *kidnapped* by Thor. Neither does Steve, but he's willing to let it slide. Lewis and Bohdi are the only two humans to go to Asgard and come back. Steve wants them to feel safe and secure, and to be on his team.

Bohdi takes a deep gulp of air.

"Because they wanted to eat him!" Lewis says.

Bohdi starts and looks at her, eyes wide.

"That's why you couldn't, isn't it?" says Lewis, putting a hand on his knee. "I figured it out…They're spider women, and some spiders eat their mates afterward…and well, I remembered Addie saying how we should fatten up…I thought she was just being mean but…"

Bohdi swallows again and smiles slightly. In gratitude… relief…or…Steve lets that explanation just hang in the air for a bit.

Not meeting anyone's eyes, Bohdi whispers, "The first words out of Addie's mouth when I walked in the door were about how delicious I looked…"

"So there's something that can turn you off?" says Hernandez.

"Shut up," Lewis snaps.

Shooting Hernandez a death glare of his own, Steve says, "Moving on." He's starting to see why Bohdi might be in a bit more shock than Lewis.

"I jumped out the window," says Bohdi, finally meeting Steve's eyes, "and landed on Nidhogg's head and bit his tentacle and ran like hell—"

"Screaming for Thor at the top of his lungs," says Lewis. "We could hear him even from camp."

Nodding, Bohdi says, "And then there was a blast of fire from the dragon—"

"It just missed him," says Lewis.

Sitting back, Steve listens as they describe their trip to Asgard. Thunder rumbles outside as they bashfully describe the Einherjar's suggestion they get married. Steve has to hide a smile behind his hand as they say how crazy that was. They've been interrupting each other's sentences from the get go and making sure the other got credit for all his...or her...heroics—just like a happy couple that's been together for years.

Lewis says, "And then Bohdi stood up so fast at the table, he knocked over the cups and everything and distracted Odin and I..." Her voice trails off.

Bohdi looks at her, looks back at Steve, and says, "Performed a Vulcan neck pinch."

Steve's brow furrows. "Really? I've been doing martial arts for years and I can't do that. You have to know anatomy really well."

"Amy is a doctor, Steve," says Bohdi.

"Of veterinary medicine," says Hernandez.

"I took comparative anatomy," says Lewis, a furrow appearing in her brow.

"It takes a lot of strength, too," says Steve.

For a few seconds, neither says anything, and then Lewis says, "Adrenaline."

Something is off, but Steve decides he'll confront them about it later—separately. "So...then..."

Bohdi's mouth falls open. Lewis's lips make a small "o."

Clearing his throat Bohdi says, "So you know...we think

Freyja, Goddess of Love, Beauty, and War, might have her sights on you."

Steve snorts, and rubs the bridge of his nose. "I should be so lucky." He waves his hand. "Back to how you got out of Odin's dining room."

Lewis's and Bohdi's eyes slide to each other. Appearing to hesitate, she says, "Well, there was another tunnel that…"

At that moment, there is a familiar rumbling voice from the hallway. Lewis and Bohdi both snap their heads to the door. Steve's phone rings. He hits accept and lifts it to his ear. "Director Rogers, Thor Odinson wishes to come in… and deliver an apology on behalf of the All Mother. He says it can't wait, and he must speak to Dr. Lewis and Bohdi immediately."

"Send him in," Steve says, eyeing the kids.

Not two seconds later, the door bangs open and Thor strides in. Eyes going immediately to Lewis and Bohdi, he bows at the waist. "My friends, the All Mother, Queen Frigga has told me about my father's shameless behavior toward Dr. Lewis's person."

"He tried to touch her cheek," says Hernandez, sounding a little confused.

Thor blinks. "Perhaps my understanding of modern Midgardian manners is deficient?" Shaking himself he says, "But she bids you know, she will make sure that Odin does not retaliate against you. She's grateful she was able to intercede in time."

Bohdi's shoulders soften. Lewis gasps, sags, and closes her eyes.

"You found a tunnel?" says Bryant.

"Queen Frigga showed us where it was and gave us

directions to the stables," says Bohdi too quickly.

"Yes," says Lewis, very fast.

Steve raises an eyebrow but lets the obvious lie slide.

As they describe their altercation in the stables, Bohdi's shoulders slump. "I might have killed the guard," he whispers. "But I didn't mean to. He was a nice guy."

Steve feels a hollowness in his gut for the kid but isn't sure what to say, surrounded by too many people.

Later, as everyone starts to leave—Lewis being led out by her grandmother—Thor says, "I would have a word with Mr. Patel, alone, in this magically shielded room."

Steve is about to say no way in hell. But he looks to Bohdi first. Bohdi's looking up at Thor, something undecipherable in his eyes. Sounding uncharacteristically old, Bohdi murmurs, "Sure."

Steve hesitates, fist tightening at his side. But then he leaves the room, shutting the door behind him. He'll catch up on the conversation later—the room has a few hidden bugs.

He turns and walks a few steps, and then stops by the little service hallway shaking his head. When they'd first brought Bohdi in, he'd wandered down the hall, looking a little dazed. When Steve had said, "We need to debrief you," Bohdi had looked confused. "Me?" he'd asked. Steve rubs his jaw. The kid must have been in shock. Steve walks toward the grimy window at the hallway's end, his mind running through all the intel Bohdi and Amy gathered. The elves are trading weapons with the Fire Giants, and they are seeking Loki too…but no one's found Loki. Steve rubs his temples. Maybe he'd kind of hoped Lewis would find the guy and bring him back—Loki was a useful ally. And Steve would rather Odin not have allies. His nostrils flare and jaw hardens. Actually,

Steve would rather Odin not have anything he wants.

Putting his hands in his pockets, he gazes out the dirty window remembering Ratatoskr's words after Loki destroyed Cera, *"The team with Loki always wins."* He shakes his head. Doesn't matter. Not a lot he can do.

He hears a bang from the conference room. Crap. Bohdi probably told Thor where the bugs are. Turning around, Steve's about to go back to the conference room when he notices that the utility closet door is slightly ajar. As he prepares to close it, he hears murmured voices from within. Blinking, Steve steps into the closet. It's empty. But Bohdi's voice comes from a vent on the wall. "Why did you lie, Thor?"

Steve closes the door gently behind him and steps over to the vent.

Bohdi jumps a little as Thor crushes the last of the bugs with Mjolnir. Turning to Bohdi he says, "Even without magic it still works as a hammer."

Bohdi's hands fist into the blanket draped over his shoulders. Pulling it tighter around him, he asks again, "Why did you lie, Thor?" Beneath the blanket he fumbles for his lighter. "And why didn't I feel it?"

Sighing, Thor sinks into the chair vacated by Steve. "Ah, you know what you are."

Bohdi bows his head. Thor's casual acknowledgment shouldn't make him feel like he's starved for oxygen. He stares at the dingy carpet beneath his feet. Being on Earth, in the drab conference room, back in normalcy...Bohdi had almost hoped believing he was the incarnation-of-chaos-thing was a product of stress, extreme circumstances, and his own slightly wonky brain.

"I did not lie," Thor says. "I told the truth. That the new Loki was destined for Hel and would be there shortly."

Bohdi's brows draw together. Lifting his head sharply, he says, "Is that some sort of fucking riddle?"

Thor snorts. "Yes, I suppose." His eyes drop. "Hel is in the realm of Niflheim, where Loki's daughter was banished long ago and then died. The story made its way into your myths… though it was twisted and convoluted…and then made its way back to Asgard." Looking up at Bohdi he says, "In Asgard, being destined for Hel means to be destined for death." He sighs. "…and you will be dead too soon."

Rolling his eyes, Bohdi tightens his fingers around his lighter. "Thanks for reminding me I'm going to die in fire and pain."

A sad puppy-dog look settles on Thor's face. "I only meant that you are mortal, and I am sad of it."

Bohdi meets the big man's gaze. He feels no need to sniffle, but maybe it is the magic sealing room?

Shaking his head, Thor says, "Why did you choose such a weak form?"

"I didn't choose it," Bohdi snips, shifting in his seat, and drawing the blanket tighter again.

Thor sits back and narrows his eyes. "You have so little magic you don't even have an aura—" The big man's jaw drops. "And maybe that's why…without an aura you can't be identified." Thor shakes his head. "It's a very clever disguise. And you have *human* magic."

Bohdi leans back against the cushions of the couch. What had the Norns said? Even they hadn't been sure it was him…

He thinks of the Valkyries who saved him from the

Norns, and scuffs his feet in the carpet. "Was there something in particular you wanted to say?" he says.

The chair Thor sits in creaks. Bohdi lifts his eyes to see Thor has straightened. The big man gives him a sad smile. "Queen Frigga begs that when you return you have mercy."

"Return?" says Bohdi, with a sharp exhale. "Believe me…I don't want to return."

Thor sighs. "But you will, or human kind will. Odin is afraid of humanity's magic and determined to put Earth under his thumb. Sooner or later, humanity at large will retaliate…and it's your nature to be in the thick of such chaos."

Bohdi, draws back. "Why would Odin be afraid of Earth?"

Brows rising, Thor stares at him a moment. Bohdi squirms under his gaze.

Putting his huge hands on his thighs, Thor draws back a little. "Truly, you don't know?"

Bohdi stares at him blankly.

Thor huffs. "Besides the fact that there are more than seven billion of you—nearly seven times as many as the other realms combined—your kind has walked upon your moon. You split atoms and rob them of their energy. You send signals through the air at the speed of light. You cruise the skies at the speed of sound."

"But we can't world-walk!" says Bohdi. "We're stuck here!"

One side of Thor's mouth turns up in a twisted smile that somehow manages to be both wry and sad. "For now…but in a hundred years, maybe less, your kind will be traveling between realms through doors that never even existed before."

Bohdi shrugs. "That doesn't make us dangerous."

Thor snorts. "Says the man who set Nornheim on fire."

Shaking his great mane, Thor says, "And when you can leave, leave you will. You will spread out through the Nine Realms and nothing will ever be the same."

Bohdi's face must be broadcasting his incredulity, because Thor leans forward and says, "The most humble among you has more magic at his fingertips than the other races would ever dream of. Why, think of the sprites you speak with in your phones!"

Bohdi gapes for a second, and then squeezes his eyes shut and rubs his forehead. "Thor, there aren't sprites in our phones."

Thor's chair squeaks again. Bohdi opens his eyes to see the space Viking's brow furrowed. Thor's lips purse. "Ah, that's right. Sprites are tiny elves, you can't squeeze an elf into your phone!"

Bohdi lets out a breath.

Thor smiles. "You have *spirits* in your phones." He looks up. "Although the word I seek may be closer to *kami*, there's no English translation precisely, but they are spirit-like consciousnesses that inhabit all things."

Bohdi blinks. "No, Thor, we've programmed our phones to do simple tasks…"

Thor nods. "Spirits are very simple. Loki said some sorcerers can communicate with them. The one time he tried wasn't very helpful…although, I truly believe the rock *wanted* to give us directions."

Bohdi feels his nostrils flare. Tapping his fingers on the couch, he says, "There are no spirits in our phones, Thor."

The big man smiles slyly. "Are you sure? Everything exists as both matter and energy, Bohdi. Your quantum theory tells you that."

Bohdi blinks at Thor. The implications of that are interesting...

And then his jaw gets hard. Thor still hasn't answered his question. "Why did you lie to Odin?"

Thor's smile melts away. "There was my oath..."

Bohdi shakes his head. "But you're not going to tell Odin now that you brought me safely home." Bohdi's not sure how he knows it, but he does.

"No." Thor frowns, and a crease settles in his brow. "The Norns...and Frigga...have given me much to think about." Swallowing, he says, "Ragnarok has begun. Heed Frigga's plea... It is mine as well."

Bohdi slumps against the back of the couch. Ragnarok? He's heard that word before...

Shifting in his seat, Thor says, "Son of Patel—there is one more thing."

Bohdi looks up. Thor is leaning forward, elbows on his thighs. There is something about the weariness in his expression that makes him look ancient. "If you know you are destined to die in pain, think hard about what you find worth dying for." He gives a weary half-smile.

With a soft exhale, and a loud squeak from the chair, Thor stands. Coming over he puts a hand on Bohdi's shoulder. "We will meet again Son of Patel. Burn bright."

Thor's eyebrows rise a little, as though he is waiting for Bohdi to say something in return. But Bohdi has no words. He just slouches into the couch and looks at his feet.

Thor turns and leaves the room, and Bohdi bites his lip. And then he remembers there was another mystery he wanted an answer to.

Exiting the women's locker room, Amy surveys the comfortable yet rather stylish workout gear Beatrice supplied her with. Yoga pants, a T-shirt that's a little too tight, and a zip-front sweatshirt that won't quite zip all the way up. She puts her hands into the pockets of the sweatshirt. On one side, Squeakers is curled up in a warm little ball. On the other side, she still has one Archaeopteryx feather—she had relinquished the other to the FBI.

"Told you it would fit," says Beatrice. She hands Amy a spare winter coat from the lost and found. Before Amy can put it on, Beatrice gives her a hug. "I'm so glad you're back. That is never going to happen again!"

Amy pats her grandmother. Something hard under Beatrice's coat at the level of her left hip catches her attention. "Grandma, are you still packing?"

Pulling away, Beatrice grins, eyes sparking beneath her straight gray bangs. "Yep. Legally now."

"Uh-huh," says Amy. From her pocket, Squeakers gives a cheep.

Someone clearing his throat nearby catches her attention. Amy turns to find Bohdi, still in Asgardian attire.

Hands in his pockets, Bohdi says, "Can we talk?" His eyes go to her grandmother. "Alone for a minute?"

Beside Amy, Beatrice whispers, "He obviously doesn't know I'm packing."

Amy shoots her grandmother a glare, but Beatrice is too busy glaring at Bohdi to notice.

"Yes," says Amy, her heart giving an extra thud. "Yes, a talk would be...fine."

Giving Beatrice what she hopes is an appeasing smile, she

follows Bohdi back into the conference room, stepping over some broken electronicky thingies on the floor as she does.

She's not sure what she expected him to ask her, but when he closes the door behind her and says, "So...when we lied and said Frigga told us about the tunnels...how did you really know the way out?" Her heart sinks a little.

Swallowing, she looks to the window, still curtained. She promised to tell him.

Shoving her hands into her pockets, she says, "Loki gave me his memories."

Bohdi tilts his head. "What kind of memories?"

Amy shrugs. "I guess...all of them?" Unable to meet his eyes, she says, "I sort of stumble on them when I need them, they're not at the forefront of my mind all the time. It kind of makes sense, the brain isn't a whole bunch of highways, it's a whole lot of side roads and—"

"He wanted to protect you," says Bohdi.

Amy stops, words dying on her tongue. Her eyes go to his. His face is very serious. But then it has been since before they left Asgard. It makes her a little sad.

Bohdi nods. Voice very somber, he says, "He knew Odin would get his hands on you eventually, and he loved you and so he made sure you were protected."

Amy's mouth drops open. And then she shakes her head. "No, no, he gave me his memories so that I could remind him who he was, and what his oath was. He didn't do it for me."

Bohdi cocks his head. "His oath?"

Amy sighs and looks down. "He keeps oaths, even across lifetimes." She smiles tightly. "His last oath was to have Odin kneel before him while all of Asgard burns to the ground."

Bohdi snorts.

Amy looks up to see him rolling his eyes.

"Well, that's kind of extreme," Bohdi says, shaking his head. "Odin's a dick, but not everyone in Asgard is." His jaw tightens…and something in Amy loosens and uncoils.

She feels the corners of her lips turn up. Bohdi isn't Loki. His highest ambition isn't to destroy a race.

"Yes," she sighs. "It's extreme…and no, Loki didn't love me…" She swallows, not sure why it's important he know that. Maybe she's just trying to keep it straight in her own mind?

Bohdi raises an eyebrow. "Are you sure? It seems to me that Loki might not be the most reliable narrator."

Amy blinks. That is possibly the nicest thing anyone has said about her relationship with Loki since…

She looks away. "You talked with Thor?" she says.

Bohdi shrugs. "Oh, yeah. They still haven't found Loki."

Amy frowns and Bohdi adds quickly, "But don't worry… I'm sure he's…you know…okay."

Amy swallows.

"He'll find you," says Bohdi, softly.

She takes a breath. It's important Loki find her, and she vowed to help him…but she's no closer to finding him than when she left for Nornheim. She shakes her head. "How…?"

Will she find him? What will she do when she does? And how can she reconcile a *life* with this burden?

Bohdi coughs, and she looks up to find a mischievous grin on his face. He gives her a wink. "You know…there might *possibly* be *magic* involved."

Amy stares at him, and then remembers those were her own words about Nidhogg's ability to fly. She laughs, and Bohdi's smile broadens. She takes a step toward him, or maybe he takes a step toward her, or maybe both, but they're suddenly very close.

There is a click, and she turns sharply to see the door swing open. It takes her a moment to recognize the silhouetted figure there. It's the pretty agent from the photo of Bohdi at the ball game.

"Am I interrupting something?" the agent says, looking between the two of them.

"No," says Amy, doing a pretty good job of not sounding guilty...even if it feels like the woman is interrupting something.

"Um," says Bohdi.

The agent rushes toward Bohdi, arms outstretched. "Oh, Bohdi I'm so glad you're back."

Amy's jaw drops as the agent wraps her arms around Bohdi.

"Erm..." he says right before the agent plants her lips on his.

Or maybe the agent hadn't interrupted anything. Face heating, Amy breaks for the door. She's just stepped out into the hallway when Beatrice's voice calls out. "Oh, there you are..."

"Let's go," Amy says quickly, heading toward the elevator.

Bohdi gently pushes Marion away. It's nice to be welcomed back, but the timing and Marion's particular brand of enthusiasm... He looks toward the doorway, and winces remembering the hurt and embarrassment he saw in Amy's eyes.

Marion follows his gaze. "I did interrupt something, didn't I?"

Bohdi's eyes snap to hers. Her brows are knit with concern. Because maybe they don't love each other, but they do *care.*

She pulls back, her eyes searching his face. He can't read her expression. She definitely doesn't look happy, but she's always been clear that the "ship" in their relationship was going nowhere. He looks to the door. He wants to chase after Amy…and he can't think clearly…and doesn't know how to spare Marion's feelings if he has hurt them. "I don't know," he says truthfully.

She gives him a smile that is knowing, and maybe a little sad. "Yeah, you do." She looks toward the door, and back to him. "Shouldn't you go get her?"

"I, uh, maybe?" Bohdi says.

Marion rolls her eyes. Inclining her head to the door, she says, "Go."

Bohdi gently squeezes the top of her arms and kisses her cheek. "Thanks," he says.

She gives him a nod just before he runs out into the hallway. He doesn't see Amy. He darts toward the elevators and hits the button. He stands for a few minutes in front of the doors, tapping his hand against his thigh.

The doors don't open. Spinning, he goes to the stairs. Barreling through the fire doors, he takes the steps two at a time until he reaches the lobby. It's nearly six thirty. There are a lot of people heading home, but he doesn't see Amy there, either. He pats his pocket and realizes he doesn't have his phone. And he doesn't even know her number.

He'll find it. Bohdi dashes back up the stairs to his cubicle.

It takes him only a few minutes to find her number. He dials it with the phone on his desk, his mind racing trying to think of what to say. He hears ringing on his phone, and then his heart leaps when he hears a corresponding ring just a few cubicles away. Leaving his phone on the desk, he races toward the sound…

…and finds Brett and Bryant holding up Amy's cell phone.

"Huh," says Brett. "It still works."

Bryant shakes his head. "But with the amount of water damage it sustained it can't be reliable."

"Where's Amy?" Bohdi says.

The two techies turn to him with what feels like agonizing slowness. They shrug. "We were just going to exchange this thing for a new phone," Bryant says. "Since hers broke in the line of duty."

From behind Bohdi, comes Steve's voice. "She and Beatrice left."

Bohdi's body sags. He turns slowly to his boss.

"What's wrong?" says Steve.

Bohdi's mouth opens. He can't meet Steve's gaze. Hadn't Steve warned him not to get involved with anyone in the office? Didn't he say that it always ended badly? Bohdi had thought he'd proven Steve wrong—but now he's lost his chance at, well, something…because of his own…

His hand goes to his pocket, and wraps around his lighter. Because of his own chaos.

Odin's voice rings in his ears. *He destroys everything and everyone he loves.*

Bohdi looks down at the floor and remembers Amy bleeding in the snow. If he cares about her even a little, he should probably stay away from her…

"Bohdi?" Steve says.

Bohdi shakes his head, remembering Steve's question. "Nothing, nothing's wrong." Even if maybe everything is.

He looks up to see Steve's eyes narrowed. "Uh, huh." Steve takes a step forward. "I could use a drink…" He puts a hand on Bohdi's shoulder. "And if I'm drinking, you're drinking."

Odin's voice rings in Bohdi's mind again. *He will die in pain and fire.*

"A drink sounds good," Bohdi says. Or more accurately, getting drunk to the point of oblivion sounds good.

"Come on, let's go," says Steve, guiding him toward the elevators.

And why not indulge in a little self-destructive behavior? Bohdi finds himself smiling tightly.

What does he have to lose?

CONTINUED IN WARRIORS:
I BRING THE FIRE PART V
AVAILABLE NOW

Appendix

The Nine Realms

Alfheim — Realm of the elves

Asgard — Realm of the Aesir, "gods"

Jotunheim — Realm of the Jotunn, or Frost Giants

Midgard — Earth, realm of humans

Muspellsheimr — Realm of the Fire Giants

Niflheim — Realm of mists, location of "Hel" — the place where Loki's daughter Helen and other plague-ridden Asgardians died.

Nornheim — Realm of the all-seeing Norns

Svartálfaheim — Realm of the dwarves

Vanaheim — Realm of the Vanir. Formerly rulers of Asgard, the Vanir retreated to their homeworld after they were defeated by Odin's forces.

Human Names & Places:

ADUO — FBI Department of Anomalous Devices of Unknown Origin

Amy Lewis — Veterinarian for ADUO. Loki's former "lover."

Beatrice Lewis — Amy Lewis's grandmother. Translator of Ukrainian and Russian, works for ADUO.

Bohdi Patel — Real name unknown. Computer programmer employed by ADUO.

Agents Brett & Bryant McDowell — Twin brothers, ADUO agents. Their specialty is technology.

Claire Rogers — Steve Rogers' ten-year-old daughter

Agent Hernandez — Agent of ADUO, second in command at the Chicago Branch Office

Laura Stodgill — Legal Counsel at ADOU

Steve Rogers — Director of Chicago's Branch of ADUO

Ruth Rogers — Steve Roger's mother.

Henry Rogers — Steve Roger's father.

Names & Places of Other Realms

Adze — Carnivorous hominids with dragonfly wings. In Ghana legends, the source of malaria.

Aesir — Denizens of Asgard, "gods."

Allfather — Another name for Odin.

Andvaranaut — Cursed ring in Norse Mythology—part of a ransom an incarnation of Loki paid to a dwarf for Hoenir's release.

Anganboða/Angrboða — Also known as "Aggie" by Loki. Loki's Jotunn wife, mother of Helen. In myths, Angrboða, meaning "grief bringer." In reality, her name was Anganboða, meaning "bringer of joy." One of the few to see through Baldur's glamour.

Baldur — Son of Odin and Frigga. Possessed a magical glamour that made him appear beautiful, wise, and kind. Tried to abduct Nanna, the beloved of the human warlord Hothur. Used enchantment to create a magical plague that killed Loki's daughter Helen.

Bifrost — "Rainbow Bridge" between realms

Cera — A.k.a, the World Seed. A being of infinite magical power, tricked by Loki into destroying itself in the In-Between.

Diar — Odin's council.

Einherjar — Mortal warriors recruited by Odin or Freyja. They are given access to Idunn's apples of immortality.

Eisa — In Norse mythology, daughter of one of Loki's incarnations and Glut.

Fenrir — In Norse mythology, Loki's wolf son by Angrboða. In actuality, just a wolf Loki and Aggie adopted when they thought they could not have children. Also the name of Amy's vicious, tailless, rat-like, Chihuahua-poodle mix.

Fire Ettin — Fire Giant

Freyr — Originally a Vanir, Freyr remains on Asgard. Associated with fertility. Former husband of Gerðr, brother of Freyja, son of Njord.

Freyja — Originally a Vanir, Freyja remains on Asgard. She is associated with love, beauty, and war. A master of magic and illusion, she can alter her appearance to match anyone's romantic ideal. She is a cunning warrior and leader of the Valkyries. Sister of Freyr, daughter of Njord.

Frigga — Wife of Odin, Queen of Asgard. In Norse mythology Goddess of Motherhood and Marriage, believed to spin clouds and to see the fates of all beings of the Nine Realms. One of the few to challenge Odin's authority and get away with it.

Frost Giant — Another name for Jotunn, the natives of the realm of Jotunheim. Not really "giants." They are tall by modern standards, but nearly giants compared to ancient humans.

Gerðr — Jotunn enchantress, former wife of Freyr. Gerðr led a team of Jotunn from Jotunheim across a World Gate on a hunt for Cera. Realizing the danger of Cera's power, she grudgingly aided humans in trying to control it.

Gleipnir — Magical, unbreakable rope. In Norse Mythology, believed to be used to chain Fenrir, Loki's wolf son. In reality, used to control Sleipnir, eight-legged stallion, and one of Loki's incarnation's children.

Glut — "Glow," the wife of one of Loki's previous incarnations.

Gungnir — Odin's magical spear. A gift from Loki to the Allfather. Broken when Loki destroyed Cera.

Heimdall — Servant of Odin. Creator of the classes among men. All seeing and hearing—if he happens to be gazing in your direction.

Hel — In Norse Mythology, Hel is Loki's daughter. It is also a place in Niflheim.

Helen — Loki's daughter, in Norse Mythology known as Hel. Half-blue, Helen had the ability to reveal the lies around her. As such, she was a threat to Baldur's power. After Baldur killed her, Loki, with Odin's approval, killed Baldur.

Hoenir — Gardner of the Asgard and a powerful enchanter.

Loki's friend.

Hothur — Human warlord, slayer of Baldur—with Loki's help.

Huginn and Muninn — Odin's raven messengers.

Idunn — An elf who lived in Asgard, and grew the magical apples they ate every year to restore their immortality.

In-Between — A place beyond space and time. Magical philosophers suspect it may be a place beyond the universe. Loki can step into the In-Between for inter-realm travel, but not for travel from realm to realm. For that he needs a World Gate (also called the Bifrost).

Jotunn — Natives of the realm of Jotunheim, also called Frost Giants — though not really "giants" per se.

Jörmungandr — The "world serpent," guardian of Asgard's seas. In Norse Mythology, the son of Loki by Angrboða.

King Billings — Frost Giant, father of Rind.

King Geirod — Frost Giant, held Loki prisoner for thirty days and thirty nights.

King Sutr — Fire Giant, one of only two beings that pose a serious risk to Odin's power.

King Utgard — Frost Giant, one of only two beings that pose

a serious risk to Odin's power.

Laevithin — Loki's magical sword. Charged with Cera's magic.

Laugauz — Loki's Fire Giant incarnation

Lopt — Female incarnation of Loki

Lothur — Incarnation of Loki

Loki — Frost Giant incarnation of chaos. God of Mischief, Chaos, and Lies. Friend of Hoenir. Associated with fire. Feels when lies have been uttered. In mythology, blood brother of Odin, destroyer of the gods and bringer of Ragnaork.

Mimir — The severed head of Jotunn, animated by Odin. Knowledgeable about all things magical.

Mjolnir — Thor's hammer. A gift for Loki offered in reparation for cutting Sif's hair.

Mr. Squeakers — A venomous spidermouse given to Amy by Loki. Hoenir used spider mice to eat cockroaches that invaded his hut.

Nari — One of Loki's sons by Sigyn. According to Loki, "the incarnation of democracy."

Njord — Vanir, father of Freyr and Freyja. Associated with the sea. Married for a short time to Skadi. His father was the leader of the Vanir before he was slain by Odin.

Norns — Watchers of fate, compared to the three fates in Greek mythology. Powerful enchantresses.

Odin — King of the Aesir, and leader of the Nine Realms. Also known as the Allfather. His magic lies in preservation. Willing to sacrifice his own son for the benefit of the Nine Realms.

Ord — Husband of Freyja.

Prometheus — In Greek myth, the titan that gave fire to mankind. In modern times, the FBI's source for information on all things magical, and Promethean wire.

Promethean wire — Magic-conducting wire. Any magical being or object placed in an unbroken sphere of Promethean wire will have its magic blocked. Blocks the eyes of Heimdall. However, a sufficient magical charge to Promethean wire can cause a tear in space time.

Ragnarok — End of the world.

Ratatoskr — Gossiping and extremely powerful, magical squirrel. Servant of the Norns.

Rind — Jotunn princess and enchantress, daughter of King Billings. Raped by Odin after the death of Baldur.

Sif — Wife of Thor. Associated with fertility and harvest. Her long golden hair was famously snipped off by Loki.

Sigyn — Asgardian, friend of Angrboða. Sigyn became Loki's wife after Angrboða died.

Skadi — Native of Jotunheim, one of Loki's former lovers. Her father was the giant that built Asgard's great wall; he was killed unfairly by the Asgardians. Seeking vengeance for his death, Skadi came to Asgard. She agreed to forgive the Aesir if one of their number could make her laugh, and if she had her choice of Asgardian men for a husband. She chose Njord, father of Freyr and Freyja, and God of the Sea. Loki was able to make her laugh.

Skírnir — A powerful enchanter and servant of Frey. Skírnir blackmailed Gerðr into marrying Frey.

Skywalker — In Norse mythology, a name for Loki.

Sleipnir — Odin's eight-legged steed, Sleipnir is the son of one of Loki's incarnations and Svaðilfari, the stallion that helped the giant build Asgard's wall.

Thor — Son of Odin and an unknown giantess. Carries the hammer Mjolnir that makes lightning and summons storms. Associated with strength, healing, industry, and fertility.

Ullr — Son of Sif by an unknown father, adopted by Thor. Became Skadi's second husband.

Valli — Son of Loki and Sigyn, twin of Nari. According to

Loki, he would be the ""incarnation of armed rebellion."

Valkyries — Winged women warriors of Asgard.

Vanir — A person from Vanaheim.

World Seed — A being of nearly infinite power. Tricked by Loki into destroying itself in the In-Between, liked to refer to itself as Cera, which translates as "power".

World Gate — Any place where the fabric of space time is weak and allows magical beings to travel between one place or another.

World Tree — Also called Yggdrasil. In Norse mythology, the "tree of life" and the connection between the realms. A way of describing the universe, worlds within it, and connection between worlds.

ALL STORIES BY C. GOCKEL

The I Bring the Fire Series:
I Bring the Fire Part I: Wolves
Monsters: I Bring the Fire Part II
Chaos: I Bring the Fire Part III
In the Balance: I Bring the Fire Part 3.5
Fates: I Bring the Fire Part IV
The Slip: a Short Story (mostly) from Sleipnir's Point of Smell
Warriors: I Bring the Fire Part V
Ragnarok: I Bring the Fire Part VI
The Fire Bringers: An I Bring the Fire Short Story
Atomic: a Short Story part of the Nightshade Anthology

Other Works:
Murphy's Star a short story about "first" contact

The Archangel Project Series:
Carl Sagan's Hunt for Intelligent Life in the Universe:
A Short Story
Archangel Down

Author's Note

Thank you for taking a chance on this self-published novel and seeing it to the end. Because I self-publish, I depend on my readers to help me get the word out. If you enjoyed this story, please let people know on Facebook, Twitter, in your blogs, and when you talk books with your friends and family. Want to know about upcoming releases and get sneak peeks and exclusive content?

Visit my website to sign up for my newsletter:
www.cgockelwrites.com

Follow me on Tumblr: ibringthefireodin.tumblr.com

Facebook: www.facebook.com/CGockelWrites

Or email me: cgockel.publishing@gmail.com

Thank you again!

Made in the USA
Las Vegas, NV
12 August 2021

27993863R00288